PRAISE FOR

cat's claw

"Callie bounces from twist to twist as she explores Benson's richly imagined world, where multiple mythologies blend, and the afterlife is run as a corporation." —***Publishers Weekly***

"An entertaining, frenzied fantasy frolic that will have the audience laughing at the chick-lit voice of the heroine, who is willing to go to heaven on a hellish cause."

—***Genre Go Round Reviews***

"Readers get another dose of the irresistibly flaky heroine. Join Calliope on another rollicking adventure."

—***Romance Reviews Today***

"Incredibly imaginative and creative, silly and fun."

—***Errant Dreams***

"Benson is back with a second helping of her refreshing take on death and purgatory as viewed through her heroine's less-than-enthusiastic eyes. Normality is what Callie Reaper-Jones longs for, but it's definitely not in the cards for this quirky and stubborn heroine. As curses and dangerous missions collide, Callie's offbeat humor and viewpoint guarantee a madcap romp." —***Romantic Times***

"A fun, snappy read to the tune of a chick-lit writing style, set in a colorful supernatural world. It's a charming mesh of several myths with an unconventional modern-day twist that hosts a cast of quirky, likable, and diverse characters."

—***Fantasy Dreamer's Ramblings***

"Sustains the style and pace of *Death's Daughter* but adds deepening characterization." —***The Monthly Aspectarian***

continued . . .

death's daughter

"Amber Benson does an excellent job of creating strong characters, as well as educating the reader on some great mythology history . . . a fast-paced and very entertaining story."
—*Sacramento Book Review*

"An urban fantasy series featuring a heroine whose macabre humor fits perfectly with her circumstances. Sure to appeal to fans of Tanya Huff's Vicki Nelson series and Charles de Lint's urban fantasies."
—*Library Journal*

"Beguiling . . . Calliope emerges as an authentically original creation . . . Benson gives [her] a wonderfully varied landscape to explore, with elements of Hindu and Norse mythology and European folklore swirling around more familiar Judeo-Christian lore . . . The humorous tone never gets in the way of the imaginative weirdness of the supernatural events."
—*Locus*

"Benson provides a fun romp that defines the rules of an exciting new universe you'll be chomping at the bit to dive back into time and again. There's action; there's intrigue, redemption, an adorable hell puppy, and even a hot guy or two. What more could you ask for?"
—*Buffyfest*

"Amber Benson writes an amusing, action-packed, chick-lit urban fantasy loaded with more twists and curves than a twist-a-whirl . . . Filled with humor and wit, this is a refreshing, original thriller as double, triple, and nth crossings are the norm."
—*Genre Go Round Reviews*

"With a creative story line as proof, Ms. Benson adds writing to her ever-growing list of talents. Set within an intriguing paranormal world, *Death's Daughter* unfolds a seductive tale of power and deception. A great start to a series that will be easy for readers to get hooked on."
—*Darque Reviews*

"Opens the door on an intriguing, fully thought-out universe, with a likable main character and the potential for mayhem around every corner. It's a lot of fun." —*Fangoria*

"The first-person point of view and the fast-paced plotting contribute immensely to creating a lively and funny story packed with nonstop action." —*The Green Man Review*

"Callie is sarcastic, smart-mouthed, and overwhelmed. I liked her a lot! . . . a lighthearted but still-suspenseful paranormal . . . The mythology and settings were unique and creepy . . . I will be eagerly awaiting more adventures of Callie, Clio, and Runt the hellhound."

—*Night Owl Romance*

"A clever and well-told story . . . It's also a step outside the current paranormal-fantasy rut but with enough elements in common to please fans of that form as well."

—*Critical Mass*

"Amber Benson has created a brash, sassy heroine oozing attitude as she deals with family, business, an angry goddess, zombie armies, and betrayal in this imaginative blend of assorted mythologies. The snappy dialogue keeps pace with the quick pace while providing a fun touch of self-deprecating humor. It should be interesting to see where Benson takes Callie next." —*Monsters and Critics*

" 'Multitalented' doesn't begin to cover the gifts of former *Buffy* TV-alumna Benson. Her quirky, cranky, and humorous heroine leads readers on a wacky first-person adventure through hell. Great supporting characters and wild antics keep the pace brisk and the humor flowing."

—*Romantic Times*

"There's a whole lot of promise here . . . enjoyable."

—*SF Site*

Ace Books by Amber Benson

DEATH'S DAUGHTER
CAT'S CLAW
SERPENT'S STORM

serpent's storm

AMBER BENSON

ACE BOOKS, NEW YORK

THE BERKLEY PUBLISHING GROUP
Published by the Penguin Group
Penguin Group (USA) Inc.
375 Hudson Street, New York, New York 10014, USA
Penguin Group (Canada), 90 Eglinton Avenue East, Suite 700, Toronto, Ontario M4P 2Y3, Canada
(a division of Pearson Penguin Canada Inc.)
Penguin Books Ltd., 80 Strand, London WC2R 0RL, England
Penguin Group Ireland, 25 St. Stephen's Green, Dublin 2, Ireland (a division of Penguin Books Ltd.)
Penguin Group (Australia), 250 Camberwell Road, Camberwell, Victoria 3124, Australia
(a division of Pearson Australia Group Pty. Ltd.)
Penguin Books India Pvt. Ltd., 11 Community Centre, Panchsheel Park, New Delhi—110 017, India
Penguin Group (NZ), 67 Apollo Drive, Rosedale, North Shore 0632, New Zealand
(a division of Pearson New Zealand Ltd.)
Penguin Books (South Africa) (Pty.) Ltd., 24 Sturdee Avenue, Rosebank, Johannesburg 2196,
South Africa

Penguin Books Ltd., Registered Offices: 80 Strand, London WC2R 0RL, England

SERPENT'S STORM

An Ace Book / published by arrangement with Benson Entertainment, Inc.

PRINTING HISTORY
Ace mass-market edition / March 2011

Cover art by Spiral Studio.
Cover design by Judith Lagerman.
Interior text design by Tiffany Estreicher.

ISBN: 978-0-441-02009-6

ACE
Ace Books are published by The Berkley Publishing Group,
a division of Penguin Group (USA) Inc.,
375 Hudson Street, New York, New York 10014.
ACE and the "A" design are trademarks of Penguin Group (USA) Inc.

PRINTED IN THE UNITED STATES OF AMERICA

10 9 8 7 6 5 4 3 2 1

For my mom,
who isn't part fish

serpent's storm

prologue

Blue sky.

She would do anything in the world to see blue sky again. The only window in her cell perpetually framed the same picture each and every day: large gray thunderheads always on the verge of spilling rain yet never seeming to deliver on their promise. She hated the window, the view from it, the cell in which she was incarcerated . . . all of which acted as a continuous reminder of the crimes she'd committed.

Yes, she'd done some stupid things—mostly she'd underestimated the people who'd sought to thwart her—but she didn't regret any of her actions. She'd acted in the right. She'd done what she knew was necessary to secure a future that was most deservedly hers, and she'd do it all again if given the chance.

She'd be smarter the next time, though. There would be no compassion for the people who'd brought her suffering. She would grind them under her stiletto heel and feel no mercy toward them. She would make them suffer as she had, and she would enjoy every second of it.

There was a rattling behind her at the heavy iron door that barred her escape, and she turned, expecting to see a guard—one of the nasty Bugbear creatures with its four unblinking, button eyes showing nothing but reproach—bringing up her breakfast. Instead, the figure at the door was humanoid and covered in a light brown shroud that obscured its face. It carried no tray in its hands.

"What do you want?" she said, her words like acid as she glared at the figure, hoping to cut short this unexpected and unwelcome visit.

The figure pulled back its hood as if in answer, revealing a sharp, feminine face and curious eyes. A pair of red, cat-eyed glasses sat jauntily on the tip of the woman's nose. A long, low-pitched laugh burbled from her throat as she smiled broadly from beneath her cowl-necked shroud.

"Why, I'm here to spring you, of course, darling. At the Devil's behest, of course."

The acid drained from her tongue as she took in her savior's words, a malevolent grin slowly spreading across her face. *How quickly things change,* she thought to herself as she followed the woman in the cat-eyed glasses out of the cell, looking forward to the blue sky she knew was very much in her future.

one

Waking up next to a deliciously hot, naked man—one who was in my bed of his own volition—was like the most glorious feeling in the entire world. Right up there with winning an all-expenses-paid trip to Tahiti on *The Price Is Right* or having someone gift you a twenty-four-hour shopping spree at Barneys, Saks, *and* Neiman Marcus all on the same day. Yes, those were the things that rated A++ in my book, and having a naked man in my bed topped every one of them.

In the past I'd been utterly opposed to the idea of buck-naked sleeping because of my "in case of fire" phobia, in which I become the dumb girl caught running around her apartment building like a naked lunatic on holiday, giving all the firemen a "Calliope Reaper-Jones Boobies on Parade" show while they try to put out the flames. I was a modest maiden when it came to giving out free jiggle shows. I did *not* want to be that girl, no way, no how.

But I guess proximity changes everything—and once I actually had a man in my bed to be naked *for*, well, all my buck-naked sleeping misgivings strangely evaporated, fireman booby parade be damned!

You see, for me, puberty had come and gone without even the possibility of a steady beddy-buddy. Sure, I'd dated a few guys here and there, but none of them had ever hung around long enough to become my boyfriend, or anything so trite. As much as I hated to admit it, this phenomenon had to be at least 50 percent my fault. It wasn't like I was ever: "Hey, male person I just schtupped, why don't you stay and watch me wash my face in the morning?" I suppose I was just as eager to have them go, as they were to leave.

I didn't understand why I behaved this way, but it had quickly become a pattern I was repeating well into adulthood. Maybe it came from being a late bloomer, or maybe I got bored easily . . . or *maybe* I just didn't have what it took to make a real connection with someone unless their last name was Prada or Versace.

But then I'd met Daniel (the naked man in my bed) and everything had changed. For the first time, I'd *wanted* a man to stay at my house, to share my space, to eat my food . . . I'd wanted him to laze around my bedroom in the mornings while I got ready for work, talking to me, telling me how sexy I was in my underwear—which I knew *had* to be a lie, but I loved it anyway. Having a man in such close quarters was at once thrilling and completely decadent, which was a brand-new experience for me. For the first time in my life, I was a wanton woman and I loved every minute of it.

But then a week into the cohabitation, I had a complete and utter change of heart.

At first, I didn't understand why my feelings had changed so abruptly. I'd been nothing but excited to have Daniel come stay with me while he got his new life started, so it was a shock when I realized my lack of happiness stemmed completely from the realization that Daniel wasn't the "bad boy" I'd assumed him to be.

You see, ever since he'd been released from his duties as the Devil's protégé (and taken up residence in my bed), he'd become a lot less exciting to hang around with. I was still ridiculously attracted to him—which I guessed was a positive—but sex was quickly becoming the only thing we had in common. Now, when we weren't doing the nasty, all he talked about was how much he wanted to help the denizens of Hell and how the Devil deserved a one-way ticket to a jail cell in Purgatory for all the misdeeds he'd perpetuated on his subjects. It seemed like every conversation was a rehash of this same subject until I could hardly stand to be around him anymore.

I'd expected James Dean; what I'd gotten was Mother Teresa.

Daniel was a do-gooder, an all-around nice guy who just wanted to help other people—including the entire population of Hell—and the truth was I didn't really see where I fit into the equation. I had needs, wants, neuroticisms—all the bells and whistles that went along with being a girl—and my man needed to be as interested in those things as he was in maintaining the balance between good and evil in the universe.

Of course, it didn't mean I wasn't interested in helping out the peeps down in Hell.

Far from it.

I'd promised Cerberus, the three-headed Guardian of the North Gate of Hell—and the father of my hellhound pup, Runt—that I'd make a trip to Heaven and take up his plight with God. And as soon as things had cooled down a little at work, I had definite plans to go to Heaven—just like I'd promised Cerberus—and make good on my tête-à-tête with the powers that be. I didn't know if I could really make God put a stop to all the nasty stuff the Devil was doing down in Hell, but I was going to give it my best shot.

But I didn't let the above-mentioned subject color everything I did. I still tried to have a real life outside my quasi-supernatural existence, unlike Daniel, who had no interest in anything from the human world—movies, clothes, eating out at nice restaurants—unless he could connect it back to the Afterlife.

Daniel was consumed with the idea of freeing Hell from the Devil, and he spent a lot of our time together pushing me to drop everything and go straight to Heaven to start bugging God for his/her help. When I explained to him how crazy work was, how I couldn't afford to piss off my boss any more than I already had or I was gonna lose my job, he just looked at me like I was the most selfish person on the face of the earth.

To Daniel, my job was unimportant, especially when compared to all the crap the Devil was doing down in Hell. Losing my job was a small sacrifice, one I should make willingly, so he could assume the Sally Struthers position in the "Feed the Downtrodden Minions of Hell" commercials.

The odd thing was that although we were having these very intense disagreements about what was more important—my job or the servitude the inhabitants of Hell were forced to endure—none of it seemed to impact our sex life. All the arguing had actually served to make the physical stuff even more heightened, which was annoying because I couldn't see the fairness in having our bedroom antics be so amazing while the rest of our relationship was slowly disintegrating.

"What're you thinking about?"

Daniel's face loomed large over mine, a grin on his handsome mug. He had an amazing smile, one that made my heart do the flip-flop dance every time he flashed it in my direction, but the smile didn't linger long. He knew I was holding something back—and I had no idea how to even begin to broach the subject with him. As the weeks had worn on and I hadn't conceded to help get the ball rolling up in Heaven, things had deteriorated to the point where nonverbal communication was a heck of a lot safer then opening my mouth.

I felt guilty. No, worse than guilty. I felt wicked and wrong for having these kinds of not nice thoughts, especially while the person I was having said "not nice thoughts" about was lovingly stroking my rib cage with his index finger and making my toes curl with happiness as he lay across my bed, his warm head draped on my exposed stomach.

"Nothing," I finally replied, glad he couldn't read my mind.

He lifted his dark, tousled head and raised an eyebrow thoughtfully.

"You're thinking about *something*."

He rested his head against my collarbone so he could kiss

the curve of my neck at his leisure, all the while stroking the flat part of my belly with his hand.

I had a hard time thinking logically whenever Daniel was touching me. As his hands roved over my body, I felt an electric shiver race from my stomach to my breasts, leaving a tingling feeling in its wake. Daniel knew what his hands were doing to me and took full advantage of the situation, running his fingers up between the smooth flesh of my rib cage then cupping one globe of trembling flesh and pinching the pink nipple so hard, I cried out in pleasure. Arching my back so the length of his body and his cock were pressed against me, I opened my mouth, willing his lips to find mine. He took the hint, letting his mouth trail light kisses across the hollow of my neck, up the smooth incline of my jaw, all the while using his fingers to lazily stroke my captured nipple until it was hard as a rock.

"Oh, God," I moaned. "You feel so good."

He liked that. I could feel him smiling against my mouth before he slid his tongue in between my lips and devoured me.

"Wait!" I said, sitting up so abruptly Daniel was forced to release me from his embrace, or risk smacking his head into the headboard in recompense.

"What?" he said as a frown creased his brow.

"I can't do this," I barked at him, pulling the covers off the bed to conceal myself with. Apparently, I'd chosen this very moment to purge all the poisonous thoughts that'd been building in my head ever since he'd shown up at my door and started harassing/sleeping with me.

"Do what?" he said, looking perplexed as I wrapped my naked self in the comforter and crawled down to the bottom of the bed, trying to put a little distance between me and his naked (i.e., distracting) man parts.

"We shouldn't be having sex anymore," I replied lamely. "I just don't think it's a good idea."

"I don't understand," he said, sitting up and, thoughtfully, putting a pillow over the distracting man bits. "I thought we liked each other . . ."

He trailed off, scrunching his forehead in confusion. I closed my eyes, trying to buy myself a little time. I didn't really want to have this conversation, but the relationship couldn't keep going the way it was going or else I was gonna tear my hair out in frustration.

"Look, I don't want to be a bitch, but you are seriously buzzkilling our relationship," I began.

"Excuse me?" Daniel interrupted, grabbing a pair of boxers off the floor where he'd dropped them the night before and slipping them on.

"You talk about the same stuff over and over again and it's hard for me to feel like anything other than a conduit to Heaven—"

"I can go there without you anytime I want, Callie. I thought it would be more effective if we put the request in together."

"Oh," I said, looking down at my hands. This was a new piece of information. "Well, then, I think you should just go now and then I'll go later—"

"Callie," Daniel said, his voice taut with feeling, demanding my attention. I looked up, expecting to find a scowl on his face, but he was only gazing at me with a quiet intensity, his countenance broadcasting nothing but sincerity.

"I know all of this is hard for you, Cal," he continued. "And I'll go to Heaven without you if that's really what you want, but I'm not gonna let you push me away without a fight."

"Huh?" I said, feeling as if the rug were being pulled out from under my feet. Here I was trying to tell him why he was ruining our relationship, and instead, he was turning it all back around on me.

"You push people away," he said, reaching out and taking my hand. "Especially when you're scared. I know I've been trying to force you to deal with the promise you made to Cerberus, but if you're not ready to do it, then I won't press you anymore."

I gulped, uncertainty distracting me from my righteous sense of anger.

"But we don't even get along . . ." I babbled, my brain searching for more words to bolster my argument, but not finding any.

"I think we get on great," Daniel said as he lifted my hand to his lips and softly kissed my knuckles.

"In the sack maybe," I replied, the words sounding rude even to my own ears, but I was feeling the pull of his physical nearness and I hoped rudeness would stave off attraction.

"You don't really mean that," he said, a grin stealing across his face.

"I do, too."

He turned my hand over and kissed the delicate flesh of my wrist, making my heart flutter pitifully.

"No, you're just scared, so you're putting together all kinds of irrational arguments in your head. You're such a *girl*."

"Whatever!" I said, resenting the implication. I might be a girl anatomically, but I hardly ever acted like one—well, at least I thought I hardly ever acted like one. But now Daniel was starting to make me feel uncertain about that, too.

"Yeah, I know you pride yourself on being surly," Daniel laughed, "but you're just a big marshmallow underneath it all."

I smacked him on the arm, but he used the opportunity to grasp my wrist and leverage me toward him, the covers slipping away as he wrapped his arms around my waist and pulled me close. He smelled yummy, like cinnamon and cloves, as he slid his hands over my breasts, cupping them and making me squirm.

"See, I told you we get on great," he whispered as he nuzzled my neck, peppering kisses across my collarbone.

As much as I wanted to disagree, I found that I couldn't. My body had betrayed me, giving in to the lull of sex as Daniel slid has hands between my legs, his fingers slipping wetly inside me. I moaned, knowing the argument would have to wait for another time, because pleasure was what my body craved now. I gave in and kissed him, our tongues entangling while his fingers worked me like a harp, sliding in and out of me, faster and faster, until I could hardly contain myself. I was in agony, on fire with the need to feel him inside me, but when I reached for his cock, he crawled on top of me.

"I want you to feel good," he said, nipping at my earlobe, then his lips roaming down until they found my breast, kneading the nipple taut with his teeth. I couldn't breathe, my brain overwhelmed by a warm, tingling sensation deep in my belly.

"You're gonna make me . . ." I moaned, my voice thick and drugged with sex as a wave of pleasure hit me, and I cried out, my back arching in ecstasy, his slick cock thrusting inside me while I climaxed. The orgasm was overwhelming, taking over my entire being with its sweetness, my body trembling as I fell against him. A moment later, he came inside me and I clutched his body tightly to my own, not wanting to ever disentangle myself from his embrace. Spent, I could hardly put together a coherent thought, but as he collapsed on top of me, I knew I was utterly satiated by what we'd done.

"Feel better?" he whispered, and it took all the energy I had left to nod my head "yes." "Good."

I wanted to close my eyes and go back to sleep, but my eye caught the face of the digital alarm clock on my bedside table and I nearly choked. It was almost time to be at work and I had left myself zero time to shower before I got dressed. I was just gonna have to be late; I reeked of sex, and a shower was the only cure.

Ugh.

"I gotta go," I said, pushing myself up onto my knees.

"You don't *have* to go," Daniel said, but I ignored him as I crawled off the bed and began searching for my robe.

"I've told you a million times, if I'm late for work—"

"Hyacinth will have your head," Daniel finished for me.

"Exactly," I said as I dragged the robe from its hiding place under my bed, slipping it over my shoulders before making a beeline for the bathroom. Worried about being late and getting my head bitten off at work, I didn't even take the time to say good-bye.

"I'll miss you, Cal . . ." he called after me, but he didn't make a move to stop me—and I was too preoccupied to notice the hurt look on his face.

Funny thing was, when I thought back to that moment, the only thing I remembered was the sense of finality I felt as the bathroom door clicked shut behind me. Little did I know then that the next time I saw Daniel, two people I loved would be dead and my whole world would be utterly changed forever.

two

New York in the late fall is a beautiful thing. It marks the beginning of scarf season, when people start hauling out their heavy winter coats from the back of the closet, digging up mittens and earmuffs from the bottom drawer of the wardrobe where they've been hibernating during the off months. All across Manhattan people shut their windows against the cold, cranking their thermostats up as high as they'll go, daring Mother Nature to catch them if she can.

I loved walking in the fall air, my breath a frosty wreath in front of my face as I marveled at the beauty of my chosen home. I loved the city with a passion, the way it made me feel as if I'd been thrust into the teeming heart of humanity and, at the same time, left utterly to my own devices. It was easy to blend in with the crowd here, to escape into the monotony of urban life and not think, just react.

I loved that I could walk or take the subway wherever I wanted. Or if I was feeling particularly blasé about my finances, I could hop in a cab and take it all the way uptown. There was so much to see here, so many people to interlock my fate with. For me, it was enough just to stand underneath a canopy of skyscrapers and breathe the salty, human-scented air.

Of course, there were bad things about the city, too, but like a love-struck schoolgirl with a myopic view of the thing she adores, I revered what I wanted about the city (and myself) and ignored the rest. I pared away the bad parts until all that was left was a fantasy world. One I could float through without really having to be engaged in what was going on around me. A place where I could be and do whatever I wanted without being judged by anyone—even when I majorly screwed things up.

In the summer, New York City was stuffed to the gills with people walking, talking, and eating. It was only as the air crisped and the leaves in Central Park started to change their color that the cacophony died away and the city began its preparation for the long, hard winter to come. The fall was that happy time between the two extremes, when people were still out on foot—albeit wrapped up to their ears in outerwear, not half-naked like in July and August—enjoying the outdoors and knowing full well as soon as the first snow fell, even they would be taking refuge indoors, where it was warm and toasty.

I personally didn't mind the cold because it was a very good excuse to trot out all my winter goodies. Today, as the wind whistled down through the construction site and the row of street vendors camped out next to the subway stop at Canal Street, I was wearing a thickly woven Prada scarf I'd gotten as a gift from my sister Clio on my last birthday. It was light gray and went splendidly with the purple plaid knee-length skirt, gray tights, and creamy charcoal leather cropped jacket I'd gotten at H&M the week before.

I know shopping at H&M might be seen as slumming it a little, but I was seriously learning that relaxing my rigid "designer only" policy was freeing to both my pocketbook *and* my psyche. My jacket may not have been culled from the finest lambskin money could buy, but it looked supercool and was definitely within my price range—no need to forgo lunch for a week because I'd plumbed my bank account of every last penny to buy it, either.

Clad in my Swedish import best, I may've looked like a

discount fashion plate, but I was so not feeling the love on the inside. I was running late from an aborted lunch experiment, and I knew if I didn't make this train, I was gonna be up shit creek without a paddle. My boss, Hyacinth Stewart, was a complete and total taskmaster. She'd just as soon put my bloody head on a pike as dock my meager pay if I wasn't back at my desk—butt in chair and furiously answering e-mails—by one o'clock.

I didn't know what I'd been thinking, going so far downtown for lunch, but I'd read on this fashion blog about a new restaurant that'd opened in SoHo—and happened to be co-owned by three supermodels of late nineties' fame—so I was exceedingly curious about getting a look at the place. Of course, you needed reservations months in advance just to have a drink at the bar; still, I had an hour to kill for lunch and I was more than willing to pop by and see if I could worm my way in for a look-see.

I'd had to settle for stargazing at the struck metal and glass sign on the front of the building—no supermodel action on the agenda for me that afternoon. I did spy a couple of polished-looking women in Armani who I thought I recognized from the society section of *W* magazine, but they only stopped on the sidewalk long enough to coo over the Pinkberry two doors down, completely ignoring the fashionable new restaurant I'd been obsessing over. After that, my highly annoyed stomach had growled three times in quick succession to remind me it needed feeding, and I'd grudgingly given up my spot in front of the restaurant I obviously was not gonna see the interior of, grabbing a chicken shawarma pita from a Pakistani street vendor I passed as I trudged back toward the subway stop.

For some reason luck was with me. I ended up elbowing my way onto the subway platform just as the train arrived. I slid in and immediately found a seat—which should've clued me in that something was amiss—because I never find a seat on a crowded train. Usually, I end up mashed underneath the armpit of some really tall, grubby guy with incredibly strong body odor, so this was a rare treat.

"Hello, Mistress Calliope," I heard a melodious male voice whisper into my ear.

I jumped in my orange plastic subway seat, spilling tahini sauce all down the front of my shirt.

"Dammit, Jarvis!" I choked, pulling a Kleenex from my purse and quickly wiping at my shirtfront. I sighed when I realized there was no helping the beige stain now front and center on my white sweater—and the Kleenex I was using to dab the stain was only sloughing off and making it look even grittier.

"What the hell are you doing here?" I asked through gritted teeth, looking over at my father's Executive Assistant, who was sitting primly on the seat beside me, fiddling with his pocket watch. He was wearing a fitted blue wool blazer with gold buttons, no pants, and a pince-nez perched precariously on the end of his aquiline nose.

"I am here to force you into finally making good on your promise," he replied in his clipped British accent. "Since you obviously were not going to come to me, I had to come to you."

"But here? On the subway? *Right now?*" I glared at him, hoping he'd at least put a spell on himself to prevent anyone of the human persuasion from noticing the cute little goat haunches he happened to be sporting.

Oh, did I forget to mention Jarvis is a faun who prefers to go around without pants—regardless of the fact that not wearing pants is tantamount to sharing entirely too much information about one's self with people one does not know?

No one sitting or standing near us seemed to have noticed that a supposedly mythological creature was hoofing it on the subway with them, so I relaxed a little. The last time Jarvis had been spotted out in public, it had been by a little boy at a Starbucks and it had almost caused a scene.

"I think the time is ripe to make the introduction you promised me," Jarvis said, interrupting my train of thought *and* ignoring the look of surprise that overtook my face.

"Oh *that*," I said, relaxing as I realized Jarvis wasn't here to badger me on Cerberus's behalf. The promise he was referring to was of a more personal nature.

"Yes, *that*," Jarvis replied, getting all persnickety.

"But now?" I repeated, no witty rejoinder finding its way into my head and out through my mouth.

"I've had my eye on the lady in question, and I feel if I am ever going to act, I must do it now," Jarvis continued, his thick black eyebrows raised in consternation.

He may have been a faun—a half-man/half-goat whose human torso balanced precariously upon cloven-hoofed lower extremities right out of the barnyard—but he was still a pretty handsome-looking fellow. He had a head of thick black hair he kept carefully pomaded in place, a Tom Selleck mustache that would be considered "sissy" on anyone else's face, and dark, luminous eyes that were always keyed in on exactly what I didn't want them to see. Still, where human women were concerned, I had a feeling his smaller stature—Jarvis was no taller than four-eleven on a good day—and lack of human-looking equipment downstairs might preclude him from catching the eye of the lady he was enamored with at the moment:

Namely, Hyacinth Stewart, my power-monger boss.

I'd graduated from Sarah Lawrence with a degree that prepared me for absolutely nothing. Sure, I knew what the term "postmodern feminism" meant, but I'd had no idea how to roll calls or make an Excel spreadsheet. I was woefully unprepared for my first foray into the workforce—despite the fact that I was starting at the bottom rung of the ladder, in what could only politely be termed an "entry-level" position.

You'd think a chimp could do my job (I'm the Executive Assistant to the Vice President of Sales at the aptly named House and Yard—the company that brings you all the house and yard crap you see at three in the morning on the Home Shopping Network), but you would be sadly mistaken. Dealing with the whims of a highly neurotic boss who wants nothing more than to make my life a living hell is *not* for the banana-slurping constitution of a primate.

Opposable thumbs or not.

I respected Hyacinth for her astute business acumen, but I had loftier goals for myself. I wanted to work for *Vogue*—or any other fashion rag that would have me—so I was kind of annoyed by my boss's unwillingness to promote me or, at the very least, put in a good word with one of her publishing diva girlfriends. I just knew she had the connections to give me a leg up if she wanted, but ever since I'd heard through the grapevine—the grapevine being my fellow Executive Assistant in crime, Geneva—that Hyacinth actually *liked* having me around, I'd known there would be no plans for advancement in my future.

A fact I was still trying to come to terms with.

With the economy in the crapper, and me being a coward who hated confrontation, there was no chance I would have it out with Hy. So instead of dealing with my future in a productive way, I spent my days at work in my cubicle silently stewing in my own juices as I answered e-mails, took phone calls, and fervently wished my boss would get run over by a bike messenger.

I knew it was a mean thing to wish on anyone, but I couldn't help it. I was a wuss.

And so, these were the myriad reasons why I hadn't made good on my overdue promise to introduce Jarvis to Hyacinth, a promise I really did need to fulfill—and soon—or else the faun might take things into his own hands, and then where would my future job prospects be?

"Okay, there has to be a smart way to do this," I said. "There has to be a legitimate way to introduce you guys without her having a freak-out and firing me."

"And pray tell, *why* would she freak out?" Jarvis asked testily.

"Oh, I don't know why she would freak out, Jarvis. Maybe it's because you're a midget with the hoofs and private parts of a goat," I shot back.

"Such terrible parenting these days," the arthritic old woman on the other side of the bench said as she raised her newspaper between us like some kind of homemade cootie barrier.

"Excuse me?" I growled at the business section of the *New York Times*, but the lady didn't even twitch.

My suspicions aroused, I turned my attention back to Jarvis.

"What kind of glamour did you put on yourself?" I said, peeved.

He just grinned at me.

"Tell me!" I said, grabbing him by the lapels of his blue suit coat.

Suddenly, a man in white coveralls and a baseball cap, who had been quietly minding his own business across the aisle, stood up and lumbered toward me.

"I dunno how you treats yo'kid in da privacy of your own home, but if you go touchin' him again on dis' train, I'm gunna show you what's what."

I gaped at the man, trying to process what it was exactly he was saying to me because apparently I wasn't fluent in what was either Brooklyn- or Long Island–ese.

"Mean it," he sputtered at me as he returned to his seat, giving me the stink eye, for all that was worth. I was more frightened of his giant, hamlike fists.

"Did that guy just threaten me?" I growled out of the side of my mouth at Jarvis.

"I suppose it could be categorized as a threat." Jarvis shrugged, all nonchalant in a way that made me want to slap him upside the head.

"You just *had* to spell yourself to look like a little kid, didn't you?"

Jarvis gave me a happy nod, and for the first time I caught a glimpse—by way of his reflection in the window across from us—of the glamour he'd put on himself. No wonder Mr. Brooklyn-ese thought I was a Grade A, primo jerk. Jarvis had chosen the most angelic-looking child in the whole of the free world to spell himself into. With big, blue button eyes, a shock of white blond hair that came to a swirling cowlick at the crown of his head, and two missing incisors right in the front of his mouth, Jarvis was unimpeachable. I would lose every battle we got into as long as he continued to look like Dennis the Menace on steroids.

"Ah, it *does* give one pleasure to see you under the gun, Miss Calliope."

"Jarvis," I started to hiss at him, then thought better of it, modulating the sound of my voice so as not to appear aggressive with the *child*. "They think you're *my* kid, don't they."

It wasn't a question.

Jarvis giggled gleefully.

"So *not* fair," I added, still keeping an eye on the guy across the aisle. He'd pulled out a tattered *MAD* magazine, but was only pretending to read it.

"Not my kid!" I said, pointing at the top of Jarvis's head. "Seriously, *not mine*."

The guy continued to ignore me, but a few of the other people on the train openly stared at my outburst. Just at that moment, thankfully, we hit a bump in the track, and the whole car was jostled sideways, so trying to remain upright took precedence over staring at Jarvis and me. Besides, I'd long since stopped being embarrassed by all the weird things that happened to me—like fauns pretending to be children, pretending to be nice to you, so they can get what they want: an introduction to your plus-sized boss.

Ew!

"If you want me to introduce you to Hy, then you have to get rid of that ridiculous glamour. No way José am I going into my building with Dennis the Menace in tow," I said. "There will be no end to the questions, and frankly, everyone at the office already thinks I'm a nut ball."

"As you wish, Mistress Calliope—"

"And none of that 'Mistress' crap, either. You call me Callie just like everyone else does," I interrupted, "or the deal is off."

Jarvis extended his dainty hand and we shook on it.

Without warning, the train hit another bump and the whole car was plunged into darkness. I squeezed Jarvis's hand, not liking this premature night thing one little bit.

"Mistress Calliope—"

Jarvis's eyes were like two shining marbles in the unexpected, inky darkness—yet they weren't trained on me, but on something outside our window. I followed his gaze and saw a creature stalking the tunnel walkway just beyond the glass. It was surreally pale, its long-limbed body fluid as it navigated its way past our car and down through another subway tunnel that splintered off our line. As it disappeared, I tried to recall exactly what I'd just seen, but found all I could draw back into my mind was a blurry afterimage of the thing. I couldn't have told you if it had a face or whether it was male or female.

As soon as it was completely gone, the lights flickered twice then returned to their full, preblackout brightness. I let go of Jarvis's hand, embarrassed he'd caught me freaking out. It wasn't like I was scared of the dark or anything . . . Okay, maybe I was a little scared of the dark, but mostly it was just being trapped in a speeding subway train hurtling through pitch-blackness toward God knew where that made me nervous.

From the looks of it, no one else in the car had seen what we'd seen—otherwise I was pretty sure there would've been a stampede for the emergency brake cord. In fact, the old lady beside me was quietly reading her paper as if nothing had happened.

Not even the blackout.

I wondered how it was possible to make a subway carload of people forget what they'd just seen, or maybe I had the whole thing backward—maybe human beings were trained to ignore the weirder stuff; like there were synapses missing inside their brains, so that when magical stuff went down, it just didn't register.

Later, I was gonna to have to ask Jarvis for a little insight into the matter, but first I wanted to know what I'd just seen outside the window.

"What the hell was that thing?" I whispered to Jarvis.

"My poor little dense child," Jarvis intoned.

I rolled my eyes. Jarvis had spent enough time in my company to know my knowledge of the Afterlife was pretty limited—mostly because I had absolutely zero interest in the subject. I suppose if I really cared, I could've taken a crash course on the topic and be a Mr. Know-It-All like him, but somehow the idea held very little appeal.

"Give me a break, Jarvi, and stop being so patronizing. You know I have no clue what that thing was, so why don't you just spill the info—"

"But you *must* know why the New York Subway System was originally built?" He sighed.

I took a deep breath and held it for a few moments before releasing it, my lips now formed into what I hoped was a condescending smile.

"Jarvi, I have no idea why the subway was originally built," I said, a smile still plastered on my face with the superglue of annoyance. "*All* I know about the New York Subway is I can buy a single-ride ticket and ride up and down any goddamned subway line I want to until I have to get off to pee."

"Well, that is *one* use, I suppose," Jarvis considered, "but the *real* reason the subway was created was to provide a more literal conduit to Heaven—"

The words weren't even out of his mouth before I was talking over them.

"No way! That's so cool—"

"Callie, quietly, please—"

"But—" I said.

"No *buts*," Jarvis said quickly, his eyes scanning the train to make sure no one was listening in on our conversation.

"Tell me—"

"We should discuss this in another environment," Jarvis said firmly, his eyes resting on a tall, cadaverous man standing beside the emergency exit. "A *safer* environment."

"Why?" I whispered, getting unsettled by the rigid set of Jarvis's shoulders. "Is that guy listening to us?"

Jarvis merely nodded at my words. I followed Jarvis's stare, taking in the cadaverous man's shabby charcoal suit, scuffed Hush Puppies, and the fact that he was staring straight ahead, his eyes looking nowhere in our vicinity.

I decided to make my own assessment of the situation.

"Are you *sure*?" I said, relaxing as I decided the cadaverous man was just some sad sack who happened to be riding the same train as us. Obviously, Jarvis needed to get over the whole "secrecy" kick he was on, because no one cared what the hell we were talking about.

"Do you *never* listen to a word I say?" Jarvis sighed.

I shrugged.

"I don't know. I listen when I think you're saying something important—"

Suddenly, there was a flurry of activity near our man—people trying to move out of his way actually—and I realized there was something very wrong about the way his body was shuddering underneath his clothing. He shrieked once, the sound like sewing pins being shoved into my eardrums, and then fell forward onto his knees, his back arching inhumanly as his body slowly started to change shape, the contours of his shoulders pushing in on themselves as they elongated.

"Oh, shit . . ." I said under my breath.

"Yes, Callie, 'oh, shit' is an appropriate response," Jarvis rejoined, scowling at me for like the three-thousandth time in our relationship.

I watched, frozen in my seat, as the cadaverous man—who now looked like a cadaverous, furry wolf-man with long, muscled forearms and a nasty set of serrated teeth—hunkered down into a crouch, a long string of drool hanging like a pendant from his elongating jaw. I watched in horror as his jaw continued its bizarre re-forming until it was more muzzle than mouth, his eyes shifting from dull gray to a piercing rain-slicker yellow.

With a sharp *crack*, the transformation was complete and the creature stretched its newly reconstructed limbs, making sure all was as it should be. Then, like buoyant fingers quickly doing an arpeggio up my spine, I felt the beast turn its head and train those strange yellow eyes onto the hollow of my throat. I gulped as the creature threw back its head and howled, a sound so chilling that one of the women a few seats down from Jarvis began to sob. Fear pulsed like a live diode through the subway car, but I had a strange feeling this man/

beast wasn't after indiscriminate bloodshed. No, he had one goal rattling around in that nasty old skull case of his and I was pretty certain it concerned me personally.

The beast began to sniff, its gaping nostrils flaring as it combed the air, searching for a particular scent tangled among the many. Its eyes flared as it found what it was seeking, but it took one more exaggerated inhalation, as if savoring what it had discovered.

"I can smell your fear, Death's Daughter," the creature rasped, human speech not so easy now. *"Come to me and spare these poor mortals."*

His words were spoken pointedly in my direction, and everyone in the car turned to look at me, a miasma of their fear, anger, and pity enveloping me. I looked around, wondering why there were never any superheroes around to save me when I happened into one of these gnarly, monster-themed situations.

"Uhm . . . no?" I said, my mouth moving without any help from my brain. "You do understand the concept of the word 'no,' right? It means that there is no way in hell am I going to come to you, wolf boy—"

I felt Jarvis clutch the hem of my scarf, yanking hard, as if to remind me of the delicate footing I was currently on.

"Beware, Calliope, the Vargr are cunning beasts," Jarvis muttered into my ear as the creature inched toward me on its padded paws.

"Come . . . to . . . me," it keened, beckoning me forward with one hairy, bloated claw. Its knuckles and sharpened, talonlike nails were deterrent enough to keep me from answering its call. I could feel the stares from the rest of the passengers and realized some of them would gladly sacrifice me if it meant their own freedom.

It was kind of a chilling realization.

Still, I was not gonna let the creature tear my throat out for fun, no matter what anyone else was thinking. I shook my head firmly in the negative, unwilling to speak again because I was afraid my voice would come out about two octaves higher than normal.

"So be it," the beast growled, throwing back its head and rending the air with another bone-chilling howl, this one causing every hair on my body to stand at rigid attention.

Immobile in my fear, I sat stiffly in my seat, my eyes glued to the naked muscles at the nape of the creature's neck as they twitched uncontrollably underneath its tufted brown pelt. The creature was annoyed by its inability to bend me to its will and it growled ferociously, the nauseating stink of its breath crossing the length of the subway car, making everyone gag.

I could sense the coiled energy seething inside the beast, compressing its physical form into a ball of tightly muscled fury as it bided its time, waiting to pounce. All it needed was a reason to attack and it was gonna be exhaling that nasty breath all up in my face.

And I am that reason, I realized grimly as the beast suddenly leapt into the air, its body a missile with canines, making a beeline straight for my Prada-clad throat.

three

Let's pause a minute for a little station identification.

I mean, it's not every day you see a Vargr throat-ripping scenario play out on a New York City Subway car, so let me just give you a little background info on myself, which will, hopefully, clarify things a bit.

My name is Calliope Reaper-Jones and I *used* to be a normal girl—okay, scratch that last part. In truth, I was *never* a normal girl. But in my own defense, I always wanted to be normal, and I really thought wanting to be like everyone else actually got you halfway to being there.

You see, I was born into a family of immortals—with my father being one of the chief immortals in all of the Afterlife. Call him what you would—Death, the Grim Reaper, the Man with the Golden Scythe, he pretty much answers to *any* of the above—his supernatural pedigree seriously put a dent in my attempts at normalcy.

Growing up, I desperately held on to the fact I was half-human on my mother's side (i.e., the Reaper-*Jones* hyphenation) with all the tenacity I could muster, but whether I liked it or not, it was the nonhuman part of my heritage that would forever assert itself in my life . . . no matter how hard I tried to keep it hidden away from prying eyes.

My own immortality—bestowed upon me at my birth—was something I despised. It made it impossible for me to do anything but outlive all my friends, and frankly, that also kind of killed my ability to assimilate: assimilation being the key to a normal existence, as far as I was concerned.

Being the denial-loving creature I am, I decided the best thing I could do in the situation was to pretend I wasn't Death's Daughter. That, in fact, I was really the offspring of some businessman who just happened to be extraordinarily gifted with money. That would explain the huge mansion in Newport, Rhode Island, called Sea Verge, which my family called home, and the funds necessary to send my sisters and me to the best private schools on the East Coast.

And so went the first decade and a half of my life: me taking all of my familial weirdness and shoving it way down deep into the darkest recesses of my mind, where it stayed, unwanted and ignored, for a very long time.

But then a few months ago my dad had to go and get himself kidnapped, and suddenly, all of the supernatural craziness I'd been suppressing came back to bite me on the ass. I was thrust headfirst into the family business, forced to complete three nearly impossible tasks by the Board of Death in order to take over my dad's position as President and CEO of Death, Inc. Plus, I had to figure out who'd kidnapped him *and* get him back before all hell broke loose.

Piece of cake, right?

I don't think so.

Finally, after ensuring order was restored to the Afterlife, I'd taken pity on my estranged family and—against my better judgment—agreed to try and get reacquainted with them, for better or worse.

So far things had been leaning toward worse, which was how I now found myself sitting on an uptown subway train trying not to get my throat ripped out by a Vargr.

"stop!" i screamed, my mouth overriding my brain as I stood up, shutting my eyes against the oncoming attack (two very disparate acts, but my body has never seemed to understand the word contradiction). I gritted my teeth and covered my face with my arms, waiting for the onslaught of violence to begin, but before any Vargr teeth could rip into the reasonably smooth flesh of my throat, my entire body was enveloped in a pulsing white-hot heat. I tried to scream—the pain being pretty damn intense—but only strangled gurgling bloomed from between my lips.

As if the subway car were moving in tandem with whatever strange energy had hold of me, it began to shudder, bouncing on the track like some irate five-year-old was playing demolition derby with it. Still hunched over, arms covering my face, awaiting my imminent dismemberment (something that would really hurt and would also make my immortality not very much fun for the foreseeable future), I swallowed hard, my nerves on fire. Pins and needles shot up my arms and legs as an intense burning sensation numbed me from the inside out. It felt as if I'd fallen into a vat of Icy Hot and was now experiencing the afteraffects of a menthol overdose.

As abruptly as it had started, the white-hot heat dissipated, leaving me with a chill that wracked every cell in my body and made me shiver uncontrollably, my teeth cracking together like nunchakus. I figured it would be a miracle if I didn't bite my tongue off before this crazy ride was over.

Trying to ignore the weird shivering that had overtaken my person, I unhunched and slowly opened my eyes to find out what was going on with the Vargr attack already in progress. But before I could get a fix on what was happening, the lights flickered then went out, sending the car into a fathomless darkness punctuated only by the occasional flash of blue light marking the places where emergency phones were hidden inside the subway tunnel—something that was of absolutely no help to me.

With the disappearance of the light, a sense of foreboding filled the car, and the people around me started to panic, terrified by the supernatural weirdness they'd just been thrust into the thick of. Most people had no idea the supernatural world even existed, nor were they prepared for some of its (heretofore imaginary) minions to make a surprise appearance on their lunchtime subway commute.

High-pitched voices, underlined by a tremolo of fear, intermixed until the cacophony of words was unintelligible. One thing I've learned about human beings is that whenever they're in the middle of a crisis, they are certain that the louder and more insistent they become, the more chance of surviving they have. I'm pretty sure this tack doesn't really work, but they hold on to the idea regardless.

Ignoring the squawking of the people around me, I reached up and felt for my face, my shaking fingers hooking into the weave of my Prada scarf and almost choking me in the process. I assessed the rest of my limbs, finding, happily, that whatever energy had overtaken me hadn't done any outward damage—even though my body continued to vibrate like a plucked string. Still, my joy at being physically A-okay receded sharply as I realized that by all intents and purposes I shouldn't be standing upright.

As great as it was to find myself all in one working piece, the Vargr had been gunning for my throat, so why the hell wasn't I lying in a pool of my own blood on the nasty-looking subway floor?

I pictured my physical body, lying in bloody pieces on the dirt-and-germ-laden fire-retardant flooring of the subway train—and then I pictured myself trying to Purell said bloody mess as it lay strewn across the floor.

Ah, the joys of being immortal.

The fact that my body had been used as some kind of magical superconductor and I was still functioning, with no teeth marks anywhere I could feel, meant that a little supernatural assistance had been thrown my way. And the only person I could think of with any magical ability within a fifty-foot radius was—

Jarvis!

I'd totally forgotten about my dad's Executive Assistant during all the craziness. Apparently, I turned into a complete and selfish bitch when I got caught up in a monster attack—not that this was any kind of a shocker. Being less self-involved was something I'd been working on as of late, but since I'd spent the last few years on my own, it was still hard for me to remember to play well with others.

"Jarvis!" I hissed, but my voice was lost in the panicked chatter of the other human beings trapped in the subway car with us. They sounded like a pack of royally pissed-off parakeets, annoyed someone had walked past their cages at the arboretum.

"SHUT UP OR DIE, PEOPLE!" I screamed and felt another pulse of energy slam into my body. Shivering, I reached out a hand, searching for the faun, but I only came away with empty air. Somewhere in the darkness I heard the tolling of a bell, thirteen times in quick succession, and I hoped that meant someone was working on getting the lights back on soon.

"Jarvis?"

Oh, God, I totally let the Vargr beastie eat Jarvis, I thought miserably, my head starting to pound. I should have put a kibosh on the whole cowardly lion act and protected my friend, whether I got turned into immortal beef jerky or not. I was immortal, for God's sake. I could live without a chunk of my intestines—and besides, who says an all-liquid diet is such a bad thing anyway?

"Jarvis, where are you? Are you here? Oh my God, did you get *eaten*?" I whispered, terrified I wasn't gonna get a response. "*Jarvis?!* Did I let you get eaten? Please don't be in someone's stomach—"

Suddenly, I felt a cold, clammy hand grasp my wrist, and I went rigid, fear turning me to stone where I stood, my feet frozen to the plastic flooring. It seemed the Vargr wasn't gonna let me off so easily. I was about to become the main course in a Vargr brunch.

I kicked myself for coming downtown in the first place. If I'd stayed in my cubicle at work, none of this would be happening. Jarvis wouldn't be the goat kebab appetizer on a wolf-man's lunch buffet . . . I wouldn't be the dessert.

"Oh my God, please don't eat me . . ." I began, trying to sound as meek and pathetic as possible. If I was going to be

Vargr fodder, then I at least wanted the creature to feel cruddy about it.

"I taste like crap . . . I swear, if you eat me, you're talking like major league indigestion—"

"Hush now, Miss Calliope."

Even though I couldn't exactly see him in all the darkness, we'd been through enough Callie-induced scrapes for me to recognize Jarvis's snooty British accent whenever I heard it. Instantly I relaxed, letting the fear slide down my back and disappear into the pitch-black ether surrounding us. I squeezed Jarvis's bony hand, exceedingly relieved to find my friend hadn't been turned into a goat kebab, after all.

Sadly, my guilt-induced headache was less easy to get rid of: it'd sunk its teeth into my brain and had obviously liked what it'd found there. It wasn't going anywhere until I got my hands on a bottle of Extra Strength Tylenol and downed its contents.

"What's going on?" I whispered, squeezing Jarvis's hand again, very happy he was alive and well, standing beside me. The darkness made it impossible to see what was happening around us, so I hoped Jarvis was more clued in to the supernatural 411 than I was.

"I'm not certain," he began, "but I believe the spell you used incapacitated the Vargr—"

"Hey, I didn't do a spell," I said, protesting my innocence. "And I'm pretty sure I would know if I *had* done one, don't you think?"

"Miss Calliope, I was sitting beside you and you definitely used a spell."

Jarvis might think I was capable of doing the kind of magic that would subdue a savage Vargr, but when he actually stopped to think about it, he would realize how highly unlikely it would be for me to pull off something so advanced all by myself. I mean, I knew me pretty well—I'd only been kicking around in this body for twenty-some odd years—and I knew there was no way I could successfully subdue a Vargr without help. I couldn't even call up a wormhole, and that was one of the most basic magic spells around.

If I was going for full disclosure here, I'd say the only advanced magic I'd ever been capable of producing revolved around me being stuck in a tight spot and magic just "popping" out of me in order to save me from sudden dismemberment.

Maybe this was what had happened with the Vargr, but I doubted it. Every other time I'd been saved by magic, there'd been no ill effects—being dipped in a vat of Icy Hot, anyone?—so I was pretty certain the magic hadn't come from me.

Pretty pathetic, huh? I could create an Excel spreadsheet, beat the bejesus out of any living creature that got between me and the sale rack at Bloomingdale's, but I couldn't pull a rabbit out of my hat without a pair of training wheels and a copy of *Magic for Dummies* clutched in my hand.

I vehemently shook my head in disagreement because I knew I hadn't done a spell, but then I remembered we were in the dark and Jarvis couldn't see me.

"I didn't do a spell. I don't know how to do spells," I said. "You *know* this about me. I'm totally magic defective."

There was a pause as Jarvis thought that one over.

"I suppose someone else could've been working the spell through you," Jarvis conceded finally. "*If* you're sure the magic didn't come from you."

"Absolutely, positively certain," I said.

As I waited for him to reply, I noticed the subway car had gone deathly silent. I'd been so busy arguing with Jarvis I'd completely missed the changeover. Part of me assumed we'd scared the crap out of our fellow riders with all our magic talk and that they were being good little church mice, recording our conversation on their iPhones to hand over to the Bellevue commitment crew who were waiting for us at the next stop. Yet deep inside I knew I was being naïve. I mean, these people had been chattering like drunkards, and now you could hear a pin drop. The whole situation gave me a funny feeling in the pit of my stomach—and I was doing everything within my power to ignore it.

"Uhm, Jarvis?" I said. "Do you hear anything funny in

here? Actually, I mean, do you hear a *lack* of anything funny in here . . . ?"

The lights flickered back on just as the words left my mouth. I blinked a few times, my eyes stinging as they tried to adjust to the sudden onslaught of fluorescent light. Jarvis's hand found mine again, and this time the crunch he gave my fingers was anything but reassuring.

"Miss Calliope . . . ?"

Jarvis's words trailed off into a very definitive question mark. I looked around the car, reaffirming that the silence I'd just registered had not been brought about by our magic-centric conversation. Nope, something a lot more insidious was responsible for the lack of human chatter on this particular subway car . . . and that insidious thing was Death.

While Jarvis and I'd been babbling our heads off, someone or something had laid waste to every single living creature in our subway car. I did a silent head count, my eyes roving over the dead bodies draped over plastic seats, faces pressed against windows, hands hanging limply in the aisles. In front of Jarvis lay the Vargr, who in death had returned to his original form, that of a tall, gaunt man. I reached out my foot and poked the man's shoulder with the tip of my shoe, hoping against hope this was all just a prank, but the man was deadweight, his body immovable. I wanted to squat down and touch his face, move his lips back to see if those nasty-looking Vargr teeth were still in residence, but something held me back. I wouldn't call it fear, per se, but more like a healthy respect for the dead.

I looked around at the other dead folks, but I couldn't tell what had killed them. From where I was standing, there appeared to be no blood on the bodies, no sense that any kind of violence had overtaken them. Their faces were peaceful, and if I chose to step into the world of denial, I could almost believe they were sleeping. There were no lines of terror etched into their skin, no glazed and sightless eyes staring reproachfully up at me, laying the blame at the dainty feet of the itinerant Daughter of Death.

I observed the thirteen corpses—men and women who up

until a few moments ago I'd shared oxygen with—and tried to put the pieces of the puzzle together. I knew it wasn't my fault, yet I couldn't help but feel responsible for the loss of life. If Jarvis and I hadn't been on this train, would these people still be alive? I had absolutely no idea, and to dwell on the question too long might bring answers I couldn't—and didn't—want to deal with.

Who was I kidding? The time to *not* deal with this stuff had passed me by about ten minutes earlier when I was walking down Canal Street chowing down on my chicken shawarma. Suddenly, a really horrible thought came unbidden into my mind and wouldn't go away. It sat there like a whiny baby, demanding I pay attention to it.

What if these Deaths had nothing to do with the situation and *everything* to do with me? I'd been set up before and I knew the hallmarks pretty well. Maybe whoever had killed these people had done it to place the blame squarely at my feet?

"Jarvis, we have to get out of here before we get to the next stop," I said, looking over at the shell-shocked faun, who only nodded. "Otherwise, you and I are going to end up locked away in a human prison for the next thousand years."

"These poor people," Jarvis said, his voice trembling with emotion.

"I know," I said, wrapping my arm around his shoulders, "but right now I need you to ignore everything in this subway car and open a wormhole so we can get out of here before the police lay their hands on us."

Jarvis nodded, but his eyes were still locked on the motionless human bodies. "Please, Jarvis," I said, feeling the brakes of the subway car engage as the train began its imminent stop at the next station.

"We have to go now."

The meaning of my words finally seemed to penetrate, and he sighed, tearing his eyes away from the grisly sight that surrounded us. The car began to jerk, wheels grinding against the track as we neared our final destination.

"I'm sorry, shall I do it now?" he asked, distracted.

I nodded my head. "Yes. Now would *definitely* be a good time."

I held on to the little faun, as much for my support as his own, while he began the preparations for the spell. He mumbled a few words under his breath and then the air around us split, revealing a gaping hole in the ether in front of us. Pulses of staticky, amber-colored lightning cascaded out of the wormhole, coursing down the metal carriage of the subway car and slithering like electrically charged worms as they shot across the floor toward us.

Jarvis let out a low moan as the light converged around his hooves and then shot up his haunches. Instinctively, I took a step back as the fierce amber light consumed Jarvis's whole body and he moaned again, painfully. The light flared and then began to burn out, its gold tones fading into Jarvis's skin. As soon as he looked reasonably normal again, I reached out for him, steadying his body as he fainted into unconsciousness.

I gasped, never having seen a wormhole behave in quite this manner before. Usually they were more like swirling masses of black nothingness that you stepped through in order to quickly get to a new location in time and/or space. Sure, it beat the hell out of traditional traveling methods as far as efficiency was concerned, but I wasn't really a fan. The whole experience always left me feeling like a load of wash that'd been tossed around too long in an overenergetic dryer.

The train jerked twice as it screeched to a stop, the doors sliding open to admit the next wave of commuters. There was a bloodcurdling scream as the people on the platform discovered the carnage awaiting them inside. As much as instinct prevailed upon me to see what was happening back on the platform, I didn't dare turn my head. I was afraid if I wasted any more time, Jarvis and I were going to get lynched by the angry mob. With as much strength as I could muster, I looped my arm around Jarvis's waist and, straining under our combined weight, dragged the two of us into the gaping wormhole.

It was only much later, as I stood on the brink of losing everything and everyone I loved, that I truly understood the omnipotence of fate. It didn't matter what choice I'd made that day—to stay or to go was irrelevant—the hands of fate had been set into motion by a chain of events I had absolutely no control over. Of course, I had no idea then that fate was actually leading us out of the frying pan . . . *and into the searing heat of the fire.*

four

The wormhole took me back to work on time—actually with *two* minutes to spare—and in a relatively economical manner. I usually likened travel by wormhole to riding a Tilt-a-Whirl on the "spin your head off setting," but on this trip there'd been only minimal trauma to my person via the wormhole's pummeling effects and I'd even managed, unbelievably, to keep my chicken shawarma pita down in my stomach where it belonged.

As glad as I was not to be on the subway car anymore, I had to say going back to work was not exactly what I'd imagined when I'd initially stepped into the wormhole. Personally, I didn't want to return to my cubicle and stare at my eye-strainingly bright computer screen while trying not to worry about whether or not the NYPD was hot on my trail, patiently waiting to take me out back and firing-squad me with a pack of Uzi machine guns. Ostensibly, my arrest would be for masterminding a full-scale terrorist massacre on the New York City Subway System—something I did *not* do and had *no* intention of taking any false credit for—but God knows what other trumped-up charges they might decide to add to the warrant.

My fear of the NYPD was then compounded by the terror that my boss, Hyacinth, would stride out of her office to ask me where her dry cleaning was and, instead, would find me nervously biting my nails as I stood over my shell-shocked and "not so imaginary" faun friend who was sitting catatonically in my rolling black office chair.

Loverly.

Lucky for us, the wormhole hadn't dropped us off at my cubicle, but had had the decency to deposit us into an empty stall in one of the office unisex bathrooms. That meant there were at least a hallway and the office kitchen between me and the end of normal life as I knew it.

"Jarvis? Are you okay?" I asked, crawling over to where he lay on the cold, tiled floor. He shrugged, his face turned away so I couldn't read his expression, but I had a feeling Jarvis was not feeling okay, regardless of what the shrug implied.

I crawled over to the bathroom door and slid the lock into place. There was another bathroom at the other end of the hall, so if someone had to pee they could just go there. I sighed, easing myself against the wall facing a bank of sinks and the long rectangular—and unforgiving—mirror that hung above them. I could finally see Jarvis's face reflected back at me and was surprised to discover he wasn't as badly off as I'd first thought.

"I really need your help," I said lamely.

He caught me looking over at him and gave me a wink, shaking off the traumatized look he'd worn ever since we'd wormholed out of the subway. He sighed and sat up, shakily brushing the dirt and debris from the subway car off his suit jacket.

"I have been racking my brain, trying to understand what happened," Jarvis said. He stood up and walked over to the bank of sinks, turning one on and vigorously washing his hands with the tropical-scented hand soap from the dispenser.

My dad's Executive Assistant was a bit of a clean freak, but then I was, too, so at least we had that in common.

"Any ideas yet?" I asked. "Because, honestly, I feel like there's some jerkoid out there trying to set me up. It's the only thing that makes any sense."

Jarvis nodded, drying his hands with a paper towel.

"And what was that Vargr thing?" I added. "And how does it figure into all of this?"

"A Vargr," Jarvis answered, "is similar to a werewolf, but with one very marked difference."

"Yeah?" I said uncertainly, really hoping this wouldn't send Jarvis off on a lecture tangent. The poor guy loved to impart esoteric knowledge the way other people loved to . . . well, I couldn't actually think of anything other people loved to do as much as Jarvis loved to lecture.

"A Vargr is never made. It is only born," Jarvis said succinctly, raising a well-shaped brow in my direction and almost daring me to comment on his lack of lecture.

I opened my mouth to comment, but immediately thought better of it. I wasn't gonna be the one to look a gift horse in the mouth—I *sorely* wanted to encourage more succinctness in the future—so I wisely let it ride.

"And what was it doing on the subway with us?" I said instead. "It obviously wanted to eat me, but someone or something intervened."

Jarvis nodded his agreement.

"You're right when you say you don't have enough control over your powers to do the kind of damage we saw on the subway train," he added. "Although please do not take that as a slight, Miss Calliope. I'm sure if you put your mind to it, you could learn to do much worse."

Someone telling me I could learn to perpetrate magical mass killings if I wanted to shouldn't have made me feel better, but it did. I'd known in my heart Jarvis would see the truth, that I really *was* a helpless magic practitioner. As a kid, my dad had forbidden my sisters and me from practicing magic at Sea Verge—not that the ban had stopped either of my siblings from doing what they wanted. They both had way more cunning than I'd ever possess, and they ascertained as long as they kept their magical endeavors "outside" the confines of my dad's house, then they weren't really subverting his wishes. I'd always been more of a stickler to the rules, and it wouldn't have occurred to me to do something that went against my dad's wishes back then. Unlike either of my sisters, I didn't even begin to *think* about rebelling until I went away to college.

I was the average kid in the family—the middle child, sandwiched in between an abrasive, supermanipulative, Type A older sister (Thalia), who embraced her supernatural birthright with way too much gusto, and a younger, computer genius sister (Clio), who also happened to look like a miniature Kate Moss in combat boots.

I guess I should've been bitter and resentful about the short shrift I'd been given in life—apparently, I got the average gene, while my sisters split all the others—but instead of lingering on my lack of excessive brains and beauty, I did the one thing I could think of that would set me apart from my luckier siblings: I became the token normal person in my abnormal family.

Literally.

I was the one who got acne, gained twenty pounds when I hit puberty, and whose brain got all hot and bothered when it looked at fashion magazines, but then short-circuited when it had to study for a test. The funny thing was, even though my sisters were both more talented and more beautiful than me, I was never actually jealous of either of them. I may have whined about the weight and the acne, but the rest of it, the normal part, I loved.

Because my family was so vastly different, all that human frailty was extremely alluring. I very badly wanted to be like everyone else, with their human problems and instinctive knowledge of just how finite time actually was—something which forever forced them to live within the constraints of the here and now, aware that Death was riding just beyond the horizon, lustily coveting their souls.

I left any thoughts of Death as a Pale Rider behind and returned to the problem at hand.

"Thanks, Jarvis. I appreciate your mass-killing support.

No matter how many times I get singled out as the bad guy, you're always in my corner. Thank you."

Jarvis waved my thank-you aside, his brow knit in concentration as I watched the wheels spinning away in his head. I could see he was as baffled by the situation as I was.

"I think what you said might be correct, Miss Calliope," he said finally. "Although there is one other possibility, I can't imagine it would be that . . ."

I ignored the last part, fixating on the idea of who could be trying to frame me.

"So who could it be? I mean, it can't be Thalia," I offered, biting my thumbnail. "She's in Purgatory under lock and key."

My older sister—and the person who had previously tried to make me the fall guy in her wicked scheme to take over Death, Inc., and all the rest of Death's purveyance—had been sentenced to one hundred years of solitude in a cramped cell in Purgatory.

And I had no doubt that were we to go take a peek, this was exactly where we would still find her. Security in Purgatory was insanely tight, something I knew from personal experience. Jarvis and I had recently been on a "research" trip to the Hall of Death (housed within the confines of the Death, Inc., building in Purgatory), and we'd had a slight run-in with the armored knights guarding the place: I'd almost lost my head to a broadsword during our visit, and needless to say, it was not something I was dying to repeat anytime in the near future.

"Yes, I suppose it would seem unlikely that she would be able to escape without help," Jarvis murmured, but his mind seemed elsewhere. "The security in Purgatory is nothing if not reliable. Also, your father made certain the original brimstone structure was retrofitted with every security allowance possible when he created the Death, Inc., offices."

"So this is what we do know," I said. "We know that we don't know who's trying to set me up. We also know we don't know what that Vargr was doing on the subway with us. And we definitely know that we don't know what the hell we're gonna do about any of this!"

I moaned at the hopelessness of our circumstances, quietly banging the back of my head against the white subway-tiled wall in frustration.

"Frankly, I can think of only one possible next step," Jarvis said, leaning against the sink. "I think it would be best if we returned to Sea Verge and consulted with your father."

I swallowed hard.

I knew Jarvis was right. The smartest thing to do under these circumstances was to go to my dad for help. He was Death, for God's sake, and I knew without a doubt he would help me no matter who or what was trying to frame me. Still, I didn't really want to go back to Sea Verge and have my dad fix all my problems for me.

Once upon a time maybe, but not now.

Things had changed. I'd been working hard to shed the old me, and this seemed like the perfect opportunity to give the new me a test spin. I would take the initiative this time and not just passively let some asshole use me as a dodge for his/her evil scheming. I was gonna fight for my good name, and if I drew a little blood in the process, well then, so be it.

I mean, I don't want to be a wuss forever, do I?

I looked around me at the white-tiled bathroom, realizing the irony of my situation. It was right here in this very spot where, only a few precious months ago, I'd begun my return to the supernatural world. It was in this very restroom Jarvis had used a magical cupcake to unspell a forgetting charm I'd placed on myself and then informed me of my father's kidnapping and begged me to return home with him. Of course, like the sap that I am, I'd relented and we'd made the journey (via wormhole) to Sea Verge that same afternoon. It was there, in the bosom of my familial home, that my mother and our family's lawyer, Father McGee, had strong-armed me into taking over Death, Inc., until my dad could be found. Little did I know the strange odyssey I would be forced to embark on—or the friends I would make along the way—as I sought to save my dad's job and my family's immortality.

"Okay, I see how talking to my dad is an option," I began,

weighing my words, "but first, I want to call Daniel. He might have some ideas and I—"

"Of course, call him, yes," Jarvis said casually, but I could see the effort it took him to let me make my own decision, especially when it went against his better judgment.

"Thanks," I said, pulling my phone out of my bag and unlocking it. I had one of those wannabe BlackBerry phones that looked and felt like a high-end PDA, but had half the power and even less reception than the big boys. Jarvis waited patiently as I dialed the number and waited for Daniel to pick up.

No matter what might be happening in our relationship, I knew he'd help me if I needed him.

Though I let the phone ring and ring and ring, Daniel never answered. I hated to end the call just in case he was in the shower or something and was racing to get to the phone, but after a few minutes I knew it was a lost cause and I gave up, disconnecting.

"Okay, Daniel's a no-go," I said, putting the phone back in my bag after double-checking I'd left the ringer on high. "I just need to let Geneva know I'm leaving, and then we can go to Sea Verge."

"What will you tell her?" Jarvis asked.

"I guess I'll say I'm not feeling well. I'm allowed a sick day every now and then, aren't I?" I said defensively.

I really wanted to be doing anything but running to Sea Verge, but I knew we had to take care of the problem now before it got too big to contain.

"I'll wait here, then," Jarvis replied. "You'll be brief?"

I had no idea how long it was going to take me to get things cleared up with work. It's not like we were running on a schedule or anything, was it?

"I don't know, Jarvis," I said, unlocking the bathroom door and steeling myself to go lie to my cubicle mate. "I'll be back as soon as I can, okay?"

"Take your time," Jarvis added dryly. "Because we have nothing but time, Miss Calliope."

He got the last words in just as the door closed behind me.

Startled, I nearly walked into our office intern, Robert, who was lurking in the hallway. A totally adorable hipster with the cutest Louisiana drawl in town, I would be seriously crushing on the guy if I weren't otherwise engaged.

"Hey, Callie," he said. "How's it going?"

I took a step back, blocking the door with my body.

"Good, great . . . perfect actually," I said, a nervous grin pinned to my face. He gave me a curious look.

"Cool," he said as he pulled at the bottom of his Pink Nasty T-shirt, but didn't make a move to leave.

"Yep, pretty cool," I said, leaning against the door and folding my arms across my chest, hoping he'd take the hint and move the show on the road.

But the hint was not taken. Robert continued to stand there, yanking on his shirt like a two-year-old. I took a deep breath and renewed my smile, anxiously drumming the fingers of my left hand against the fatty part of my upper arm. We stood in silence and then Robert scrunched his face up like he was getting ready to tell me something really important.

God, I hope he isn't going to ask me out. That would be really awkward.

"Uhm, can I use the bathroom, Callie?"

Not what I was expecting, but not a complete surprise, either.

"This one's got something wrong with it," I imparted conspiratorially. "I was just getting ready to go call maintenance."

"Oh, but there's more than one stall in there—"

I didn't let him finish.

"Yeah, but the smell is pretty fierce," I said. "Know what I mean?"

Robert began to nod his head, but then he stopped, thinking.

"Okay, but I gotta go kinda bad, so I guess I'll just grin and bear it," he said, trying to push past me.

"Not a good idea," I said, continuing to physically block his way with my body. I probably had about fifteen pounds on the guy—which I thought would give me the advantage, but I didn't count on him being as wiry as a cheetah. He took me by the shoulders, squeezing my wussy deltoids with way more power than was absolutely necessary, and easily shifting me out of the doorway.

I lost my footing and fell, my ass hitting the floor with a loud *crunch.* Robert didn't even look down to make sure I was okay—he just stepped over me.

"Stop!" I cried, rolling on my hip and grabbing both his legs in a bear hug. I yanked my body backward with as much force as I could muster, and the little shit went down, falling almost on top of me.

Now who's the cheetah?

My triumph only lasted a moment before I realized I was now pinned to the ground by Robert's body . . . and from the snarl on his face, I could tell he was pretty pissed about the change in plan. He thought he'd be through the bathroom door already. He hadn't expected me to actually put up a fight.

"You are a pain in my ass, Calliope Reaper-Jones," Robert spat, his face red with anger. Then before I could stop him, he'd reached out and grabbed me by the throat, wrapping bony fingers around my neck and squeezing. I gripped his wrists, trying to rip his hands away from my fragile trachea, but he was a lot stronger than me. It wasn't that I was worried about him doing any serious damage—*uhm, immortality?*—but I didn't want to black out and leave Jarvis unaware that an enemy was at the gates.

"Jarvis!" I tried to croak, but I only succeeded in making Robert put more energy into his task. I was starting to lose consciousness, my vision tunneling to a pinpoint.

This is so not happening right now, I thought as I redoubled my effort to pry his hands from my throat. *Seriously, we're in a place of work here!*

I tried to call out again, to get someone's attention, but I was fading fast and my body didn't seem to want to do what my mind was directing it to do. I was really worried I was gonna pass out right there on the floor—which was so not pretty.

"Who . . . are . . . you?" I managed to squeak out in the

brief second that he relaxed his fingers before increasing the pressure again.

He leaned forward, pushing his face right into mine. I almost gagged on the stench issuing from his open mouth. It smelled exactly like rotten eggs, but with the foulness factor ratcheted up to the three-millionth degree.

"You don't *recognize* me?" he hissed, spraying spittle in my face—which frankly was so gross that if I could've died then, I might've gone for it.

"No," I squeaked.

"No?" he repeated back at me in a nasty imitation of my own strangled rasp.

"But doesn't this give it away, Calliope?" he continued, referring to the feel of his hands on my neck. I drew a blank, which I'm sure showed in my eyes, and he only ratcheted up the throat squeezing.

Even if I knew what he was talking about, I couldn't have responded anyway because my larynx was being crushed beneath his fingers. This time I really did start to black out, but being a cat who wasn't ready to stop playing with his little rat (me), Robert released his hold on my neck and I began to cough, trying to draw in as much air as possible before he changed his mind and started choking me again. I was giddy that I could finally breathe, but now my throat ached so badly I wanted to cry with every inhalation.

I was too exhausted to move—though my brain was still racing a million miles a minute trying to formulate an escape plan—so I watched, transfixed, as Robert reached up and slid his hands into his hair, giving a quick aggressive tug that peeled the flesh away from his face in one cohesive chunk. I gasped (painfully) as he held the flaccid skin forward so I could see his true face grinning down at me. Then, pleased by my reaction, he let the flesh slip from his hands and flop onto his chest, where it hung like a discarded Halloween mask.

"Now do you recognize me, sweetheart?" he asked gamely.

All I could do was nod as I stared up into the victorious eyes of my dad's archenemy . . . *the Ender of Death.*

five

"You again?" I croaked, anger very much at the top of my emotional list as I glared up at the Ender of Death.

This guy was a Class-A prick: one I'd tangled with twice before and both times had kicked his ass into tomorrow. His primary raison d'être was to get rid of Death (i.e., my dad) and free the rest of us from the Wheel of Samsara—basically he was looking to end the concept of death entirely—and he would not be satisfied until he'd accomplished said task. He had a real Javert-from-*Les Miz* quality about him, and by that I mean he was totally obsessed with taking my dad down . . . and me along with him.

"Hello, Calliope," he said, grinning.

I felt funny calling the guy "the Ender of Death," so I went for one of the other names I'd known him by.

"*Marcel*, you little shit," I said, eyes narrowing to slits as I used both fists to start pummeling his chest. "I'm gonna kick your ass!"

He easily grasped both my wrists and held them tightly to my chest until my fingers started to go numb from the lack of blood flow. I got tired of being on the losing end of the struggle and gave up, letting my body relax, hoping it would encourage him to let me go. This seemed to do the trick and he released me. My hands free, I sank back against the floor, my whole body exhausted from the exertion, and then rolled over onto my side. I immediately started massaging my wrists to get the blood flowing again, and then I scowled back up at Marcel, feeling defeated and pissed off with myself for not knowing any good magic spells to levy at him. Still, with his patrician face—modeled on one of those gaudy Roman Catholic effigies of Jesus suffering up on the cross—and heavy-lidded eyes, I had to admit that Mr. "Ender of Death" Marcel was kind of a good-looking guy. That is, if you ignored the one blemish on his face—a fresh cut across his cheek—and liked assholes who had nothing against choking a girl to get her attention. I knew that while I could appreciate his good looks, I was *never* gonna love the asshole-ier aspects of his character.

"Where's Robert?" I demanded. "What did you do to our intern?"

Marcel smiled, using a long, square-tipped finger to point down the hall toward the office kitchen. I quickly rolled away from him and used the wall to pull myself to my feet. My legs were shaky as I took the first few tentative steps, but I felt my adrenaline kicking back in with each footfall. From my vantage point, the kitchen looked completely normal; the small fridge was where it was supposed to be, the coffeepot was still burbling on its attached hot plate, and the box of mostly eaten pastries still sat on the counter where I'd left it after I'd ravaged it earlier in the morning. Maybe Marcel was just pulling my chain, making me walk all the way down the hall for absolutely nothing, but a niggling voice in the back of my mind was telling me otherwise: I had a very bad feeling about the fate of our poor office intern.

My heart was in my mouth as I rounded the kitchen counter, hoping against hope I wouldn't find Robert sprawled on the floor, a half-eaten bear's claw stuffed down his gullet, but thankfully, the floor was empty.

"There's nothing here," I said, turning around to find Marcel standing directly behind me—I hadn't even heard him get up from his spot on the floor, let alone cross the rest of the hall.

Creepy.

He didn't deign to answer me, just shrugged his shoulders and looked down, his long eyelashes fluttering. I followed Marcel's gaze to the bottom cabinet, the one that usually held coffee accoutrements like filters, wooden stirrers, Sweet'N Low, etc.

"You wouldn't—" I began, but I didn't finish the sentence. I knelt down, my sweaty fingers fumbling to grasp the plastic handles and throw open the cabinet doors.

I found the intern crammed down inside the bottom kitchen cabinet, naked except for a pair of bright yellow boxer shorts hanging low enough on his hips to reveal the crack of his ass. His head was tilted at a very odd angle . . . one that was not natural to any living human I'd ever seen—and the niggling feeling I'd had about the intern's fate blossomed into full-scale panic. This was entirely my fault. If I hadn't been working at House and Yard, our poor intern would never have had any cause to run into the Ender of Death.

Shit!

I slammed the cabinet door shut, the sound reverberating in the empty hallway.

"You killed him," I growled, guilt and rage bubbling up inside me, making me want to scream. Not wishing to draw any more attention to the situation than I already had, I worked hard to maintain my indoor voice.

"Why would you do that? You're the *Ender* of Death, for God's sake!" I added, staring at Marcel like he was some kind of nasty little bug under a microscope, one I would've happily exterminated right there on the spot.

"Calliope, you must have some idea of what is happening," Marcel said, leaning against the bone white refrigerator. "Greater forces than you are at work and you *will* have to bend to their will sooner or later. So why not save yourself the suffering and do it now."

"Greater forces of what?" I said, slowly inching away from him. Marcel might think I was playing dumb, but I really had no clue what the jerkoid was talking about.

"Who do you think sent the Vargr welcoming party?"

"That was you?" I said as I stepped out into the hallway, putting a little more distance between us. I did not want to be trapped in a tiny U-shaped space with Marcel.

"Me and the greater forces, babe. They're responsible for putting your little friend in the cabinet, too. I'm just here at their behest to offer you the chance to capitulate before something even worse comes your way."

"I don't think so, asswipe," I said, reaching forward with both hands and shoving the son of a bitch as hard as I could. He wasn't prepared for my surprise attack, and the force of the blow sent him backward into the thick plastic door handle of the refrigerator. He howled in pain as the handle rammed into the soft flesh of his lower back, but I didn't stick around to see what happened next. I turned on my heel and ran back to the bathroom, my body slamming against the solid door, knocking the wind out of me. I tried the door handle, adrenaline keeping me on my feet, but it was locked. I began to hammer on the doorframe instead.

"Jarvis!!! Let me in!!! Emergency!!" I yelled.

I felt my hackles rise at the sound of someone clearing their throat behind me. I shivered, my mind racing as I tried to figure out how to defend myself against Marcel's next attack.

I stopped banging my fists against the wood and slowly turned around. My breath sat like a lead weight in my lungs as I waited for Marcel to wrap his fingers around my throat again. But to my surprise, the Ender of Death was nowhere to be seen. Instead, my boss, Hyacinth Smith, loomed before me, her carefully manicured hands planted firmly on her wide hips. With her black jersey Donna Karan dress and (newly) white-blond hair, she looked like a Valkyrie on speed. She raised an eyebrow in my direction—and I could see her brain trying to process what she was seeing.

I didn't need a mirror to know I looked like something the cat dragged in. My hair was totally out of place, with strands hanging down into my eyes, and I could feel the red welts from Marcel's fingers starting to swell around my neck like a blood blister necklace.

Gross.

"Callie, you do know there's another bathroom down the hall, don't you?" Hyacinth said. Her voice was like cream silk, but with an undertone of derision so fierce, it made me feel like *I* was now the nasty little bug under the microscope in need of extermination.

I didn't know how best to respond, so I just nodded my head. My eyes flicked over to the kitchen to make sure Marcel was missing-in-action—and this insubordinate behavior did not please my boss.

"What are you looking at?" she asked with aggression as she followed my gaze.

I shrugged.

"Uhm, nothing, Hy," I said, swallowing hard as I tried to replenish some of the saliva that had mysteriously disappeared from my mouth upon her arrival.

I let my gaze return to her face and she unwillingly shifted her eyes back to mine.

"What's wrong with you, Jones?" she said, choosing to ignore my lie.

I shook my head.

"Nothing's wrong," I squeaked. "I promise."

She narrowed her eyes, but didn't reply. Suddenly, she was swishing away from me, down the hall, toward the kitchen.

"No!" I screamed, taking off after her. "You can't go in there!"

She picked up her pace when she heard me cantering down the hall after her, but I was younger and in better shape (surprisingly) than she was. I passed her with seconds to spare, blocking the bottom kitchen cabinet with my body.

"Stop!" I cried, thrusting my hands out in front of me like a shield, leaving Hyacinth to either obey my orders or get forcefully shoved backward. She went for the less violent alternative, waiting in the hallway well out of my arms' reach, her face perfectly composed except for the bright shade of fuchsia staining the apples of her cheeks. This was, I recognized, an early predictor that my boss was becoming exceptionally pissed off by something—and that something was *me*.

I'd never been on the receiving end of one of Hy's angry outbursts before, but I'd seen it happen to a number of other people in our office and it was not a pretty sight.

"Calliope Reaper-Jones, put your hands down and get out of my way," Hyacinth said, her even tone belying the fact she was near her boiling point.

Still, I didn't move. I couldn't. I was frozen in place, unresponsive to the impulses my brain was sending down to my body telling me to move out of the way and let Hy do what she wanted. I took a deep breath and it was like I was inhaling poison instead of air. I felt light-headed, as if I were somewhere above my body watching the proceedings tick by while I acted as a conscientious objector to my own life. All I could do was stand there while the things I'd worked so hard to attain all my adulthood slipped inextricably out of my grasp. The thump of my heart skipping a couple of beats brought me back to myself, but this return to reality just reaffirmed the one thing I already knew: I was quickly running out of options. I could either let Hyacinth find the body (and go to jail for a human lifetime) or I could lose my job (and my human existence) while keeping my immortal freedom intact.

I stared at my boss, willing her to back down first, but I knew it was useless. She'd never backed down from anything in her life—and she wasn't about to start with her unruly Executive Assistant.

"If you do not get out of that kitchen right now . . ." Hyacinth said, taking a dramatic pause to give more weight to her words. This was her way of making me understand that she didn't *want* to issue a definitive ultimatum, but that I was forcing her hand.

I opened my mouth to acquiesce. An apology was right on the tip of my tongue, but before I could form the words, a giant belch issued from the depths of my belly. I covered my mouth with my hand, but the damage was already done.

Hyacinth's nostrils flared at my rudeness.

"Then consider yourself fired."

It was like getting sucker punched right in the gut while being concurrently poked in the eyeballs with a pointy stick.

Still, my unresponsive body stayed wedged in between the kitchen cabinets, blocking Hyacinth's way. It appeared that my decision had been made for me. My body, apparently, would rather see the end of my so-called "normal" life than allow me to rot in jail.

I sighed and felt my eyes smarting with tears. This time my thoughts seemed to flow from my mouth in a flood of words.

"I've really enjoyed assisting you, Hy, and I'm sorry that our working relationship is ending this way." My throat ached from the throttling Marcel had given me—and from something else, too. Something that, if I'd been forced to describe it, I would've likened to despair.

"I accept that you're firing me, but I will not move from this cabinet," I continued, clearing my throat in a last-ditch effort to not emotionally lose it in front of my (now) former boss. "So, that's it, then."

Finished with my speech, I bit my lip, trying to channel the pain I was feeling into a physical outlet. I hoped it would pull me back from the brink of the full-scale tear-fest I was on the precipice of having.

For the first time since I'd known her, Hyacinth Stewart (the woman with the mad skill set for figuring out a person's weakness and then exploiting it) was speechless. She'd pegged me for a total pushover—which normally would've been a correct assumption—only she'd chosen to confront me during the most transitional period of my entire life. She had no idea I was in the process of extracting myself from the "normal" world so I could return to the bosom of the Afterlife. All the years of trying to change myself, to fix the quirks that made me different from the human beings who surrounded me, were fast becoming irrelevant. The past few months had been the brine, changing the consistency of my soul until I was ready to step out of my old skin and become someone new.

Hy's mouth worked open then shut, then open again, her brow furrowing in intense concentration. Finally, she cocked her blond head at an angle and said:

"Clean out your desk."

No sooner had the words cleared her lips than she turned around and sashayed back down the hallway, hips swinging in time to the click of her heels. I watched her go, all the tension I'd been holding in my jaw and shoulders dissipating with her exit. I felt the countertop pressing into the small of my back and I closed my eyes, letting my body sag against it, elbows resting on its smooth, laminate surface for support.

My moment of respite was interrupted by the crack of knuckles against wood. I surmised that it was coming from somewhere in the direction of my feet and immediately slid away from the cabinet, stepping out into the hallway, where it was ostensibly safer. The door to the bottom cabinet flew open and the very alive body of our nearly naked office intern crawled out, gasping for breath like a deep-sea fish caught on a line. He grasped at the floor with both hands, using leverage to disentangle his limbs from the cabinet's embrace. He flopped onto the ground, his pale white torso covered in splotchy red patches where it had pressed into the wooden interior of the kitchen cabinet.

I wanted to look away, to give the poor guy some privacy, but he reached out a shaky hand and wrapped it around my ankle. I instinctively took a step backward, easily slipping out of his infirm grasp.

"Sorry," I said, feeling bad I had recoiled from his touch. I hadn't done it on purpose. It had just happened unconsciously.

He stared up at me, eyes wide as saucers, bare body shivering despite the fact the building's ancient heating system was going full blast. It took me a moment to realize that, while he might be disoriented by his experience, he wasn't the least bit angry with me for my reaction. He was just totally confused by the situation as a whole.

"What happened to me?"

The sentence came out in a rush, his lower lip trembling as if he was about to cry. I wanted to kneel down beside him, the picture of calm reassurance, and promise him everything was going to be all right. But since I had no guarantee this was actually the case—and my body didn't seem to want to touch his flesh anyway—I decided against the Florence Nightingale act. The truth probably wasn't something I should be sharing with the poor guy, either, so instead I opted for a hybrid of the two:

"Help!!" I screamed as loudly as I could. "Man down in the kitchen! Help!"

This only seemed to add to the nearly naked intern's terror and confusion. He made a keening sound low in his throat and closed his eyes as if forced blindness were the answer to all of his problems.

"Look," I said, crouching down on my heels so I was closer to his level, but still just out of reach. "Someone is gonna come out here any second and help you. I'm sorry it can't be me, but you give me the willies when you touch me and that *can't* be a good thing."

My honesty seemed to do the trick. Robert stopped making the pitiful noise deep in his throat and cracked his bloodshot eyes open just wide enough to get a fix on my position.

"Please don't leave me," he begged, and I sensed he was about to pounce seconds before he actually did. It was enough lead time to stand up and rest my leather-clad foot right in the middle of the intern's solar plexus. The impact—I tried not to push him too hard—sent him sprawling, and I watched guiltily as his head bounced against the cabinet door, knocking him out.

I can't believe it—I'm two for two in the kitchen/fight arena.

"Hang in there," I offered meekly, hoping someone would find Robert's prostrate body where it lay flat on the floor sooner rather than later.

Then, feeling as though I were the new Heavyweight Boxing Champion of the World, I jogged away from the kitchen and back toward the bathroom, where I used my newfound moves to smash the crap out of the bathroom door with two well-aimed kicks—and this time, the puppy opened right up for me.

It was like I was made of magic.

six

"What the hell, Jarvis!" I said as I stepped through the bathroom doorway, my eyes scanning the white subway-tiled space for my dad's Executive Assistant. I had a bone to pick with the meddling faun and I was itching to get started.

But what I found in the bathroom stopped me dead in my tracks. The room had been ransacked—sinks ripped from the wall, toilet stall doors hanging askew on their metallic hinges, cracked subway tile on the wall caked in scarlet streaks that could only be blood. Water from the dislodged pipes spewed from underneath the busted sinks, flooding the floor and pooling in red eddies where Jarvis lay propped up against the base of one of the toilets. A ragged gash in the side of Jarvis's head gaped open, revealing the pulpy-red tissue that lay just beneath the faun's skin.

"Jarvis?" I said, speaking his name again, but this time without a trace of anger in my voice. Now the anger had been replaced by worry. I knew a normal human would've been dead ten times over from a blow of that magnitude, but Jarvis was an immortal, thank God. Still, the gash on his head was pretty gross, and I felt terrible knowing how badly his head was gonna hurt once I roused him.

Ignoring the mess around me, I navigated my way through

the torrent of water to where the unconscious faun lay, and knelt down beside him, turning his head so I could get a better look at the wound. I noticed a fleck of blue-gray metal protruding from the gash and plucked it from the abraded skin, tossing it across the room. This action caused Jarvis to stir beneath me.

"Mistress Calliope?"

His voice was weak, but firm.

"Are you okay?" I asked as he lifted his chin and gave me a snaggle-toothed grin. I inhaled sharply at the sight of his three front teeth, each of which had been cracked in half, the stumps remaining stubbornly fixed in his upper gums.

"Been better," Jarvis lisped, keeping his tongue away from the jagged edges of his ruined teeth. He coughed, and the spittle that came up was a shade of pink that did not bode well for the faun. The way he winced when he coughed—or even when he drew a breath, for that matter—informed me he probably had a few busted ribs and other internal injuries, too.

"What happened?" I asked as he slid his hand into mine. His pulse was thready under my fingers, but at least I could still feel it.

He tried to shake his head, but the effort was too great. Instead, he swallowed back another cough and closed his eyes for a moment to conserve his energy. While I waited for his answer, I looked around the room, trying to figure out my next move. We couldn't stay in this bathroom forever, but I wasn't good enough with magic to open a wormhole and get us out of there.

"The Ender of Death," Jarvis said finally, opening his eyes. "He came in to call up a wormhole. Caught me by surprise. I tried to stop him, but—"

"I know," I said, squeezing Jarvis's hand. "He got me out in the hall."

Suddenly, Jarvis's eyes flew open and he looked hard at me, his eyeballs nearly popping out of their sockets.

"Calliope," he said, gripping my hand so hard I thought he was going to squeeze off my wrist. *"What have you done?"*

I stared at Jarvis, aghast. Not because his words had penetrated my consciousness, but because something else—something exceedingly strange—had caught my eye. At first, I had assumed it was a trick of the light. Yet the more I looked, the more I began to believe that the gash on Jarvis's head *was knitting itself back together right before my eyes*. He may have been immortal, but I'd never seen anyone, immortal or not, heal this quickly. Amazed by what I was witnessing, it took me a second to process Jarvis's words. When they finally did penetrate my thick skull, I immediately picked up on his disapproving tone.

"Hey, wait a minute," I said, confused. "What did you mean by 'What have you done?' I didn't *do* anything—"

In response, the faun reached up and probed the gash on the side of his head with his fingers.

"My head wound," Jarvis said, ignoring my outrage, "is healing, is it not?"

I nodded.

"Why do you suppose it's doing this?" Jarvis continued.

"I don't know." I shrugged, not sure what the faun was driving at. "Why?"

Instead of answering my question, Jarvis merely shook his head then closed his eyes again, exhaustion overtaking his features.

"Tell me why it's doing that," I demanded, pointing at the gash. Even though his eyes were closed and he couldn't see what I was doing, I didn't care. I was in awe of his miraculous recovery and I wanted answers.

Jarvis slid open his lids and found my eyes. It was as if he were plumbing their depths for some answer I would never verbally be able to give him.

"You truly don't know, do you?"

I shook my head. I wasn't lying to the faun. I really *was* completely in the dark about whatever was upsetting him.

After a moment he released his death grip on my fingers, seemingly satisfied by what he had found in my gaze. I pulled my hand away and massaged my numb digits against my thigh. Aside from the fact that his wounds were spontaneously healing of their own accord, something else was not quite right about my friend—and his odd mood was contagious. Shivers of fear pulsed up my spine.

"We need to get out of here," I said finally, gesturing to the ruined, watery mess of a bathroom we were sitting in. "Any suggestions?"

Jarvis nodded.

"A wormhole would be best."

I totally agreed with him. A wormhole that took us directly to Sea Verge (and my dad) would be perfection. I could get Jarvis all bandaged up, throw on some fresh clothes, and hit up my dad for some information about the bizarre situation I now found myself in the middle of.

"I know I was hedging before, but I think you were right about asking my dad for help—" I was in the middle of saying, when Jarvis roughly grabbed my arm.

"No! We cannot go to Sea Verge," he said, his voice harsh.

I stared at him, openmouthed, shocked by his stern reprimand. I'd *seriously* tried Jarvis's patience on a number of occasions, and he had *never* been this aggressive with me before. He must've realized how brusque his tone had been because his next words were issued in a breathy whisper:

"It is just that now would not be a . . . *prudent* . . . time, Miss Calliope."

"Uhm, okay . . ." I said, though I did *not* understand at all. Was I crazy or hadn't Jarvis been bugging me to go back to Sea Verge ever since the subway fiasco? Now here he was telling me *not* to go home? I was beginning to suspect the beating he'd taken had scrambled his brains a little.

"Please trust me," Jarvis said, resting his hand over mine. "It's very important. I know you have a difficult time accepting things without an explanation, but this one time, please, you must."

Jarvis had me pegged. He was dead right when he said I hated to be told what to do—especially without any kind of explanation. But there was something about the tone of his voice that made me want to do what he asked of me, as much as my nature might struggle against it.

"Okay, fine," I said, resigned to staying in the dark a little longer. "I'll go wherever you want."

"I promise to explain myself when we get to a safer location," Jarvis replied, relaxing now that we were in agreement. I noticed how much better he looked now than when I'd first entered the bathroom. His cheeks had regained some of their previous color, and the gash was knitting itself back together nicely as the magic that was healing him continued its impressive work.

"Good," I said. "Because I expect a thorough explanation—and when I say 'thorough,' I mean it. I want the whole damn story—"

"Of course," Jarvis said, cutting me off as he added: "You deserve nothing less. Now take my hand. I shall need to draw from your power in order to call up the wormhole."

Without any of the hard-core, question-everything attitude I was usually guilty of, I did as the faun said and slipped my hand back into his. I felt a jolt of stinging electricity flow from my fingers directly into the faun. The raw power was so intense I could literally feel Jarvis's body spasm as it flooded into him. He gripped my hand hard, his jaw clenched tight against the pain, but he refused to cry out even though he was clearly suffering. In all my Afterlife adventuring, I'd never personally been on the tendering end of anything as potent as the power surge we were experiencing. I had hopes that the catalyst was the three inches of water we were sitting in while trying to open the wormhole, but I was pretty sure this was only wishful thinking.

Another burst of energy shot through my body—I was beginning to wish I had a circuit breaker—and my head began to throb as a deafening crack split the atmosphere around us, charging the air with electricity. All the hair on my body bristled and I could taste the electrical current with my tongue. Another booming crack split the air, almost as if a mini thunderstorm had found its way into the bathroom, and a pinprick of light appeared, hanging like a crystalline teardrop in the middle of the room. The overhead lights began to strobe and then went out completely, which should have reduced my visibility down to zero, but I found I could see just as well in the dark as I could in the glare of the fluorescent light.

I watched, fascinated, as the wormhole began to unfold like a lotus flower, each petal of light ripping apart the darkness until it had rent a gaping hole right in the very fabric of time and space, enticing us forward. I was entranced by the wormhole, the way its edges sputtered and twirled with energy as it continued to eat away at the darkness. It seemed to grow larger with every second, consuming more and more of the matter surrounding it.

"You ready?" I asked, slipping my arms around his rib cage and lifting him onto his hooves. He didn't answer me, merely nodded his head. Together, we stepped forward, the humid heat from the other side of the wormhole steam-cleaning my pores.

"It's like a sauna in there," I said, my voice starting to go hoarse from all the beating my throat had taken. "Where does it go?"

Again Jarvis didn't answer me but, instead, took another step toward the wormhole. I grabbed him by the arm, pulling him back to me. I wanted some kind of assurance we weren't going back to Hell. I'd spent a good chunk of the last few months wandering around the place, and I had no intention of going back there without my knowledge.

"If that thing's going to Hell," I began, digging in my heels, "then I'm staying in the flood plain."

Jarvis raised his head so he was looking into my eyes.

"I swear on my life that we will not be visiting Hell," Jarvis said.

"Okay," I replied, feeling like I'd gotten back at least *some* control over the situation. "Let's do this thing."

I let Jarvis take my hand, giving him no resistance as he pulled me toward the light. Suddenly, the bathroom door flew open and my now former boss, Hyacinth Stewart, stood framed in the doorway, her spun white gold hair like a halo around her head. She wasn't in the same outfit I'd last seen her in—apparently she was a quick-change artist—but instead had donned a thin white sheath dress and a flowing cloak of what appeared, upon first glance, to be falcon feathers.

"Stay away from the wormhole," she intoned, forcing her way through the door and into the bathroom, the bottom of her cloak seeming to magically float just above the waterline.

"Okay, hold on there—" I began, but Hyacinth placed one meaty hand on my shoulder and the other on Jarvis's and physically drew us away from the wormhole.

"They are monitoring all the wormholes. It isn't safe for you to travel this way," Hyacinth said to Jarvis, who stared up at the hulking woman, glassy-eyed—with lust or pain, I couldn't have told you which.

"Come away from here before they discover that you were the ones who called it," she continued, pointing to the fast-growing seam of light.

"I had no idea," Jarvis whispered, more to himself than to Hyacinth.

"It wasn't for you to know," she barked back at him. "Come."

She didn't wait for us to respond before she spun us around, dragging us out of the war-torn bathroom like two limp rag dolls. Hyacinth slammed the door closed behind us, a muscle-relaxing sense of relief flooding my body. I hadn't realized how tense the situation had made me until I was out of it.

"Where can we go?" Jarvis asked as we followed Hyacinth down the hallway.

"This way," she urged, guiding us away from the crowd of office workers who were surrounding the kitchen—obviously, someone had found Robert's prone body.

As we ran, it seemed like Jarvis and I were forced to take two steps for every one of Hyacinth's. Call me crazy, but I was pretty certain my boss had grown like five inches since I'd last seen her. After all the weird stuff I'd been exposed to since Jarvis had unspelled me from my Forgetting Charm, I knew that when someone presented themselves as completely normal and then suddenly did something totally abnormal right in front of you, it meant they were *not* totally human.

"I have a way out. It's not magical, but it should do the trick," Hyacinth—who wasn't really Hyacinth, my boss, anymore—said. She led us to the emergency exit stairwell and pushed open the door, setting the alarm off. It began to screech like a banshee, but this didn't faze Hyacinth—she merely waved her hand across the doorframe and the sound instantly ceased.

"Nice," I offered as she held the door open for Jarvis, who was standing unsteadily on his hooves.

"Easily done," came her reply, but she wasn't really paying attention to me. Instead, her gaze was fixed on Jarvis as he paused beneath the door lintel, trying to catch his breath. The head wound may have healed, but the faun still looked drawn. His skin was pasty and dry, his eyes encircled by dark purple bruising. He gave a ragged cough that sent him reeling, but Hyacinth had anticipated what was coming next and reached out, catching him just as his legs gave way beneath him.

"Jarvis," I cried, but the faun only shook his head for me to be quiet. Hyacinth stared at the creature in her arms, taking in his haggard appearance and lack of strength. Then she fixed her steely gaze on me, and under the intensity of her glare I felt like an impaled bug trying to wriggle its way off a specimen board.

"What have you done, Callie?" she asked. Her words came evenly, but I didn't believe for a second there wasn't malice underneath them. I took a cue from the rigid set of her shoulders and the faint lines ringing her mouth and decided not to be a smart aleck.

"Look, I don't know what I'm supposed to have done," I said, my thoughts all jumbling together as I spoke, "but I swear to God I didn't do it."

Hyacinth pursed her lips, but didn't respond.

"I'm serious, I didn't do whatever it is you think I did," I said again. "I mean it."

Hyacinth shook her head.

"I believe you, Callie, because I don't think you would have knowingly wrought this thing upon a friend."

"Excuse me?" I said, my voice going up an octave. I didn't like being accused of something . . . especially something I had no knowledge of having done. I wanted an answer from her, but Hyacinth didn't seem to think now was an appropriate time for further discussion. Instead, she turned her back on me, slinging Jarvis's barely conscious body over her shoulder as if he were as light as a sack of foam packing peanuts.

"This way," she intoned, crossing the threshold and taking the fire stairs two at a time, leaving me with nothing to do but follow her.

"Crap," I said under my breath as I stepped into the stairwell, letting the fire door close behind me with an ominous *click*. I paused, the sense that I was closing the door on my past, now and forever, overwhelming all other thought. I let this feeling linger inside my brain, hoping time would give it clarification, then I picked up my pace, grasping the handrail with a shaking hand as I blindly followed Hyacinth's retreating back.

The stairs seemed to go on forever. This was only compounded by the fact I was in mediocre physical shape, and with each step, my lungs flailed in my chest, waving the white flag of surrender. But I couldn't stop. Hyacinth was still barreling up the stairs ahead of me, Jarvis in her arms, and I was determined not to let them out of my sight. Occasionally, I would have to stop and lean against the railing, gasping for breath, but then I would marshal my waning strength and begin the climb again. Each time, Hyacinth got a bit farther ahead, but as long as she stayed within eyeshot, I wasn't too worried.

Finally, above me, I heard a door opening, and a shaft of light cut across the head of the stairwell. I picked up speed, pushing my body to power its way up the remaining flight. When I reached the topmost landing, I found the door to the roof propped open, encouraging me forward. A blast of chilly air pounded through the doorway and I took a small hop backward to avoid the brunt of it, almost stepping off the landing's edge.

"Are you coming?" Hyacinth bellowed as she stuck her head back through the doorway to hurry me along. I could tell by the look of annoyance she wore she was fast running out of patience.

I never said I was a damn Olympian, lady, I thought to myself, but I kept my attitude in check, replying with as much saccharin as I could muster:

"On my way!"

I huffed my way across the landing and out onto the rooftop. Because of the height, the wind was vicious, tearing at my clothes and hair and pushing me bodily toward the lip of the rooftop.

"This way," Hyacinth called, her voice carrying on the wind. I followed the sound of her words to the far side of the rooftop, where she stood hanging from the cockpit of a gunmetal gray helicopter, beckoning me forward with her free hand. The other was clutching a flight headset already plugged into the control panel.

I jogged over to the helicopter and crawled into the passenger seating, slamming the door behind me. I saw Hyacinth had already buckled Jarvis into the backseat and I sighed with relief. Hyacinth handed me the other headset and I fitted it over my head, filling my ears with the hiss of static.

"Where are we going?" I asked as Hyacinth closed her door and began flipping switches at—what seemed to me to be—random. Suddenly, the blades above us roared to life and the helicopter thrummed with burgeoning energy.

"Somewhere safe," she replied as she gripped the cyclic stick, which resembled a giant joystick and controlled the steering. The helicopter gave a sharp jerk, then lifted off the ground, and I couldn't help but grin with surprise as I realized we were airborne.

While the helicopter gained speed and altitude, I marveled at the bird's-eye view of Manhattan spread out before me. I didn't think I'd ever seen anything so beautiful.

"This is amazing—" I started to say, but then some strange instinct for the macabre made me turn around to look at Jarvis. What I saw in the backseat of the helicopter made the rest of that sentence disappear completely from my mind. I gagged as the bile rose in my throat and I had to look away before I got sick right there in the cockpit.

I felt my hands instinctively cover my face as I shut my eyes and tried to blot out the image I'd just seen—although I was pretty sure it was gonna be ingrained in my memory for the rest of my immortality anyway.

"What's wrong?" I heard Hyacinth's words echo in the headset I was wearing, but the disembodied quality freaked me out and I ripped them from my ears. I didn't care that the roar of the helicopter blades was deafening. I wanted the sound to overwhelm my brain and block out the image etched in my mind.

"His face," I moaned, letting the headset fall to the floor of the cockpit. "It's sloughed right off the bone."

seven

I twisted around in my chair, my eyes settling on Jarvis's prone body, where it sat, strapped to the bench like a child in a car seat. The pale bone of his exposed skull reflected back the golden sunlight streaming in through the transparent shell of the helicopter like fire. I stared at his tattered body and, for my trouble, was gifted with the spectacle of cloth-covered skin and muscle sloughing off his right arm bone before slipping past the seat and pooling on the floor with the rest of his already-melted flesh. I was glad the whir of the blades made it impossible to hear anything above their din, so I wasn't subjected to the sound of Jarvis disintegrating before my eyes.

"*Jarvis,*" I whispered, my ability to speak compromised by the sight of him.

From the collarbone up, he was skeleton, the flesh having melted away like butter in a pan, leaving only pristine bleached-white bone in its stead. For some strange reason, Jarvis's eyeballs had remained fixed inside their sockets, but since his eyelids and eyelashes had fallen away with the rest of the delicate skin of his face, it was hard to gauge what my friend might be thinking, trapped inside his putrefying body. I knew he was still sentient by the wild twitching of his eyeballs inside the smooth orbital bones of his skull, but I really needed the other aspects of the face—facial muscles, eyebrows, etc.—to give me the emotional context.

It's amazing what your mind decides to settle on during times of high stress, I thought to myself as I tried to remain clinical about my friend's situation—as if that were really possible.

Another piece of Jarvis's flesh detached, denuding his right shoulder of skin and muscle. Like a fool, I tried to catch the blubbery stuff in my hands before it could splat on the floor, but it was no use. The subcutaneous fat was as slick as baby oil, and the gelatinous skin and muscle slithered right through my fingers, splattering against the leather of the adjacent seat like tallow.

Jarvis's metamorphosis was moving at an accelerated rate and I deduced that his skeleton would be stripped clean of flesh within the hour. A school of piranhas couldn't have done a more thorough job if they'd tried. Jarvis's skin loss problem was gonna need a very quick fix—the word "superglue" kept flashing in my mind—or I was going to be left dealing with a silent skeleton instead of a helpful faun.

What do I do? I thought, frantically racking my brain for some kind of an answer, but I didn't have any experience with a situation like this.

In the pilot's seat beside me, Hyacinth spoke abruptly into her headset, gesturing at me wildly, but in my freaked-out state I couldn't understand what she wanted.

"What are you saying?!" I yelled over the cacophony of the helicopter blades, but Hyacinth only shook her head and gestured again, pointing down to the floor of the cockpit where my headset lay, twisted in its own cord. I swallowed hard then reached down and scooped up the offending thing, sliding it back over my head.

". . . can't do anything for him right now," Hyacinth said, the last half of her sentence crackling into my ears as I eased the headset in place. "Please stop freaking out and collect yourself. You're behaving like a child."

I started to protest, but I knew she was right. I was acting like a little shit. I needed to calm down and put everything into perspective. Jarvis's face may have fallen off, but that didn't give me permission to lose my shit.

"What's happening to him?" I asked, aiming my words into the headset's protruding mouthpiece, having a bit more control over my hysteria now. There was a moment of radio silence—and I assumed Hyacinth had decided not to answer me—but then she began to speak:

"He was dead, Callie, and you roused him out of Death to do your bidding."

"He can't be dead," I said, my voice rising. "He's immortal. You can't kill an immortal with a blow to the head. Besides, he was healing, I saw it myself, and FYI, if I were going to 'rouse' someone out of Death, I think I would know about it!"

"Yes, I would hope that that would be the case, but you're very unskilled in the art of Death, so who knows what you're capable of," Hyacinth said, her disembodied words like thoughts being implanted into my brain. "And what you saw earlier was the beginning of the *turning* process. You should at least know from your own experiences that immortals don't heal that quickly."

As much as I hated to admit it, I deserved the disparaging tone Hyacinth was using on me. I *was* a kindergartner when it came to the supernatural world. I knew next to nothing about the subject. I know being the Daughter of Death should've made me an expert on that kind of stuff, but I don't think you can ever learn about something you're not interested in. Like in school, you see kids who hate being there, and no matter what you do, you just can't inspire them to retain the information they're supposed to be learning. As far as I could tell, you had to *want* knowledge; you had to be really interested in a subject in order to absorb it.

And the last thing I had ever been interested in as a kid—or as an adult—was Death and the supernatural world it encompassed. But because I *had* experienced the healing process of an immortal firsthand (I'd banged myself up pretty good here and there growing up), I did recognize it didn't happen as rapidly as what I'd observed in Jarvis. If, like

Hyacinth said, this *turning* thing was really happening to Jarvis, then it explained a lot.

"Okay, say it's true," I said, "and Jarvis is turning. What does that actually mean?"

Hyacinth sighed, which translated into a loud *hiss* in my headset.

"I won't know for certain this is what is truly transpiring until we arrive at Sea Verge—"

"We're going home?" I interrupted, excitement and relief flooding my body. "Thank God!"

"Let me finish," Hyacinth said in a sharp tone, deflating the good vibes I'd just conjured up. "As I said, I won't know the veracity of this hypothesis until I can verify that your father is no longer among us."

"What!" I cried, the meaning of her words like a sharpened stake plunging into my soul. I may've been oblivious at times, but I wasn't an idiot. I understood what she was driving at.

"Callie, you can't *turn* the dead unless you *are* Death."

She didn't even bother to look at me as she let this callous statement hang in the air. Not even an iota of compassion from the woman. She continued to pilot the stupid helicopter like nothing had happened, the rigid set of her shoulders and unbroken line of her mouth giving only the barest hint that there was emotion bubbling somewhere inside her—a fact that was hardly encouraging.

"I think you're full of shit," I said after a protracted silence. "I think it's all bullshit, so there. My dad is immortal. No one can kill him . . ."

The syllables streamed from my lips without thought. I sensed this nauseous rush of invective was an intuitive reaction to information I wasn't ready to process yet, but I had no control over it. It was like if I could just keep talking, just keep my lips in perpetual motion, I could purge the growing terror Hyacinth had stoked inside my gut. For her part, my former boss remained silent—although I did notice that her grip on the steering shaft was so intense the skin of her hands was bloodless.

All around us, the sky began to darken, going from pale blue to foreboding gray in an instant. The change in air pressure screamed that the threat of rain was fast approaching, and as if to prove its point, the helicopter was snared in a massive downdraft. Caught by the unexpected violence of the encroaching storm, we lurched to the left, my head slamming into the side of the door. Mind-numbing pain engulfed every synapse of my body as the metal hinge on the side of the door sliced into the thin skin of my scalp. I felt something warm and viscous on my face, shrouding my vision in a blurry haze. I tried to wipe the stuff away with my hands and clear my vision, but I couldn't seem to get my fingers to do what I wanted them to do. It took me a few moments to comprehend that it was blood pouring from the gash in my scalp and not some unknown liquid cascading into my face. I wanted to scream, to rage against the stupidity of what was happening to me, but my throat was like a vise, allowing no sound to escape. All I could manage was a strangled gurgle—which did nothing to relieve the pressure enveloping my brain and sending me into a miasmic veil of nausea.

I closed my eyes, fighting back the urge to puke. I didn't think my getting sick would help the situation very much. Opening my eyes again was like trying to pry open two rusted window frames. All I wanted to do was to sink into a black abyss and then wake up back in my bed in Battery Park City, but the rocking of the helicopter wasn't helping my wish one bit. It only seemed to stoke my nausea, dragging me back into a more alert state.

"*Crap,*" I moaned, reaching up with my right hand to feel around in my scalp for the bloodied gash.

I winced as my fingers palpated the tender skin around the cut, biting my lip against the pain. When my speculative probing got too intense, I yanked my hand away and wiped my blood-coated fingers on the underside of my seat. The wound didn't seem very deep, and if I remembered correctly, the scalp tended to be a heavy bleeder even when the wound wasn't really that bad.

More like a dog's bark being worse than its bite, I thought miserably.

While I was musing about scalp wounds and barking dogs, Hyacinth was working hard to hold the steering apparatus steady, keeping the helicopter on an eastwardly course. As my eyes refocused on my surroundings, I realized the rocking sensation I was feeling stemmed from the terrible lightning storm our tiny helicopter was entering. I watched, surprised at how quickly the storm was enveloping us.

Rolling black rain clouds had eaten up all of the sky, making it hard to see farther than a few feet into the distance. A flash of white-hot lightning split the horizon, producing enough light, at least for a few seconds, to verify that the darkness around us was absolute.

"What's going on?" I asked uncertainly. The intensity of the storm was making my arm hair stand on end.

"What did you say?" Hyacinth asked, not daring to breach her concentration by peeling her eyes from the windscreen. It was taking everything she had just to pilot the helicopter away from the encroaching rainstorm.

"What's. Going. On?" I said again, slowing down my speech and enunciating as best I could.

"I don't know where this storm came from, but it's not a good thing," Hyacinth replied, flicking a few switches on the control panel as she spoke. "Makes it really hard to keep the helicopter steady."

There was another bump and the helicopter went into free-fall. My stomach migrated into my throat and I screamed—just as the helicopter righted itself again.

"Where are we going?" I asked after my stomach had slid back down my throat.

"It's not much further now," Hyacinth said as she banked a sharp left, sending us careening into pitch-black airspace.

I knew I wasn't going to get a straight answer out of Hyacinth about where we were going, so I turned my attention back to Jarvis. The poor little guy looked the worse for wear, his jawbone hanging from the rest of his skull by a thin filament of flesh. I wanted to do something to help him, but I didn't think trying to get into the backseat while we were in the middle of an aggressive rainstorm was the smartest course of action. It wasn't like I was gonna be able to hold his hand or anything.

"I'm sorry, Jarvis," I said, even though I knew he couldn't hear me over the drone of the helicopter and the rain splattering against the windscreen.

I sat back in my seat, feeling lost and terribly alone. Usually in these situations I had Jarvis's steel trap of a mind to lean on, but now, left to my own devices, I didn't have a clue as to what was happening around me—or why it was happening. Was what Hyacinth said true? Was there something wrong with my dad, and had the power of Death somehow transferred to me? I thought back to when I'd first entered the bathroom and found Jarvis. I remembered barging into the room, seething with anger, only to find my friend lying on the ground in a half-inch of water. I knew he was immortal, so I hadn't been concerned about checking to see if he was breathing or if he had a pulse. No, I'd just squatted down beside him and made sure he was all right . . . but had he *really* been all right? I racked my brains, forcing myself to remember any bits of minutiae I might've missed.

And then it hit me. Something I'd totally forgotten in the heat of the moment: There'd been a piece of blue-gray metal protruding from Jarvis's head when I'd first gotten there. I hadn't paid it any attention then, having no idea the stuff might be important, and had just brushed it away with my hand so I could get a better look at the gash on my friend's head—but I did remember that it was at this very moment that Jarvis had returned to consciousness.

Only, he *hadn't* returned to consciousness, I realized with horror. No, I had roused Jarvis from a sleep much deeper than anything this reality had to offer: I had woken my friend out of Death.

Whatever that blue-gray metal was, it was Jarvis's weakness—like Superman, all immortals had one that could kill them. That was the only thing that made any sense. The Ender of Death hadn't come to my office just to harass me—he'd come to assassinate Jarvis, and like a fool, I'd let it happen. But if that were the case, then if, like Hyacinth surmised, I was now Death, why hadn't the Ender of Death killed me, too?

None of it made any sense.

But I did know that if I'd been smarter, I would've protected my friend instead of leaving him alone in the bathroom. I'd let myself get distracted by bodies in the cupboard and illusions of police brutality, condemning Jarvis—who now sat in a pool of goopy skin and muscle because of me—to a new life as a sentient skeleton.

"We're here," Hyacinth said into the headset, interrupting my thoughts, and I felt the helicopter begin its initial descent.

The storm had moved on, so now only the fingers of gray thunderclouds were visible above us. Hyacinth had done a pretty incredible job of piloting us through the thick of it, and I couldn't help but feel kind of indebted to her for her quick thinking. If she hadn't hustled us out of the House and Yard offices when she did, Jarvis and I would've been in a wormhole going God knows where when his skin had started to melt, and I just didn't think I would've been able to deal. I had no idea where we were or what plans my former boss had for getting us home, but I was willing to give her the benefit of the doubt because of all of the above.

I gazed down at the landscape taking shape below us and was surprised to find we were in the middle of a large marsh. I could see nothing around us but empty land stretching out as far as the eye could see. It was totally desolate out here, with no signs of human habitation, and I couldn't quite imagine what'd made Hyacinth choose this isolated place as her landing strip.

As we touched down, the land gave way beneath us and I could feel the helicopter's legs sink deep into silt and mud. Hyacinth pressed a series of buttons on the flight control panel, and the whirring blades above us slowed their pace and then came to a gentle stop. The helicopter lurched forward as the mud it was now shackled to settled, sucking the machine farther into the morass.

"Where are we?" I asked as I pulled my headset off and let it fall to the floor of the cockpit, glad to be rid of it. It'd put unnecessary pressure on my scalp, so that the gash on my head hadn't been able to scab over yet.

"A safe place."

That was all I could get Hyacinth to tell me as she opened her door, letting a torrent of fresh air into the stuffy compartment that made me shiver. I could smell the tang of the sea in the air, the rotting saltiness of seaweed and ocean water putrefying just out of sight. I knew we had to be near water for the smell to be so pungent, but since Manhattan was an island, this bit of information wasn't very helpful in gauging our position.

I stayed in my seat while Hyacinth slipped out of the helicopter, landing with a *squelch*—that made me cringe for her shoes—in the marshy muck that had served as our landing strip. I watched as she took a cell phone from her cleavage and dialed a number from memory. While she waited for whomever she was calling to pick up the other end of the line, I made a mental calculation of my "personal space" situation.

I could *feel* the matted blood in my hair without having to touch it, and I was pretty sure I looked like the remains of a fatted calf after a trip to the slaughterhouse. I was glad I didn't have a mirror. I didn't want to see the monstrosity I'd become: the blood all over my face, my clothes all torn and bloodied, my scarf gone. I just wanted to curl up in a ball and pretend none of this was happening. And if I couldn't have that—which, at this point, was looking highly unlikely—then I wanted a nice, long, hot shower to wash away the dreck, so I could be returned to a state of quasihuman normalcy.

Oh, and I wanted Jarvis not to be dead anymore.

"Miss Calliope?"

I whirled around in my seat, almost giving myself whiplash in the process.

"Jarvis?" I cried, not daring to believe what I was hearing until I saw it firsthand. Jarvis—the Jarvis I knew and loved, flesh and all—was sitting in the backseat. I looked down at the floor, expecting to see a pile of discarded skin and muscle, but there was nothing, just the faun's adorable little hooves.

"Are you alive again?" I asked, feeling tears I hadn't even known were there pricking at the backs of my eyeballs.

But Jarvis only shook his head.

"I don't want to be your shade," Jarvis said, his big dark eyes full of sadness. "I know you didn't intend to do this to me—"

"No, I didn't," I said, my voice stretched thin as I tried not to cry. "I don't want you to be my shade."

Jarvis nodded. He knew I would never hurt him on purpose. He was my friend—probably the only one I had in the whole world besides my hellhound pup, Runt, and my sister Clio—and I would undo whatever terrible thing I'd done to turn him, even if it killed me.

"You must let me go, Miss Calliope," Jarvis said, his voice calm.

"But I don't want you to go," I begged, understanding the finality of what the faun wanted. "I need you, Jarvi. I can't do this without you. You're my rock."

Jarvis tried to give me a reassuring smile, but it was a grotesque approximation of what a smile like that should be, more of a grimace really—and it broke my heart. I clutched the seatback, my fingers digging into the buttery leather as if it were a lifeline.

"I'll always be with you, Calliope," Jarvis said softly. "You're my friend. And even in Death no one can change that."

I would never make Jarvis my shade. I would never steal his body so his soul would be forced to do my bidding. It was a horrible existence—lonely and utterly cruel—and I would never allow it to be Jarvis's fate.

Even if it meant I lost my friend forever.

"What do I have to do?" I said, breathing hard as I wiped

my nose on the back of my bloodied hand. "Just tell me what to do."

"So simple . . ." Jarvis began, but faltered as another grimace of pain distorted his features and the illusion of his former self—something he'd been magically projecting for my benefit, I realized belatedly—flickered long enough for me to see the skeletal frame beneath it. I understood that somehow, using whatever vestiges of magic were left in his body, my friend was trying to make me remember him as he had been in life, not as what he had become in Death.

I reached out my hand to touch him, but my fingers slid through the phantom image of Jarvis's former self, and the skin of my fingertips brushed only rigid bone. I let my hand rest there, as close to my friend as I could get. I wanted him to know I would help him, whatever the cost.

"Tell me, Jarvis," I said, the lump in my throat threatening to choke me.

"So simple, Calliope," the faun answered, his words a soft whisper from desiccated lips.

"Wish me dead."

eight

Tears slid down my face. I closed my eyes, my heart thumping sluggishly in my chest as time slowed and I did the hardest thing I'd ever had to do in my entire life.

I killed my best friend.

"Good-bye, Jarvis," I whispered, my fingers brushing only empty bone where there had once been a shimmering, beautiful soul.

"I wish you dead, my friend."

As the words left my lips, I felt the power I held inside me intensify until I was thrumming with it, making the air around me heavy with prickling energy. Suddenly, the sky went black above us and the heavens split apart, sending a shower of rain tumbling down to the earth. The deluge was followed by a screaming wind—like someone plucking the taut strings of a piano in frantic sixteenth notes—that made the fragile hairs on the back of my neck stand at attention. I looked over to where Hyacinth had been standing to see what she made of this new development, but to my surprise, she was gone, or more likely, she hadn't been transported into this strange break in time with us. I scanned the horizon, but a wave of darkness had inked us in, leaving Jarvis and me alone in our helicopter cocoon.

I fumbled with the catch, pushing open the passenger door as I tried to look farther into the murky shadow enveloping us. A jarring crack of thunder sounded overhead, followed by a flash of lightning that illuminated the darkness for a split second, heralding the arrival of two strange men. It was as if they had been there, waiting just outside the door of the helicopter, forever. But only by the intoning of those six words—*I wish you dead, my friend*—had they been made visible to me. Like mirror opposites, one of the men was tall and fat, the other short and stout. Each wore a black Victorian-style suit with a wide black cravat cinched so tightly around his throat it would've strangled a living person. Each man had a black watered-silk top hat perched at a jaunty angle on his head and a black silk handkerchief stuffed into his suit pocket. It was then that I recognized them for what they were: Harvesters, come to collect the dead.

The larger man had a sparse red goatee that nicely set off his dead-white pallor, and two black holes floating in his face where his eyes should've been. He carried a thin-poled butterfly net in his left hand and a tiny silver bell in the other. When he saw me, he gave me a low, proud bow, then rang the miniature bell without further ceremony. The small iron clacker swung with abandon, clattering into the sides of the bell with a cacophonic *tinkling* sound. The hair on the back of my neck prickled as the notes rang, clear and true, a sensuous call from the dead, beckoning a fellow comer home—but even the living like me were chilled by the haunting report. As the last ring faded into silence, Jarvis's skeleton twitched in place, and a pale gray wisp unspooled itself from inside Jarvis's skull, wafting out of one of his flattened nostrils as if it were a smoky snake called out of its bamboo basket by a snake charmer. It circled around the faun's head, floating in the air like a cloudy halo.

The smaller of the two men pulled a pint-size glass jar from his pocket and twisted off the intricate brass lid to reveal a pale, golden gelatinous substance swirling inside it. He, too, was missing his eyes, but he wore no goatee like his partner—only a fat Fuller Brush mustache that failed to give his round, piggish face the hint of respectability he was obviously trying to engender.

The cloud gathering around Jarvis's head began to undulate, faster and faster, until the frenzied pace made my head swim, and then, like a phalanx of energetic bees, the cloud buzzed toward the jar. With a practiced ease, the tall man lifted his net, swooping up the cloud before it could reach the glistening contents of the jar.

"Wow," I breathed, watching as the tangled cloud disappeared, leaving only empty net behind it.

Now the smaller man bowed, sinking even lower to the ground than his partner had. Before I could tell him he didn't need to do this, he popped back up and the two men saluted me.

"Long live the Reign of the New Death!" they said in harmony, each open mouth revealing rows of ruined and decaying teeth. Then, in tandem, they stepped back into the darkness, fading away into the murky shadows until I was left alone again in the helicopter.

Only *this* time, I was truly alone, because Jarvis was gone.

Forever.

I closed my eyes and sat back, letting my head rest against the cool of the leather seat. I felt the tears flooding my eyes, seeking an outlet I didn't want to give them. I pressed the backs of my thumbs into my eye sockets, holding the tears at bay by sheer will, but it was a losing battle—they leaked out anyway, scalding my hands and cheeks, burning my eyelids with their evil saltiness.

I didn't want to cry. I wanted to be happy I'd released Jarvis into a better existence, but it didn't feel like that was what I'd done at all. I felt more like I'd failed him.

It shouldn't have gone down this way, I thought to myself, feeling miserable.

"Don't do this to yourself," Hyacinth said.

I sat up with the abruptness of someone caught doing

something embarrassing—I guess *crying* does rank somewhere on the embarrassing scale—and as punishment, I banged my elbow on the frame of the door.

"Dammit," I said under my breath, clutching my bruised elbow in my hand. In the time between closing my eyes and reopening them, the world had returned to normal—only Jarvis wasn't in it anymore and there was nothing *normal* about that. I started to cry again, but my eyes were still wet from my first bout of tears, so it wasn't like anyone but me would know the difference.

"You did the right thing," Hyacinth said as she held out a large but very feminine hand to help me out of the helicopter. "Your father would be very proud of you."

"Who cares if he's proud of me," I said, ignoring her hand so I could clamber out of the aircraft by myself. I didn't want her help; I just wanted to be left alone.

"Callie . . ." Hyacinth warned, but I was having none of it. I brushed by her proffered hand and jumped out of the helicopter without any help—only to catch my foot on the side of the door and go skate-sliding onto the muddy, grassy marsh floor, where I then tripped on a piece of exposed driftwood and landed hard on my butt.

"What's the point of all this?!" I yelled, flopping back onto the muddy ground, not caring that my whole backside was now an impromptu mudsicle. "I mean, why are we *doing* this? It's so stupid. Life. Is. Stupid. We go around and around and we learn *what*? Seriously, what do we learn?"

I looked over at Hyacinth for an answer, but she remained silent, her cornflower blue eyes ever watchful.

"That's right! *Ding, ding, ding!!* You got the correct answer," I crowed. "Human beings learn *nothing*! They live, they die, they're reborn, and then they do it all again . . . and for what? What is the goddamn *point*?"

I was possessed. The words poured out of me like poison and I couldn't stop myself. As far as I was concerned, the hypocrisy of life and death, the stupidity of the system, had been laid bare before me, and I wanted to stomp on it, crush it, destroy it so it could never hurt me like this again.

"I hate it!" I screamed at the mottled gray sky above me. "I hate Death and I want it to stop!"

I lay in the muck, exhausted, my throat raw from screaming. My breath came in short, staccato bursts and my face was covered in blood and mud and tears. I rolled over on my side and retched into the grassy marsh. There wasn't much in my stomach, but what was there came out fast and without fanfare. When I was done, I rolled onto my back again and stared up at the sky, bleary-eyed. I could see the clouds, long grayish cotton fluffs of varying shapes and sizes, but they didn't really register.

"Are you done now?"

Hyacinth stood above me. Her fair hair was a wild and staticky puff around her head, while her eyes remained calm seas in her pale face.

"I don't know," I said, teary again. "I just feel so bad. I just . . . my heart *hurts* . . . you know?"

I rubbed at my eyes with muddy fingers, my stomach a gurgling knot.

"I know right now everything seems pointless," she said, "but I promise you that there is a purpose."

"What? You mean *fate*?" I said, scoffing at the word. "That *God*—or whoever created this roulette wheel of a universe we live in—has some big tapestry of fate hidden somewhere, and it's this stupid 'wall hanging' that demanded Jarvis die? So he did? That's the answer to everything?"

I smacked my fist into the mud as hard as I could, and the muck replied with a satisfying *splat*. It felt good to vent some of the anger brewing inside me while I waited for Hyacinth to reprimand me or tell me I was being juvenile.

"Aren't you gonna tell me to stop acting like a brat?" I said finally, baiting her.

She didn't take the bait. Instead, she knelt down in the muck beside me and sighed.

"I think you have every right to be upset, Callie."

This gave me pause. It was so rare to have someone validate what I was feeling that it cowed me.

"You do?" I asked.

She nodded.

"I do."

As I lay there, waging war with my own disparate emotions, another bank of thunderclouds passed overhead, blotting out the sun and sending a gray pall over the marsh. The wind picked up as if in answer, and an icy shaft of foreboding, matching the swirling mass of grief and anger all tangled up inside my brain, shot through me. All my instincts said to feed the anger, to stoke it as high as possible, so I wouldn't have to deal with the grief, but I knew it was a cop-out, an excuse to, once again, not have to be responsible for my own feelings.

Hyacinth seemed to sense my turn of mood. She gave me a weary smile, then held out her hand for me to take, a peace offering. I stared at it, making my decision.

"You just have to have a little faith, Calliope."

This time I took her proffered hand and let her pull me up, so that now I stood above the muck . . . instead of wallowing in it like a baby.

"So where are we and what are we gonna do about that bastard, the Ender of Death?" I said, wiping my hands on my jacket. "I want to rip his guts out and make him eat them."

"All right," Hyacinth said, unfazed by the gore factor of my revenge plot. "But first, we need to get rid of the helicopter and the faun's body."

I wasn't prepared to hear someone refer to Jarvis as "a body" yet, but I held my tongue. The Jarvis I knew and loved was gone, and his skeleton wouldn't care what we did to it now. It was a simple shell that had once housed a good and loyal friend. And so, it was with grief-stricken body and soul that I merely nodded in response when Hyacinth informed me what she intended to do next.

Together, we gathered as much exposed driftwood as we could find, piling it inside the interior of the helicopter and around what was left of Jarvis's body—his skeleton had already started to desiccate, the bones of his haunches crumbling into a chalky powder on the floor. With a level of strength I'd never seen in a woman, Hyacinth ripped the gas tank out from underneath the transmission and doused the driftwood kindling with its contents. Next, she held up the lighter she'd taken from one of the compartments in the cockpit and flicked open the lid.

She paused before igniting the spark.

"Would you like to do the honors?" she asked. I started to shake my head *no*—then I changed my mind.

"Yeah, I wanna do it." I took the lighter from her hand and pressed my thumb into the cold, metal wheel. It was heavier than I'd imagined and I felt its weight settle in my hand.

As much as I wanted to pretend this wasn't happening, I didn't think I could bear to *not* be the one who set Jarvis's funeral pyre alight. Somehow, it would be wrong not to do this service for my friend.

With a shaky breath, I depressed my thumb against the spark wheel and the pale gold flame flickered to life, singeing the delicate skin at the tip of my finger. I flinched at the pain, but I didn't drop the lighter no matter how badly it hurt me.

I didn't dare.

I allowed it to burn for a moment, shielding it from the wind with my left hand, then I let it fly. My aim was good and it sailed into the cockpit of the helicopter. With a seductive *whoosh*, the fire took hold of the aircraft, lighting it up like a tinderbox. I watched as the flames lapped at the metal body of the machine, turning it black and sooty, while the intense heat cracked the tempered glass with a loud popping sound before finally melting it into a twisted hunk.

It was a fitting good-bye for my dad's Executive Assistant, Jarvis de Poupsy.

Something inside me broke . . . and I giggled. I couldn't help it. I stifled the indiscretion, covering my mouth with my hand, but then I stopped trying to control anything and just let the smile that was threatening break over my face. For as long as I had known Jarvis, just the mere mention of his full name gave me the giggles. Jarvis would've hated me for my lack of decorum, but he would've understood. He would've known it was a giggle of love and that it was the best way I had to say good-bye.

Good-bye, Jarvi, I thought to myself, but I knew, wherever he was, he'd heard me.

Hyacinth waited for the last of the flames to extinguish themselves then she indicated that I should follow her as she picked her way through the marsh grass toward the sea. Silently, we traversed the muck until we came to the edge where the marsh fell into the water and we stopped. A seagull screamed above us, but I barely noticed because my eyes were transfixed by the sprawling view of the Manhattan skyline that greeted me once we'd left the confines of the marsh.

"Where are we?" I breathed, my eyes sucking in the beatific vision of the city I loved so well.

Hyacinth, too, seemed in awe of the view.

"We're in Queens, on an island right across from the city."

"Really?"

She nodded.

I couldn't believe that here, in what appeared to be the middle of nowhere, we were still in the Triborough Area. It was amazing. A drop of rain fell from the darkening sky, hitting me squarely in the eye. I blinked and wiped it away. The air was getting colder, and the way the wind was blowing, it appeared we were gonna be in for another pummeling rainstorm.

"It kind of blows one's mind, doesn't it?" Hyacinth said. "That something so pristine and untouched like this protected marsh—that we have now desecrated—can be so close to one of the largest man-made rattraps in the world."

I didn't take offense at Hyacinth calling New York City a rattrap, but in no way did I agree with her.

"What are we doing here?" I asked, shivering as the heavens opened up and the rain came down, drenching us before we could do anything about it. I didn't care. In fact, I was happy for the free shower—maybe it would wash away the blood and grit I was covered in.

The sea turned choppy before me, licking at the marsh grass, inching closer and closer to where we stood. I took a few steps back, but Hyacinth held her ground.

"We came here to get some help," she called over to me

as the rushing wind stripped the words from her mouth almost before I could make them out. "And we're not leaving until we get it."

There was an emptiness, a desolation to this place we had come to that frightened me. Not because I was going to die here, but because I was afraid of what kind of creature would call this place home.

"We have come for guidance!" Hyacinth screamed into the wind, which whipped her bright gold hair around her face and tore at the white sheath dress she wore. *"We will not leave until we are satisfied!"*

I half expected Hyacinth to pull out a knife and sacrifice a goat or something to whatever monster she was calling up from the depths of the stormy sea, but instead, she took out a small white bone and held it up for the wind to take. Instantly, the bone was funneled into the sky, where it hovered in the air for a few hesitant moments before it was flung into the water by unseen hands.

The second the bone hit the water, the winds died down and the sea became calmer.

"Where did you get that bone?" I asked Hyacinth, but she ignored me.

Dammit, I knew exactly where she'd filched it. Where else but from Jarvis's poor desiccated corpse? *What a bitch!* A powerful surge of adrenaline slammed through my veins and I very nearly tackled the Viking-like woman beside me, but seeing as she outweighed me by about two hundred pounds, I decided it would be safer to just let my anger go.

"We have offered you a gift," Hyacinth bellowed. "Now show yourself, you old bastard!"

The seawater began to churn and froth, the wind screaming around us like a banshee, and I covered my ears to block out the terrible wailing. Then, like the return of the Leviathan from the very depths of Hell, the sea split apart and a solid wall of water crashed over us, washing me away from the safety of the land and out into the foaming sea.

nine

Like a freight train running at full throttle, the wave crashed over me, knocking my legs out from under my body and sucking me into a swirling vortex of saltwater and seaweed. I was so surprised by the turn of events that I went under with my mouth wide open—and let me tell you, having your lungs inflated with saltwater is never a pleasant experience. I went into shock, the cold and the inability to draw a breath causing my brain to default into panic mode. I started struggling against the pull of the tide, clawing at my amorphous captor as if I could break its watery embrace by sheer dint of will. Which was totally ridiculous; I wasn't going anywhere the water didn't want me to go.

I felt a tug on my leg and I realized I was no longer being dragged as viciously by the water as I'd initially been. Now I was free-floating, with very little tidal pull working over my body. I also discovered—though it freaked me out to no end—that my lungs weren't screaming for air anymore. I was perfectly fine to hold my breath—or not hold my breath—while I sailed through the murky seawater. I opened my eyes, the saltwater stinging the delicate vitreous humor, but after a few moments my eyeballs adjusted and I was able to get a better look at my new surroundings. To my surprise, I found myself in a massive underwater grotto, miles away from the frightening wall of blackness that had originally captured me. Encircling me on all sides were mountainous embankments of coral in varying shades of blood orange and cream, their strange squiggly outcroppings like skeletal branches of a denuded forest. Marveling at the intricate beauty of the cavern, I used my arms and legs to propel myself forward, careful not to get caught on the intricate outcroppings of coral, which were sharp enough to slice open my skin like a razor blade if I was unlucky enough to get too close to them.

As I maneuvered around the coral cavern, the lack of available light made it hard to get my bearings. To add to that, the farther forward I trekked, the less light filtered down, making it nearly impossible to discern which way was "out" and which way led deeper into the impenetrable ocean depths. To my relief, a smack of tiny Day-Glo purple jellyfish swam out from the gray shadows ahead of me, surrounding me with their luminescent bodies. Shimmering like neon blossoms in the dusky gloom, they beckoned me to follow them—and together we raced through the coral caverns.

I didn't know why I felt safe following the miniature jellyfish deeper into the underbelly of the ocean, but there was just something pleasant about them, calming even as we moved inextricably farther away from my normal habitat of earth and air.

Finally, after what seemed like eons, the darkened cavern gave way to a brightly lit chamber full of twinkling rainbow-colored jewels in a multitude of sizes and shapes. They were everywhere: littering the floor, crammed into every available nook and cranny, the plethora of colors contrasting sharply with the bloodred coral that made up the circumference of the chamber.

In the middle of said chamber, on a throne made out of the protracted jaws of a great white shark, sat a wizened old Japanese man. A black kimono hung limply from his thin frame while an odd grass skirt cinched in at his waist then flared primly to his ankles. A thick piece of black linen peeked out from underneath a mop of gray hair and wound around his forehead, almost obscuring his bushy salt-and-pepper-colored eyebrows.

The jellyfish, having delivered me in one piece to their master, turned as a smack and swam back the way they had come. As soon as they'd gone, the chamber began to vibrate, and the entrance I'd just arrived through disappeared behind a quick-grow wall of bone white coral. This new wall acted like a lock, slowly sucking all the salty water out of the chamber, as if someone had pulled the plug on a slow-draining bathtub.

Cool, dry air filled the chamber in the water's wake, and I discovered I could breathe again. I found the gentle rise and fall of my chest as I drank in the sweet-tasting air to be an incredibly reassuring thing.

"Why have you disturbed my slumber?" the old man growled at me, his voice projecting menace as he spoke, the deep lines around his jaw sagging and puckering like an angry fish.

"*I* didn't disturb you," I said firmly. "I was just standing *next* to the lady who did."

The old man's brows compressed in thought as he meditated over what I'd said.

"Is that so?"

I nodded.

"I don't even know who you are," I added.

This elicited a grin, exposing a nice set of pearly whites.

"Seriously," I continued, "I don't know who you are or why I'm here, and I'm truly sorry about disturbing your 'slumber,' so if I you just want to send me back up to the surface, I'd be mucho appreciative."

"Hmm," he said, resting his chin on his fist as he surveyed me.

"Look, it's been a rough day," I said, as honest as I could be. "I look like crap, I feel like crap . . . I probably *smell* like crap, and I'd appreciate it if you could just help get back up onto dry land—"

Something I said made the old man giggle, squeezing his eyes shut like a little kid as he enjoyed whatever I'd said that had tickled him. I grinned back at him, enjoying our strange little back and forth. I don't know what it was, but when someone laughed at my stupid schtick, I felt compelled to totally debase myself in order to make that person laugh harder.

"Oh, you like that, huh? When I said I smelled like crap?"

The old man's head went up and down like a pogo stick.

"How about this one?" I said, enjoying myself. "I look like poopie pie and I taste like one, too."

Now the old man was snorting with laughter at the absurdity—I supposed—of what I'd just said.

"You're funny," he said between guffaws. "Like a tuna fish."

I had no prior experience with tuna fish, but if the man said they were funny, then who was I to argue.

"I *have* eaten tuna fish in the past," I said. "But now that I know we have a similar sense of humor, I'll only eat salmon."

He found my comparison of tuna and salmon hysterical. Once again, I couldn't tell you what he found so humorous, but he was obviously enjoying my company immensely.

"I like you," the old man said abruptly. "You don't take things too seriously. That's a good way for Death to be."

That sobered me up.

"I'm not Death."

"You might be," he said matter-of-factly.

"Not if I don't have to be . . ."

"You are who you are." He grinned back at me, sounding very philosophical. But since I was a purveyor of pop culture, not Pericles, I just shrugged.

"Look, I don't know why Hyacinth was trying to call you out of your slumber, but maybe you can just send me back up top now and we'll call it even-steven?" I asked, hoping the idea would appeal as much to him as it did to me.

He wrinkled his brow.

"This Hyacinth . . . big tall lady with golden hair?"

I nodded. "That's the one."

"She sent this?" he asked, pulling a small white bone from his kimono pocket and holding it up for me to see. It was the pinkie bone Hyacinth had nicked off Jarvis's corpse while we were preparing the funeral pyre.

"It belonged to a friend," I said softly, biting my lip.

The old man seemed to sense that this was a touchy subject and slid the bone back into its hiding place in the folds of his kimono.

"Okay, we go up top, then," he said, answering my earlier question.

"Uhm, you don't need to go with me—" I started to protest, but he held up his hand.

"I need to confer with the lady up top, see what she has to say. That would be the right thing."

"I guess so," I said uncertainly.

"All right, then," he said, standing up and moving toward me, the magnificent shark jaw throne devolving into a pile of bones behind him. "It's all settled."

"If you say so—"

"This is for you," he said, pulling a small uncut stone the color of heart's blood from inside the magical folds of his kimono. He presented it to me, but at first I didn't take it.

"Oh, that's really nice of you, but I can't really—"

"Take it!" He scowled at me, pressing the jewel into my hand, then wrapping my fingers into a tight fist around it. Satisfied, he stepped past me, waving his hand dismissively at the coral, indicating that it should get out of his way. Without a sound, the wall of coral receded, revealing the entrance through which I'd first arrived.

"This way," he said, waving for me to follow him out into the cavern.

I took a deep breath, expecting to be inundated with seawater, but the old man had created a magical air pocket that ran the length of the cavern. I barely knew this strange man, yet here he was trying to make me comfortable.

"Come along."

He was already halfway down the cavern, almost out of sight, so I picked up my speed to catch up. The guy moved pretty damn quickly for an old man, and I had to jog to keep up with him, my feet crunching against the unprotected coral. The old man didn't seem to mind the mess I was making, he just kept encouraging me forward.

"Stop," he said when we had reached the entrance to the coral grotto. "I will call the tuna."

I thought he was joking, but within ten seconds of him snapping his fingers, we were surrounded by a school of huge, bulbous-eyed tuna fish. They came over to the air pocket like hesitant goats in a petting zoo, and at the old man's urging I grabbed hold of two of them. Suddenly, I found myself racing through the ocean, eyes shut tight against the sting of the saltwater. Air bubbles streamed from my nose as we flew, my body slicing through the cool water like Esther Williams on speed—but only a million times cooler because I was tuna skiing!

As we got closer to the surface of the water, I released the friendly tuna, letting them return back to the depths while I swam the last few feet on my own. Relief filled my brain as my head broke through the water and the cold air plastered my wet hair down to my scalp. I wiped my eyes and looked around, certain I was back where I'd started and that land was within easy reach, but I was mistaken.

To my horror, there was nothing but empty ocean for as far as the eye could see in any direction.

"Shit!" I said, treading water like a maniac. After a few minutes, my limbs started to ache and, teeth chattering, I came to the realization that it was really cold out on the open water.

"Help!" I cried, scared I was gonna be stuck in the middle of the ocean all by myself. *"Help me!"*

The only response was the lone cry of a gull circling somewhere overhead.

I felt something brush by my feet, and I instantly pulled my legs up to my chest, protectively wrapping my arms around my knees and floating on my back. Instinct was telling me to make myself as small as possible in the presence of whatever was lurking in the water below me, that I would be safer that way. With bated breath, I waited for something else to brush past me, but after a few minutes of nothing but calm seas, I chalked the whole thing up to a random fish drive-by and started to relax—until I saw a red fin break the surface tension of the water a few feet away from me then disappear again.

I decided to stay in the tiny ball position for a little while longer.

Too bad tiny ball position wasn't enough to dissuade whatever was stalking me not to attack—before I even knew what was happening, something big had come up from underneath me, lifting me bodily into the air.

Terrified, I screamed as I was hoisted skyward onto the back of a monstrous red sea serpent, replete with scales the size of roof tiles and a huge forked tail. Ascending far above the water, I started to slide down the beast's back. It was all I could do to flip onto my stomach and grasp at the smooth red scales as they slipped between my fingers. Finally, I was able to catch hold of a scale, and getting as much purchase as I could, I held on for dear life.

The beast reared, its giant head swiveling on its neck so it could get a better look at me. Crystalline blue eyes goggled in my direction, and I wilted under the creature's fierce gaze—and then to my utter shock, *the damn beast winked at me!* I nearly lost my grip and slid all the way down the creature's back; only a hundred feet or so of scaled slip-sliding and then I'd be free again.

"Do you have a strong grip?" the serpent hissed.

I had a hard time processing the fact that the beast's voice was pure "old man from the coral grotto," but the accent was unmistakable.

"Yes!" I screamed in the direction of the monster's flat, square head, making the assumption there were ears somewhere in the vicinity.

"Hold on, then," the creature growled before rearing its head and plunging back toward the water.

I've ridden a few roller coasters in my time, and frankly, the experience is not something I overly enjoy. The theme-park feeling of having your stomach plunge from your abdomen down to your toes is awful, and riding a sea serpent as it slithered through the water was tantamount to getting on the biggest, scariest roller coaster ever. It made me think that the beast was probably better suited to traveling underwater, but since I was onboard, it was choosing to swim well above the waterline.

Moving with a bizarre, rolling motion that started at its head then oozed down the line of its body until it reached its tail, the sea monster pushed against the water, propelling itself forward with a steady velocity. I likened it to a crazy sea-monster version of the butterfly stroke.

Not fun.

"Where are we going?" I screamed up at the beast's head, but the monster didn't answer me. I wasn't even sure it had heard the question.

I gritted my teeth and settled in for the ride.

As we sliced through the endless seascape, I lay my head against the creature's flesh and closed my eyes. Everyone kept telling me I was Death, but something didn't feel right about the whole thing. If something *had* happened to my dad and I'd unwittingly been imbued with his powers, then the Ender of Death would've killed me back at my office—but he hadn't, and that gave me hope. Besides, Daniel and I were both born with the propensity to become Death, and until one of us beat out the other to drink from the Cup of Jamshid, then neither of us could fully take over the job anyway.

Both of these insights made me feel better, but then I started obsessing over the Jarvis situation and that made me feel crappy again. I'd unconsciously willed Jarvis back into life (and then killed him again), which was a point on the Death-side, so that just sent me back to square one.

If only I still had Jarvis's brain to pick, I thought angrily, *then I'd have a much better understanding of my situation.*

By murdering the faun, the Ender of Death had destroyed my only source of knowledge about the Afterlife and all its strange rules and regulations. Without Jarvis, I was pretty much flying blind.

It was frustrating to be at the mercy of Hyacinth and the odd little Japanese man/sea serpent when what I really needed to be doing was going to Sea Verge, finding my dad, and making damn sure he and my mom and Clio were safe and sound.

When we were near the shore, I heard someone call my name.

"Calliope?"

It was Hyacinth. I opened my eyes—I was so high in the air that the Amazonian woman appeared to be a tiny speck below me. I gave a tug on the creature's scales and it began to gently lower itself below the waves. When I was only a few feet from the water, I clambered off the beast's back and slid into the sea. I'd had just enough time to dry out during the journey, so hitting the cold water was a bit of a shock. Teeth chattering, I shivered and set off toward shore at a modified dog paddle. Once I'd reached the point where the surf breached the land, I happily let Hyacinth haul me out of the water. I felt like a beached whale as I sat back in the marsh grass and caught my breath. Exhausted from my adventure, I could hardly move.

Hyacinth hovered over me like a nursemaid. I'd never seen the woman be so solicitous before, and it struck me as funny—like she had some hidden ulterior motive for making sure I was all right. Also, she kept asking me if I needed anything—which really didn't make any sense because we were in the middle of nowhere, so I wasn't really sure what it was exactly she thought she could "get" for me out here. I shook my head and told her I was fine.

"I just need a nap," I said as something sharp poked me in the side.

I fumbled in my pocket, pulling out the burgundy jewel the old man had given me. I held the sparkling gem up to the sun, marveling at the way its many facets flashed in the light. As I stared into the heart of the jewel, I began to relax, my eyes closing as I enjoyed the bristle of the marsh grass poking into the back of my head. It was a pleasant, relaxing sensation . . . a marsh grass head massage, if you will. I'd been through a lot during the past few hours, both emotionally and physically, so it wasn't a shocker when relaxation quickly metamorphosed into sleep.

The last thing I remembered hearing as I drifted off into the land of Nod on a bed of massaging marsh grass was the old Japanese man's voice, like a low hiss in my ear, intoning these words:

"Rest now. There will be no chance for sleep when the time comes to slay the challenger."

ten

I dreamt I was in a room with no windows and no doors. The walls, the floor, and the ceiling were made of pale gray stone, so smooth that when I ran my palm over it, it felt like water. I was sitting in the middle of the room, Indian style, wearing a white nightdress right out of a BBC/Jane Austen flick. The sleeves were long and puffy, buttoning at my wrists, the neckline encircling my throat in a lacy poof that tickled the underside of my chin.

The nightdress was made of sheer linen, which left nothing to the imagination, and was in direct contrast to the modest cut of the gown. I found the garment both revealing and constricting at the same time, two sensations I'd never experienced together before.

At first, I stayed where I was, observing the space, trying to discover any escape routes, but the more I looked, the less likely it seemed I would be leaving the place of my own volition. So, I stood up and began pacing out its dimensions, running my hands across the walls and floor, marveling at how even they were to my touch. I couldn't feel any groove marks, any place where a tool had touched the stone. I'd seen craftsmanship like this before in Purgatory, when I'd gone to the Hall of Death with Jarvis. That gave me a pretty good idea of the room's location: I was probably in the bowels of Purgatory in one of the holding cells housing political prisoners before they went to trial. My sister had been held here while she awaited sentencing for our dad's kidnapping *and* the attempted coup on Death, Inc.

I still hadn't been able to forgive Thalia for what she'd done, so I hadn't visited her while she was there. But Clio and our mother had taken pity on the scamp and had gone to see her. After their visit, Clio had given me a pretty thorough description of the cell—one that made me glad Thalia was the sister locked up there, not me.

Suddenly, I felt a low rumbling, like stone grinding against stone, vibrating underneath the soles of my feet. I assumed something was happening on the floor below me, but when the vibration didn't dissipate and, instead, seemed to grow in pitch, I realized I was actually feeling the reverberation of the door in the far right wall as it slid open. From my vantage point, I could see a well-lit office hallway—beige Formica floors, peach walls, and the nastiest brown-spotted acoustic ceiling tile I'd ever seen—just beyond the lip of the doorway. When I saw who was coming down the hallway, I took an involuntary step back, trying to blend into the wall I'd just backed myself against.

The Jackal Brothers, who should've been in a holding cell of their own after the body-stealing episode they'd attempted on yours truly only a few weeks earlier, strode down the Formica-tiled hallway as if they owned the place. They wore traditional Egyptian loincloths of white and blue linen, their deeply tanned bodies toned and supple. Their jackal heads betrayed no discernible emotion as, between them, they half carried, half dragged a limp human body toward me. I held my breath as they stopped in the doorway, doing a visual scan of the cell. Their cold, dark eyes slid right over my cowering form as if I weren't even there—which made me think that this was some kind of bizarre dream I'd haplessly wandered my way into.

Satisfied that the cell was empty, they threw the body inside, where it crumpled at my feet, the side of its face pressing into the stone floor. Then, with a rumbling *screech*, the large stone door clapped shut, blocking my view of their retreating backs. I stayed where I was against the far wall, waiting for some kind of movement from the body, but it just lay there, lifeless. I started thinking maybe this was a dead body I was dealing with, but then one of the feet spasmed and I knew it was a living being.

"Hello?" I whispered, stepping closer to the prone body, but I got no response. I took another step, this time getting within kicking distance, and I reached out a bare toe, poking the man's T-shirt-covered shoulder.

Nothing.

I poked harder, but my touch still didn't register.

I was prepared, a few minutes later, when the stone doorway began to rumble again, grinding its way open. I ran back to my corner, trying to blend in with the stone—I wasn't 100 percent sure of my invisibility, so I thought it better to be safe than sorry.

A woman stood silhouetted in the hall light, tapping her heel on the Formica as she waited for the door to open. I squinted, hoping to make out more of the woman's features, but she still had her back to the light. It wasn't until she stepped into the cell that I had to stifle a cry . . . standing before me in a prim Louis Vuitton minisuit was my older sister, Thalia.

I didn't realize I was holding my breath until I felt the bump and grind of my heart, racing for air. I didn't want to hyperventilate, so I took small, measured breaths until the shock wore off.

Thalia.

This was my sister, the one who hated me so much she'd tried to steal my birthright (which I hadn't even wanted in the first place) and kidnap our dad, sending our family into a tailspin. She was supposed to be in the towers of Purgatory doing penance for her crimes, but instead she was out, wearing a goddamn *Louis Vuitton* minisuit and looking smugger than a cat who'd eaten a cage of canaries. She looked amazing—smoky makeup, bloodred lipstick, and her hair wrapped in a severe chignon that pulled the skin of her face so taut you could bounce a penny off it. The black minisuit she wore was open at the neck, showing off the pale white skin of her cleavage, and her Jimmy Choo stilettos (she was partial to the brand) click-clacked like someone had spilled a box of tacks on the smooth stone floor.

The door closed behind her and she made her way across the room, stopping when she reached the prostrate man so she could stare at his unconscious form. I expected her to kneel down beside the body and try to rouse it, but she surprised me by turning back around and walking over to the far wall. There, she leaned her hips against the stone and waited.

I wanted to speak to her, to ask her why she hated me so much, but I was scared of what she might say . . . of what I knew she would say. Her reply no doubt would be full of nastiness and vitriol—and after what I'd just gone through with Jarvis, I didn't think I could handle unbridled hate being loosed in my direction. Besides, it seemed as though I could kick and scream as loud as I wanted and Thalia wouldn't notice, so there wasn't any point in trying to connect with her now.

"Wake up."

Thalia was talking to the body, a brittle thread of anger running through her otherwise calm voice. If it were possible, she'd become an even colder creature than when I'd last seen her, all the humanity burned out of her by hate. A chill radiated from her very core, invading the cell with its frozen majesty, making me shiver involuntarily. It was an emotional response rather than a visceral one, because my body felt no colder than it had before. I'd heard of psychic vampires, people who dined upon the strong emotions of others, but I'd never met one before. Yet it wasn't hard for me to make the leap, to believe that this was what my sister had become. It was as if she weren't even a person anymore, just a cipher for her anger and hatred, subsisting on what energy she could scavenge from those around her.

Somehow this transformation was more frightening than if she had become a real, physical monster. At least it was a change I could see and touch. That was something I could handle. This alien coldness was a different thing entirely and much harder for me to wrap my head around.

"I said," she cooed, "*wake up*!" The "wake up" part was spoken with a lot of hostility and it definitely did the trick. The man began to stir, his body lengthening as he rolled onto his side and then immediately contracting again as he clutched his head in pain.

"*Ah* . . ." he cried. "Make it stop. Please."

Oh, Jesus, I knew the voice and I knew the man. My stomach roiled with nausea, but I just kept telling myself this was some surreal dream—*but is it really a dream or is it something else,* a voice whispered in the back of my head.

This new development was not palatable. Never in a million years would I have guessed the man I'd watched the Jackal Brothers manhandle into the cell, whom I had poked with my toe and taken for dead, who was now being tortured by my criminally insane older sister, would end up being someone I knew.

Yet there it was, the proof sitting right there before my disbelieving eyes.

Daniel is in Purgatory.

I didn't know how he had gotten there or who was responsible—other than Thalia—but I wanted to run over and beat the shit out of my sister for toying with my man. It didn't matter that he and I were fighting or that we might not even make it as a couple. Daniel belonged to me. He was mine, and all I could do was stand there and watch, helpless.

"Yes, I can make it stop," Thalia said, her tone mild. "But you have to ask the right question, Daniel. Not *can* I stop it, but *will* I stop it?"

Daniel continued to hold his head in his hands, pressing against the flesh of his scalp with his fingers.

"Please, I beg of you . . . Will you make it stop?"

I could tell by the evil grin she tried to suppress with a studied frown that Thalia was pleased with his response.

"Because you asked nicely." She waved her hand and Daniel convulsed on the floor.

"Now isn't that better," she purred, finally stalking over to where he lay, dazed. She waved her hand and—like magic, because that's exactly what it was—a chair appeared beside her. She sat down and crossed her legs, the tiny skirt riding up her thigh in a very deliberate fashion. It was so gross to watch my sister parading herself over Daniel, flaunting her skin and limbs as a lure.

"What do you want?" Daniel asked, sitting up now that the pain had seemingly evaporated. He was wearing a torn white V-neck T-shirt I recognized and a pair of ratty burgundy cords I hadn't been able to get him to part with when he moved in, no matter what bribe I offered him.

"I think you have an idea of what I'm after," Thalia said, playing with the thin gold watch on her wrist. I'd never seen it before and I wondered who'd given it to her. Now that she was a widow—months ago Daniel and I had made short work of her demon husband, Vritra—I didn't doubt there were a number of suitors willing to drop a fortune on baubles in hopes of winning her heart, whether she was in prison or not.

"Why don't you just cut the bullshit," Daniel said, his face scarlet with anger, "and tell me what you want from me?"

Thalia laughed, peals of staccato burbling that made me want to retch. I watched Daniel, to see how he was taking it all, and he looked perplexed.

"You're so precious," my sister cooed again. "I couldn't imagine what Calliope saw in you until right now."

Yuck, I thought.

"But that is neither here nor there," she continued. "I want what you want, Daniel. I want to rule the Afterlife."

Daniel snorted in derision.

"That's not what I want—"

Thalia didn't let him finish, interrupting him midsentence.

"You want the Devil out of Hell, and the only way to do that is to put him in Heaven, where he rightly belongs."

Daniel stood up and began to pace. He was like a caged lion, all muscle and swagger. I wanted to go to him, wrap my arms around his waist and kiss his sweet lips. I wanted his ice blue eyes holding mine, reassuring me that everything was going to be okay . . . but that might never happen again. Mostly because I'd done everything in my power to push him away during the course of our relationship, since I'd been scared of what he really meant to me. I was an idiot and now I was gonna pay for my stupidity.

"Explain," Daniel said, stopping in the middle of the room to stare at my sister.

She nodded, sensing that he might just be amenable to her plans after all.

"The Devil wants to challenge God for the rule of Heaven. To do that, he needs help. *My* help—which he will receive so long as he holds up his end of the bargain we've struck. What that bargain entails, of course, is none of your business. Suffice it to say, none of this will be possible until we are assured that there will be no opposition from Death, Inc. This is where you come in," she purred. "I need *your* help and I am prepared to offer you the presidency of Death, Inc.—once the Devil has assumed his new position, of course—in order to get it."

Thalia paused, waiting for Daniel to weigh in—which, to my utter shock, he did.

"But I have no interest in running Death, Inc. My allegiance is to the minions of Hell."

Thalia nodded.

"Yes, I assumed as much. I'll make a deal with you, then. One, I assure you, you will have a hard time turning down."

She paused for effect and the whole show was so calculatedly pretentious that I really wanted to gag myself with a spoon.

"I will give you Hell. You can do with it whatever you want," she continued finally, "with no one looking over your shoulder or challenging your wishes. You just have to do one teensy thing for me first."

"And what's that?" Daniel asked.

Thalia shrugged.

"Now that my father is gone—"

I didn't like where my sister was going with this one bit, and Daniel, thankfully, had the decency to look uncomfortable with this train of thought, too.

"Right now, Death is ineffectively split between you and Calliope, so neither of you wields ultimate control," Thalia continued. "Things will remain this way until you challenge my sister, best her, and assume total control of the job by drinking from the Cup of Jamshid. Until this is accomplished, she will remain a threat to everything I hold dear."

I froze, unable to breathe as I waited for Daniel to tell my sister where she could go shove it.

"And all I have to do is fight Callie and drink from the Cup of Jamshid?"

Thalia nodded, but didn't push the issue, letting Daniel come to his own conclusions. He appeared to be mulling the idea over in his mind, weighing all sides of the proposition.

"And she won't be hurt. She'll be allowed to continue with her life, no strings attached? A real human being like she's always wanted?"

My sister grinned mischievously—and Daniel, the trusting nimwit, didn't have my invisible vantage point, so he couldn't see Thalia crossing her fingers behind her back, making any promises she agreed to effectively null and void.

"Of course, Daniel," Thalia said, looking indignant. "She's my sister. I wouldn't harm a hair on her pretty little head."

"I still don't know—" he started to say, but Thalia closed the gap between them, resting her hand on his muscular chest—which only made me want to tear her eyes out with my fingernails.

"Why don't you ask me what your alternative is, Daniel, darling?" she murmured, her lips inches away from his. I could see Daniel struggling against the urge to kiss her—and Thalia smiled, knowing she had him in the palm of her hand.

"What is my alternative?" He gulped.

She reached down and grabbed his crotch, her bloodred nails like sharpened talons digging into his most delicate man bits.

"I'll tear your balls off with my bare hands and make you eat them while I watch," she said matter-of-factly. "Not much of an alternative, is it?"

Daniel shook his head and she released her hold on his balls, stepping back to admire her handiwork. She'd definitely put the fear of ball-less-ness in my usually fearless fellow.

"Okay, then." Daniel nodded, swallowing hard. "I guess I have no other choice."

I wasn't sure I'd heard him. I shook my head and willed him to repeat what he'd just said, but in the negative.

"You'll do it?" Thalia breathed, clapping her hands together in happiness.

"I'll do what you want," Daniel said, wary now. "So long as Callie goes free."

Like an ax to my heart . . . his words split me in two, severed my soul from my body, sent me spinning into space like an errant satellite. I'd been betrayed, and by the person I'd expected it from the least. I was on fire with heartache and it was the most miserable feeling I'd ever endured. I couldn't even begin to process the rest of what Thalia had said about my dad, about Daniel and me splitting Death . . . I couldn't focus, I felt myself sliding back into the wall, letting the smooth stone envelop my body, steal me away from the horrible betrayal I'd witnessed.

I closed my eyes, the scene repeating itself on the backs of my eyelids, etched in my memory for all eternity—and then a cool, soothing blackness fell upon me and I ceased to think anymore. I let my brain shut down, and as I let my soul fall away . . .

I opened my eyes.

I was lying in marsh grass, the itchy plant sheaths poking into the back of my neck and shoulders. At first, it was pleasant just to lie there, looking up at the sky as it graduated from the blue of day to the orange of sunset. My brain was free of any conscious thought; all I could do was marvel at the beauty blossoming above me. Then, like a knife slitting apart my reality, the memory of Daniel's betrayal bloomed inside me and I almost cried out because the physical pain of my heart breaking was so terrible.

"Are you all right?" Hyacinth said. I turned my head to find the giant woman sitting on the grass beside me. Concern was rife on her face and I guessed I'd been pretty vocal while I was dreaming. I reached out and took Hyacinth's hand, squeezing it as hard as I could to blot out the hurt.

"Daniel . . . He . . . It's over," I cried, the tears leaking from eyes, unbidden. "And my dad, too. Something terrible—"

I couldn't get the words out. They got stuck in my throat and I couldn't breathe. I sat up, putting my head in between my knees so I wouldn't pass out. Hyacinth didn't question me; she just put her hand on my back and rubbed the tension away as best she could.

"What am I gonna do?" I whispered, my voice cracking as I fought down my grief. "I don't know what I'm gonna do."

"That's why your father asked me to be your guardian," Hyacinth said. "To look after you and protect you if something . . . like this should ever happen."

I lifted my head to look at her.

"He thought something bad was going to happen?"

She nodded.

"He hoped not, but he made arrangements just in case."

That made me feel a little less worried, but it wasn't enough to rest any real hopes on.

"Daniel is going to challenge me," I whispered. "And I don't think I can win. I don't think I want to."

Hyacinth didn't seem too unsettled by what I was saying.

"You love him. Of course you don't want to hurt him."

"Isn't that just the worst?" I said, smiling wanly. "I'm just like every other girl with a shitty boyfriend: in denial."

Hyacinth patted my back.

"When the time comes, you'll do the right thing, Callie."

I hoped she was right. I didn't know how I felt anymore. I just wanted to see my mom and dad and my little sister. I wanted to help them if I could before Thalia did anything else to destroy our family.

"I just want to go home, ya know?" I sighed, some of the pain receding a little when I realized what I wanted. "Right or wrong, I just want to find out what's happened to the rest of my family."

Hyacinth was smart enough to remain silent, knowing that nothing she could say would make things any better for me—because she understood something I did not: My life had changed irreparably . . . *whether I liked it or not.*

eleven

We stayed on the shore, the clear blue sky stretching out into the horizon above us while I watched the water foam around the edges of the marsh. The sea looked as lonely as I felt, empty of any life on the surface, but a tumultuous mess of activity below the cresting waves. My brain couldn't stop rehashing everything I'd seen, all the crappy bits compressed into one big ball of awfulness. I saw Jarvis propped up against the toilet, his head hanging forward, lifeless. I saw Daniel pacing his purgatorial cell, choosing power over love. I saw my mom and dad, just a still frame of the last time we were together: my mom sitting on the living room couch, my dad sitting in an armchair reading a book. The image faded to black and I felt terror at what that might mean. I chose not to think of my little sister. If anything had happened to Clio . . . I couldn't bear to think about it.

There was one positive thing. Our hellhound pup, Runt, was still down in Hell with her three-headed dad, Cerberus, the Guardian of the North Gate of Hell. That meant she wasn't at Sea Verge, and that if anything bad had happened there, then at least she was okay. I couldn't see Cerberus letting anyone touch his little girl as long as he was guarding her. This thought gave me the first glimmer of hope I'd had in hours. It wasn't enough to dispel the depression settling over me, but it was a beginning.

Hyacinth was a good thinking companion, silent and ever watchful, never pushing me to pull myself together, letting me take all the time needed to find my way back on my own terms.

"What was my dad's plan?" I asked as I picked at a piece of marsh grass, shredding it. "I mean, his contingency plan if anything bad happened."

"I was to bring you here and call out Watatsumi from his coral palace," she said. "He would give you a gift, one you might need to assume control of Death."

"What gift?" I asked as I fingered the jewel the old man had given me.

"The one you're holding in your hands right now," she said. "It will help to restore the power of Death to its rightful owner."

"What will *I* have to do?" I said, not sure how one jewel and one girl could fight both the Devil and my sister.

"You must make sure the Devil is not allowed to install Daniel as the head of Death, Inc. He has groomed his former protégé for many years to usurp your father's position from you. If he were to succeed, then the Devil would control Daniel and, through him, Death—which would be disastrous."

After all those years in service, I'd guessed that the Devil might still have some control over Daniel. It only made sense, especially in light of what I'd witnessed between him and my sister.

"Why? What does the Devil have on Daniel?" I said. I was really hoping Hyacinth had the answer. I'd spent many nights quizzing Daniel about his past, but I'd never been able to get much out of him, especially when it came to why he'd been the Devil's protégé.

"I don't know the whole story, only the gist of what happened," Hyacinth said.

"Tell me," I said, standing up and walking off some of the pent-up energy ricocheting around inside me. I paced in front of the shoreline, anger fueling my movements as I waited for Hyacinth to tell me what she knew.

"Your friend—" she began, but I interrupted her.

"He's not my friend anymore."

Hyacinth nodded, conceding.

"The Devil knew exactly who the young man was, and what possibilities lay in his future, so he went all out wooing Daniel, promising him Heaven and Earth in order to steal his soul. I don't know what compelled Daniel to accept the Devil's offer, but he did and he was bound to Hell for all eternity unless . . ."

"Unless what?" I asked, my feet crunching the marsh grass with viciousness.

"You saved him, Callie," Hyacinth murmured. "By allowing him to make the ultimate sacrifice—his life for yours."

"I didn't do it on purpose," I offered, but Hyacinth shook her head.

"And that's why the Devil's bond was broken. Daniel sacrificed willingly, in the moment, to save you, an innocent. He was not compelled to protect you; he did it of his own free will."

"But now he's doing what the Devil wants—"

"Yes," Hyacinth said, interrupting me. "And he must be stopped at all costs."

"I promise to do what I can to protect Death, Inc.," I replied, "but I want to go to Sea Verge first. I need to speak to my dad, see what he wants me to do."

Hyacinth pursed her lips then nodded.

"You will need someone to take you there. Wormholes are no good to you," she intoned.

I could only think of one person I trusted enough—and who was powerful enough—to help me. I closed my eyes and screamed the first name that came into my brain out across the heavens.

"*Kali!* I need your help!"

A crack of thunder skated across the sky and my senses prickled as the air filled with electrical tension. The ceiling of sky remained intact, but a skeletal arm of lightning broke through the clouds and shot toward me, sizzling as it passed within a few inches of my head. The lightning struck the marsh, igniting the dry and brittle grass with a *pop* that made me and Hyacinth scurry out of the way. I waited for the fire to ramp up in intensity and start spreading, but it didn't act how I had expected. Instead, it flamed upward, a column of undulating orange and red flame flickering wildly as it funneled smoke into the atmosphere.

There was a loud *crack* like the sound of an iceberg calving on a lonely stretch of the Arctic Ocean, and then Kali was standing before me, wrapped in a bright purple sari, henna tattoos covering her olive body from the nape of her neck to the tips of her purple-painted toenails. Around her throat hung a fiber necklace strung with tiny human teeth that glinted like opals in the fading sunlight.

Her dark hair was tied up at the crown of her head, revealing a streak of oxidizing blood that ran across her cheek and down to her collarbone. At first, I thought it was Kali's blood—that she'd been wounded and had bled out—but when I realized she was intact and unblemished, I knew it must've come from someone else. Then I noticed the rest of the blood on her sari that the deep color of the fabric had camouflaged from me.

We both spoke at the same time:

"Kali, you came—"

"You're safe, white girl—"

I was so ecstatic to see my old friend, I grabbed her in a giant bear hug, which she totally slipped out of as fast as she could, her dark eyes narrowed in an angry glare that sliced at me like a sharpened knife.

"Uhm, this is my boss, Hyacinth—" I started to say, but she interrupted me.

"I was in the middle of kicking some serious ass, white girl," she seethed. "So this had better be damn important."

I swallowed hard.

"Jarvis is dead and I think my dad may be, too. I can't use the wormhole, so I need someone to take me to Sea Verge."

Kali's mouth fell open.

"The little faun? They got him?"

I nodded, a tear spilling from the corner of my eye before I could wipe it away.

"I need to find out what's happened to my family—"

Kali shook her head.

"Your mom and dad—along with your dad's lawyer, Father McGee—were taken hostage at Sea Verge earlier today. We were under the assumption you might be with them—"

I walked over and took her by the wrists.

"Then I have to go there and help them," I whispered, holding her wrists in my firm grasp. *"Please . . ."*

Kali rested her chin on her chest, unable to look at me.

"There's a war on, white girl. And now that we know you're still free," she said, her voice hoarse, "you gotta stay out of harm's way."

"Kali, please," I said, begging.

Torn, my friend sighed, her brown eyes ringed with exhaustion.

"All right, white girl, I'll make you a compromise. I'll send your spirit back so you can see what's happening—"

"Thank you," I said gratefully, knowing it was the best I was going to get.

"Don't thank me, dipwad," she glared. "Just keep your lily-white ass out of trouble."

"I hate it when you call me that," I laughed, releasing her wrists so I could wipe away the tears of gratitude.

"Then don't be a dipwad, dipwad," the Hindu Goddess replied matter-of-factly.

"You said there was a war on?" I asked. "What's happening?"

"Your sister and her minions are colluding with the Devil and the Ender of Death to take over Heaven, as you may or may not know," Kali said, gesturing to the blood on her sari. "This is from fighting a whole horde of Hellspawn outside of Purgatory. And you better believe my ass when I say it's been a bloody mess. They've overrun the building and taken prisoners, holding them hostage so they can lord it over us."

"And Sea Verge?" I asked.

Kali shook her head.

"We've been out of contact with them since this morning. We sent Clio over to do reconnaissance once we heard there had been trouble—"

I grabbed Kali's shoulders, almost shaking her.

"Watch the sari, white girl—"

"You said you sent Clio. That means she's not with you now . . ."

I trailed off.

"She was with Indra, but she volunteered to scout out Sea Verge for us," Kali confirmed.

"She was with Indra?" I sputtered. "Wait, you mean she was *with* Indra . . . like having a *sleepover with him* with him?"

Kali shoved me aside and walked over to the water.

"I don't go messing in other people's nasty business, white girl."

"Okay, totally doesn't matter," I offered, following her over to the water. "As long as she's all right—"

"I didn't say that, either, dumb girl," Kali shot back, raising an eyebrow. "I don't know what Clio's found, because we haven't heard from her, so I don't know if she's A-okay or not."

"Take me there, then," I said. "Let me find my sister."

Pulling a razor-sharp blade from her cleavage, Kali faced me and plucked my hand from my side. She raised it high into the air, holding the knife out with her other hand. I watched, transfixed, as the steel blade caught the light, reflecting the mottled sky.

"You know what happens next, Death's Daughter," Kali said—and then she plunged the blade toward the meat of my palm. At the last moment, she slowed her momentum, letting the blade only kiss the skin as it drew a straight red line of blood across my hand.

She dropped my wrist and pressed the blade into her own hand, the blood burbling up like an oil slick. She wiped the blade on her sari before resheathing it in her bodice, leaving another bloodstain to dry on the matte purple fabric of her dress.

"I have to sever your body from this plane, hold on . . ." She grabbed my bloodied hand and squeezed, our blood comingling like we were two children completing a blood brother ritual.

"Ow!" I cried as she ratcheted up the pressure, the tiny bones in my hand cracking like kindling being thrown into the flames of a fire. I could feel the cartilage and tendons being ripped out of place as Kali twisted my hand in hers. The last time this happened, the pain had been so intense that I'd blacked out. This time, I was prepared for what was to come, so it wasn't as bad.

"Close your eyes, dipwad," Kali hissed in my ear, yanking my wrist with enough force to dislocate it. I did as she asked, shutting my eyes so tight you couldn't have pried them open with a crowbar. My hand ached like a bitch and I was sure the Goddess of Destruction had permanently crippled me, but I didn't care. I was grateful for her help.

"Thank you, Kali," I whispered, my body going numb as a subarctic wind whipped by from out of nowhere and enfolded me in its wintery embrace. My body became light as a feather and I drifted in the air, my fragile soul floating on the back of the wind. I spun in the air, faster and faster, until I was a human top dancing on the slipstream.

As the wind dropped and I felt myself falling, I ignored my fear. It was a controlled fall and I relaxed into it, consciously working to ease the tension from my muscles. I hit the ground hard, my left hip taking much of the brunt of the fall, but there was no pain.

"Get up!"

Adrenaline coursed through my veins, making my heart beat like a metronome set to an "extra fast" tempo. My eyes flew open and I found myself lying on my side in the backyard of Sea Verge. Only, it wasn't me anymore. At least, it wasn't my *body*—my body was back at the marsh in New York. My *soul* was here at Sea Verge, enmeshed with someone else's soul.

And that someone else was my dad!

I was filled with joy—my dad was alive and kicking! I couldn't believe I'd listened to any of those false pronouncements, that I'd let them trick me into thinking my dad was dead. I wanted to tell them all where to stick it, but I put my anger on hold to deal with more pressing matters: namely, why was my dad lying on the ground in the backyard with the Ender of Death standing over him?

"I know what your weakness is, Death," Marcel said as he stood over me/my dad, grinning like an idiot.

I wanted to kick the guy right in his pointy little eyeteeth, but I wasn't in control of my dad's body, so I was forced to sit back and, like a passive spectator, do nothing. It was pretty frustrating, but I told myself to relax, because it was a futile waste of energy to get worked up about it. Luckily, my dad seized the moment himself, rolling away from the Ender of Death before crawling back onto his feet.

"You are the Ender of Death," my dad said, lifting his hand to wipe away a smear of blood from his nose. "It's your job to know my weakness."

Apparently, there'd been some kind of fight before I'd gotten there—which was where the bloody nose came from. Once my dad was standing, Marcel lunged, but my dad sidestepped him, slamming his fist into the Ender of Death's cheekbone and giving the crazy man a nasty-looking cut on his cheek.

Wait a minute, I thought, something clicking in my brain. *I saw that cut on Marcel's face back at my office. But if my dad had just given it to him . . .*

And that's when I understood that Kali, the crazy Goddess, had sent me back in time. It shouldn't have surprised me because it had happened to me before. Frustrated, I wondered if she'd even realized what she'd done, but I didn't have time to linger on that thought because the Ender of Death was attacking me/my dad again.

"I am going to fulfill my destiny right here and now, Death," Marcel said, both fists raised as he smashed into my dad, sending him sprawling back onto the ground.

This time my dad just lay there in the grass, looking resigned.

"It doesn't matter what you do to me. My daughter will find you and destroy you."

It took me a minute to realize my dad was talking about me. I was shocked. He was putting his faith in me, the daughter who'd shunned his work and run away from home so she wouldn't get suckered into the family business. I'd never done anything to earn his trust, but here he was giving it to me anyway.

"I will give your daughter a chance to relinquish her power," the Ender of Death said, nonchalantly pulling at the bottom of his T-shirt. "I will offer her a way out, but I hope she will not take it. Then she will die by my hand, just as you will."

My dad began to laugh, his whole body shaking with it. He was tickled by something the Ender of Death had said, but for the life of me, I couldn't have told you what. Actually, I wanted to tap into his brain and see what was so goddamn funny, but I found that it wasn't an option.

"What's so funny?" Marcel barked, assuming he was the butt of some secret joke. Fueled with anger, he struck my dad in the shoulder with his foot. I felt my/my dad's shoulder bloom with pain and I suspected the Ender of Death had broken our collarbone.

This was crazy. Why wasn't my dad fighting back? Why was he allowing Marcel, the insane Ender of Death, to hurt him?

I got my answers in rapid succession:

"Don't hurt him!"

My dad turned his head and I saw my sister Clio and my mother kneeling in the dirt a few feet away. My mother was sobbing and her head hung forward so I couldn't see her face. Beside her, my dad's attorney, Father McGee, looked on, his face composed. Clio, defiant as ever, knelt at attention, hatred oozing from every pore in her body. Her left eye was a swollen purple mess, and a fierce blow to her face had split her lower lip almost in two. Standing on either side of them, keeping them restrained with papyrus rope, were the Jackal Brothers.

"Quiet, Clio," my dad started to say, but one of the jackal-headed bastards took matters into his own hands. He slammed his fist into the side of Clio's neck and she slumped forward, dazed.

"I'll ask you again," Marcel said, leaning in toward my dad's face for maximum effect. "Why are you laughing at me?"

My dad shrugged.

"I laugh because you will never win. It's very simple. Calliope will kill you and then the next incarnation of the Ender of Death will be called up and she will fight them, too."

It was nice to hear how confident my dad was about my prowess as a killer, but I thought he was going a little overboard—I was as much a crack assassin as I was a Nobel Prize–winning microbiologist.

Ha!

The Ender of Death sneered at my dad, not liking what he was saying one teensy bit.

"Well, then," the Ender of Death replied, "it's a pity you won't live to see it."

Marcel turned on his heel, making his way over to where the Jackal Brothers stood with their hostages.

"Let me have it," Marcel said, extending his hand. With horror, I watched as one of the Jackal Brothers drew a clear-bladed scythe from a sheath at his hip and laid the iron handle in Marcel's outstretched palm.

So this is my dad's weakness, I thought, staring at the scythe. I'd never have guessed that something so simple could end my dad's immortal life forever.

Marcel turned around, a smirk lifting the corners of his mouth as he walked back over to where my dad waited.

"Good-bye, Death."

He lifted the scythe high in the air, the diamond blade so clear I could see the sun—a tiny orange ball shimmering on the horizon—through it. Time froze and then began again, but in slow-mo, so that I could enjoy the delicate curve of the scythe as it sailed through the air toward me/my dad.

"NO! Please don't hurt him!!" I heard my mom scream, but it was like her words were being strained through a sieve so that I could hardly understand their meaning.

I knew my dad couldn't hear my thoughts. I was reliving something that'd already occurred in the past and I had no ability to change its outcome, no matter how desperately I wanted to. Still, I urged my dad to get up and flee, to save himself from his own impending death, but he was immovable. His body remained prostrate in the dirt before the Ender of Death's diamond-bladed scythe even as the *whoosh* of the blade cut through the air and the sound of death filled my ears. I caught a glimpse of the diamond blade in my peripheral vision, moving so quickly I could only hold it in my gaze for a second.

Then everything went dark . . . and then I could not see to see.

twelve

It was jarring to be back in my own body—even more so to have been a mute witness to my father's murder. Everything Jarvis and Hyacinth had said was true: I was Death again, well, at least partly, until Daniel came along to challenge me—then all bets were off. The strangest part of the experience had been hearing my dad tell the Ender of Death that I would avenge him. My dad had never spoken to me like that before. In fact, he'd done everything to dissuade me from using magic, almost as if he were protecting me from my birthright . . . something I'd never considered before.

With the obstinacy of a child, I'd railed against joining the family business . . . but maybe that was just what my dad had intended, what he had wanted all along: for me to be as far away from Death as possible—but thinking the idea was my own. He'd been shielding me from the supernatural world, letting me have a real life while it was still humanly possible to do so—and I'd completely misunderstood his intentions. I'd been living under false pretenses, existing in the land of denial not because I wanted to, but because it had been engineered that way by my parents.

I had this odd feeling I'd never really known my father—

and now I was never gonna get the chance to remedy it, because he was gone. I had already done so much crying I didn't think I was capable of any more tears, but I was wrong. The tears came freely, and once they'd begun, they didn't want to stop.

"He's dead." I shuddered. "They killed him with a diamond-bladed scythe, cut his head off."

Kali was gone—back to Purgatory to help try and reclaim Death, Inc.—or else she would've laughed in my face when I continued with: "They have my mom and sister and I have to go back and save them."

Hyacinth was much kinder. She merely shook her head no.

"You'll do them no good dead. You have to prepare to face the challenge ahead of you. Only then can you save your family."

Hyacinth was right.

If I wanted to help anyone else, I had to help myself first.

"I'm ready," I said to Hyacinth, but she merely nodded and pointed to the sea.

"Ask for his help."

"Help me—" I started to scream, my voice sailing across the waves, but it proved to be unnecessary. Watatsumi had many ears listening to our conversation, and within seconds the water at the marsh's edge was alive with bubbles.

"I heard tale you were looking for guidance," the old man said as he dredged his human body out of the water and flopped onto the brittle grass in front of us.

The upper part of his body was as I remembered it—a long, lean torso wrapped in a kimono—but the lower half was now nothing more than a flat fish tail made up of thousands of sparkling red jewel-like scales. As soon as he had beached himself on dry land, the glittering scales began to fade until they were gray and lusterless. The old man reached down, catching hold of the scaled fish tail and shedding it as if it were a second skin to reveal the grass skirt he was wearing underneath. The old man hoisted the fish tail back into the sea, where it sank below the waves. He stood up and walked toward me, moving with as much ease on dry land as he had underwater.

Hyacinth took the opportunity to go, disappearing behind the shell of the burnt-out helicopter and leaving me in the old man's capable hands.

"I want to learn how to beat my challenger," I said, "I want to kick his ass. I hear you can help me."

The old man giggled, pleased with my irreverence.

"Good, that makes things easier," he replied. "Think fast."

I felt something heavy fly into my midsection, knocking me backward onto my ass.

"What the—" I started to say, but out of the corner of my eye, I saw something large and silvery escape the waves and shoot toward me. On guard now, I rolled over onto my side so that the silvery thing shot past me and landed on the grass, flopping around wildly.

"A fish? You're attacking me with *fish*?" I managed before another sea creature flew through the air, flinging itself at me like a berserker.

"This is gross!" I said, sidestepping another flying fish and glaring at the old man. I didn't care that he looked pathetic and harmless in his ratty grass skirt. I knew underneath the sweet old man exterior was a scaly sea serpent biding its time until it could show its true form and chomp me in two.

"Stop throwing fish at me!" I screamed as I bent down and picked up one of the floundering creatures, its gills working overtime as it tried to suck some air out of the alien and inhospitable environment.

"You're gonna kill them," I said, throwing the projectile fish back into the water, where it swam out of sight—only to have three more leap out at me for my trouble. One of the fish slammed into my shoulder, knocking me down hard. But it was really on the losing end of that proposition, dying on impact, a smear of blood marking my shoulder as the murder weapon.

"Enough!" I yelled, picking my way through the dying

fish littering the marsh floor. I couldn't look at the heaving bodies and drying silver scales without feeling annoyed about all the waste of life.

"What's your problem?" I said, stalking over to where the old man sat cross-legged in lotus position, skimming the surface of the water like a Japanese Jesus. He'd moved to this position out on the water because it was just out of my reach—but that didn't stop me from picking up one of the dying fish and lobbing it at his head.

To my surprise, it wasn't a fish but rather a harmless clump of seaweed that landed in the water and floated at the old man's feet. I scanned the ground around me, but the fish had magically disappeared. In their place: rotting clumps of dark green seaweed that stank to high heaven.

"So, what was the point of that?" I bellowed from the edge of the marsh. "What does that do for me, buddy?"

The old man sighed. I guess he was expecting a little more brainpower from a Death-in-Waiting.

"Why don't *you* tell *me* what this exercise teaches us?" he said, rephrasing my question back at me.

"I don't know." I shrugged, feeling as if I were in the middle of a pop quiz I'd forgotten to study for. The old man floated farther away from the edge of the land, enjoying my profound discomfort.

"You're the bloody guide," I said. "Guide me to the answer."

"Nope," he said, grinning. "*You* guide *me*."

I didn't like this word game bullshit. If he wanted to teach me something, then he was gonna have to do it the old-fashioned way. I was much better at accomplishing things once someone had told me what needed doing. I guess that was what made me such a good assistant—not much thought involved in getting someone's dry cleaning, is there?

"Look, you tell me what I'm supposed to think and I'll think it," I said, hoping honesty would get me somewhere. Instead, the old man just covered his eyes with his palm and shook his head.

"You are Death's Daughter." He groaned. "But you act

like Death's idiot. What do you have against thinking for yourself?"

I shrugged.

"It's easier the other way."

He couldn't believe what he was hearing. I could feel the disgust radiating out at me.

"That is the idiot talking again," he said. *"Think!"*

I sighed, feeling a bit overwhelmed by the whole situation.

The man wants me to think. Well, even if I'm not aces at it, I can at least give it a shot. Now, what am I supposed to be learning from the fish/seaweed incident?

Just calming my brain down for two seconds and not putting up any "I can't do this" roadblocks freed my mind enough to let the answer come to me. It was so simple that I had to agree with the old man: I was being an idiot. It wasn't that I *couldn't* do what he asked of me. My problem was that I was so used to coasting through life I'd gotten lazy, letting things happen around me rather than being a willing participant. I knew this about myself. It'd been pointed out to me before, but I'd never had a reason to change it. Now I had four good reasons: my dad, my mom, Jarvis, and Clio. If I wanted to avenge the people I'd lost and save the ones who still had a chance, I was gonna have to get myself together and start acting like a real person who gave a shit about what was happening in her life.

"You wanted to me to think about illusion," I said. "To understand that things are not always what they seem."

The old man clapped, the sound as dry and brittle as the marsh grass I stood on.

"You're finally using your brain, Death's Daughter. Does it hurt?"

I gave him the finger, which got him tittering like a schoolgirl.

"What's next? You gonna teach me how to gut a fish, Sensei?" I said, rolling my eyes. "Or maybe you can teach me how to turn into a big red sea monster—"

"Good idea," the old man giggled. "You want to be like Sumi and get big, huh?"

"Like *who*?" I asked.

The old man pointed to his own chest.

"Get big like Sumi. *Sumi.* That's me."

Did I want to get big like Sumi? Heck, I wasn't opposed to it.

"Sure, tell me how to get big like Sumi," I shot back. Sumi grinned, his teeth flashing in the fading sunlight.

I hoped "learning how to get big" would be the last item on the Sumi "guidance counselor combination plate," because twilight was fast approaching and I didn't want to spend the night chilling on the marsh.

"You have the jewel I gave you?" he asked and I nodded, retrieving the scarlet stone from the pocket I'd slipped it back into.

"Good," he said, pleased I still had the stone in my possession. "Now put it in your mouth—"

"Put it in my *mouth*?" I replied incredulously. "You've got to be kidding me."

The old man shook his head.

"Why would I kid you? You have no sense of humor."

"Excuse me?" I said, taking umbrage at the implication.

"Put the stone in your mouth or go home."

I glared at him—he knew I couldn't go home and he was just being contrary.

"Fine," I sniffed, putting the jewel in my mouth. "Appy ow?"

The jewel tasted like seawater and mud, but I kept my features slack, not giving Sumi the satisfaction of seeing the disgust I felt.

"Now swallow it," he said as if it were the most commonplace suggestion in the world.

"Oo!" I said, the jewel rattling against my teeth. "Oo way!"

Suddenly, the old man was standing beside me, his grass skirt and kimono akimbo. I had no idea how he'd gotten out of the water and onto dry land so quickly, but before I could ask him, he'd slapped me hard on the back, sending the jewel flying down my trachea. I choked, my gag reflexes kicking in, but the jewel went down anyway. I could feel it hit bottom, sitting in my stomach and taking up space among the remains of the shawarma I'd eaten for lunch.

"Uck!" I squeaked. "That's disgusting!"

"A necessary evil." Sumi shrugged. "Now you can get big like Sumi."

The jewel had left the lingering taste of the bottom of the sea in my mouth. I spat, expecting a little spittle to hit the grass, but instead a burst of flame shot out of my mouth, scorching the ground in front of me.

"What the hell—" I said, startled by this strange development.

"Now you get big like Sumi." The old man grinned, pointing at me.

I looked down to find my body changing: my pale peach flesh became mottled with shimmering scales the color of a melted orange sunset, my arms shrinking then disappearing entirely into the folds of my orange-scaled torso. I was growing at an alarming rate, my body lengthening unnaturally as I transformed from human into sea serpent. Not wanting to be caught on dry land in monster form, I flopped forward, using my extended torso like a snake to slither into the water.

The transformation process generated a lot of heat and the cold water felt amazing on my new skin. I glided through the silken seawater at a brisk pace, propelling myself forward with the elongated forked tail I'd just grown. It was so freeing to be out of my human form, shooting through the water like a sailboat hewn from sea serpent flesh. I could taste the pollution in the water as I swam, and I wanted nothing more than to leave the human defilement of the bay behind me, in favor of the deeper, uninhabited waters of the ocean. My human mind knew this wasn't possible, that I was needed back on dry land, but I let myself swim for a while longer before turning back around.

When I resurfaced, I was still a good distance from the marsh where I'd transformed. I let my body float, basting in the brine for a few minutes. I'd never been so relaxed before, had never felt so free. Now I understood why Sumi was always in such a good mood: He could turn into a seagoing beast anytime he wanted. Even though I'd fought him on it, I was glad he'd made me swallow the jewel. In retrospect, I wouldn't have been so hesitant about the whole thing had I known the wonders of the sea serpent lifestyle that were ahead of me.

Being a creature from the deep, I was utterly satisfied with my lot in life. Being a human? Not so much. Still, as much as I liked riding the waves and looked forward to kicking ass and taking names as the baddest beast in the ocean, I knew that duty called—and I had to listen.

My brain high on happiness endorphins, I flipped onto my stomach and jackknifed my way back through the water toward the marsh, picking up speed as I went. I was going so fast that I didn't notice the churning water above me until I was in the thick of it.

I tried to stop short, but my velocity was too great and I caromed into the side of a tour boat, slamming into the hull with enough force to almost capsize it. I could hear the human screams reverberating through the water and I tried to sink deeper into the darkness. Above me, I sensed the flash of digital cameras as the tourists from the tour boat worked frantically to document our run-in.

Dammit, I thought. *This is so not good.*

I sunk even farther into the water, but not before the tourists were able to get a decent look at me. I had been a sea serpent for less than an hour, and already I'd wrecked the mystique for all the other sea serpents out there. I started to panic, my brain trying to figure out a good escape route, but I shouldn't have bothered. Nature took over, shrinking my body back down to human size. It was strange to be my old self again—my muscles felt rubbery and unwilling to bend to my control, and even my brain protested against the change. My human body fought against being pressed into service, but I forced it forward, away from the boat, doing an easy breaststroke in the direction of the marsh.

I was definitely ready to get out of the water now that my sea serpent body was gone. Swimming just wasn't as much fun without it.

I reached the edge of the marsh and hauled myself up onto dry land. I was exhausted and it took me a few moments to catch my breath. When I could move a little more easily, I squinted out toward the horizon, my eyes spying the tiny tour boat I'd rammed. It was still idling where I'd left it, probably hoping I'd make a repeat appearance, but it would be forced to return to port soon because twilight was fast approaching.

"You and Nessy. You give us a bad name," Sumi said as he squatted down in the grass beside me. I'd thought he was going to be superangry about my tourist attack, but that comment proved to be the only one he made on the subject.

"Time to feed you and get you dressed for your trip," he continued, offering me his hand. I took it, letting him help me stand up. I was wobbly on my feet, my whole person exhausted from my adventure, but I followed Sumi as he trudged across the marsh, his grass skirt crunching with every step.

I thought we'd run into Hyacinth on our walk, but she never appeared. Darkness was our only companion as we pressed onward, and I found it only slightly harder to see as night stole around us like a predatory cat.

"Where are we going?" I asked as my feet hit pavement and we left the marsh in favor of a road.

"Not far," Sumi replied. "We can rest then."

We followed the curve of the road to the inhabited part of the island, the lights from the houses we passed dissipating the darkness we'd enjoyed out on the marsh. In lieu of the darkness, a heavy fog descended, shrouding the landscape like a thick gray blanket and chilling me to the core. I wrapped my arms around my torso and tried to stay as close to Sumi as possible. No way José did I want to get left out in the cold on my own.

Suddenly, I felt a chill at the nape of my neck and my entire body gave an involuntarily shiver. The wind blew across my face, the ripe bouquet of animal musk blossoming into stench as it hit my nose and I nearly choked on the foulness of it.

"Get back," Sumi said, thrusting me behind him as an inhuman howl cracked the night wide open.

thirteen

The Vargr moved so quickly they were like gray and brown streaks racing through the moonlight. Before I knew it, we were surrounded by five of the slavering beasts, each one more hideous looking than the next. They were similar to the gaunt man/beast I'd dealt with back on the subway, but these guys were larger and more intimidating, if that was possible. I could see rippling rhomboid muscles working angular shoulder blades as they stalked closer, encircling us. Taut strips of muscle held their jaws in check for now, but I knew it was only a matter of time before they attacked, using their elongated snouts and serrated teeth to tear our flesh into ragged pieces.

"Vargr," Sumi said. "They belong to the Devil."

I nodded.

"Yeah, one attacked me and Jarvis on the subway this afternoon."

Sumi raised an eyebrow but never got a chance to question me further because the pack leader—a huge black beast with bright yellow corneas floating inside bloodshot sclera—chose that moment to attack. There was no warning howl, just the sound of its talonlike claws ripping through the dirt as it sprang forward, all coiled energy and aggression.

Sumi opened his mouth as if he was going to yell at the creature, but no sound escaped his lips. Instead, an arc of fire poured from his mouth, sailing across the sky and engulfing the Vragr midair. The creature screamed—the sound so piteous it chilled me to the bone—then dropped to the ground like a stone, its frantic yelps growing in intensity as the fire burnt through its black pelt. The acrid stink of sizzling fur and flesh filled the air as it died.

Now that their leader was an out-of-commission Vargr shish kebab at Sumi's feet, the other beasts broke rank and attacked. There were four of them left, too many for Sumi to take on at once, and besides which, they weren't just mindless beasts; they knew exactly where and what the old man's weakness was:

Me.

I suck at hand-to-hand combat, I thought miserably as one of the Vargrs broke free of the pack and came bounding in my direction.

I knew I was on my own, because Sumi didn't even glance in my direction to see how I was faring. I guess he figured I was immortal, so I could stand a little mauling while he took care of the other three.

"Go away, beastie!" I cried as the creature barreled toward me.

Beside me, Sumi spewed another arc of fire at the creatures, but they'd learned from watching their leader get baked and stayed just out of the fire's reach.

A low growl sounded in my left ear, demanding my attention. I whipped around to find the Vargr who'd been sent after me crouching at my feet, a long string of drool hanging from its massive jaws. I froze, my eyes riveted by the sheer power radiating from the beast—and it was then that I noticed the heavy teats protruding from the soft fur of the creature's belly.

Great, they sent the bitch after me, I thought bitterly. *A bitch for a bitch.*

Dammit, just knowing the beast was a female—who might have little Vargr kiddies waiting at home for her—changed the situation. I didn't care that the creature wanted to rip my throat out. I mean, I was immortal, so it would hurt like hell, but I'd survive.

"I know you may have kids somewhere," I sputtered, trying to get my words in order. "What's gonna happen to them when my friend over there turns you into doggie flambé?"

This only elicited a growl from the bitch.

"Okay, fine, I just wanted to put that out there—"

Interrupting me midsentence, she leapt forward, the sheer weight of her muscled form forcing the two of us to the ground, where we tussled like angry children. She bit at me, her serrated teeth sheering the skin off my forearm, exposing a strip of bloody muscle directly to the night air. I screamed. The pain was awful. I could hardly catch my breath as the nerve endings in my arm flared in response to the injury.

"DROP DEAD!" I shrieked as the Vargr went for my throat.

Instantly, my whole body was enflamed with the same pulsing white-hot heat I'd experienced earlier when the other Vargr had attacked me back in the subway car. My limbs went numb and my skin burned like fire—then a moment later it was as if my entire body had been plunged into a bathtub full of ice water. I ached as the power slowly drained out of my body and I was left shivering on the ground, breathless. The pressure on my sternum increased tenfold as the bitch's body ceased moving, flattening me into the ground with its mass. I gasped and tried to roll the beast off me, but the deadweight was nearly impossible to shift.

"Damn," I cursed under my breath, marshaling the energy I had left in hopes I could shove the bitch's body onto the ground. But before I could exert myself, Sumi was above me, lifting the dead body off so I could breathe again.

"Thank you," I said, wheezing.

Even though I was now free from the beast's weight, I was still having trouble catching my breath. I realized that something inside me had to be out of whack, so I looked down and instantly saw what the problem was: the entire left side of my chest was concave where it should've been convex.

Instinctively, I reached down to press my fingers against my rib cage, then quickly pulled my hand away, nauseous at what I'd discovered. I knew without being told that the bones had been crushed beyond recognition, leaving only shards that slid easily underneath the rubbery skin of my chest.

I felt like someone had hit me with a Mack truck, then left me on the side of the road to die slowly.

I groaned, my arm still aching where the skin had been ripped away by the Vargr's teeth, but when I checked it, I saw that the flesh was quietly re-forming itself over the wound, knitting together as if it were made out of wool instead of living tissue.

Suddenly, the sky went dark, the clouds overhead blocking out even the meager light from the moon. A lone bolt of lightning cracked the heavens in two, slamming into the ground in front of me as I scurried backward, trying to escape its reach. The sizzle of electricity frizzed out my hair and made my teeth sing in my head as the energy discharged into the ground around me.

When I looked up again, Sumi was squatting beside me, and together we watched as a man and a woman, both in black Victorian mourning clothes, strode across the dirt. They had come on the heels of the lightning strike, but they moved independently of the strange weather as another lightning bolt struck the ground behind them. When the smoke cleared, two more women in Victorian mourning garb were in lockstep with the first couple.

My eye was immediately drawn to the man, to the shock of white hair that stuck out in frothy bursts from underneath his watered-silk top hat. There was a skeletal bent to his tall frame, and the round, smoky glasses he wore made it impossible to tell if he had eyes or not. He carried a tiny platinum bell, which he rang as he walked, four sharp bursts that called out to the dead, beckoning them homeward—even though I counted *five* dead Vargr, not four.

The three women who followed in his wake pulled long-handled butterfly nets from their backs, making preparations to capture the souls they were obviously here to collect. All three women wore high-necked collars with cameos fixed at their throats and had empty coal sockets for eyes—but that and the color of their clothing were the only things they had in common.

One of the women was more than six feet tall with a flaming nest of red hair that encircled her head like cotton candy. Another of the women was very tiny, her birdlike fingers almost too small to grasp the neck of the butterfly net she was holding. The last woman was my height, blond hair curling around her face in ringlets as she pulled a silver-lidded jar from her pocket and slid it open, all while still holding the butterfly net rigidly in her other hand.

I didn't recognize any of them from my previous encounters with the Harvesters.

The man pulled his own butterfly net from his shoulder, holding it aloft like a sword while the little bell did its work. Behind me, the other three Vargr lay in various positions on the ground, their limbs splayed at whatever odd position they'd assumed when death had claimed them. In response to the bell's call, pale swirling tendrils of soul pooled out of the bodies, eddying around the emptied corpses like tiny hurricanes. The blond woman waved the jar in the air, attracting the souls' attention, compelling them forward. They oozed toward her, making a beeline for the honeyed substance inside the jar, but the other Harvesters moved swiftly, swooping in and capturing the souls with their nets before they could reach the jar.

The blond woman caught her soul last, using the butterfly net in her hand like a scythe, then she screwed the top back on the jar and curtsied.

"Long live the Reign of the New Death," she murmured, the sibilant hiss of her words setting my teeth on edge.

That's nice of you, I thought, amused by the women's display. *But I'm only part Death right now. No "long live" anyone just yet.*

The other women curtsied, too, and the man bowed, then they turned toward the water as if they could walk across the sea like it was a paved roadway.

"Wait!" I said and the four stopped, stiffening at my demand. "You only collected four souls. I want to know why you didn't collect the soul of the Vargr my friend, Sumi, killed."

Only the blond woman turned to face me, her blackened eye sockets giving me the chills.

"You will only see us when you have made the kill yourself, Madame Death," she said. "To remind you of the power you hold over those who cannot defend themselves against you. You have no need to see us collect the others."

"Oh."

That was all I could think to say in response.

"May we go?" the blonde asked, looking at me askance. I nodded and she curtsied again, turning her back on me and joining the others. Then, as the clouds dissipated and moonlight flooded the sky again, the four soul collectors faded away into nothingness.

"Shit," I murmured when they were gone.

The realization that I had just unintentionally killed four Vargr without using a weapon any stronger than my own words forced me down an even thornier path, one that I did not want to tread. With only a presentiment of how terrible the end of the path was going to be, my brain started to reel—and it was then that I finally understood the full magnitude of what I had done, of what I had become: *I am now a mass murderer.*

And I killed all of those people on the subway.

Here, I'd been thinking someone was out to get me, framing me for those innocent humans' murders, but instead, I'd been the true culprit. I thought back to the moment on the subway when I'd first experienced the numb feeling, the pins and needles of hot and cold shooting through my limbs—and I understood that it must've correlated exactly with the very moment of my dad's murder. That was when the power of Death had been split between Daniel and me, but since he'd been surrounded by immortals in Purgatory, he hadn't had a chance to abuse his power. I, on the other hand, had been murdering innocent people left and right for hours . . . and hadn't even *noticed.*

For a moment, a glimmer of hope knifed through my fevered thoughts: Why hadn't I seen the Victorian soul-collecting mafia back on the subway car? Did that mean I hadn't killed all of those people? Maybe I wasn't a murderer after all? But then I remembered how dark it had been in that subway tunnel, my night vision not yet having kicked in, and I had to concede that I probably just hadn't seen the Harvesters making their rounds because of the blackout, though I had heard their bell.

"Oh my God," I whispered as I sank to my knees, my legs giving out as the truth of what I had done overwhelmed me.

I was a loose cannon. I had killed indiscriminately and obliviously—two words that could deftly be applied to all the mistakes I'd ever made in my life. I wanted to cry, to scream at God, to ask why he/she had done this to me, but nothing came: no words, no tears, *nothing . . . absolutely nothing*.

As if none of what had happened had just happened, Sumi pointed to my chest:

"You're healed now."

I looked down. He was right, my rib cage looked normal again, but I didn't care. I just wanted to disappear, to have someone put me out of my misery so I could cease thinking. I didn't want to keep company with myself anymore . . . but I knew I didn't deserve the freedom of nonexistence, either.

No, what I deserved was to spend the rest of my immortality thinking about what I'd done to all those people so I'd never do anything like it again. I honestly didn't feel so bad about the Vargr because they'd been gunning for my throat and were *hardly* what you'd call innocent.

But for the human murders, I deserved to be punished for all eternity.

If I make it that long, I thought dryly.

Sumi patted my arm. He must've sensed the dark tone of my thoughts and was trying to make me feel better. As stunted and indifferent as this "kindness" was, it did make me feel slightly less like a shit heel.

"We should go," Sumi said as he helped me to my feet. "The food will be cold."

"I wish I could be so glib about all this death stuff," I muttered under my breath.

"Life and death are merely a spiral with no end and no beginning," Sumi replied sagely. "Though he who controls it controls all."

I sighed. It was like dealing with Yoda, only without any of the little green creature's charm.

"I'm not feeling all that hungry anymore," I said, but Sumi didn't answer. He'd already started walking again—and since I didn't want to be left to my own devices after my latest "murderer" epiphany, I trudged onward, following his footsteps in the dirt.

"What did the Vargr want?" I asked as I caught up to my guide. "I mean, what were they gonna do to us?"

"They were sent to slow you down, incapacitate you so you would not be capable for the challenge."

I nodded. It made sense.

"What I don't understand is why the Ender of Death is involved in all this?"

Sumi shrugged.

"Your sister offers him things, things he cannot get on his own—your dad on a silver platter, for one—and I bet other gifts will be forthcoming."

"Like what kind of gifts?" I asked. Then jokingly: "Maybe I should get in the gift-giving business myself, so everyone'll leave me alone."

"The Ender of Death is the yin to your yang, Little Death," Sumi said. "He wants whatever it is you *don't* want."

"I don't want to be Death." I shrugged. "That's what I want."

"Then," Sumi sighed, "the Ender of Death wants to *be* Death."

"But he can't," I cried. "It's impossible. He's not one of the chosen ones—"

"Stranger things have happened," Sumi replied as he chewed on the end of his thumbnail. Obviously this conversation was making him nervous for some reason. "The Ender of Death is so close to Death that it might be possible. A faraway possibility, but still . . . a *possibility*."

I felt Sumi's eyes settle on me then and it was a strangely uncomfortable feeling, like he hated me but needed me at the same time. His dark eyes seemed to plumb the very depths of my soul, searching for something inside me. It was a feeling I didn't enjoy one little bit. Finally, I looked away and the spell was broken.

"Let's go," Sumi said, and without another word, we continued onward toward a better-traveled stretch of the road.

After a few more minutes of walking, we stepped out of the night and into another world, one inhabited by powerful streetlights illuminating every detail of the scenery we passed. Soon the last remnants of the marsh gave way to human dwellings and I stopped feeling as nervous as I had back in the darkness. At least now, between the lights and the houses, no attacker could sneak up on me again. Still, I continued to scan the road as we went, wary that something far worse than the Vargr would decide to come keep company with us. I'd been reacquainted with the Afterlife long enough to know there were a lot of nasty creatures out there, ones who made the Vargr look like miscreant puppies on a puppy holiday.

Not a very nice thought.

My disquiet did ease some as we walked between the rows of tiny cottages, but not because my spidey senses felt any less tingly. No, my brain had just found something more intriguing than fear to find purchase on: the surreal architecture we were encountering.

The dwellings we passed may have resembled tiny Maine fishermen's cottages in their simplicity, yet these homes were anything but simple. With much forethought, they'd been built upon gangling stilts that hoisted their frames high above the reach of the water to prevent against flooding. There was something skeletal about them, spooky even, and I moved closer to Sumi as we walked among them, catching one leg of my gray tights on an errant piece of his grass skirt and shredding the cotton fabric beyond repair.

"Wow, this place is crazy-looking," I said, pointing at one house in particular. It was more than three stories high, but only about ten feet across. I marveled at how it was able to stay upright on its stilted foundation without falling over into the waiting water.

As if I'd asked a question, Sumi answered:

"We are here."

Then he stopped in front of the strange house I'd just pointed to.

"No way," I said.

"Yes, way," Sumi retorted.

Then the little old man in the grass skirt stepped off the road and started up the rickety steps, disappearing inside the gaping front door of the deformed house.

fourteen

I stood out in the fog, my wet body chilled to the bone, trying to decide what to do. I couldn't stay out in the cold all night—it was freezing—and besides that, I was starving. I hadn't eaten in hours and my stomach was making frustrated gurgling noises deep in my belly as a reminder to feed it.

"Dammit," I said under my breath as I stepped off the asphalt and onto the dirt path that led to the rickety front steps. I felt like I was walking into a horror film, one of those H. P. Lovecraft, attack of the frog/fish people scenarios with all the atmospheric fog and creepy fishermen bidding you to leave town before it's too late.

I didn't want to end up in Davy Jones's locker, but I also didn't want to stand out in the fog like a nincompoop, either.

"Wait for me!" I called as I placed one foot on the bottom step and grasped the wooden railing for support. As soon as my fingers wrapped around the splintered railing, I felt a jolt of electricity shoot up my arm. A painful current zapped through my body, completing some unseen circuit, and I gritted my teeth against the pain. My hand was riveted to the wooden rail—and no matter how hard I tried to pull away, my fingers remained frozen in place.

The light on the porch flipped on and a voice I didn't know said:

"Stop that!"

Instantly I could move again. My instinct for self-preservation kicked in and I yanked my hand away from the rail, but with a little too much force, causing me to lose my balance and fall backward into the dirt, my tailbone taking most of the impact.

"Ow!" I screeched as I hit the ground hard, my teeth rattling together like maracas.

"Are you all right?" Hyacinth said, thudding down the stairs to help me, concern flooding her face and making her normally pale skin pink with worry.

"She'll be fine," someone drawled above me. I looked up to find a guy with pale blond hair and muttonchops staring down at me. From my vantage point on the ground, the man appeared to be upside down, his pale orange sweater bleeding away into darkness. This gave his brown eyes and yellow eyebrows an alien appearance, while the light pouring from the porch cast a deep shadow across his face, making his already prominent nose seem even larger.

"So glad you're psychic," I said as I probed my backside to see if anything was busted—thankfully, nothing was—and glared at the man. "Maybe you can tell me how this whole Death thing is gonna work out for me, too. I'd love to hear your opinion."

The man grinned down at me.

"You're a real spitfire, ain't ya."

I rolled my eyes but took the hand he extended, crawling to my feet while trying not to look like a total spaz. The guy seemed nice—if kind of studious in his burnt orange wool sweater and charcoal pants. Very J.Crew, which was a total departure from what I normally was attracted to, but it kind of worked with the muttonchops.

"The house is warded against enemies," the man said to Hyacinth, who nodded as if that made perfect sense.

"Why is the house warded against enemies?" I asked, confused.

"Wouldn't want a little lady like you catching me unawares," he said, winking as he offered me his hand to shake. "And by the way, I'm Frank."

"Callie," I replied, letting him take my hand. At his touch, my heart started racing and I found it hard to breathe. Of course, I attributed all of this to the very firm grip that almost crushed my fingers.

"I already knew that." He winked, and God help me, I blushed. He had a real Southern charm I found hard to ignore. I discovered I didn't even mind the muttonchops that much—as Lynyrd Skynyrd as they were—which again was totally out of character for me. I was usually hard-core anti–facial hair on my men.

"Why don't we take this inside," Hyacinth said, interrupting the meet-and-greet and forcing Frank to drop my hand. "I think it would be safer."

My new friend nodded in agreement.

"Good idea."

He clapped his hands together and the sound was like flint sparking against steel. In response, the lights on the porch began to flicker, taking on a bluish tinge that turned Frank's pale skin ashen.

"That's that," he said, offering me his arm.

As nice as Frank was, I didn't feel comfortable letting him touch me. I was an emotional wreck and I didn't want to encourage him or in any way make him think he had a chance with me.

"I'm okay," I said, trying to be gracious. "But thanks."

I had to admit I was attracted to the guy, but I knew it was just my body responding on a purely physical level. Emotionally, I hadn't even dealt with Daniel and the feelings of hurt and betrayal I was holding at bay, so there was no way I was gonna even go there with Frank. I wasn't a glutton for punishment. I knew flirting with some poor guy because the man I'd thought I might be in love with had sold me down the river wasn't gonna make me feel any better.

"Well, you can't say chivalry's dead." Frank grinned, gesturing for me to go ahead of him.

"You are chivalry personified," I said, ignoring the handrail as I trooped up the stairs after Hyacinth's retreating back.

"I should put that on my tombstone," Frank said from behind me.

I took the stairs slowly. After the partial electrocution I'd undergone, I wasn't taking any chances. I kept my hands at my sides and made sure each stair would hold my weight before I stepped fully on it.

"Is this your house?" I asked Frank as I neared the landing.

"Nah, I've just been squattin' here for a little while," he replied. "I saw which way the wind was blowin' and decided to get out while the gettin' was good."

We were on the porch now and I stopped, facing him.

"What does that mean?"

Frank cocked his head, thoughtful.

"You don't know what's going on out there?"

I shook my head. "The Devil and my sister want to take over Heaven. That's all I know."

Frank laughed, then leaned against the porch railing with a casual fluidness. He crossed one leg over the other and I saw, for the first time, that he was wearing cowboy boots.

"Nice boots," I added without even thinking.

"They're old friends," he said, his smile so wide I couldn't help smiling back. "Anyway, you asked what was what."

"I did." I turned around, checking to see if either Hyacinth or Sumi were watching us. Except for the fog and the whistling of the wind as it blew in from the open sea, we were alone on the porch.

"You're prettier than I expected," Frank said abruptly and I blushed again.

"Look," I said, twisting my hands together nervously. "I think you're very nice and under different circumstances I'm sure I would enjoy all the vibes you're throwing in my direction—"

"But your man threw you over for another filly and now you're hurtin'."

The saliva dried up in my mouth. The guy had just turned

my life into a bad country song, making me feel embarrassed and exposed at the same time.

"How did you know about that?" I said, looking around for Hyacinth. She was the only one who knew what I'd seen and she'd gone and opened her goddamned mouth—

"Hyacinth might've let a little something slip," Frank said, covering my hand with his own. I yanked it away, his touch like fire against my frozen skin. "She says he sold you out."

"He didn't sell me out," I almost yelled at Frank, hating that he—and everyone else in the Afterlife apparently—knew my personal business. "He may even have his reasons for what he did—"

"I don't care what reasons he's got." Frank scowled. "You don't ever treat a lady the way that scumbag treated you."

"Thank you, I guess," I said, hating the pity I saw percolating behind his eyes. "I appreciate that, but I don't know whether I'm coming or going right now, so . . ."

I let my words trail off. Frank didn't seem at all bothered by my rudeness.

"Let's get you inside, 'cause I bet you're starving."

I nodded, knowing he couldn't have said a truer thing if he'd tried.

the house was as tiny on the inside as it appeared on the outside, the front room doubling as an entrance hall with crackling fireplace and an eat-in kitchen. When I came in, I discovered Sumi and Hyacinth already sitting across from each other at a small square dining table, plates of steaming food in front of them. I took the seat facing the door, not wanting to have my back vulnerable. Plus, someone had been kind enough to drape a woolen blanket over the chair back and I was particularly eager to wrap myself in it and warm up a bit. Frank nodded at my choice and took the seat directly across from me.

The food looked amazing: mashed potatoes drenched in brown gravy, gently steaming meatloaf, glazed carrots, and a glass of iced tea to round the meal off. I wanted to tuck into the food and put my stomach's growling to rest, but I found my imagination stirred by the room.

I wasn't a gourmet and the best I could manage while in chef mode was frying an egg, so the kitchen behind me didn't really whet my interest. Instead, I was drawn to the entrance hall and the seafaring paraphernalia gathered along its wide-planked, whitewashed wooden walls.

My eye settled first on the blazing fireplace cut into the far wall and its beautiful concrete mantel fashioned from broken shells and bits of brightly colored sea glass. Above it were fishing nets of various shapes and sizes all suspended just below a giant metal trident, the sharpness of its prongs glittering brightly in the firelight. On the opposing wall, high up near the ceiling, hung a wooden mermaid, obviously once upon a time the figurehead of some large seagoing ship, now just a pretty piece of memorabilia casting shadows in the firelight. As I looked at her, taking in her long, flowing blond hair and the sensual curving lines of her figure, I found myself thrilling at how lifelike she appeared. Someone had carved her with love, imbuing her with as much humanity as one could give a statue. Her skin was luminous, a gleaming honey that sparkled in the firelight as if she were covered in a coat of gold-flecked paint. Her pale blue eyes seemed alive, full of mischief and cunning, and her face was nothing short of gorgeous, all cheekbones and pouting pink lips. Her gaze was so compelling I could've easily left my place at the table, crossed the room, and stood beneath her, marveling at her beauty for hours on end—hunger pangs be damned.

"Let it rest, Starr," Frank said, not even bothering to look up from his plate. "The little gal's hungry and her dinner's getting cold."

"I was only having a little fun," a tinkling voice cried. "Why do you always have to be so mean?"

Startled, I stared at the mermaid as she tilted her head in our direction and pouted prettily at Frank. He ignored her, which only turned her gaze murderous.

"You stick me up on this wall and then you don't let me have any fun," she twittered, her voice shrill. "You stink!"

Frank continued to ignore her, as did everyone else at the table, so she crossed her arms and turned her head away rudely.

I wanted to ask who and what the mermaid was, but I restrained my curiosity, not wanting to get caught up in conversation when I should be eating. I pulled my gaze away from the mermaid and focused on my food.

I found myself inhaling my dinner as if I were in a contest and all the food I hadn't eaten before the timer went off would be taken away. The meatloaf was delicious, all warm and ketchupy, and the mashed potatoes went down like silk.

"This is fantastic." I grinned, my mouth full of carrots. "I haven't eaten like this in ages."

It was true. I hadn't had a home-cooked meal in I didn't know how long. I hadn't realized it until the second week of his stay, but Daniel was a closet junk food freak. I guess there was no delivery down in Hell, so the poor guy had been junk free for years. Of course, that was remedied once he started shacking up with me—and we'd been on a steady diet of pizza and Chinese takeout ever since. I'd depleted a good chunk of my savings in the process, but I really hadn't minded. In the beginning, it'd been heaven to have him at my house, sleeping in my bed and sharing my life.

My praise made Frank sheepish.

"It was nothing," he said.

I wasn't having any of this false modesty crap. He was a fine cook and I wanted him to know it.

"No, seriously," I pressed on. "You're an excellent cook. Really, I can barely make mac and cheese without burning it."

"Ha!" Starr harrumphed behind me.

I turned in my seat to face her, not liking her one bit.

"Why don't you take a look at what you're *really* eating?" she trilled.

I looked down at my place setting and saw that, instead of

the meatloaf and mashed potatoes I'd *thought* I was eating, my plate was half filled with gelatinous sardines. I wanted to gag as I stared at the dead-eyed fish, but I fought to keep my stomach in check. I didn't know when I was going to get another meal, so I needed to keep this one down. I may have been an immortal, but if I didn't eat, I'd waste away to nothing—and an eternity spent as a wraith of my former self was not a life.

"That's gross," I said, pushing my plate away.

"Not gross," Sumi said, his mouth full of the silvery skinned fish. "Yummy, yummy."

"It's what Sumi likes to eat," Frank said. "I tried to put a glamour on it so it would be more appealing to you—"

"Appreciate the effort," I interrupted, raising an eyebrow, "but I'm done."

Like Sumi, Hyacinth didn't seem bothered by the sardine development, so I figured I was the only one who didn't like the nasty buggers.

I hate jellied meats of all kinds. I'd spent Passover with my friend, Noh, and her then boyfriend, Haskell, and I'd nearly thrown up when Haskell's mom had plopped gefilte fish on my plate. Anything jellied and fishy that comes out of a can is a no-go for me.

"Well, if you're finished," Hyacinth said, setting her knife and fork down, "then I think we need to get our game plan in order."

"Okay," I said, feeling nauseous. "I'd love to know the plan—whatever it is."

"Are you sure about that, Death?" Starr chimed in from her perch on the wall.

"I don't care what your deal is," I said, turning in my chair again, "but I'd seriously appreciate it if you'd shut up now."

Starr opened her mouth in indignation.

"How dare you!?" she shouted. "How dare you talk to me like that—I've crushed boats on the rocks for less!"

"Wait, you're a Siren?" I asked, surprised I hadn't put it together sooner. "Of course, you are! You just said as much."

"I said nothing," Starr growled at me, then shut her mouth.

"I think my mom is part Siren," I said to no one in particular.

Starr took offense at this.

"Your mom is no more a real Siren than you are, Death," she bellowed, her high girly voice lowering about three octaves in anger. "You're nothing but Anglo-Saxon trash on two legs!"

I snorted, not really able to give her old-school insult much credence. I supposed we were all Anglo-Saxon white trash to a Siren.

"So, how did you get her on the wall?" I asked Frank, but Sumi raised his hand for silence.

"The Siren's fate is neither here nor there," he said, sucking down the last fish on his plate before reaching for my leftovers. "We have to discuss your battle strategy, Death's Daughter."

"The challenge will come soon," Hyacinth chimed in. "You'll be forced to comply, whether you're ready or not. And you must stop Daniel from winning, whatever the cost."

"Okay," I said, surprised at the larger woman's vehemence. "What do I have to do? For the challenge, I mean."

I'd been on a quest before, looking for the three objects the Board of Death had required me to find in order to save my family's immortality during my dad's kidnapping fiasco. I'd been successful then and I knew I was down to find even more magical objects, if that's what the Board of Death wanted.

"This is open combat—a duel," Sumi piped in. "And immortality becomes superfluous—"

"Hold on a minute," I interrupted. "What did you say?"

Hyacinth rested one meaty hand underneath her chin, thoughtful.

"Sumi is saying," she explained, "that your immortality is superfluous during the challenge and you will be forced to fight until the death."

I'm going to have to fight Daniel to the death? That is bullshit!

"Look, Daniel may be on my shit list right now," I said,

slamming my hand down on the table. "But that doesn't mean I want to kill him—"

"You do not decide how things are run," Sumi said abruptly, talking over my protests. "You will defeat your challenger . . . *or you will die*."

I shook my head, anger boiling just below the surface.

"Then I'd rather die."

"Don't be stupid—" Frank began, but Sumi held up a hand as if to say that he would take care of this.

"You love your mother and sister, yes?"

"Yes," I nodded.

"And you love the hellhound you call Runt, yes?"

I sighed, getting annoyed by the repetition.

"Yes, of course."

Sumi nodded, thoughtful.

"If what you say is true, then you would want them to continue to exist, correct?" he asked.

"That's a given—"

"Then you must choose," Sumi said, spearing a sardine from Hyacinth's plate and slipping it into his mouth. "The life of the Devil's protégé . . . or the lives of the people you say you love. It is your choice."

I didn't answer—I couldn't.

There was nothing I could say because I knew I'd been checkmated by the old man from the sea. I was, for all intents and purposes, well and royally screwed. I pulled the blanket up around my shoulders, trying to fight off the chill that had overtaken my body.

Somehow, the blanket didn't help nearly enough.

fifteen

I didn't have time to ponder the catch-22 I'd been railroaded into because a thundering *boom* from outside shook the house, rattling the dishes and sending the metal trident above the fireplace crashing to the floor. Starr, stuck on the wall like an insect pinned to a specimen board, gave a high-pitched scream, then began begging Frank to release her from her prison.

"Frank, free me! Please!" she howled as another loud *boom* shook the walls. "How can I protect myself if I'm stuck on this wall!?"

Frank shot a warning look in Starr's direction, then jumped out of his chair, knocking the wooden seat over in his haste. Ignoring the Siren's pleading cries, he headed for the front door, throwing two heavy iron dead bolts I hadn't even noticed were there, before turning his attention to the windows.

"What's happening?" I asked Sumi as another *boom* sounded in the distance and our dinner plates crashed to the floor, sending the remains of the jellied sardines scattering.

"The time is nigh."

"We can hold them off for a little while," Frank shot back,

flipping the lock on a window that looked out onto the porch. "The house is warded against magic—"

"I thought it was just warded against enemies," I interrupted, getting a little panicky.

"Enemies, too," Frank answered, giving me a wink.

"You're no match for them, Little Death," Starr said suddenly, all the melodrama wrung from her voice. "Free me and I will fight on your side. I can be *very* persuasive."

Frank shook his head. I turned to Sumi, but the old man shrugged.

"You unleash a Siren, then you will be responsible for putting her back where she belongs," Sumi said, pulling a piece of straw from his skirt and wedging it in between his teeth like a makeshift toothpick.

The old man was less than helpful.

"Let me just figure this out first," I said, walking across the room to peep out one of the windows so I could see what the hell was happening outside. I wanted to know exactly what I was dealing with before I leapt blindly into the fray—or released a Siren from bondage without proper cause. No way did I want to be responsible for Starr unless I absolutely needed her. She'd already gotten on my last nerve with all the whining she'd been doing.

I lifted the white lace curtain away from the window, expecting to see an army of bad guys waiting to rip me limb from limb, but instead I found that the house was totally fogged in. I couldn't see two feet in front of me, let alone tell if there was an armada of evildoers lurking around the yard or street.

"There's a whiteout," I cried, spinning back around. I caught Frank's eye first and was instantly sorry I had. He was giving me a strange look, like I was speaking gibberish at him.

"There's no fog out there," Frank said, taking a step toward me. I didn't want him to touch me, so I slid out of his way, moving toward the dead-bolted front door.

"Yes, there is," I nearly shrieked at him. "I'm not imagining it—"

"There's nothing but the sea out there, Death's Daughter," Sumi said, gesturing to the front door. "See for yourself."

I took another tentative step in the direction of the front door.

"Are you nuts?" Starr screamed. "Don't encourage her to open the door—"

Frank tried to rush me, to keep my fingers from unlatching the dead bolts, but Sumi and Hyacinth sprang at him, restraining him before he could reach me. Possessed by an irrational need to prove to Frank that I wasn't crazy, I forced my shaking fingers to undo the dead bolts and then threw the front door open—without a thought to the fact that I might be putting myself *and* everyone else in the room in danger.

I gasped as I stood in the open doorway, the doorknob still in my quivering hand. On the porch directly in front of me stood Daniel, the Devil's (former) protégé, wearing a creamy gold suit of armor and looking so delicious I wanted to cry. The pounded metal armor was molded to his muscular frame like a second skin, revealing every curve and "protrusion" he possessed. A glittering gold helmet in the shape of a bullet covered his head, except where the visor was raised to reveal his fine-boned face and pale, ice blue eyes.

I couldn't believe what I was seeing. I couldn't even begin to form words to express what I was feeling. I swiveled around to escape, but stopped when I saw that Frank, Hyacinth, and Sumi had all vanished. The room that lay behind me was empty—no table and chairs, no dishes, no nets or trident hanging from the wall. Even the fireplace had gone cold, as if there had never been a fire there. Only Starr remained behind, the last link to the world I'd left behind me. Only she was no longer the living, breathing creature that had begged me to free her from her walled prison. Now, she had magically become the wooden embodiment of a ship's figurehead and she was as silent as the dead wood she appeared to be hewn from.

There was no help to be found inside the house. The fog had merely been a lure to get me to open the door—but Hyacinth and Sumi had known this. That's why they'd held Frank back. They'd wanted me to answer the call, to do what was expected of me. I wondered if Jarvis would've been so cold-blooded had I been left in his charge, but I didn't think so. He would've been my friend first, and my guide second.

I was just a tiny cog in a much larger machine, as far as Hyacinth and Sumi were concerned. Hopefully, I would win my challenge, but if I didn't, maybe they'd go after Daniel and try to bend him to their will. I had no way of knowing.

We stood in the doorway, each silently appraising the other. I was curious what Daniel thought about our awkward situation. Did he even realize that I knew about his betrayal? I didn't know how he could stand there, looking so adorable and bewildered, while my whole world was crashing down around me.

"Hi," I said, biting my lip, nervous as a kitten at a kill shelter.

"Hey," he said, giving me a sheepish look. "You look nice."

He had to be joking. I'd been dirtied, bloodied, almost drowned, then turned into a giant sea serpent, and he had the audacity to say I looked nice?! Then I looked down at myself and saw something I wasn't prepared for. I was wearing a gleaming golden suit of armor, the twin of Daniel's except for one thing: Mine had the image of a sea serpent etched on its breastplate.

"So, what's the dealio?" I asked, wanting to reach out and touch his face, but stilling my hand before it could act. I'd cuddled up beside this man night after night for weeks, and wanting to be as close as possible to him now was just my body's reaction to his nearness—and a weakness, too, I supposed.

"Well, I'm here to challenge you, Cal," Daniel said, his tone serious.

"Okay."

He seemed surprised. I guess he'd been waiting for me to protest, or maybe even to tell him he should just get it over with and end my existence right here and now—neither of which I was going to do.

"Should we do this outside?" I asked, and Daniel nodded.

"Yeah, we need to take a little walk," he said.

I followed him onto the porch, but before I'd gone very far, I turned around and I did something crazy. I made a snap decision about the Siren, something I hoped I wasn't going to regret later.

I swallowed hard then whispered:

"Wake up, Starr."

Silence greeted my whisper.

"Okay, fine, be that way," I said. "Just know that I release you from bondage. Go and be free!"

The stupid creature just hung there on the wall, still as a piece of driftwood—which I guess she kind of was—ignoring me. I rolled my eyes in annoyance.

"Ugh," I mumbled, rethinking my possibly unsound snap decision.

"You coming?" I heard Daniel say from the head of the stairway.

"On my way," I called back, wishing I were anywhere but right there on that porch with Daniel.

Of course, as usual I had no say in my fate.

Typical, I thought to myself as I closed the door behind me, hoping I wasn't closing the door on the innocent part of my life forever. Feeling uncertain about what the future held, I followed Daniel down the rickety stairs, careful not to touch the railing. My last experience with the stairs had not been positive, and though I doubted the gold armor was an electrical conductor, I wasn't taking any chances—I didn't want to get flambéed.

For the first time since I'd been dragged back into the supernatural world, I was on my own. There was no Jarvis, no Hyacinth, no Clio or Runt to help guide me anymore. I just hoped I had what it took to do the right thing and save the people I loved.

The old me would've sat down in the dirt and cried, lamenting the unfair predicament her family had entangled her in . . . But the new Callie? Well, she was made of tougher stuff.

I took a deep breath and let it out slowly, marshaling every ounce of willpower I possessed. Then I did exactly what I knew Hyacinth and Sumi wanted me to do:

I started jogging after my competition.

"Wait up," I called, chasing after Daniel, who was keeping an Olympic record–setting pace down the dirt sidewalk. He didn't seem worried about having his back to me, not that I would play dirty and jump him while he wasn't looking, but it still made me feel funny, like he didn't really consider me a threat even though I was wearing the exact same suit of golden armor that he had on—

My thoughts were interrupted when, without warning, my body tensed, my fight-or-flight response triggered by something I couldn't see. The hairs on the back of my neck bristled and I spun around, my breath coming hard and fast as fear, more palpable than the air I was breathing, invaded my body. My skin responded to the perceived threat by breaking into gooseflesh, but I ignored my cowardly body and took a visual scan of the surrounding space, my eyes testing every nook and cranny of darkness for signs of life.

I found nothing.

Then out of the corner of my eye, I saw something or someone waiting in the shadows underneath one of the stilted houses. Two sets of violet eyes, their tapeta lucida reflecting back at me under cover of night, were watching me with an intensity that was unsettling. My senses itched and I tried to figure out what was causing me to feel so unhinged.

I swallowed, fear making my mouth so dry the flesh felt smooth, and let my attention wander back to Daniel. He'd put more distance between us than he'd realized and had to turn back around to reclaim me.

"What's wrong?" he asked, but I shook my head. I had no words to describe the *crawling* sensation I felt.

He didn't seem to mind my silence, shrugging off my unwillingness to confide in him and gesturing for me to follow. At first, my body didn't want to comply, but I picked up my feet and made them fall into sync with Daniel's steps.

I was still having trouble keeping up, so my former love slowed even more, giving me an opportunity to catch him, and together we headed back down the street. The fog was long gone now, allowing me to see more of the island as we walked. We were very close to the water here, and the surf was like a lullaby, gently rocking the land to sleep. I wanted to shuck off the heavy armor, run to the shoreline, and slip into the waiting embrace of the sea, but the human part of my brain held the impulse in check, reminding me that running away now meant letting my whole family down.

We continued on the same road Sumi and I had taken, only going in the opposite direction, the asphalt giving way to dirt under our feet. Once again I began to feel kind of spooked by our setting, by all those houses on their crazy stilted legs, the gaps between their skeletal foundations casting shadows on the ground around us.

Every so often, I thought I caught a flash of violet keeping pace with us, but when I turned my head to investigate, there was nothing there but empty night. My brain was trying to put the "violet-eyed creature" puzzle together as we walked, but it wasn't having very much luck.

"You all right?" Daniel asked after we'd trudged along for a few minutes in silence. "You're usually a regular old chatterbox."

I knew he was trying to be cute, but all his little comment made me want to do was smack him. I took a deep breath and let it out slowly to stymie the violent impulse.

"We don't have to do this, you know," I offered instead. I was half serious and half just hoping to distract myself from the creepy feeling I had in the pit of my stomach. I was pretty certain that nothing I had to say was gonna sway Daniel from fighting me and getting Hell as his reward.

"You're wrong," he replied, shaking his head. "We *do* have to do this. We have no other choice."

Angry, he picked up speed and I had to trot to keep up with him.

"We were going to go to Heaven and ask God for help," I pleaded, but the pounding of the surf picked up just then, dulling my words. "We can still do that. It's not too late."

Daniel stopped abruptly and grabbed my wrist, aggressively yanking me into him.

"Ow," I cried, trying to wrest my arm out of his grasp.

"You don't understand," he rasped, gritting his teeth in frustration as I glared at him. "There are creatures counting on me to help them and time has run out. I have to do this or the Devil will do terrible things in Hell."

I couldn't believe the bullshit he was spewing. How could he possibly believe the Devil and his cohorts would leave Hell alone if he just did what he was told and handed them Death on a silver platter?

"So, you kill me and then they give you Hell," I said, marveling at his naïveté. "You *really* think that's what's gonna happen?"

He stared at me, his face riddled with confusion.

"Kill you?" he asked, incredulous.

"Damn straight, kill me," I said, annoyed at his stupidity. "What do you think this armor is for? We're supposed to battle it out for supremacy and that means death, buddy."

Daniel looked horrified. Apparently, he hadn't taken the time to think the whole thing through.

"My sister can never be Death, Daniel. She isn't one of the chosen ones."

In every generation there were two or three people who were fated to possibly become Death, but only one would reign supreme by besting the others at three tasks set by the Board of Death. Daniel was aware of the 411 on how someone got to be the Grim Reaper, and he knew my sister was ineligible—a detail that had been one of the contributing factors in why she'd kidnapped my dad all those months before.

"You challenge me and win? Well, then *you're* Death," I said, stabbing my gloved finger into his armored chest for emphasis. "You'll be my sister's plaything, and you'll never get anywhere near Hell."

I was telling him the truth, as I knew it, and I could tell he believed what I was saying. If he defeated me, he'd be at the mercy of the Devil *and* my sister—and he'd actually be in a *worse* place than when I'd first met him.

"So what do we do, then?" he asked me finally.

I wished I could've told him I had a plan, but I didn't even have the beginnings of one.

"We gotta at least look like we're down for doing this thing," I said, letting my arms drop to my sides. "Just don't kill me until I can put all the pieces together."

He nodded, flashing me a brief smile.

With a truce of some sort in place, we continued walking down the derelict path. A few minutes later Daniel stopped abruptly in the middle of the road and declared:

"We're here."

I let my eyes sweep across the empty lane, following the curve of the land until it bowed to the sea. I couldn't imagine what was so important about this random, uninhabited stretch of road that meant we had to stop and make our little battle party here.

I didn't have to wait long for an answer.

The ground began to rumble like a freight train, the earth heaving beneath my feet in undulating waves that played havoc with my balance. Before I knew what was happening, I'd lost my footing and fallen flat on my ass in the middle of the road.

"Come on, not fair—" I whined, but I shut up when I saw what had caused the tremor.

Above me, in all its opalescent glory, rose the gleaming white seascape of Atlantis.

I goggled at its majestic beauty, the creamy marble pavilions silhouetted against the agate swell of the sea. I'd always been in awe of the mysterious Lost City of Atlantis ever since I'd come across a picture of it in a book when I was a kid. I can still remember bugging my parents to take us there for summer vacation, only to be told we couldn't actually go there because it was "lost." I also remember the very strange looks I got from the other kids in school when I told them I would rather go to Atlantis for my vacation than dumb old Disney World.

It seemed that the venue for our battle had been chosen for a reason. And though I was leery about fighting Daniel, period, I didn't think I could've picked a better battle site.

Atlantis was where I would make my stand.

Hopefully it wouldn't be my last.

sixteen

As I steeled myself for the battle ahead, I realized that, though it appeared to be daytime in Atlantis, I could still feel the coolness of the night at my back. I turned around and was shocked to find my feet still firmly planted in the marshy backwater of New York.

"Whoa," I said, the word escaping from my lips of its own volition. I was having a hard time wrapping my mind around the disorienting feeling of being in two places at once.

"Pretty weird, huh?" Daniel said, giving me a nervous smile.

"Yeah, weird," I agreed.

"Look," Daniel said suddenly, grabbing my armor-clad arm with a *clank*. "I feel terrible about all of this. I really had no idea it would be a battle to the death—"

"It's okay," I said, interrupting him. "I know you're one of the good guys, Daniel."

I wasn't sure if I really meant what I said or if the last bit had been laced with a hint of sarcasm. Daniel took it at face value, shaking his head, his handsome face creased with worry.

"I meant everything I said this morning. I'm not gonna let you run away from me."

Because I was so not expecting to have a conversation about our relationship, I just stood there, dumbfounded.

"Callie, I have very strong feelings for you," he continued, taking my silence as an open invitation to keep talking. "And I want to make our relationship work, no matter what happens."

"Uhm, I don't know if this is really the right time to be having this conversation," I said, looking around uncomfortably. I was starting to feel like I was the guy in our relationship: all terror at having to talk about feelings and other intimate things.

"Just know that whatever happens," Daniel said with an air of finality in his voice, "I'll be waiting for you."

He lifted my arm, pressing his lips to the top of my golden glove–encased hand—and even though there was no skin-on-skin contact, I had to say it was one of the more erotic experiences I'd ever had. He released my hand, his pale blue eyes raking my face for some sign of capitulation—which he must've found, because the taut muscles of his jaw visibly relaxed.

"I love you, Calliope Reaper-Jones. With all of my heart."

He gave me a wan smile as he closed the face flap on his golden helmet and walked into Atlantis.

I had no recourse but to follow him, so I flipped my own visor forward—and found that I couldn't see a thing in front of me because the helmet was entirely too big for my head. Resigned, I flipped the visor back up in place and took a deep breath. The visor immediately fell forward, covering my face again and making my ears ring.

"Dammit," I muttered under my breath, my voice reverberating hollowly in my ears as it echoed inside the helmet.

I reached up and shoved the visor into what I thought was a secure position, but the stupid thing just clanged back over my face again, obscuring my vision.

"Dumb visor!" I said, grappling with the golden face guard and trying to force it into a raised position. Apparently the armor didn't like being trifled with, because no matter what I did, I could *not* budge the faceplate. It remained locked in place, making me feel slightly claustrophobic while also giving me a new appreciation for what sardines go through.

"Fine," I said, deciding if I couldn't beat 'em, I'd join 'em. "You wanna stay shut? Then just move the stupid eye-holes down so I can see out of 'em."

Instantly, the helmet began to heat up, scalding the top of my head.

"Ow!" I screeched, reaching for the burning metal, my first reaction to get the offending object as far away from my scalp as humanly possible.

I hooked my hands around the smooth edge of the helmet and started yanking, but when I realized the helmet wasn't trying to immolate me, I relaxed, letting it resize itself to fit my head. The eyeholes realigned over my eyes, and—my sight restored—I found Daniel waiting for me down by one of the gleaming, bone white pavilions. I clomped over to where he stood, grunting in exertion as I felt the armor getting heavier with every step, the short walk leaving me as winded as a jog on a treadmill would. It appeared that engaging the faceplate had triggered some kind of magical response, increasing the protection factor of the armor a hundredfold and making it much harder to maneuver in.

Where Daniel stood, the surrounding pavilion was empty except for a long marble table overlooking the azure sea. I craned my neck, curious to see if any of the Board of Death had decided to put in an appearance, but Daniel and I were alone next to the pavilion—in fact, we seemed to be the last people in all of Atlantis, because there were only empty promenades and pavilions stretching as far as the eye could see.

I inhaled the raw scent of salt and seaweed as the wind cantered across the perfectly crested waves, eddying around us and rattling our armor.

"I'm gonna check that stuff out," I said to Daniel, indicating the marble table. When he didn't reply, I shrugged and clomped over without him.

Laid out for our perusal was an arsenal of weaponry—totally old-school stuff: forged metal weapons right out of the Middle Ages, with no gun or flamethrower in sight. Since I was outfitted like a knight of the Round Table, I figured being forced to wield a sword was just par for the course. Along with a pair of swords, there was also a mace, a crossbow, a double-sided ax, and two bronze daggers.

"Amazing," I said, reaching for one of the long swords, its gilded hilt carefully crafted to resemble a mass of trailing grapevines.

To my untrained eye, the blade looked like it was made out of polished steel, its stone-sharpened edges so precise that the blade glistened like quicksilver in the sunlight. Curious now, I wrapped my mailed hand around its bas-relief hilt and tried to lift it, but the stupid thing was so heavy I couldn't move it. Frustrated, I threw everything I had into the endeavor, leaning back so my body weight would act like a fulcrum and lift the sword off the table into the air—but still, no dice. The sword might as well have been cemented to the tabletop because no amount of effort on my part could budge it.

"Here, let me help," Daniel said, sidling up beside me. Startled, I jumped, my armor rattling. I hadn't even heard him walk over.

"No, that's all right," I said, frustration mounting as I tried to yank the sword from its resting place to no avail. "I've got it."

Ignoring me, Daniel slid his armored hand around mine. Instantly, the sword was light as a feather, and together, we easily hefted it into the air.

"Whoa," I cried, the now much lighter sword swaying in our clasped hands as if it were a reed in a rainstorm.

"I won't let go."

As Daniel said this, his eyes—the only part of his visage I could see through his faceplate—grinned mischievously at me, and I was struck, not for the first time, by how magnetic his gaze was. The eponymous "they" say a man's eyes are the windows to his soul; if that was the case, then Daniel's soul was made of ice blue steel.

"You have pretty eyes," I blurted out before I could stop myself. This made Daniel grin sheepishly.

"The better to see your beauty with, my dear," he replied, making me blush.

It's funny how things happen sometimes. Daniel and I were *supposed* to be beating the shit out of each other with medieval weaponry so the victor could then reign supreme over Death. Instead, we were standing on the battlefield trapped in gold-plated tin cans, flirting with each other like a couple of teenagers in heat.

"So, what happens if you let go of the sword?" I asked.

Daniel shrugged. "It would probably flop onto the ground."

It was a totally benign statement, but my mind went right to "flaccid penis land," and I giggled.

"What?" Daniel demanded, but I merely shook my head.

"You don't even want to know."

Daniel rolled his eyes, exasperated.

"You're right. I don't want to know," he said finally. "You have a very juvenile mind."

You can say that again, I thought. I wondered what alternate, immature scenarios Daniel and I could be partaking in if we weren't trapped in the middle of a pernicious battle between Good and Evil right then. The images that thought conjured made me blush again.

There was just something about Daniel I couldn't get out of my head. He may have driven me nuts as a live-in boy toy, but when our bodies were in close proximity to each other, well, all bets were off.

"Enough canoodling!" a clipped voice boomed from behind us. We both whirled around to see who was yelling at us, and I gasped as I lost my grip on the sword's hilt. Daniel grabbed the blade of the sword with his free hand, balancing the weapon delicately across both of his palms.

"Sorry," I mouthed, worried I'd almost skewered him, but I got a flirty wink in return for my apology, so clearly Daniel hadn't taken offense.

"If you two are through fooling around . . ." the voice

continued. I looked up to find a thin woman standing on the opposite side of the marble table from us, her brown hair piled on top of her head in a modified beehive.

Sensing that she now had our undivided attention, the lower half of her face split apart in a protracted grin. There was something about the way her pearly white teeth glinted so fiercely in the sunlight that reminded me of a piranha's dilacerating maw.

"I will be proctoring this battle for the Board of Death, as its members are indisposed at the moment," the woman purred, the rhinestones on the temples of her cat-eyed glasses twinkling merrily as she fingered the lapel of the vintage pink mohair suit jacket she was wearing. The tailored, high-necked jacket and skirt combo cinched in at the woman's waist, creating the illusion of generous curves, but the woman's shapeless calves and delicate ankles belied all the hard work the suit was doing.

"I know you," I said suspiciously. "You worked for Thalia when she was at Death, Inc."

I'd met the woman—Evangeline, Jarvis had called her—when I'd gone to the Hall of Death looking for my friend Senenmut's Death Record. Even though she'd been completely pleasant when we'd bumped into her, Jarvis had been leery of letting her know our business, because she'd worked with my sister before all the crazy dad kidnapping stuff had gone down. Needless to say, the faun hadn't thought her very trustworthy.

And neither do I, I thought, agreeing with Jarvis's estimation of the woman.

"Yes, we have met before," Evangeline replied, shooting me a tight smile that was anything but friendly. "Under more pleasant circumstances, I'm afraid. By the by, how *is* your little faun friend doing these days?"

She knew! The bitch *knew* Jarvis was dead and she was flaunting that knowledge in my face. It was pure evilness—and as much as I wanted to grab the mace off the table and slam it into her nasty grin, I wasn't going to give her the satisfaction of knowing she'd hurt me.

"Oh, you know Jarvis. He's hanging around somewhere."

Yeah, hanging around Purgatory waiting to get recycled into a new body, so I can never find him again.

"Really?" She tittered. "How nice for him, then."

Evangeline didn't press the issue; I guess she'd noticed my interest in the mace.

"So how does this work?" Daniel asked, changing the subject. "We each choose a weapon and then we fight until someone concedes?"

Evangeline picked up a tiny clipboard from the marble table—one that hadn't been there the last time I looked—and consulted the top page as if it were a manual on car repair. She flipped the first page then the next and the next until she found what she wanted.

"Yes, it seems that under the normal rules, one of you would concede and that would be that, but since those rules no longer apply," she murmured, tossing the clipboard over shoulder, where it sailed past the marble balustrade and was swallowed by the welcoming sea, "I'm afraid you're just going to have to fight to the death."

"That's bullshit," Daniel stammered. "You can't change the rules like that."

Evangeline shrugged.

"Rules are made to be broken."

"I won't kill anyone," Daniel growled. "Thalia promised me that Callie would go free. Killing her was never part of the deal."

Evangeline raised an eyebrow.

"You gave your word, Daniel. You can't back out now. Besides," she purred, "I'm sure Calliope would love to know what you and her sister were up to in Purgatory this afternoon . . ."

If the bitch thought she was gonna drive a wedge between Daniel and me, she was wrong. I knew exactly what my sister had promised him.

"Shut your mouth, bitch," I said, sick of hearing her smarmy voice. "Let's just get this over with."

I made a grab for the other sword, trying to lift it from where it lay on the table, but like its sword brother, it appeared to be superglued to the marble.

"Not again," I said, ignoring Evangeline's gleeful smirk as I worked to pry the weapon from the tabletop.

"I think they're magically drawn to a single combatant," Daniel offered. "Look at the weapons and then take the one that calls to you."

"Ugh." I groaned. "This is why I hate magic."

But I did as Daniel said, releasing my grip from the sword and stepping away from the table. I waited impatiently for one of the weapons to call out to me, and when my gaze finally settled on the mace, I plucked the heavy instrument of destruction from the tabletop and lifted it into the air, testing its weight. As far as weapons go, it was a pretty fine looking—and deadly—piece with a flanged morning star–shaped head and a long, thin handle of hammered iron that fit perfectly in my grip. I swung the mace over my head a few times to get a feel for the weapon, then I let it fall to my side.

"You look good, Cal," Daniel quipped as I hefted the mace back over my shoulder. I had to admit I did feel pretty badass just holding the lethal-looking weapon.

"I don't think this is gonna work out the way you thought," I said suddenly, turning my gaze on Evangeline and swinging the mace menacingly in her direction.

"I know what you're thinking, Calliope Reaper-Jones," Evangeline said, taking a wary step backward. "And it's not going to happen."

"Really?" I said, using both hands to lift the mace over my head. "You don't think so?"

With all my strength, I slammed the morning star mace into the tabletop, the marble splintering as the weight of the weapon struck it full force. I heard a barely perceptible *crack*, and the table split into two neat pieces of veined white marble as it buckled under the strength of my swing. All of the other weapons tumbled to the ground at Evangeline's feet, but since she wasn't one of the challengers, they were useless to her.

"Don't touch me!" she shrieked, holding her hands up to protect her face, her back pressed against the marble balustrade that looked over the sea.

I lifted the mace over my head, my arms straining underneath its weight, but before I could slam it into the bitch's head, I felt Daniel's arms around me, pulling me away from my prey.

"That's enough," Daniel whispered in my ear, my armor-plated heels sending up sparks as he dragged me backward across the floor. I was too shocked by Daniel's sneak attack to put up much of a fight, but I did manage to elbow him in what would've been his very vulnerable gut if he hadn't been wearing protective armor.

"Let me go!" I cried, flailing.

"It won't help anything, Cal," he whispered in my ear. "They'll just send someone else to take her place."

"So?" I replied, trying to wiggle out of his grasp.

When that didn't work, I slammed the heel of my armor-clad foot down, hard, on Daniel's instep. I knew the blow would be glancing at best because of the armor, but that wasn't my main thrust of attack, so I didn't care. It was merely a diversion so I could keep Daniel off guard for the big-ticket maneuver.

"What the—" he blurted out in surprise.

I whirled around and slammed the butt end of my mace into his upper chest as hard as I could, knocking him off his feet and onto his ass. The beauty of Daniel wearing all the heavy body armor was that he had about as much mobility as a turtle when he lay spread-eagled on his back. Swinging his arms and legs wildly, he tried to right himself, but I was pretty sure it was gonna take more than the modified Macarena rehash *he* was doing to get himself back on his feet.

I took my moment of freedom, racing back across the marble floor, my eyes locked on Evangeline. She was crouched like a cowed dog behind one end of the broken table, as if that would somehow protect her from my wrath.

"Please don't hurt me!" she cried, covering her beehive with her arms. "I'm not immortal!"

I stopped in my tracks, morning star mace raised in my right hand as I let her words sink in. If what she said was true, then I didn't even have to bloody my mace in order to end her pip-squeak existence. All I had to do was wish her dead and she would be . . . *dead*.

There was something very appealing about that proposition.

I crouched down in front of the broken slab of marble, glancing back to see if Daniel had been able to right himself yet—nope, he was still on the ground, floundering—then I leaned in close, the grille covering my lips inches from Evangeline's ear.

"I wish . . ." I began, my mouth curling in a mischievous smile as Evangeline's whole body began to shudder, fear emanating from her pores like honeyed ambrosia.

"I wish you would tell my sister that I'm gonna go to Heaven and have a little chat with God and *then* I'm gonna go down to Purgatory and kick her big, flabby ass from here into eternity."

I swiveled back on my armored heels as if I were going to leave, but then I went back in for more.

"I don't wish you death—no, that would be too easy," I sneered, watching as the tension eased from her shoulders and she lifted her head to look up at me.

"What I wish for *you*, bi-atch," I continued, "is that every hair on your body should die and never, ever, ever, *ever* grow back."

Evangeline gasped, covering her mouth in horror.

"You wouldn't dare," she said, reaching for her beehive.

"Weren't you listening?" I said, disdain dripping from my tongue. "I just dared, honey."

There was a terrible cry of anguish as Evangeline slid her shaking hands into the crown of her beehive, *only to have them reemerge with her hairdo wrapped around her fingers.*

seventeen

They say the best way to cripple a lady is to take a potshot at her vanity—and *this* lady had a goddamned beehive on her head. There had to be a heck of a lot of vanity going on if she really thought anyone (outside of Amy Winehouse—and she was on fashion probation) could pull off that hairdo and still be relevant in the twenty-first century. As far as I was concerned, she deserved every ounce of pain and suffering she'd received at my hands—and would continue to receive from the Afterlife at large as she went about her hairless way.

She was in my sister Thalia's thrall, and because of that I considered her a party to the murder of my dad and Jarvis. Whether she did the actual killing or not, I hated her for her participation in these heinous crimes. Believe me, I would've done more than just depilate her if I could've, but Daniel had been right to stay my hand. Killing Evangeline would've done nothing but bring down a rain of crap from my sister, the Devil, and the Ender of Death. Much better to keep the proctor we knew: especially now that she was a cowering, sniveling mess.

"Get up," I said, ignoring Evangeline's high-pitched screams of dismay as she ran her fingers across her hairless brow. It felt incredibly nice to be the responsible party for turning my sister's henchman into a Baldy McBalderton.

"I told you to get up!" I said as I shook the morning star in her face, threatening her with more than just magic-induced alopecia if she didn't do what I wanted.

"Callie?"

I felt Daniel's hand on my armored shoulder. I guess he'd managed to right himself after all.

"Are you okay?"

"I've got everything under control," I replied, turning my head to give him a quick wink, even though I didn't really want to take my eyes off Evangeline.

He returned the gesture—and I was glad to see he wasn't mad at me for stomping on his toes and forcing him to do the upside-down turtle dance. I hadn't wanted to hurt or humiliate him; I'd just wanted to give Evangeline a piece of my mind.

"We can't go through with this," I said to Daniel, still waving the mace in Evangeline's face. She took the hint and stood up. "I don't want to fight you and you don't want to fight me. We're not fighters. We're . . . I don't know, lovers or partners or whatever."

I paused, not sure where I was going with my little speech.

"I just—"

But I didn't get a chance to finish my thought because Evangeline took the opportunity to shove me as hard as she could, knocking me sideways as she pushed past me and sprinted across the pavilion. Luckily Daniel was able to catch me before I hit the ground, but Evangeline had managed her escape beautifully. When she was far enough away from us to feel safe, she turned back around, her bald pate glistening like a sunburst, and shook her fist at me.

"Get them!" she screamed, gesturing wildly, her face beet red as she glared back at us. I didn't know whom she was talking to, but my ignorance was soon remedied by the arrival of a troop of Bugbears who magically materialized beside her.

Under normal circumstances, I would've been glad to see

the hulking security guards from Hell, but these Bugbears were under Evangeline's command, and from the determined look in their brown eyes, they meant business. With their reptilian, prehensile tails, four sets of eyes (two of which were situated on either side of their heads), and humanoid-looking—but backward-bending—legs, they were monsters in the most standard definition of the word. Yet if you took a second glance (after you were done freaking out), you would see that they actually possessed very cute velveteen noses, plush teddy bear ears, and kindly brown eyes that flashed with a violet sheen in the sunlight.

As they descended on us, I realized what an idiot I had been: The flashes of violet light I'd seen in the darkness had belonged to them.

"They don't look very happy to see us," Daniel murmured under his breath.

"You were the Devil's protégé once upon a time," I said back at him, thrusting my mace forward and assuming what I hoped was a threatening stance. "Won't they listen to you?"

Daniel only grimaced.

"This is exactly why I wanted to go to Heaven, Callie. These guys have families down in Hell, and I'm sure your sister and the Devil are using that fact to make the Bugbears do their bidding."

"I'm sorry," I said meekly.

"It's my fault, Cal," he said, trying to take the sting out of his last comment. "I could've gone on my own at any point. It was my call."

I still felt horrible—and exceedingly guilty. Daniel wasn't just a do-gooder trying to get an audience with God to stroke his own ego. He'd had *very* specific reasons why it was imperative to help the denizens of Hell—like keeping the Bugbears out of Thalia's hands—and I'd done nothing but act like a selfish ass at every turn, making things impossible for him. Once again, I'd been acting like everything revolved around me, and there was no excuse for it. As God was my witness (literally), I was going to go to Heaven and make things right.

"Look, you were right," I said, grabbing Daniel's gloved hand. "We should've gone to Heaven weeks ago when you wanted to—"

"Callie," Daniel said, interrupting me, but I shook my head.

"No, listen to me. I was an ass and I'm really sorry—"

Daniel nodded.

"But I really think we should cut our losses and make a run for it. We can go to Heaven right now and get help . . ."

I trailed off. I could see Daniel's eyes behind the faceplate of his helmet, and what I saw in them made my heart break into a million little pieces of pulpy pink muscle.

"I can't go with you, Cal," he said sadly.

"Why not?" I pleaded.

"Because someone has to deal with the Bugbears and Evangeline so you can get out of here . . ."

As we'd been talking, Evangeline had goaded the Bugbears forward with an insistent snarl. I knew I was supposed to do something, to make some kind of calculated offense so we could both escape the quickly escalating situation, but my mind was not built for military strategy. And the Bugbears weren't your run-of-the-mill enemy. You couldn't just fell them with traditional weapons.

"Daniel, we *could* just wish them dead—" I started to say, but he shook his head aggressively.

"No, that's not how we play this, Cal," he said. "You and I aren't the Devil and your sister. We don't kill indiscriminately."

"Because we're the good guys," I said, nodding.

"Exactly," he said, his eyes smiling at me. "Now whatever happens, just run as fast as you can."

Then, before I understood what was happening, Daniel had shoved me backward and I was flying. The mace dropped from between my fingers as I sailed through the air. I felt untethered, like I was floating outside of my body, watching the situation from above as everything took on a bizarre surreality. Airborne, my body was propelled in a graceless arc toward the phalanx of Bugbears, the power of Daniel's push hurtling me through their unsuspecting ranks like a bowling ball taking out a row of tenpins—which was kind of cool until the weight of my armor dragged me back to earth. I landed hard on my side, my helmeted head smacking into the marble floor of the pavilion with a gut-churning *crunch.* I couldn't catch my breath, I couldn't think; the impact had knocked the air out of my lungs and the sense out of my head. Behind my helmet, my head pounded with the beginnings of a violence-induced headache.

"Run, Callie!" Daniel screamed as he raised his sword from his hip, pointing it at one of the Bugbears.

Daniel was once again sacrificing himself in order to save me—and if I didn't get my ass out of Atlantis pronto, it was all going to be for nothing. I drew a ragged breath and rolled away from the shining daylight of Atlantis, rattling like a tin can as I went, until I felt the cooler, damper New York night waiting at my back.

I picked myself up and took off, the heavy armor slowing me down and making it harder to run. As I stepped out of Atlantis and back into reality—or what I hoped was reality—I judged the line of the sea to be only a few yards away. Headache thrumming in time with my carotid artery, I forced myself forward, hoping when I hit the water the armor would magically disappear—or else I'd sink down to the bottom of the sea like a stone and wouldn't be able to help anyone. Behind me, I heard the *whoosh* of Daniel's sword and I could only hope he was holding his own. Since he was the Devil and Thalia's champion, I didn't think Evangeline would allow the Bugbears to hurt him, but still I prayed he'd be able to escape.

Almost there, I thought, relief flooding my body. I was so close to the water's edge now that I could taste the salt in the air. I reached out, using every ounce of energy I possessed to drive myself toward the sea—and freedom—but before I could make good my escape, my body was engulfed in a searing violet light so hot I thought my skin was going to melt off right there on the beach. Shock at the pain I was feeling echoed through my body and I pitched forward, my knees jackhammering into the ground with enough force to crack my jaw together, embedding my teeth into the meaty pulp of my tongue. Blood pooled in my mouth, salty and viscous like molasses, but I was already in so much pain, it barely registered.

The pain gradually lessened as I lay there panting in the sand, but now I found myself trapped like a bug in amber, the violet light pinning me into place where I lay. I had hoped that the armor would afford me *some* protection from the Bugbears' wrath, but as soon as the violet light had tractor-beamed me, the armor had disappeared as unobtrusively as it had come.

Great. Just great, I thought as I found myself back in my ratty old clothes.

As much as I'd disliked being encased in a golden exo-skeleton, not having the armor for protection left me extremely vulnerable. Panicked, my hands shot out of their own accord, fingers clawing the wet dirt and sand as I tried to breach the last few remaining inches that separated me from the cool seawater. Yet no matter what I did, the violet light prevented me from reaching my goal.

I heard Daniel scream in agony somewhere behind me, and another wave of violet light shot through the air, joining the first one and pinning me even more firmly to the ground. The pain was once again ratcheted up to the highest level, and dark splotches appeared in my peripheral vision, condensing my vision down to a tiny pinprick, then blinding me entirely, my singed eyeballs broiling away inside my eye sockets like eyeball filet mignon. I screamed, my lungs exploding as fire coursed through every cell of my body, cooking me from the inside out. My brain was having trouble cognizing, but with what little clarity I had left, my mind begged me to escape.

Then, as abruptly as the pain had begun, it stopped. I let out a ragged breath and opened my eyelids. I expected my eyeballs to gush out into a puddle in the sand, but instead, they stayed where they belonged, in their sockets completely unscathed.

"I told you releasing me from Frank's spell was a good idea."

I lifted my head in response to the tinkling voice in my ear. Starr, her human upper body wreathed in seaweed and half-beached in the sand, grinned at me like a lunatic, her left hand held aloft while she crafted a water-based protection spell that spun around us like salty cotton candy, deflecting the violet light that was being emitted from the two Bugbears on the beach behind us.

"Yes," I said, bone-tired from the Bugbear attack. "You have every right to say: 'I told you so.'"

"Ha, ha, ha!" she laughed, enjoying the irony of our reversed roles. I had saved her and now she was returning the favor.

"Let's am-scray!" she trilled suddenly, throwing her head back and cooing like a bird. She slid her right arm around my tender rib cage and, with the strength of a baby sumo wrestler, dragged me into the frothing sea.

The water was like a balm on my still sizzling skin, glorious and soothing as silk, and I luxuriated in the feel of it, my limbs enjoying the weightlessness of the saltwater.

I could loll around in the water all night, I decided, giddy with my newfound freedom.

Sure, I was being dragged farther into the deep by a Siren I barely knew and I was "Death challenger incommunicado" back up on land, but screw it, I didn't want to die and I didn't want Daniel to die, either. So the safest place for me, at least for the moment, was down here with Starr, the nutty Siren. Besides, I was fast becoming an ocean junkie. I'd never known how great the sea was before I'd been forced into making nice with it. Now, if I managed to get out of this fiasco with my body intact, I was gonna get friendly with the water and spend a lot more time swimming around in sea serpent mode.

The minute I'd thought the words "sea serpent" my body

stretched to attention and I began to change. The process was hyper–sped up this time, and before I knew it, my skin was crackling as it transmogrified from pale peach flesh into sparkling, molten orange scales. The water wrapped around my new body like a baby's blanket, keeping me warm and cozy as I finished the transformation. My cells sang in happiness as the damage that had been inflicted by the Bugbears was repaired by the change.

I'd seen the Bugbears in action down at the North Gate of Hell, using their violet light to subdue demons and other creatures who tried to escape the bounds of Hell—and their own fates. I knew how powerful the creatures were, and I knew that allowing the Devil to keep them under his control during the battle between Hell and Purgatory was a serious mistake. I needed to get to Heaven, talk to God, and put a stop to the Devil and my sister's machinations, ASAP.

As much as I would've loved to stay in the water and ignore all the craziness swirling around me, it was time to go back to the real world.

"Starr," I said in a booming sea serpent voice I hardly recognized as my own. "I need to go to the city. Can you take me back?"

I was intrigued by the way sound traveled in the water, the milliseconds of time delay between the eliciting of words and the arrival of these same words to the listener's ear. It was a very different way of hearing, one that took me a few sentences' worth of talking to get used to.

The Siren, still easily matching my speed even though I was much bigger than her now, nodded then shot ahead of me like a bullet in the water, her billowing green fish tail giving her the edge over any human feet.

"Where are you going?" she asked, swimming around me like a giddy puppy dog. "Can I go, too?"

I'd spent enough time in Starr's company to know it was easier to placate her than to tell her a truth that would only incense her.

"Sure," I said, in what I hoped was a casual manner, "you can come with. That's, uh, fine by me."

Starr giggled, blowing air bubbles out into the water as she clapped her hands together happily.

"You're the best!" she said, tickling the side of my massive sea serpent head. "I knew Hyacinth and Sumi were wrong to doubt you."

I didn't know exactly what that meant, but I didn't like the implications.

"Doubt me?" I asked. "What do you mean?"

Starr shrugged, continuing to loop around me like a high-strung mutt.

"I don't know."

"Yes, you do," I said. "Explain."

"I don't want to," she said, and then she suddenly stopped swimming, instantly falling behind me. I slowed my forward progression, hoping she'd catch back up with me, but of course, she wasn't at all interested in making anything easy, so after a few seconds of floating and waiting, I turned my whole bulk around and swam back to where she was treading water.

When I finally reached her, I found her howling like a waterborne hyena, her head thrown back in the current's wake, blond hair swirling around her head like a halo. The laughter ceased with a calculated abruptness as soon as she saw me, and she pursed her lips.

"What's so funny?" I said, working hard not to show any annoyance. I wanted her to talk to me, not clam up and refuse to volunteer information that might prove to be important.

"*You!*" she cried, pointing at me and repeating the whole laughter/howling thing all over again. "You really think anyone but me is gonna help you?!"

Apparently my situation was knee-slappingly funny to the Siren.

"And why are *you* helping me?" I asked.

She snorted, blowing air bubbles all around her face.

"Because I have to. It's the law."

She tossed her hair so that it rippled behind her.

"I don't understand," I said, and it was the truth. I had no idea what she was talking about.

"It's the law of the sea." She sighed. "I have to help you

because you released me from the spell and because you're part Siren and—"

"Back at the house you said I was Anglo-Saxon trash on two legs."

"Oh, please, Little Death, grow a set." She yawned, her usually twinkling voice flat with derision. "I lied to you. Big whoop."

I decided silence was the appropriate response.

"Actually," she continued when I didn't rise to take the bait. "Frank *did* leave me in the house on purpose, so he was either trying to ditch me . . . or maybe he was just giving you a little under-the-table help."

"Because he knew that by the law of the sea you would be forced to help me?" I asked.

Starr nodded.

"Who *is* Frank?" I asked, realizing the only things I knew about the guy were that he worked for Sumi and he didn't mind eating jellied sardines—not much info on a guy who might or might not be trying to help me survive.

"Oh silly, Little Death," Starr burbled, putting a shapely hand on my scaled flank. "They give you a wish-fulfilling jewel and all you wanna do is swim around like a big baby and ask ridiculous questions, when you should be asking *smart* questions."

Who did this Siren think she was? I made twenty of her and I had no qualms about giving her the boot with my tail if she didn't learn some manners.

"I don't want to swim around in the water all day getting my jollies off," I said. "And what 'smart' questions are you talking about?"

"Don't be mad," Starr said abruptly, giving my taut flank a wallop with her palm. "I like you anyway."

I could handle a goddess like Kali who lived in a perpetual state of PMS, but Starr was giving me emotional whiplash. She was the most mercurial creature I'd ever encountered. One minute, she was tittering, helpful mermaid girl; the next, she was an annoyingly smug Siren who enjoyed making me feel small and stupid. I hated women who behaved like that, who always prefaced their digs by announcing, "I don't mean to be rude, but . . ." and then saying the rudest thing humanly possible.

"We were discussing Frank," I said, soldiering on. I decided that ignoring her ruder comments was the easiest course of action.

"He's nobody," she giggled. "Not royalty like Watatsumi or your Valkyrie friend. Just a guy with lots of magical ability, that's all—now no more information for you, Little Death."

I had my suspicions that there was more to the story than Starr was letting on, but I didn't press her. The Siren was like an oyster, taking a piece of sand—or in her case, information—then layering a whole lot of nacre over it until you didn't know what was real and what was just expensive crap.

"Look," I said. "I appreciate your help, but I think I can find my way back to Manhattan without you. So you're free to go on your way now. I discharge you from service. Go be free and multiply."

"But we were having fun," she said, narrowing her eyes at me. "I don't want to be 'discharged.' I wanna stay and play with you! Besides, you said I could go with you, and if you do a takeback now, well, then you're nothing but a big fat liar, Little Death."

To my surprise, she began beating on my elongated neck with her girlish fists, almost like a small child having a temper tantrum. In the back of my head, I remembered someone saying if I freed Starr, it would be at my own peril; that I'd be responsible for her until I could return her to where she belonged—but they couldn't have meant I was supposed to *babysit* her, could they? The dull thumping I felt on my scaled body said otherwise. It looked like I might be stuck with the Siren for the time being.

"Look, you can come with me as far as the shoreline, Starr," I offered, trying to appease her. "But I have to go back on land and I don't think it's really possible for you to go with me—"

She stopped thumping me and cocked her head curiously, her eyes wide as she digested what I'd just said.

"Why not?" she asked, putting a long finger in her mouth to suck on. More and more she was becoming like a spoiled, human child.

I inclined my sea serpent's head in the direction of her fish tail.

"I don't think it's physically possible to walk on land with a fish tail. So . . ."

I trailed off, thinking I'd done a nice job of dissuading her, but when she grinned up at me, a fiendish look in her eye, I knew I'd screwed up.

"You have the jewel," she said, batting her long, feminine eyelashes in my direction. "You can wish me a pair of legs."

Shit, I thought. *Somehow I walked into playing the Tom Hanks role in a very unfortunate remake of the movie* Splash.

"Look, I just don't think it's a good idea. What if you got hurt?"

Starr merely rolled her eyes at me—which was the first time I'd experienced an underwater eye roll—then shrugged.

"You don't really care if I get hurt," she pouted. "You just don't want to do what you promised."

"Honestly," I said, letting the cold current roll over my body, "you're right. I don't want to be responsible for you, especially when I don't even know what I'm doing right now. I know Heaven is the next destination, but as far as my ultimate fate is concerned, well, I'm totally clueless."

"Well, you can't just be a wuss and let everyone push you around—"

Like what you're doing right now, I thought, not amused.

"Fate is an important thing," she continued, moving her tail in lazy circles. "But you have to make your own destiny, Little Death. You aren't just a will-o'-the-wisp. You are a strong, powerful woman who has to live her life like she's large and in charge."

I sighed. I'd been hoping to use this opportunity to disengage myself from the Siren, but it seemed like Starr was in for a penny, in for a pound.

"Besides," she added mischievously, "your mother would kill me if I let you wander off all by yourself."

"Hold on, are you saying—"

But Starr didn't let me finish the question.

"Yup, that's Auntie Starr to you, pip-squeak."

eighteen

From the look on my face, Starr must've sensed that she'd opened a Pandora's box. Since she'd been hanging up on a wall for God knew how long, I guess there was no way for her to know my mother had been passing herself off as a human being since she'd become the Grim Reaper's wife. Sure, there'd been rumors that with her ridiculous beauty and slim physique, she *had* to be part Siren, but she'd always laughed them off.

Still, it made sense that she and Starr were related: they both had the same stunning facial structure, liquid blue eyes, and pale, spun gold hair. Starr's face was rounder than my mother's and her pale pink lips were fuller, but otherwise the similarity was remarkable.

"Achelous is father to both your mother and I, but while I was born from a sea nymph, her human mother died in childbirth," Starr said, her demeanor serious now that she'd realized what an impact her little bon mot of information had had on me. "Your mother was raised in a human orphanage and knew nothing of her birth parents until she was sixteen. Achelous found her and told her of her parentage. She came and stayed with us for a while, but the sea was never really your mother's home, so she left and returned to land."

My sisters and I had never been privy to much information about our mother's family history. She'd always been pretty cagey about her past: to the point where the only thing we knew about her was that she was an only child who'd lost both of her parents when she was very young.

And even that turned out to only be a half-truth, I thought.

"Why don't we get to land, and then I promise I'll explain myself more fully," Starr said coaxingly. This mellower version of Starr was a marked improvement on the impulsive Siren I'd first encountered back on land.

"Okay," I said, waffling. Every time I thought I had a handle on my family, they turned my world upside down all over again.

"This way," Starr said, pointing north with a long, girlish finger. She shot out into the current, her tail pin-balling away from me as she streaked like lightning through the murky depths of the water. When she realized I wasn't following her, she stopped.

"Aren't you coming, Little Death?" she said curiously.

I was torn.

Part of me wanted to follow suit, to slalom through the blue sea after the Siren . . . but then another, more persistent voice—one that spoke in a clipped British accent reminiscent in tone to the late Jarvis de Poupsy—begged me to stop looking to other people to solve my problems, insisting that my downfall would always be listening to others rather than following my own instincts.

It wasn't a hard call to make. Not after I took a moment to really think about it.

"I can't go with you, Starr," I said suddenly.

The Siren stared at me, her blue eyes hard to read.

"You're not a very nice niece," she pouted.

"I promise when this is all over, I'll make it up to you," I said.

The Siren perked up at that.

"Really? You promise you'll make it up to me?"

I nodded my big sea serpent head.

"If I had a pinkie, I'd pinkie swear it."

Starr clapped her hands together happily.

"Goodie!" she trilled then she threw her arms around my scaled flank, hugging me tightly to her breast.

"Be safe, Little Death, and ask yourself the smart questions," she murmured. Then, using my flank as a starting block, she pushed off and shot out into the deep, dark sea.

I waited until Starr was only a tiny speck way out in the distance then I turned around and I swam back the way I had come.

somewhere in the back of my mind I had an uneasy feeling about leaving Starr to fend for herself. Frank's warning about becoming the responsible party for the Siren if I let her go free echoed in my head. Still, I tried my best to put those thoughts away as I swam through the shallow waters leading back to the strange island I'd just left behind me.

I circled around the shoals until I reached the island's far eastern side. I didn't know if I would find what I was looking for this far east, but it was better than going back and getting caught by Evangeline and the Bugbears. Just the thought of leaving Daniel to shoulder all the heavy lifting made me feel terrible, but he'd sacrificed himself in order to get me out of there—and the best thing I could do to thank him was to go to Heaven and secure God's help.

As the water got shallower, it became almost impossible for me to navigate in my sea serpent form, so I wished myself back into my normal body. It felt odd to swap out the power of the larger animal body in favor of my much weaker human shape, but I was glad to be small again as I dog-paddled closer to the shore, my feet dragging across the bottom of the sand bar. I could've swum farther down the coast, beaching myself in a more desolate setting, but I needed something only the inhabited part of the island could provide.

I made my way along the beach on foot until I found an unmanned dock and clambered up the weathered wooden ladder. It was still dark out, but morning and the sunrise were fast approaching, so I knew I had to get where I was going soon or else deal with the onset of the human morning, which was about as appealing as eating a plate of sea slugs. Having to weave in and out of morning commuters in my dingy clothes while they sipped their coffees and checked their BlackBerrys was not how I wanted to spend my morning.

The dock I'd climbed on to was deserted; a boarded-up bait-and-tackle shop and a CLOSED FOR THE WINTER sign on Betty's Fried Oyster Shack gave evidence as to why. My feet squelched in my shoes as I walked down the empty boardwalk, the sea breeze making the gooseflesh on my exposed skin stand at attention like little hair follicle soldiers. My teeth decided to get in on the freezing action, doing nothing to warm me as they chattered away in my skull. I decided I was much better suited to warmer environs—so long as they weren't of the Hellish variety. I'd spent enough time in Hell to know I could do without the type of heat the Devil employed down there: namely, the kind that made you sweat out body oil, rather than just plain old saltwater and electrolytes.

I stuck to the boardwalk, following the curve of the shoreline rather than turning off onto one of the residential throughways I passed. As amazing as a warm bed and a cadged bowl of cereal and milk sounded, I wasn't skilled enough in the criminal enterprise of breaking and entering to give one of the houses a try. And being of the klutzy persuasion, I could easily imagine myself caught in a half-open window, my ass hanging out in the breeze for the whole world to see, while inside, a lady in a brown housecoat smacked me upside the head with a toilet brush. Besides, the boardwalk appeared to be where all the commerce in the village happened—and that was where I'd find what I was looking for, if it existed at all.

After a ten-minute walk, though, I was no closer to finding what I sought than when I'd begun.

I was starting to get annoyed with myself—and the part of my brain that'd told me to go with Starr was now lobbing self-recriminations at me. I was in the middle of nowhere, looking for something that probably didn't exist, it was cold, and I was wet and I smelled like old leather and fish. Definitely the kind of aroma that would get you killed out in the wild by a pack of feral dogs.

"This sucks," I muttered in between the teeth chattering.

I'd done what I *thought* was the right thing, but I'd just screwed myself up. Depressed by the wretchedness of my current situation, I was sorely tempted to crawl into a doorway and take a nap, hoping that things would look brighter in the light of day.

Brighter, but not better, I thought uncharitably.

I checked the empty doorways as I passed them, looking to see if any of them would be appropriate for sleeping in, but then something caught my eye and I instantly changed my intentions.

At first, I thought it was only a shadow, but when I turned my full attention on the image, it refocused into something more tangible. My heart stopped for the span of two heartbeats—I know this because I counted—and then everything slid into slow motion. The air around me grew heavy with promise, my brain electrified by what it was processing. Then the world clicked back into normal speed and I was jogging toward the shade, fighting back tears as I ran.

"Jarvis!?" I screamed, my eyes locked on the petite shade barreling ahead of me like a nor'easter. I knew in a way that I couldn't give voice to, that this was Jarvis . . . or at least some incarnation of him.

"Jarvis! Wait for me!" I called, a stitch forming in my side as I raced to keep up with him.

I was having trouble navigating the uneven boards of the wooden boardwalk as I scampered after the shade, but it still came as a surprise when my toe caught in a gap and I pitched forward, my arms pinwheeling uselessly as I went down, my knees taking the brunt of the fall. I slammed into the decking so hard I cried out in pain, but ignoring my bruised knees, I used the boardwalk's guardrail to hoist myself back onto my feet. My lungs heaving, I searched for Jarvis's shade, but it was no use.

I've lost him.

"Jarvis?" I took a few hesitant steps, but there was no response. I was alone again on the boardwalk, not a soul in sight, not even on the paved pathway that led away from the sea and into the heart of the residential area.

"Damn," I said, slamming my fist into my upper thigh in frustration.

It was easy to fall back on old habits. I could've sat down on the wooden treads and thrown myself a high-end pity party, tears would've flown, I would've rued the day I was born, yada, yada, yada . . . and I would've been about as effectual as a hangnail.

Instead, I closed my eyes and counted to ten in my head. With each number, I found myself relaxing as the tension and bad vibes left my body. I opened my eyes and looked around, noting that the sun was just starting to peak over the horizon, shooting streaks of orangey-yellow light into the faded gray-blue patchwork sky. The path I stood on led directly to a normal suburban street, tiny cottages bordering the sidewalk like overgrown white, gray, green, and blue wood-washed flowers. I noticed that the porch lights had begun to melt into the morning light, leaving only tiny halos of illumination around each lightbulb, but that the few cars parked higgledy-piggledy in driveways and on the street itself were still as silent as giant, sleeping beasts.

"Okay," I said. "What happens next?"

And that's when I noticed that the paved walkway beside the boardwalk forked into two separate paths. The first path fed away from the boardwalk and into the suburban sprawl, where it dead-ended at the street. The other, more oddly shaped path—it resembled the curling body of a coiled snake—turned away from the sleeping population of the island, its final destination a wrought iron spiral staircase that led upward into the sky.

I held my breath, my body frozen in place as I realized I'd arrived at my destination. Jarvis—or whatever I'd been chasing—had led me right to the very place I'd been seeking since I'd crawled out of the freezing water earlier that morning:

This was the entrance to a New York City Subway station.

"Thank you, Jarvis," I whispered, hoping that wherever he was, he could hear me. It was strange, but I had the funny feeling I hadn't seen the last of the faun; that not even Death would be powerful enough to keep him out of my life.

A shock of cold air hit me in the face as I stepped onto the first stair, making me shiver involuntarily. The black wrought iron railing was cold to the touch—further chilling my body—and I felt the whole structure tremble under my weight as I climbed the next couple of steps. The stairway had been constructed in pieces, each stair connected to its brother by a series of thin iron joists, giving it the appearance of a discombobulated black skeleton rising up into the air.

I felt the prickle of eyes, the stare of a stranger drilling a hole into the back of my head, and I picked up speed, my feet pounding against the rickety stairway as I pulled myself up the last few steps. I heaved a sigh of relief as the stairway opened out onto the subway station, but my relief was short-lived when I found my way to the platform obstructed by a gleaming silver, full-height turnstile. If it had been one of the normal turnstiles you usually see in a subway station, I could've just jumped over it, fare be damned, but this revolving-door style of turnstile made that impossible.

"Shit," I mumbled, reaching into my pockets but coming up empty—I was wet, bedraggled . . . and without a cent to my name.

I felt my hackles rise as the sense of being watched intensified. I looked both ways, hoping to find a manned ticket booth as I scanned the space, but there was nothing. Only one primary yellow MetroCard machine to my left, which was useless to me without cash or a credit card. Right now, I was alone on the wrong side of the station, but I had the impression this wouldn't last for very long. Something, or someone, was stalking me, waiting for just the right moment to slip out of the shadows and attack.

"And just where do you think you're going, dollface?"

I whirled around at the sound of the Ender of Death's voice. The tips of my fingers went numb and my whole body began to shake. I didn't know if it was fear or all-consuming rage that was making my body react so intensely.

The Ender of Death was the last creature I'd expected to find leering at me from the other side of the turnstile in this subway station to nowhere, but I shouldn't have been surprised. He'd murdered my dad and Jarvis to fulfill the dogma of his appellation—so adding another name to his kill list wasn't really a big deal. But I sensed there was more to it than that.

He looked just like any normal human being to anyone who saw him walking down the street, all fluffy hair and patrician features, but it was only a mask. I could see the raw obsession in his eyes as he stared at me from the other side of the turnstile. The years spent trapped in Hell at my dad's discretion had gnawed away whatever humanity he'd originally possessed, leaving only compulsive hatred behind, whittled like a sharpened stick ready to destroy whatever lay in its path.

"I'm going to Heaven," I spat at him. "Bite me."

The blood pounded in my temples. My vision tunneled into a pinhole: with Marcel's face as the bull's-eye. If I'd had the capability to destroy him, I would've done it right then.

Believe me when I say I tried.

"Die, you bastard!" I screamed. Of course, nothing happened, and Marcel laughed loudly at my pathetic attempt to get rid of him.

"I won't go that easily," he said, his long fingers grasping the bars on the other side of the turnstile. "Besides, when my time here is over, there'll be another and another and another of me after that to take my place."

"Whoopee," I said dryly. "Isn't that just peachy keen for you, then."

He raised an eyebrow.

"I told you that you should've given yourself up back at your office," he replied. "Then maybe all of this could've been avoided."

"Bullshit. You'd already killed my dad before that."

Marcel shrugged.

"Yes, you're right about that. Your father deserved to be dispatched from this existence. He had no right to do what he did to me . . . But your friend, Jarvis, well, that one was all you, Calliope. We needed to stop the flow of information in order to keep you in the dark."

I swallowed hard, my throat dry as a bone as the weight of his words slammed into me. There was no way of knowing if he was telling the truth or not, but it didn't matter. He'd hit a nerve, and all the pent-up guilt I was harboring broke through. It was all I could do to gulp back a sob. I may not have hurt Jarvis with my own hands, but I was just as responsible for his death as the Ender of Death was.

"What do you want from me?" I asked, my hands shaking.

Marcel smiled like a crazed saint bound on a pyre, his face lit from within by his own madness.

"I just want what I want from every Death I meet," he murmured, his voice low and malevolent.

"I just want you to die."

nineteen

Way back at the beginning of time as we know it, God created the Heavens and the Earth and things were good. All the angels and demons (demons didn't get a bad rap until way later in the future) lived happily together, enjoying their immortal existence by spending their days creating beautiful works of art, singing, dancing, and just having a grand old time. The angels were the good stewards of Heaven, and the demons, who were in charge of the day-to-day running of the place, kept everything in perfect working order. Everyone, regardless of their place in Heaven's hierarchy, was grateful to God for creating them, and they paid their creator homage in their works of art, their music, and their poetry. There were no conflicts, no aggression, no bad vibes; Heaven was a splendid place to live.

Now back then, Hell was just a suburb of Heaven—a quiet place with beautiful gardens and an overabundance of fruit and veggies that was used for recreational purposes only. The denizens of Heaven loved to take day trips there to frolic in the gardens, eat the fruit and veggies, and just, you know, chill. It was a nice place to visit, but no one wanted to live there full-time because it was in another dimension of time/space and kind of far from all the hubbub of Heaven.

But then one day, totally out of the blue, God decided to do something nuts. He/she proclaimed from on high that he/she was going get rid of the original inhabitants of Earth—the dinosaurs—and in their place he/she was going to people the Earth with these weird little furry creatures called *Homo sapiens*. When God showed the first *Homo sapiens* prototype (he/she called the very apelike creature "Adam") to the assemblage up in Heaven, everyone was aghast. They couldn't understand why God would want to get rid of the lizards—which were always a gas to watch because they attacked and ate each other in spades—and replace them with those weird furry beings.

God didn't like being second-guessed, especially when it came to the *Homo sapiens*—or "human beings," as God had nicknamed his/her newest creations—and he/she got very mad. He/she decreed that anyone who said anything bad about the human beings would be stricken from the Record of Heaven and unceremoniously tossed out into Hell, where they could spend their immortal eternity weeding vegetable beds and watering plants. It seemed that God had chosen to lavish all his/her love and affection on these new human beings, totally forsaking the angels and demons he/she had created first. The demons especially felt God's cold shoulder. They had less magical ability than the angels, which put them closer in origin to the human beings, so it was particularly hard for them to accept a new hierarchy where they were placed at the very bottom of the pecking order.

The majority of the angels accepted this new kink in the system, but a large chunk of the population—mostly demons, but a few angels, too—didn't like how hot and bothered God had gotten over the ape-men, so they decided to confront God directly with their displeasure. They selected a spokesman from among their number—an angel called Lucifer, who had immaculate oratorical skills—and they descended on God, en masse. Needless to say, God had not made an empty threat. Upon their arrival, the protesters were counted and tagged, and then their names were duly stricken from the

Record of Heaven and they were banished to Hell—all without getting a word in edgewise.

As you can imagine, this was a real blow to Lucifer and the others, who'd just wanted to speak their piece. It twisted them, made them full of rage against the God who'd given them a taste of Heaven and then thrown them into the eternal damnation of Hell. They swore that though they might have to live under God's rule, they would not like it. In fact, they would do everything in their power to undermine God and make the furry little human beings who had caused their downfall suffer as they had suffered. Lucifer was elected to lead the fallen of Hell, choosing "Devil" as his kingly name. Under his reign, the once-bountiful gardens were transformed into a desert wasteland, and a huge, enchanted forest was erected around the interior of Hell to mirror the darkness and hatred that consumed its people.

And if that wasn't enough to punish the minions of Hell, God did something even worse: he/she made Hell, the newly anointed land of wastrels and misanthropes, into a staging ground for the human Afterlife. Now the creatures of Hell would be responsible for meting out punishment to the naughtiest of the human beings from Earth before their souls were then recycled back into the human populace. On principle, the citizens of Hell refused the job. They didn't want anything to do with the stinky fur balls God had chosen over them, but since he/she was the all-powerful Creator, in the end they were forced to do his/her bidding, whether they liked it or not.

To add insult to injury, God created the office of Death to oversee the transmigration of the human souls—and to keep the balance between the good of Heaven and the evil of Hell, something that infuriated the Devil and his minions to no end. It drove them crazy to think that one of God's *Homo sapiens* might have any kind of power over them—and they definitely didn't need some immortalized human being reporting back to God about their comings and goings. So in secret, the Devil and his closest companions used their magic to create the Ender of Death, a soulless wraith sheathed in the body of an unsuspecting human being, whose job it was to find and destroy any and all incarnations of Death.

The Devil was pleased with his creation, but he did think that it was too little, too late. So as the first of the human souls invaded Hell for punishment and processing, the Devil swore that one day Hell would have its bloody revenge on God and his/her cherished human beings.

as i stood alone on an empty subway platform in Queens, my way to Heaven blocked by a revolving, full-height turnstile and the Ender of Death, I realized that the Devil's revenge had finally begun.

And I was the only person who could put a stop to it.

the sun had risen by now, and even though the subway platform itself was covered by a metal shell, streaks of sunlight had started to filter in around its edges.

"So, what's the point of you getting rid of me," I asked, "if another Death is just going to rise up and take my place?"

The Ender of Death, or Marcel, as he had once asked me to call him, grinned at me.

"I will take great pleasure in destroying the child of the Death who hid me away in the deserts of Hell for over twenty years," he purred, his voice echoing in the empty platform.

"Okay, I get that," I said. "But what then? If the Devil and my sister have their way and they control Death . . . what's that do to your job description? You really think they're gonna put a stop to Death entirely? Imagine the backlog of souls that would create."

Silence.

"Fine," I mumbled. "Don't answer my question. I don't care. Once I get over onto that side of the platform, I'm gonna kick your ass six ways to Sunday anyway, so I don't give a shit."

Marcel laughed. "You do have a certain way with words, Calliope."

I shrugged. "Just a God-given talent, I suppose."

Just then I heard the clattering of human feet on the stairs behind me. A man in a blue business suit, briefcase held protectively under his arm, emerged from the stairwell. He paused midstride when he saw us, but then he put his head down and picked up his pace, ignoring us as he walked over to the turnstile, a golden MetroCard in his extended hand.

"Excuse me?" I called to the man. He paused again, this time with the MetroCard at the lip of the turnstile card reader.

"Look, I know you don't know me," I began, "but I really need to get on the other side of this turnstile."

The man didn't look up as I spoke, just stood there uncertainly.

"Normally, I wouldn't ask you to help me, but the fate of the world as we know it is at stake and I'm totally broke. Please, will you let me go through on your card?"

I waited expectantly for the guy to respond, but he just rammed his MetroCard through the reader and pushed through the turnstile as if he hadn't heard a word I'd just said.

Marcel found the whole exchange hysterical.

"The human beings are a selfish bunch."

"Oh, shut up," I shot back, watching the man with the briefcase move as far down the platform—and away from us—as possible. I'd probably totally freaked him out with my apocalyptical ravings, and now he was just gonna pretend like our conversation had never happened.

Ah, denial, what a wonderful place to live, I thought.

"I told you that there were greater forces at work here," Marcel said suddenly. "You should've listened to me when you had the chance. Of course, I told all of them that you would never do their bidding. That you were too stupid to see the advantages one side or the other could afford you."

I walked over to the turnstile and put my face up to the bars.

"I'm not scared of you, Marcel. Besides," I continued, "I'm not Death yet. The job is being split between Daniel and me until one of us drinks from the Cup of Jamshid."

Marcel stepped up to the other side of the turnstile, his

face separated from mine by mere inches . . . and a few metal bars.

"You think that will stop me from ending your pathetic existence? You think because you aren't Death in its entirety that it will keep me from snuffing you out like I did your father?"

I glared at him.

"Like I said. When I get on the other side of that turnstile, I'm gonna make you wish you'd never been created."

Marcel just shook his head.

"And what's stopping me from coming over there to your side, Calliope? Hmmm?"

"I don't know," I said, goading him on. "But I think it's 'cause you're just a big, old, fat coward."

"I'll show you what a coward is . . ."

Marcel pushed his way through the turnstile, but I was ready for him *and* I had the advantage because he was coming after me, not the other way around. As soon as he hit my side, I grabbed him by the forearms and yanked him out of the turnstile. I held on tight, my hands like meat hooks digging into his flesh, and I began to swing him around and around in a dizzying circle, using my body as the fulcrum point. I spun him as fast as I could, my feet doing a modified two-step as I gathered momentum.

"Gonna kick your ass!" I screamed. The words ripped out of my mouth as we spun with more and more abandon. I could see the uncertainty on Marcel's face. The Ender of Death couldn't quite get a handle on what I was doing. He probably thought I was out of options and that this was some kind of Hail Mary pass I was trying in my desperation.

I abruptly released my grip and he went sailing into the white subway-tiled wall, slamming into it with enough force to crack the tile into jagged little pieces that clattered to the floor around him.

He was immediately back on his feet, hands balled into fists at his sides, a new gash on his other cheekbone—to match the one my dad had given him—where he'd hit the wall. He glared at me, his eyes full of fury.

"You bitch," he growled, his face frozen into a rictus of rage.

"Come and get me, asshole," I spat back at him.

He took me at my word. Using his hands to push himself off the wall, he snarled as he raced toward me, his teeth bared in a frightening grimace. I threw my arms over my head, covering my face as if I were seeking protection from his attack—which only made Marcel believe he had the upper hand. Lucky for me, his ego was too big to ever consider I might be faking it. Taking the bait, he barreled toward me with enough forward motion to knock out an NFL linebacker, but I waited until he was just past the failsafe point and then I slid to my left, stepping out of his way and allowing him to crash headfirst into the revolving turnstile with a horrific gristle-and-bone-shattering *crunch.*

Dazed, he crumpled to the ground, blood from his broken nose pooling around him. He didn't stay down for long, though. Like a half-beaten boxer who's about one minute from a knockout but doesn't realize it yet, he slammed one fist into the ground and used it to leverage himself into a sitting position. I caught a peek at the other side of his face and saw that the skin above his eyebrow had split in two. Blood, like a string of black pearls, beaded in the tear.

The Ender of Death doesn't look nearly as handsome as he used to, I thought happily.

Grasping at the bars of the turnstile like it was a trellis to climb, Marcel crawled to his feet and glared at me.

"Had enough?" I asked.

He ran at me again and this time he was close enough to do some damage, ramming me in the stomach with his head. The soft tissue of my belly screamed in agony as the velocity of his body slam threw me backward. Before I could right myself, Marcel grabbed me around the waist and hoisted me in the air so I was upside down, my feet kicking furiously at his face. He held me aloft so that the blood drained to my head and I could feel my heartbeat in my temples.

"Let me go!" I screamed at him, my head throbbing painfully.

"As you wish," he said, flecks of coagulating blood raining down on me.

As if my body were made out of foam, not flesh and blood, he hefted me high in the air and then, in a maneuver right out of the WWE, smashed my head into the cold concrete floor, compressing my vertebrae like a squeezebox. Pain radiated up from the crown of my head and I almost passed out, but then I was being hoisted back in the air again for another round of pile driving. I kicked with my legs, hoping to dislodge myself from Marcel's cruel embrace, but it was no use. He was merciless. My forehead connected with the concrete this time, the cords of my neck snapping taut with the force of the impact.

To my surprise, Marcel released me—he must've thought he'd subdued me with the second head slam—and I crashed to the ground, my chin colliding with my clavicle as my head twisted underneath my weight. I lay there on the cold subway floor barely able to string together a coherent thought because the pain in my head and neck was so intense. My nerves screamed at me to take some kind of sedative and put myself out of my misery, but I knew that wasn't going to be happening anytime soon, so I ignored the pain and tried to focus instead on getting my eyes open. I'd unintentionally closed them at some point during the attack—I've found that violence is much easier to endure when you don't have to see it—but now I needed them in good working order so I could get a better lay of the land and hopefully figure out a way to turn the tables on the Ender of Death.

Fat chance of that, I thought to myself.

Sure, I'd participated in a few catfights during my career as a woman and sister, but I'd never tried to take on a full-grown man before. Besides, Marcel seemed to have a lock on the whole "physical punishment" thing, at least where I was concerned. I'd sadly underwhelmed even myself by letting Marcel have the upper hand in our fight—and I didn't know if you could really come back from a psychological defeat like that.

I didn't have much time to ponder these philosophical

musings because Marcel chose that moment to hammer the small of my back with his boot as hard as he possibly could, pounding my vertebrae into smithereens with every blow he landed. It took me a few seconds to understand that the odd, guttural sounds I was hearing were actually coming from my own lips.

"Still conscious?" Marcel whispered, dropping to a crouch beside me, his lips grazing my ear as he spoke. His mouth was so close to my face I could smell his gnarly breath.

Someone needed to hit the gum before his big fight, I thought dreamily. My thoughts were becoming more and more disjointed with every lungful of air I took. If I'd been a normal person, I'd probably have been dead from the beating I'd taken, not just maimed.

"Fack ew," I slurred back at him, my eyes rolling up into my eye sockets as I fought off unconsciousness.

"Well, now," Marcel said thoughtfully as he rammed the toe of his boot into my cervical spine. "That wasn't really the answer I was looking for."

The next time Marcel spoke to me, I chose silence as my default response—but only because I couldn't have managed a verbal reply even if I'd wanted to.

I was out cold.

twenty

I returned to consciousness with the sound of human caterwauling tickling my ears. I didn't think I'd been out of commission for very long, but apparently it'd been long enough for the commuter at the end of the platform (yes, the same one who'd previously ignored my pleas for help) to finally take an interest in the abuse I was receiving and threaten to call the police.

I rolled over, pain shimmying up my body like an irate hula dancer, and I cracked my right eye open so I could get a look at the man as he stood on the other side of the turnstile, waving his cell phone with enough abandon to prove he was seriously freaked out by what he'd just witnessed: chiefly, a thin yet well-muscled seraphim-looking dude beating the crap out of some girl.

"If you don't get out of here, I'm calling the police!" the man said, his voice shaking with fear. Still, the fact he'd taken it upon himself to get involved after he'd totally blown me off was a good sign.

Marcel stood a few feet away from me, grinning like a lunatic at the hysterical commuter. Having left my prone body behind him—I guess he'd beaten me to the point where he wasn't worried I was gonna get up again anytime in the near future—he'd now turned his full attention to the terrified man on the other side of the turnstile.

"You don't want me to come over there, do you?" Marcel said, blood still running freely from both nostrils. He was wearing the stupid injury like a badge of honor, which only made me wish I'd bloodied his nuts instead, 'cause he couldn't very well show *those* off, could he?

"Stay on your side!" the man yelled, pressing the buttons on his phone as he spoke. The place was so quiet I could hear the dial pulses echoing in the empty subway station.

"I wouldn't do that if I were you," Marcel replied, his voice as smooth as polished chrome—but I could sense the razor's edge of rage lingering just beneath the surface. He did *not* like being threatened by a mere human peon.

The man, who couldn't have consciously known how dangerous a situation he'd stumbled into, reeked of fear as he defiantly put the cell phone to his ear in direct odds to Marcel's threats. His unconscious mind must've understood the danger, though, because his whole body shook uncontrollably while he waited for the call to engage.

"I told you not to do that," Marcel growled as he snaked his MetroCard from his back pocket and inched toward the turnstile. "And I don't like being disobeyed."

The man ignored him, concentrating instead on whoever had picked up the other line.

"I'd like to report an attack—"

Like a slinky black cat with a bone to pick, Marcel stalked over to the turnstile, the MetroCard in his hand extended toward the card reader. The Ender of Death was obviously a creature that did not like to be ignored—and from the gleam of malice in his eyes, I could tell the poor commuter was not going to fare well if Marcel made it to the other side of the turnstile.

"No!" I yelped, the words issuing from my mouth totally of their own accord. I don't know where I got the energy—or which God/Goddess had smiled down on me and granted me another chance at salvation—but suddenly I found myself back on my feet, my nerves screaming incoherently from all of the abject pain I was imposing on them by just standing up like a normal human being.

All the rage and hate and pain welled up inside me, giving me the power to put one foot in front of the other, gathering speed as I went. My vertebrae ground together with each step I took, sending searing pain up my spine and down my legs—and I'm not gonna even talk about how badly my head was hurting. I couldn't see my face, but I got the distinct impression that there was a rather large—and only getting bigger—blood blister smack dab in the middle my forehead. I don't know how anyone else feels about blood blisters, but give me an out-and-out gash any day of the week and I'd be a much happier camper. I hated the idea that fresh blood was pooling underneath a thin layer of delicate skin, just waiting for me to make a wrong move and pop the bejesus out of it.

Ewww!

Just as I closed in on him from behind, Marcel turned his head, his eyes wide as he tried to reconcile the beating he'd given me with the fact that I was back up on my feet and still looking for punishment. Lucky for me, I had the "sort of" element of surprise, so before he could lift a finger to defend himself—and just as the MetroCard in his hand slid through the card reader on the turnstile—I body-slammed him out of the way, sailing past him and ramming my broken self through the revolving turnstile.

As I sailed through, I just happened to look down at the digital card reader where it was flashing the most beautiful sentence in the English language (at least it was to me at that moment): Balance: $0.00.

I wanted to cry with happiness as I collapsed onto the concrete floor on the *platform* side of the full-height turnstile, my whole body on fire with pain.

"Screw you, Marcel!" I screamed through the grille.

Marcel glared at me, climbing to his hands and knees and crawling over to where the MetroCard had fallen after I'd knocked it out of his hand.

"No, screw you, Calliope!" he growled back at me, dragging himself to his feet with the help of the turnstile bars.

"Good luck with that one," I jeered at him through the metal grating, trying not to smile—only because it made my forehead throb—but having trouble suppressing my glee.

"I'm going to end you," Marcel said, holding up the MetroCard for me to see.

I shrugged—which only made him madder.

"You're dead," he growled, jamming the MetroCard through the card reader.

The look on his face was priceless when he realized there was no more money left on the card. Still, he just couldn't seem to accept the reality of his predicament, so it was with utter triumph that I watched him repeat the process of sliding the card through the reader two more times before finally giving up.

"Ha!" I screeched at him. "You lose, jerkoid!"

Shoulders hunched, he cradled the empty MetroCard in his hand then turned away from me so I couldn't see his face anymore.

"Don't cry, Marcel!" I taunted. "You'll get me someday!"

I was starting to feel better, my immortal blood going to work on my wounds, healing me from the inside out without me having to do anything more than just breathe. Just knowing the blood blister on my forehead was going to magically go away—sooner rather than later—made me glad I was immortal. This was something I'd never have copped to before, but from the moment I'd learned my mother was really part Siren, I'd started to feel differently about my supernaturalness. I wasn't exactly ecstatic about it, yet, but I was beginning to accept it for what it was.

"Are you all right?"

It was the commuter, cell phone still clutched tightly in his hand, but flipped back now to the "closed" position. He'd retrieved his briefcase from the other end of the platform, where he'd left it when he'd decided to play "hero," and now he was standing behind me, his face full of concern . . . and frankly, disgust.

I guess I looked like shit on a stick, and who could blame him for not hiding his dismay at the state of my, uhm, person, especially my nasty forehead blood blister.

"I know it looks pretty terrible," I began, "but it's not as bad as it, uh, seems."

He nodded, but I could see he was having a hard time reconciling how I *looked* with how I *said* I felt.

"Well, you don't look very good, so . . ."

It was more of a statement than a question.

"Thanks," I said dryly.

Now that we were up close and personal, I realized the error in judgment I'd made. Based on the guy's height and nervous energy, I'd assumed he was just another uptight, middle-aged businessman, but I'd been wrong. Probably only in his very early twenties, with a hint of stubble on his chin and the kind of emaciated physique and wet, droopy eyes that made one think of the hollow-eyed Eastern European Jews lost to Hitler's death camps, he was really more of a boy than a man.

His blue suit was threadbare and ill-fitting, his white shirt was made of cheap polished cotton, and a skinny tie was knotted at his neck like a noose. I wouldn't have been surprised to learn the kid had inherited the getup from an older brother or uncle. Even the briefcase had seen better days. Its handle had been repaired in several places with silver duct tape, which someone had tried to color brown with a sharpie to match the calfskin spotted leather—my guess at the coloring culprit was the kid himself, but I could've been wrong—and the brass clasps that held the case together were edged in rust. The kid's dark brown hair was pomaded back from his face, revealing faint traces of acne scarring on his upper cheeks and forehead.

I looked like crap 'cause I'd just gotten my head pounded into the concrete by the Ender of Death, but what was the kid's excuse? He looked like crap because of neglect, not physical injury. I mean, he was so damn skinny I could see his wrist bones protruding below his shirt cuffs, and his cheekbones jutted out from beneath his pockmarked, olive skin like sharpened knives.

A sudden movement back on the other side of the turnstile forced me to put my speculation about the kid's circumstances on the back burner.

Marcel is on the move.

Having discovered the only MetroCard machine in the station, he was now in the process of feeding dollar bills into the machine's cash slot.

"Crap!" I breathed, grabbing the kid's arm and propelling him away from the revolving turnstile.

"Is he gonna kill us?" the kid asked, his Adam's apple bobbing up and down as he swallowed nervously.

I didn't have the heart to tell him he was hanging out with Death's Daughter, so he should probably worry more about *me* accidentally killing him than any damage Marcel might inflict on him. That just being in close proximity to me was enough to raise your "sudden death quotient" by about 100 percent, a ratio about on par with that of a shutter-happy American tourist on vacation in Kabul.

"Do you know when the next train is coming?" I asked, ignoring his previous question, but the kid only shook his head.

"I've never been here before. Wow," he said, pointing at my forehead. "The thing on your head's almost gone!"

I reached up, my hand probing the skin where the blood blister had been only minutes before, but finding only firm, smooth flesh in its place.

"Told you," I said, grinning at him. "Wasn't as bad as it looked."

The kid took a step away from me, trying to put a little distance between himself and the rapidly healing crazy lady.

"Whatever you say."

But he didn't look convinced.

There was a muffled thud from across the platform. Marcel was having a little trouble with the MetroCard machine and in his frustration he had decided that kicking the heavy metal apparatus might yield some kind of benefit. Of course, kicking or thumping something big and metal and full of computer circuitry is never a good idea. Machines don't like to be poked and prodded by human appendages; that's when they eat your money and then tell you they're "out of order."

Which was exactly what I hoped was happening right at that very moment to Marcel.

"Do you hear that?" the kid asked.

I shook my head.

"It's the train. It's coming."

The kid was right. I could feel the low rumble of the approaching subway train as it shook the platform. Our only hope was that the train arrived before Marcel worked out how to get the ticket machine to do his bidding.

Too late.

Marcel kicked the machine one more time then froze as the machine made a funny gurgling noise and spat something yellow and paperlike out onto the concrete floor.

"Damn," I murmured under my breath as Marcel squatted down to pick the thing up. My hopes were dashed when he whirled around to face us, hoisting the yellow card above his head and waving it around so I could see that he'd triumphed over the ticket machine.

"Stay behind me," I said to the kid, stepping in front of him like a mother bear protecting her cub.

"Do you want to know what your weakness is, Calliope Reaper-Jones?" Marcel sang as he sashayed over to the turnstile and slid the newly topped-up MetroCard through the card reader.

The rumbling was getting louder. A blast of warm air wafted out of the tunnel's yawning mouth and I knew the incoming train was very close.

"No," I shot back at him as he pushed through the revolving turnstile.

The whole platform was starting to shake now, the air billowing around us like curling fingers of warmth.

"Are you sure about that?"

I nodded.

"Totally sure."

The kid grabbed my arm and squeezed just as the subway train pulled into the station with a startling squeal of brakes.

"You guys are nuts," he breathed in my ear. "Complete wackos."

I had no argument. Instead, I focused all my attention on Marcel. The Ender of Death was trying to decide what to do. Should he rush me? Keep me from getting on the train? Or should he move to one of the other doors and then wait and see whether or not I got on the train before making his move?

The doors of the subway train slid open in a burst of steam, but no one got off. There wasn't a soul on the train.

"Get on the train," I growled at the kid, shoving him back with my elbow.

He hesitated, unsure whether he should leave me out on the platform or not, but when I kicked back at him with my foot, he took the hint and scurried onto the subway car.

"Sacrificing yourself for a kid, huh?" Marcel laughed. "Pathetic."

"There's nothing pathetic about it," I shot back at him. Behind me, I heard the conductor ease up on the brake, preparing to close the doors and shove off for the next station. "Particularly because, like I said earlier, I'm just gonna use the opportunity to kick your ass."

Marcel laughed so hard, he snorted.

"Nice snort," I said.

"Oh, Calliope," Marcel said as he shook his head. "You really are a bitch, aren't you?"

I opened my mouth to reply, but a sharp tug on my collar constricted my throat and suddenly I was airborne, my body yanked over the threshold and into the subway car just as the doors slammed shut. I saw Marcel's shocked face gawping at me from the other side of the window as the train shuddered to a rolling start then sped up—leaving him standing alone on the empty platform.

I felt a pair of strong arms wrap around my waist and hoist me back up onto my feet. I turned around to find the kid standing behind me, a big smile covering the bottom half of his face. I stared up at him, my gaze boring into his large brown eyes as my mind tried to piece together what was happening to me.

"Who are you?" I asked, my brain reeling.

The kid shrugged uncertainly.

"David . . . ?"

"Just David?" I asked. "Are you sure?"

His eyebrows scrunched together and I could see him thinking hard, trying to figure out what I wanted him to say.

"What are you doing here?" I asked, trying another approach.

This made him scrunch his thick eyebrows together even harder.

"I don't know," he said. "Honestly, I don't."

I decided not to press him for any more information. He looked really confused and I didn't want to freak him out more.

"Why don't we sit down," I offered, gesturing to one of the plastic benches. He seemed relieved by my suggestion, and he let go of me so we could move the party to a more recumbent position.

I sat down, thinking he'd take the seat beside me, but he chose one that was across the aisle, plopping his skeletal body down like it weighed a ton. We sat across from each other, David looking down at his hands where they sat clasped in his lap, and I stared straight ahead, exhausted by the insane almost-twenty-four hours I'd just experienced.

As the train rocked away on its tracks, I felt it lulling me into a calmer, more relaxed state. The pain in my back was almost gone and I knew I looked better now than I had even ten minutes before. I looked over at David and saw the train had worked its magic on him, too. He was slumped over, his head resting on the metal bar next to his seat. I took the opportunity to change places, swapping my seat for one across the aisle, next to the unconscious kid.

But when I sat down, I realized that there was something wrong. The kid was so still, more still than any sleeping person had a right to be. I reached over and poked his upper arm, got no response. I poked harder. Still nothing.

"David?" I said, my voice soft. "Hey, kid?"

Only silence greeted my efforts.

I put my hand under his nose, hoping to feel the steady stream of air moving in and out as he breathed, but once again I came up empty. The kid wasn't moving, he wasn't breathing, he (obviously) wasn't responding to my prods and pokes . . . the only answer that made any sense was that I had somehow done the unthinkable:

I'd unwittingly killed the damn kid.

twenty-one

"Not again!" I yelled as I covered my face with my hands and screamed into my palms, not caring that I looked like a total lunatic. I mean, I *was* sitting on an empty subway train, next to a big, dead kid talking to myself—so, yes, "lunatic" was definitely the correct word.

"I don't understand," I said to no one in particular. "I mean, I did *not*—not even *once* at any point in the like ten minutes I knew the kid—say the word 'death' or use the phrase 'I wish you would die.'"

I stood up and started pacing, occasionally grabbing the long metal handrail that ran the length of the train to steady myself as the car rocked underneath my feet. I didn't know what to do. Twice, the kid had saved me from the Ender of Death—putting his own existence on the line both times—and now I'd killed him. I knew I was supposed to get to Heaven and start harassing God, like *pronto*, but I just couldn't leave the poor guy riding up and down the subway line until someone discovered he was dead and not, uhm . . . sleeping.

Frustrated, I sat back down next to the body and gave the kid a slug in the upper arm, punching the dead flesh as hard as I could. I don't know what possessed me, I guess I was just annoyed with the pathetic-ness of the whole situation, but boy, did I get the shock of my life when the kid sat up, rubbed his arm where I'd punched him, and stared at me, large, wet eyes alert and questioning.

"Oh, crap," I said, standing up and taking a few steps away from the living/dead man. "I didn't know . . . Sorry about that."

The kid continued to stare at me, brow wrinkled with consternation.

"Really, I'm very sorry," I stammered, not sure who or what I was dealing with.

"Whatever possessed you to hit me like that?" the kid whined as he continued to rub the spot on his arm where I'd punched him.

Honestly, I hadn't punched him *that* hard, but he was milking it for all he was worth.

"*And* after all the trouble I've gone to for you, Miss Calliope. It's rude. Yes, extremely rude."

I froze, unable to speak, my mouth opening and closing, but no sound coming out. The voice issuing from the kid's mouth was *not* the voice he'd used the last time I'd heard him speak. This new voice was more clipped, more *British* even . . . a different beast entirely.

"Seriously, you have no idea how difficult this young man is to manage," the kid continued. "It's like working with a very large, very overwrought marionette puppet."

I gulped, my head spinning, as I realized that all the strange thoughts that'd been running through my head ever since I'd met the kid were not strange at all. I'd known there was something different, no, something *wrong* about the kid, but I just hadn't known what it was.

Until now.

"Jarvis?" I said, my voice quavering. "Is that *you*?"

The kid turned and stared at me, exasperated.

"Of course, I'm Jarvis. Who else were you expecting—Jesus Christ?"

I opened my mouth to respond, but instead, I just shrugged helplessly. The kid rolled his eyes and the gesture was so

Jarvis—and so *bizarre* in the kid's ungainly body—that I had to laugh, but then the laughter quickly turned to tears as I found myself hugging the big galoot for all he was worth.

"I missed you so much," I said, wiping at my eyes with the back of my hand.

The kid—I mean, *Jarvis*—patted my hand.

"I missed you, too, Miss Calliope."

"But how did you . . ." I began. "I mean, how are you *here*, right now? I killed you."

Jarvis nodded.

"Yes, you did put an end to my life, but I haven't been your father's Executive Assistant for all these decades without learning a thing or to about what to do in case of an emergency."

"An emergency?" I asked.

Jarvis nodded.

"We were set up, Miss Calliope. That's why I was so surprised when your boss, Hyacinth, said that she was there looking after you under orders from your father. It made no sense, but of course, I was in no condition to protest, I was half-dead myself."

"What are you talking about?" I said, confused. "I don't understand."

The train slowed down as we approached the next station then came to a shuddering stop. A few commuters climbed on board, mostly men, but a couple of women, too, all carrying briefcases similar to the one sitting on the floor next to Jarvis's feet. As the doors closed, the conductor called out the next station and Jarvis resumed his story.

"Hyacinth must be working for your sister and the Devil," he continued. "She must've alerted the Ender of Death when she sensed that you had arrived at the office. It has to be how he knew where to find you."

"That can't be true," I said, dropping my voice as the man across the aisle from us raised an eyebrow at the tone of our conversation.

"I would've been alerted had your father made any kind

of order like that, Miss Calliope," he said with a sigh. "I managed every aspect of his office. I was involved in every decision. I would've known. No question."

"Wait a minute," I said. "So if Hyacinth is a bad guy, then Sumi and Frank and Starr are playing for the other side, too."

Jarvis blanched when I said Sumi's name, and I got a very bad feeling in the pit of my stomach.

"Oh, jeez, it's bad, isn't it? Really bad."

Jarvis swallowed.

"Watatsumi works for no one but himself," Jarvis said. "He is the epitome of a 'free agent,' as they say. Offer him power, or some other prize that he craves, and he will work for anyone. I don't know who these Frank and Starr characters might be, but if they *are* in cahoots with Watatsumi, they're completely untrustworthy."

I felt sick—and not just from the information Jarvis had imparted. My stomach was on fire, burning with a painful ferocity that made me involuntarily open my mouth and release the smelliest, nastiest, most god-awful burp the free world had ever been exposed to. Jarvis, who was sitting closest to me, gagged. The other people on the train covered their mouths and noses with their hands or their suit jackets.

"Sorry," I breathed, nausea still burbling inside my belly.

"Oh, Miss Calliope, you didn't."

"I didn't *what*?" I cried.

Jarvis shook his head and ran a large hand through his dark hair.

Oh, shit, the jewel, I thought miserably.

"Sumi said it was a wish-fulfillment jewel," I stammered. "He said it would help when Daniel challenged me."

"Well, that explains how the Ender of Death tracked you to that subway station," Jarvis said.

"Crap," I muttered.

"And it is only a 'wish-fulfillment' jewel in the sense that Watatsumi *wishes* to bind you to him and that that wish is now being fulfilled."

"Double crap," I said.

"Yes, I do believe a double—possibly a triple or a quadruple—crap is in order."

The pain intensified in my gut and before I could cover my mouth with my hand, I had burped again. The smell was putrid. So foul, in fact, that as the train pulled into the next stop, every other person in the subway car but us got off to wait for another train.

"Well, you definitely have a unique way of clearing a subway car," Jarvis said.

"So, what do I have to do to get rid of the stupid jewel?" I asked, ignoring Jarvis's snide comment. Normally, I would've been snarky right back at him, but I didn't want to do anything that would give him cause to disappear again.

"I honestly don't know," Jarvis said. "I have little experience with that type of binding charm."

"Dammit, I don't want to be a sitting duck for the Ender of Death—or any other bad guy—anymore," I said. "This sucks."

"We are just going to have to be *hyper*vigilant," Jarvis offered. "And hope that the jewel will be rendered ineffective while we're traveling in Heaven—"

"You're going with me?" I interrupted.

"Of course I'm going with you, Miss Calliope," he replied. "How else did you think you were going to get there?"

"I was just gonna ride around on the subway until, you know, I was struck by divine intervention," I said, feeling sheepish.

"That's what I'd supposed," Jarvis said. "Well, consider yourself struck. It's why I grabbed the closest available body I could find and made my way back to you."

"Speaking of bodies," I said, pointing at Jarvis. "Nice choice. You look like a gangling schoolboy playing dress-up in Daddy's clothes."

"Don't you dare, Miss Calliope," Jarvis replied, pulling up his jacket sleeve so I could see the track marks up and down the kid's arm.

"Holy shit."

I guess I was just too much of a "nice girl" to have ever been introduced to the kind of hard-core drug taking this kid was doing. I mean, I'd watched that show *Intervention* on TV, but I'd never seen anything like it in real life. Trust me when I say the TV version is a lot safer—the real-life stuff is just gross and sad.

"It's the only reason I was able to get inside the body," Jarvis said sadly. "It made controlling him very difficult. But now that he's dead—"

"I didn't kill him, did I?" I asked warily.

Jarvis shook his head no.

"The combination of drugs and the shock of your fight with the Ender of Death caused him to have a heart attack."

"Well, I'm sorry he was a drug addict and I'm sorry he's dead." I sighed. "But I'm really glad you're here."

I leaned over and gave Jarvis another hug.

"And I promise I'll be less annoying and less obnoxious in the future, okay?"

Jarvis snorted. "I'll believe that one when I see it."

As the train hit the brakes for the next stop, Jarvis stood up.

"Where are you going?" I asked.

"Time to change trains."

The doors slid open and I followed Jarvis out onto the subway platform. It was getting late enough in the morning that the place was now teeming with commuters, some of whom hopped on our old train as it departed. I watched one woman wrinkle her nose as she took her seat, turning around in her chair to glare at the man beside her as if he were the cause of the offensive odor. Apparently, the stench of my burps lingered long after my exit.

"Where are we going?" I asked, following Jarvis through the crowded platform toward a flight of stairs that led upward, but the sign above the stairway pointing toward the J, Z, and L lines clued me in to the idea that we were heading for Manhattan and leaving the outer boroughs behind us.

We were halfway up the stairs, Jarvis in the lead, when I

felt someone grab a hank of my hair and yank me backward. I lost my balance, my ankle twisting painfully underneath me as I went down.

Not again, I thought, reaching back with my right hand and grabbing a handful of my attacker's shirt to steady myself.

"Jarvis!" I screamed, but there were so many people on the stairs with us, and the sound of the trains pounding down the tracks was so pervasive, it obscured my cry.

"Don't worry," a male voice whispered in my ear. "I've got you, little one. You won't fall."

I breathed a sigh of relief when I realized my attacker wasn't the Ender of Death—but then I remembered that Frank, the owner of the Southern drawl I'd just heard, was as much my enemy as Marcel was, so I started kicking. Frank jerked away from me, but he still had hold of my hair, and when he moved, he unwittingly snapped my head back, sending a wave of pain up through my neck into my jaw.

"Ow!" I cried as Frank pulled me close and wrapped an arm around me. Anyone walking around us would think I'd just gotten woozy and Frank was the Good Samaritan keeping me on my feet.

"You don't need to fight me, little lady," Frank breathed in my ear. "We're on the same side here."

"Then why are you kidnapping me," I growled back at him.

I got no answer. Which left me wondering how long it would take Jarvis to realize I'd disappeared.

"Sick lady coming through," Frank repeated as he duck-walked us back down the stairway, eliciting some nasty comments from the people trying to get up the stairs to make their transfers to other lines.

Frank, cowboy hat in hand, ignored the comments, an apologetic smile on his lips. When we got to the bottom of the steps, he made a hard right and dragged me behind the stairwell, which, while not being totally hidden from curious eyes, did afford a bit of privacy. Holding tight to my waist, he pushed me up against the wall, pressing his hard-muscled body into mine. I glared at him, but that only seemed to amuse him more.

"Calliope Reaper-Jones, you are one spitfire of a little lady," he said, grinning at me. "Yes-sir-ee, a real hellion."

And then he leaned in and kissed me.

I wish I could say I didn't respond to the kiss, that it made me feel gross and dirty and evil, but the truth was much more confused . . . and complicated. And by "complicated," I mean it was *electric*. When he slid his tongue into my mouth, I felt like a pork loin simmering away on the stove, all warm and mushy, my body melting into his. He grabbed my ass and hauled me up, my legs wrapping around his waist of their own accord. The kiss deepened, his mouth devouring mine, tasting my tongue and nipping at my lips.

We fell back against the wall, his crotch hard against the softness between my legs. He pulled at my shirt, snaking his hands past the flimsy material so he could get at my naked flesh, his hands burning me where they touched my skin . . . but it was the good kind of burn. He slid his hand up my sides, tickling the flesh as he searched for a way to get at my breasts.

When his nimble fingers found my bra, he sighed.

"Oh damn, baby, you feel nice," he moaned into my neck as he pulled my right bra cup down, freeing my aching breast, the nipple already hard and ready.

"You're as soft as silk, honey," he rasped, kneading my breast with his hand. He traced his thumb over my nipple, again and again, making it stand wantonly.

I moaned when he stabbed his crotch furtively into mine; dry humping me right there in the middle of midmorning commuter traffic. I didn't care that we were on a subway platform doing things to each other's bodies that should only be attempted in the privacy of one's own bedroom, because I felt like I was on top of the world, or at least on top of a very sexy hunk of manhood.

He started kissing my neck, sucking on the delicate skin below my car.

"Oh, Callie, honey," he mouthed into my neck, then he pulled his head away, smiling up at me as I sat astride him.

Without a word, he released me from his embrace and my body slid down the length of him. We stood there staring at each other for a full ten seconds, our eyes locked together like two dogs fucking, then he spun me around, slamming me face-first into the subway-tiled wall. It should have hurt—scrap that, it *did* hurt—but I was too overheated to notice or care. Especially when he stuck his hands up under my skirt and yanked down my tights. I was still wearing underwear, but it was so thin and filmy that it was like having nothing on at all.

"Baby," he said as he slipped his fingers underneath the lacy edges of my panties and plunged his fingers inside me. He slid his fingers in and out of me, and I groaned with every thrust, my entire body quivering as he had his way with me.

"Oh my God," I moaned, straining against him as I unexpectedly climaxed, my legs going all limp and useless underneath me.

He caught me in his arms before I could hit the ground.

"Good girl," he whispered, kissing my temple before hauling me back up onto my feet.

I was drunk on sex—dazed and confused, totally out of my gourd. I hadn't done anything so hot and sexy in my entire life. It was like I'd stepped into some soft-core Showtime movie—which had absolutely *nothing* to do with my real life—and been mistaken for one of the sex extras. It was insanity.

I pulled up my tights and readjusted my skirt, but there was nothing I could do to hide the flush of sex that was ripe on my face. I felt giddy with it, wanton and completely satiated—but then a little niggling feeling of guilt crept into my head, buzz-killing my sex high.

Daniel.

I'd just cheated on the guy I was supposed to be in love with . . . well, at least, the guy I *thought* I was supposed to be in love with.

I groaned, letting my head drop into my hands.

"What's wrong, honey pie?" Frank said, stroking my hair.

"I'm a jerk," I said from in between my fingers.

I let my hands fall to my sides and lifted my head, looking up into the face of the man who'd just tempted me away from the straight and narrow. He was still as handsome as he'd been before I'd let him touch me, muttonchops and all, and I was still attracted to him, even though I felt terrible about it, but deep inside, I knew I'd just done something really stupid.

"Don't feel bad, little one," he said, running his thumb across my cheekbone—I could smell my own sex on his fingers, which only made me feel ill. "This is how it's supposed to be."

"How it's supposed to be?" I said, pissed at myself for letting things get so out of hand.

"Uh-huh," he answered, grinning at me before reaching down to pick up his discarded cowboy hat from the floor.

"Yeah?" I said, getting annoyed by his lack of explanation. "What's that mean?"

"It means that . . ." he said, lazily cupping my chin in his hand.

"That you can take a bloody hike!" Jarvis finished for him before slamming one large, heroin-addict fist into Frank's face.

twenty-two

Jarvis grabbed my arm, pulling me behind him as Frank fell to his knees, clutching his busted nose. Blood poured through his fingers, some of it dripping onto the floor, where it made a Rorschach pattern on the concrete. Eyes wide, he looked up at me askance.

"Callie, honey?" he murmured, his voice thick from all the blood.

But Jarvis didn't give me the opportunity to answer him. He took me in hand, ushering me away from the scene of the crime and back onto the platform, where we quickly disappeared into the crowd.

Jarvis was silent as we threaded our way down the platform, using the opposite staircase to take us to the next level of the station. Wordlessly, we followed the subway signs to the J, Z, and L lines. This platform was even more crowded than the previous one, but I allowed Jarvis to guide me to a quieter spot by one of the columns. It wasn't as busy here and I could lean my head against the cool of the metal. Across the track, a young man with a pale yellow Afro was busking for change, his saxophone case open to catch the quarters and dollar bills people lobbed at his feet, the melancholic strains of "Nature Boy" mixing with the clamor of the commuters and the throb of the incoming and outgoing trains.

"So, what was that all about?" Jarvis said finally.

"I don't know," I said—and it was the most honest answer I could give him.

"Who was the young man? Obviously . . . *hopefully* . . . someone you know?"

Well, at least I knew where I stood with Jarvis; he thought I was a total ho-bag.

"That was *Frank*," I said. "One of Sumi's people."

I expected Jarvis to get really upset and castigate me for fraternizing with the enemy, but he merely wrinkled his brow thoughtfully.

"Strange," Jarvis said after a pause. "I cannot place the man. You would assume with those . . . *muttonchops* . . . he would be hard to misplace."

"I don't know the first thing about him." I shrugged. "He could be Charles Manson for all I know."

"*Him*," Jarvis said, shaking his head, "I would remember."

I sighed, banging the back of my head on the metal column.

"I can't believe I did that, with him, in *public*," I breathed, tears of frustration snaking out the corners of my eyes. "Dumb, dumb . . . *dumb*."

Jarvis put his hand between my head and the column. It was a sweet gesture, but one I didn't deserve.

"I'm a terrible person, Jarvi," I said, looking over at the stranger's face that now housed my good friend's soul. "How could I have *done* that?"

Jarvis took my hand and gave it a squeeze.

"Shit happens, Calliope."

It was such a un-Jarvis statement that I couldn't help laughing.

"You can either beat your head against a metal subway column, or you can own up to your mistakes and take responsibility for them," he finished.

"That's much more Jarvis-like," I said, smiling at him,

although I still felt like a total shit heel. "And you're right. What's done is done."

Our train chose that very moment to materialize at the end of the track. It quivered to a stop, a set of doors lining up exactly with where we were standing.

"God, I sound like a Hallmark card," I said as the doors opened in front of us.

"Yes, you do," Jarvis said, taking my hand again and leading me onto the standing-room-only train.

i felt like we were on the damn train forever, but maybe it was just my imagination. Either way, the train was so crowded—and I kept getting jostled farther and farther away from Jarvis by the people standing around me—that it became impossible to talk. Needless to say, I had a lot of downtime to think about what I'd just done.

I didn't know why I felt like such a heel. It wasn't like Daniel and I were married. We were just dating each other nonexclusively—but I could only say that because we'd never "officially" talked about it one way or the other.

Oh, crap, I thought, *that makes it sound even worse. I am such a finger-banging cheater. Bad, bad, bad!*

The next time I saw Daniel, I just had to man up and do the right thing. I had to tell him what I'd done and then we'd see how it went from there. Maybe he wouldn't hate my guts too much. Maybe he'd understand that I hadn't meant to hook up with an almost total stranger in the middle of a crowded subway platform, that it'd just happened . . . by accident.

Fat chance of that, I thought miserably.

"We're getting off here."

Jarvis had worked his way back over to me, but I was so lost in my own thoughts that it took me a minute to remember it was Jarvis standing there, not some strange, gangling kid I didn't know.

We waited for the doors to open, then followed the crowd out onto the platform. It was the 14th Street Station, a station

I frequented, but I didn't think I'd ever been on this particular track before. Like a newborn lamb, I followed Jarvis and the crowd toward the exit stairs, but instead of climbing up the first step, Jarvis circumvented it, leaving the flow of foot traffic behind us.

"Where are we going?" I asked, but when Jarvis put his finger to his lips for silence, I shut up.

He pointed to the mouth of the subway tunnel and then pointed to us. It didn't take two guesses to figure out where we were going. He checked to make sure we weren't being observed then he stepped into the subway tunnel, his gangly body disappearing into the inky darkness. I followed suit a moment later, plunging into the unknown with only my trust in Jarvis to guide me.

For some reason, my night vision didn't work in here, and after only a few steps into the tunnel, I was engulfed in a blackness so absolute and impenetrable—and improbably comforting—that it was like being refolded into the universal womb. All the tension in my body melted away, and even though I couldn't see two inches in front of me, I had no fear of walking into or tripping over anything unseen. I felt weightless as I danced through the darkness, unfettered from all the human worries that had plagued me during the past twenty-four hours, all the guilt and doubt dissolving like sugar into boiling water.

I could've stayed in that lovely state of stasis forever, but just as soon as my body—and mind—had arrived at the apex of relaxation, the dark became less inscrutable, a murkier shade of gray rather than pitch black. It was like I'd been walking among the blind and then someone had turned on the light at the end of the not-so-proverbial tunnel and I could see again.

Jarvis waited at the edge, his back to the light, beckoning me forward. Shedding the last remnants of the darkness like a shroud, I left the tunnel behind me and came to stand beside my friend, my eyes feasting on the beautiful, brown-tiled subway station that magically opened up before us.

The station was bathed in an ethereal golden light that

bounced off the wheat brown tiles and filled the whole space with a burnished glow. A row of gold-leafed ticket windows lined the far wall, stretching as far as the eye could see. Above the central ticket windows hung a gigantic electronic destination board with so many sets of arrivals and departures—some for places I'd never even heard of before—that it boggled the eye. Every few seconds the board refigured itself, platform numbers lighting up beside new arrivals and impending departures.

To our left, two arched walkways bore signs above them indicating that one tunnel led to the departure platforms while the other led to arrivals. This made me wonder, since we obviously hadn't come by way of either arched tunnel, how we had gotten here. I crooked my head so I could look behind me. To my surprise, there was no darkened tunnel behind us, only a large black door with a plaque above it that read EMERGENCY EXIT in large block letters.

"This way," Jarvis said, taking my arm and leading me into the thick of the crowd.

The station was swarming with a plethora of interesting creatures—many that I'd never seen before—intermingling with humans and humanoid-like beings that probably didn't have a molecule of humanness in their entire body. Some were buying train tickets, others huddled in small groups talking worriedly among themselves. I saw three Bugbears, one with a large gash in his tail, waiting at one of the ticket booths, and I wondered how many family members they'd left behind when they'd made their escape. There were also fauns and satyrs, a tiny red dragon, some mermen—I could tell by their gills—all waiting for tickets or pointing determinedly at the destination board.

As I marveled at the startling variety of life around me, at the utter uniqueness of each of God's bizarre creations, I was forced to wonder why he/she had lifted Man to such a lofty place among this pantheon. And I realized, as I stared at the veritable Tower of Babel surrounding me, that I couldn't think of one good answer to my question.

"Is it always this busy?" I whispered.

Jarvis shook his head, but it was a tall, bearded man in a top hat, horns, and black tails walking in the same direction as us who responded to my question.

"No, this stampede is because of what's happening in Purgatory. Death has been beheaded and the Devil and one of Death's Daughters, along with the Devil's loyal minions, have overrun Death, Inc. This mad rush is on their way to help fight them."

I thought of my father, who'd done nothing wrong but had been destroyed nonetheless, and my mother and baby sister who were alive (maybe) only at the Devil's behest—and I felt ill.

"What about Hell?" I asked, thinking of Runt and Cerberus now. "What's happening down there?"

"We don't know," the man said, shaking his head. "There's been no word since yesterday."

"Thank you," I said, grateful for any information I could get.

The man tipped his hat to us before veering off in another direction, losing himself in the crowd.

"Where are we going?" I asked as Jarvis led us to an unoccupied ticket booth.

"Two tickets to Heaven," he intoned into the booth's window.

"Uhm, there's no one there," I said, but Jarvis raised a finger for me to be quiet.

Suddenly, two tiny pink tickets magically appeared on the counter in front of us.

"Thank you," Jarvis said politely. As he pocketed them, I peered into the booth to see if there was anyone hiding inside, but no matter how I squinted, I couldn't see anyone or anything.

"Who's in there?" I asked, curious. "It looks empty."

"It's not," Jarvis replied, turning away from the window—and since he seemed to know where we were going, I let him lead us back into the crowd. "You remember when your friend Daniel was a shade, his body trapped in Hell so he would be forced to do the Devil's bidding?"

I nodded.

"That was what was inside of that ticket booth: a damned soul who has chosen to let its body rot in Hell rather than do what the Devil demands."

"Oh," I said as comprehension flooded my brain. "Gotcha."

We picked our way through the throng, our footsteps and those of the people around us melding together into a cacophony of echoing sound as we moved toward the arched tunnel marked DEPARTURES. Other people/creatures around us were carrying train tickets in a rainbow of hues, but I saw no one else with pink ones like ours.

"How come everyone is here?" I asked, picking up my pace to keep up with Jarvis's longer strides. "Why aren't they just using the wormholes?"

"Because it's through Purgatory that all wormhole activity is monitored—"

"So?" I asked, interrupting him.

"If you'd let me finish, Miss Calliope," he said, rolling his droopy eyes heavenward in a signature Jarvis move. "What I was going to say, before you rudely interrupted me, is that all wormhole activity is monitored and *regulated* through Purgatory. If the Devil has taken over the building, then he's disabled the system so no one can get in or out of Purgatory."

"Shit."

"Yes," Jarvis agreed with me. "Shit is definitely apropos."

We crossed the threshold of the Departure's archway, leaving the station behind us as we followed the crush of bodies down a wide brown-and-white mosaic-tiled walkway. The arched ceiling soared twenty feet above us, and long pewter pendant fixtures cast in an art deco chevron motif dangled from the ceiling at ten-foot intervals, bathing the chamber in pale yellow light. Spaced between the light fixtures were tall, arched doorways with corresponding platform numbers embedded in the overhead tile work. The doorways were shrouded in darkness so that whatever lay beyond them remained in shadow. To keep myself occupied as we walked, I started counting doorways, but stopped when I hit one hundred and fifty-seven—and the tunnel still had no end in sight. With each subsequent doorway we passed, we lost more and more of the crowd as they peeled away to find their platforms.

Soon, only Jarvis and I remained, trudging forward like two refugees from a modern-day civil war. Jarvis, wearing his cheap business suit and thin addict's body, looked the worse for wear. He had dark smudges under his puppy dog eyes, and the pomade in his hair had started to dissolve, leaving a tuft of dark hair sticking straight up in the back. I didn't even want to think about how I looked. Suffice it to say, I could smell my own stench and it told me I was fit for a Dumpster and nowhere else.

When we reached doorway number three hundred and seventy-five, I stopped in protest.

"My feet hurt and you look like you're gonna fall over," I said to Jarvis. "Can we just take like a two-minute break . . . *please*?"

"We only have one more to go," Jarvis said, shaking his head and pointing at an arched doorway on our left.

"Okay." I sighed and picked up my feet.

Jarvis got there first but waited for me.

"Here's your ticket," he said, thrusting one of the pink things at me. I took the proffered ticket, and then together we entered the darkened doorway, stepping out from behind a column to find ourselves on a normal New York City subway platform with people milling about, reading the paper and playing with their cell phones as they waited for their train to arrive.

I heaved a sigh of relief, glad we hadn't ended up somewhere strange . . . and then I started looking around me. After that, I wasn't so sure *how* I felt anymore—definitely not relieved.

There was something *odd* about the people—humans only now—that surrounded us. An older man reading a book on one of the benches to our right was so transparent I could see the brick wall through his head. Down at the end of the platform, two skinny young women in yoga gear and thick hoodies casually held their yoga mats at their sides: one woman was slightly transparent, while the other was almost totally gone.

A Hispanic nanny and her tiny Caucasian charge, both wrapped in medium-weight coats as they waited hand in hand by the turnstiles, weren't very see-through at all.

The station itself looked normal, with dirt on the concrete floor, smears of God knew what on the white-tiled walls, and a stack of grubby newspapers sitting on the floor by the turnstiles. Beyond the turnstiles, a heavy African-American woman in an MTA uniform sat inside the information booth, reading over some paperwork. She was almost totally solid, like the nanny and her charge.

"What's wrong with them?" I asked Jarvis as I took a seat beside him on one of the empty benches.

"Nothing is wrong with them, Miss Calliope," Jarvis said.

"No," I argued, shaking my head. "There is definitely something wrong with them. I can see right through that guy."

I pointed at the guy on the next bench over, reading his book. I could see the book's title—Dostoevsky's *The Double*—through the man's transparent hands.

Jarvis sighed.

"Yes, I forgot, you're seeing their deaths—"

"What?" I growled back at him.

"These are human beings, Miss Calliope. You are Death, well, at least, half-Death right now, so your powers are growing. I suspect what you are seeing right now is how long they each have left to live on this earth."

My stomach, which was already a burning mess, flipped over with an acidy gurgle, and I fought another burp that was crawling up my throat.

I didn't want to know how long these people had left on the earth, I didn't want to see their impending deaths—this was an awful, awful thing!

"This is the way of Death," Jarvis said, continuing his explanation in the vacuum of my silence. "It's not as bad as you think, though. Having done it before."

I felt terrible. I hadn't asked Jarvis anything about what

he'd been through. Granted, things had been a little nutty since we'd hooked back up together, but still, I'd acted thoughtlessly.

"What happened to you when you died?" I asked. "I mean, I'd like to know, if you'd like to tell me."

Jarvis shrugged.

"It wasn't so bad. The Ender of Death knew my weakness and there was nothing I could do to protect myself. Right before he murdered me, he intimated that he might've dispatched your father, as well, and that was the hardest blow."

Jarvis paused, his throat constricting.

"Your father was my friend and he deserved better than that," Jarvis continued, his brown eyes filling with tears.

I nodded, my heart squeezing tighter with every word he uttered.

"Luckily," Jarvis continued, a lighter tone in his voice now, "I was dispatched by an incompetent."

"Huh?" I said, not understanding.

"You do a terrible job as Death. You aren't committed to the job—"

"No, duh," I shot back.

"So, you leave a little spark of life in the souls you dispatch."

I sat up in my seat, pleased.

"I do?"

Jarvis nodded.

"In my case, it was a positive thing. It gave me enough power to escape from the Harvesters and find my way back into another body."

"And why would it *not* be positive?" I asked nervously.

"All souls must transmigrate," Jarvis said. "You give them the power to fight against the system, and if they try hard enough, you give them the freedom to escape."

"Oh," I said. "I can see how that might not be a good thing."

Neither one of us had anything else to add to the conversation, so we sat in silence, waiting for our train. Jarvis was right, though. If I was gonna be Death, I was gonna have to commit myself to the job, or else I was going to ruin everything my dad had worked so hard to achieve.

Definitely food for thought.

Looking for something to do while we waited, I checked out the ticket I was holding. It was one of those rectangular, mass-produced paper tickets like you see at school raffles or at cheap carnivals, only this one was in a blistering shade of hot pink instead of the requisite red or yellow. It had the word TICKET on one side and KEEP THIS COUPON on the other, with no reference to what the ticket was supposed to be used for anywhere on it.

"Budget cuts?" I said, pointing at the ticket. "Or are they just cheapos?"

Jarvis laughed, looking down at his own ticket.

"Yes, I *have* always found these to be a tad bourgeois," he said with a smile.

We sat in silence, each of us lost in our own thoughts. I knew so little about Jarvis's life that I couldn't have told you what he was thinking about, but I was still trying to wrap my mind around my indiscretion with Frank and why I'd let it happen. Jeez, if Jarvis hadn't been there to wrest me out of Frank's control, who knew where I would've found myself?

"I'm glad you came back," I said to Jarvis unexpectedly. "I don't think I could've done any of this without you."

"Well, that's not entirely true, Miss Calliope," Jarvis said, an evil grin spreading across his face. "You did manage to accomplish the 'getting jiggy in the subway' part all by yourself."

And before I had a chance to properly respond (i.e., smack Jarvis upside the head), our train arrived.

twenty-three

With a loud *screech*, the train pulled into the station, the doors opening to unload its burden of passengers onto the subway platform.

Except no one got off this train.

I looked in both directions, thinking maybe it was just the cars in front of and behind us, but from what I could tell, *no one* had disembarked.

"This is ours," Jarvis said, standing up. "The pink train."

I had no idea what he was talking about. The train was silver like all the other subway cars I'd ever ridden on, and then I noticed the number on the side of the car:

Three hundred and sixty-seven.

In hot pink neon.

I'd seen trains with red numbers—and white numbers, too—but *never* ones in neon pink.

Interesting, I thought. Very *interesting.*

We climbed through the doors and sat down on a two-seater bench. I was still waiting for other people to get on with us, but no one did.

"I guess it's just us, huh?" I said finally when the doors slammed shut and the whole train shuddered to life.

"To them," Jarvis said, pointing to the people still waiting in the station, "the sign says this train is out of service."

"And what do those people make of me and you getting on an out-of-service car?" I asked deliberately.

Jarvis pointed at the window across from us. If I'd expected to see my reflection, I was sadly mistaken. Instead, a tall Asian man in stained beige coveralls, a buzz cut revealing the topography of his bumpy skull, had taken my place. Beside me, a short Hispanic man in matching coveralls sat primly in his seat, hands clasped in his lap, a silly little smile playing on his lips.

"Interesting choice of disguise," I said dryly.

"The tickets choose the costume," Jarvis shot back, "but we're only borrowing, not keeping."

The car lurched forward and we took off down the track. As soon as we were out of sight of the station, Jarvis pointed to the window, and I saw that our reflections had returned to normal.

"Whew," I said, though returning to my former state of mess wasn't an improvement. I was gonna have to take a dip in a pool full of bleach if I wanted to remedy the most serious of my cleanliness issues.

"Jarvis?"

"Yes, Miss Calliope?"

"What do I ask God when I see him/her?"

I'd been wondering how best to approach this question ever since we'd left the Ender of Death hanging out on the first subway platform earlier that morning. But now that God had already sent help to fight down in Purgatory, then what was it I was really asking for? Dethroning the Devil seemed like a moot point now.

"Well, I suppose the first thing I would ask God, if I were in your position, would be for him/her to put a stop to the challenge," Jarvis said thoughtfully. "Ask him/her to appoint someone to the Presidency of Death, Inc., so that neither you nor Daniel end up dead."

"Will God make me Death, or will he/she choose Daniel instead?" I asked, the question tentative.

Jarvis shook his head. "I really don't know. It could go either way."

"But if I'm not Death, then what happens to Clio and my mom?" I said. "Will they still be immortal?"

Jarvis looked down at his hands uncertainly.

"No," he said with an air of finality to his words. "Their immortality relies on your immortality."

"And if I'm not Death, then I'll be a full-fledged human being?"

"Not entirely, because your mother—"

"Is part Siren. I know," I said glumly.

"It's such a small percentage that I don't think it would make much of a difference, though," Jarvis said, sensing my melancholy. "It *is* where you and your sisters derive your magical abilities. Sirens are known as the Witches of the Sea—something your father detested. He always hated your mother's family."

"She told us she was an orphan," I said, my body swaying with the movement of the car on the track. "Yup, today has been a very interesting day."

"Don't ever tell your mother I said that about her family," Jarvis said suddenly, raising an eyebrow. "I'll deny everything."

I sighed. "I promise never to tell my mother what you said so she doesn't kick your ass."

"Thank you," Jarvis said primly. "Honestly, I have to say that your mother does frighten me at times."

"Me, too," I said, grinning, glad we were both in agreement on that one.

My mother *was* a severe and strange woman.

"I think we're here," Jarvis said as the conductor eased on the brakes, the train gliding to a stop in front of an empty subway platform. It was the smoothest train arrival we'd had all morning.

Jarvis and I stood up as the doors slid open, and then we stepped out onto an empty platform. There were no other riders disembarking, nor were there any waiting to board in our place, but the lack of other passengers wasn't really surprising, given that this subway station wasn't even really a station—more like the waiting room in a snazzy uptown doctor's office. Instead of benches, there were two canary yellow overstuffed leather couches against the back wall, each with its own matching white pine side table and egg yolk–colored, corded telephone. Running the length of the station floor was a rectangular pile carpet—in a shade best known as "eggshell"—which was so plump and clean that I found it had to believe it hadn't just been laid down that morning, let alone that anyone had ever walked on it before us.

Instead of the standard turnstiles one found in a typical subway station, there were two potted rubber plants, their clay planters glazed pale yellow like icing on a lemon bundt cake, leading you toward the exit.

"This place is wild," I said, pointing to the plants. "I like those way better than the stupid turnstiles back home."

Jarvis snorted.

"Let's go upstairs. I'm sure you'll be intrigued by what you find up there."

As we passed the couches, both of which looked unbelievably comfortable, I was tempted to sit down and take a nap, my sleepless night finally catching up with me. I slid my fingers along one of the arms, marveling at the buttery softness of the leather, but I quickly yanked my finger away when one of the phones beside me began to ring.

"Should I get it?" I asked, being closest to the squealing phone. I looked over at Jarvis, who shrugged, so I reached down and picked up the phone, cradling the Bakelite receiver to my ear.

"Calliope Reaper-Jones?" a woman's voice barked at me through the phone line.

"Yes?" I said. "This is she. I mean, this is me."

"I'm God's secretary and he/she asked me to call you and tell you not to bother. He/she is too busy to see you."

"Oh," I said.

"He/she says thank you for coming and to have a nice day."

The voice was nasal, clipped, and very efficient. So efficient, in fact, that I almost said "Thank you" and hung up the phone, but something, some voice in my brain, told me not to take "no" for an answer.

"Wait!" I said, sharpening my tone. "I want to see God. I'm not just gonna hang up and go away."

There was silence on the other end of the phone. Finally, the clipped voice said, "Fine. Then come up to the office."

The dial tone buzzed in my ear and I hung up the phone.

"What was that all about?" Jarvis asked, eyes wide with curiosity.

"That was, I think, God's secretary. She told me to go home."

Jarvis's face fell.

"But I told her no and she said to come up."

"That was very presumptuous of you . . . and very wise," Jarvis said as he gave a sigh of relief.

I was cheered by the compliment. Jarvis had never called me wise before.

"Have you ever been here?" I asked him. He looked sheepish and shook his head.

"I've never been past this anteroom. You father always went alone to see God."

"Good," I said. "That means neither one of us knows what we're doing."

Jarvis cocked his head, my words confusing him.

"And why should I presume this is a 'good' thing, as you say?" he asked.

"Because it means that no matter what I choose to do," I replied tartly, "neither of us will know when I'm messing up. That way I can do what I think is right, instead of worrying about what I *know* I'm doing wrong."

Jarvis stared at me then he said something that made me wanna cry:

"Your father would be so proud of you, Calliope."

"Yeah?" I said.

He nodded.

"Yeah."

The Jarvis in front of me might not be in the package I was used to, but it was still Jarvis through and through.

"Thanks, Jarvis," I said, giving him the biggest smile I could manage. "Now, let's go find God—and not in a scary Jesus freak kind of way."

beyond the potted rubber plants, we found a set of white-lacquered spiral stairs that disappeared into a cutout in the ceiling above us.

"After me," I said to Jarvis, putting my foot on the first stair and hoisting myself up.

Jarvis, who for the first time in our relationship was bigger than me, had a hard time managing the rickety staircase. His large feet slid uneasily on the smooth white-lacquered stair surface, and more than once I heard him cursing under his breath as he gripped the handrail with both hands to keep from falling off.

We reached the ceiling without incident and I popped my head through the cutout. To my shock, I discovered that there was nothing but more stairway above us. I leaned back down to give Jarvis the bad news.

"Hey, Jarvis," I said. "I don't want to be a bummer, but there's like nothing but stair ahead of us for a while."

Jarvis groaned—and I finally understood what it was like to have to deal with me: the girl who groaned, whined, and pooh-poohed everything.

"It's not as bad as it looks," I said, trying to be helpful, but I could see that Jarvis wasn't buying it.

"Just keep going," he said, resigned to his fate. "I'll be right behind you."

I popped my head back up through the cutout and began to climb again, my body quickly getting winded as we climbed higher and higher, the stairway spiraling away below us. I looked down, shocked to realize how far we'd already come.

"I feel like we're in that song, 'Stairway to Heaven,'" I called back down to Jarvis as I paused to catch my breath.

"Oh, the irony," Jarvis said as he leaned against the stairwell, breathing heavily through his nose.

Pleased with my little bon mot, I continued climbing up the stairs, using my hands to pull me from one stair to the next.

"Stop being lazy and climb," Jarvis said, poking me in the butt.

"Inappropriate," I screeched, but I took the hint and sped up.

I wasn't wearing a watch, and I've never been good at guessing ages or the time, but I know we had to have spent like at least five hours on that monstrosity of a stairwell.

Stairway to Heaven? I thought. *Ha! More like Hellway to Heaven.*

"Are we there yet?" Jarvis wheezed below me.

Just as I was ready to chuck the whole endeavor and go back down the way we'd come, the seemingly endless stairs suddenly gave way to another ceiling. This one was a lot more promising than the last because I thought I could see the end of the stairway above me.

"I think I see the exit," I yelled back down to Jarvis, who managed a quiet "Yay" in between wheezes.

I closed my eyes, whispering a tiny prayer for this to be the end of our journey.

Please don't make us climb any more stairs to find you, God. I promise to take your name in vain less often. Amen.

I popped my head through the opening in the ceiling and found that the stairway had led us into another waiting room. Although I didn't think my hasty little prayer had anything to do with the improvement in our situation, I was giddy.

"We're here," I called back to Jarvis.

I climbed the last of the stairs, exhaustion overtaking my body as I stepped into the room, then I waited for Jarvis to follow me up. Now that we weren't climbing stairs anymore, I could finally relax.

I saw that we were in another pale white waiting room, the mirror image of the one below, with the same two couches, two side tables, and two phones; one designer had obviously decorated both spaces, because the two rooms were almost identical in their blandness. The only difference between them was a white pine desk that sat on the far side of the room just beyond the carpet—*and* the large woman who worked behind it.

To my surprise, I realized that with her flaming red hair—pulled into a tight bun at the back of her neck—full peach lips, milky white skin, and arresting green eyes, the woman was beautiful. Pleasantly round, her large bosom rested just above her desk as she plucked away at an old Remington typewriter. Her pale cream sweater tied in well with her bleached environment, but the bright green scarf tied jauntily around her throat added a touch of flair to her ensemble—and showed that she had a very definite personality.

Hoping to get her attention, I walked over to one of the canary yellow couches and plopped down into its overstuffed embrace.

"I'm pooped," I said as Jarvis joined me a moment later, the apples of his cheeks red from exertion.

I'd expected the woman to look up from her work, to acknowledge our arrival somehow, but she was fixated on what she was doing and ignored us. Out of the corner of my eye, I caught Jarvis perking up like a flower that'd just been watered after a long drought. His eyes got bigger and he sat up straighter, or as straight as an overstuffed couch would allow, running his hands through his messy hair as he tried to smooth it back into place. I'd forgotten what a sucker he was for the larger ladies, and now, with this new body, he was more than a match for the girl behind the desk.

Continuing to pretend we weren't there, she typed furiously, her focus on the *click-clack*ing keys and the spooling ribbon as it set inky letters down on the white paper. After a few minutes, she finished the page, ripping it from the typewriter and setting it down on a neatly arranged stack of pages.

"I'm working on my book," she said unexpectedly, looking over at us. Her voice was as clipped as I remembered it from the phone.

"What kind of book?" Jarvis asked, wrapping his arms around his legs and leaning forward to show he was interested.

The girl shrugged, slipping another piece of paper into the typewriter.

"It's just a modern love story. About two people who live in different worlds and can't be together, but they still love each other desperately."

"Star-crossed lovers," Jarvis added. "Like Romeo and Juliet."

The girl nodded.

"But modern. 'Cause I'm a modern kind of girl."

Jarvis nodded like he knew what she was talking about, but I knew he was full of shit. *I* didn't have a clue what the girl was talking about, so I knew for a fact that he didn't, either—but *I* wasn't gonna be the one to call him out. He obviously dug the girl, clipped diction and all.

"I'm Calliope Reaper-Jones," I said, hoping this would move the proceedings along, but the girl wasn't having any of it.

"I know who you are and you're just gonna have to wait like everyone else."

"But I don't think you realize what's happening down in Purgatory—" I began.

"We know what's happening in Purgatory," she said, cutting me off. "God knows everything."

"But time is of the essence," I continued, gesticulating with my hands. "You see, we need to talk to God and—"

"Oh, *he's* not talking to anyone," the girl said, referring to Jarvis. "He's not authorized."

"That's bullshit," I said, but Jarvis grabbed my arm.

"It's okay, Miss Calliope, relax."

I took a deep breath.

"Fine." I sat back in my seat, the plush cushions fluffing out around my head, and sighed angrily.

Ignoring us again, the girl went back to her typing—but now the *clickety-clack* just got on my nerves.

"Jarvis, bad stuff's happening down in Purgatory and we're just gonna *sit* here?" I moaned, frustrated.

"This is God, Miss Calliope," he said. "I assume that God works in God's time."

"But that's nuts," I said.

Jarvis had no answer for me, which kind of sucked because he *always* had an answer for everything.

"Don't you think we should demand to see God?" I asked.

Jarvis shook his head.

"I think we should just wait and see what happens—"

I stood up. I was sick of "waiting and seeing." It hadn't served me well in the past and it certainly wasn't serving me well now.

"I'm sorry, Jarvis," I said. Then I walked over to the girl and slammed my fists down on the desktop. She stopped typing and looked up at me. She didn't seem particularly annoyed, but she didn't seem pleased, either.

"What do you want?" she asked.

I raised an eyebrow.

"I think you know what I want."

"The bathroom," she said, pointing at the stairway, "is back down the way you came."

I reached down and grabbed her typewriter out from under her, marveling at how much heavier the thing was than it'd looked. I swung my body away so it was out of her reach and glared at her.

"You want your typewriter back, then you tell God I want to see him/her, and I mean right now."

"Don't get your panties in a bunch," the girl said. "The door's right there. Be my guest."

I turned around to make sure she wasn't pulling my leg—she wasn't. A pale cream door with a white ceramic doorknob had magically appeared in the wall behind me.

"Careful with that," she said, clucking at me like a hen as I hefted the Remington back onto her desk.

"Sorry to be such a bitch," I said, "but please don't let my bad behavior reflect poorly on my friend Jarvis over there. He thinks you're cute."

The girl raised her eyes to mine, studying me for a moment—probably trying to decide if I was bullshitting her or not—then pursed her full lips and flicked her gaze over to where Jarvis was sitting on the couch, his face bright red. I gave the former faun a wave, which he halfheartedly returned, then I walked over to the doorway, wrapped my hand around the knob, and opened the door to God's office.

twenty-four

I stepped into God's office, expecting to find, I don't know what . . . a white office with a yellow couch and maybe an egg yolk–colored phone or two? But what I discovered was the opposite of that.

No, it was worse than the "opposite" of what I'd expected: *It was my room.*

Not my tiny apartment in Battery Park City near the missing Twin Towers, the Financial District, and the Statue of Liberty, but my bedroom at Sea Verge, where I'd lived—minus time away at boarding school—for the first eighteen years of my life. I'd spent my first "alive in this world" night here as a newborn—although the room hadn't been very different then than it was now: The carpet was still the same shade of dusty rose and the white wicker desk, dresser, and nightstand had been with me from the beginning, too. The double bed came later, after I'd graduated from the cradle. The comforter set and walls had changed colors and themes numerous times during my occupancy, but I'd gotten the deep rose bedding that was on the bed when I was sixteen—and it hadn't been changed since.

I'd dreamed in this bedroom: While I sat at the desk "pretending" to do my winter break homework or lay on the floor staring up at the pale cream ceiling, imagining what my life might be like when I grew up. I'd had pillow fights with Clio here, and I'd lain on the bed and cried my eyes out for two days straight when I'd lost my two best friends in a car accident. This room, whether I lived in it now or not, was me, was everything that I'd been . . . that I'd hoped to be. It was like walking into a ghost, but one whose every moan you knew by heart.

Overwhelmed, I sat down at the foot of the bed then I instantly shot back up, thinking I might find some clothes in the closet that I could change into. I got to the closet door before remembering I'd taken all my stuff with me the last time I'd visited, so I sat back down on the bed and waited.

I didn't have to wait long.

"Calliope Reaper-Jones."

I sat up, my spine straightening as God's voice punctured the silence, its honey timbre palpitating in my ears and tickling the tiny hairs on the back of my neck. I'd experienced God's dulcet tones before, but I was still surprised by the RuPaulish quality of his/her voice, the brassy low end mixing nicely with the high-pitched purrish vibrato.

"Why am I here?" I asked, cutting to the chase. I didn't have time for pleasantries.

"Because you asked to see me," God said.

"But I don't *see* you," I said. "I don't see anything but my old room."

Suddenly, I felt a chill race up my body. It started at my toes, rushed up my calves, through my midsection, and into my jaw before settling inside my head. I blinked twice, my thinking clearer than it had ever been before.

"Look in the mirror," he/she said, using my lips to give body to his/her words. I turned my head, catching my reflection in the white wicker mirror above my dresser. I looked like me, only a more "knowing" me.

"Are you inside me?" I said, but I knew the answer.

"When I was that I was," God said, *"I found myself to be a very lonely creature. So, I created this universe—and all the other universes—so that I would not be alone anymore.*

My first attempts yielded the angels and then the demons, but both of them lacked a spark, an ability to be both perfection and imperfection at once. They were rigid, inflexible, and so the perfect ones stayed in Heaven and the imperfect exiled themselves to Hell—"

"They make it sound like you kicked them out," I said, marveling at the oddness of having God speaking to me through my own body.

"They exiled themselves by their very nature, but that's neither here nor there," God said. *"You want to know why I created humans . . . it's a question I can feel resonating inside you, even now."*

"It's one of many questions I have, actually," I said.

"I created Man in my image, Calliope, because I am a mercurial, fickle, and unknowable creature myself. I created you so that I might experience myself in every one of you. The good and the evil, the wisdom and stupidity; that Man is a living, breathing contradiction in terms thrills me . . . it is my ultimate masterpiece."

"I don't want to be Death," I said suddenly, selfishness welling inside me. "I know it's selfish of me, that my family is depending on me, but I'm so scared to be something more than . . . just *me*."

In the mirror, I watched God laugh (using my body).

"This is why I enjoy you so much, my dear," I (God) said. *"I spend entirely too much time losing myself in your life, in your choices. You please me more than you will ever know."*

"Is that why you've helped me with the Demon Vritra and the Devil and my sister?"

I nodded to myself in the mirror.

"It's why I have helped you, yes. Sharing your experiences has cheered me a great deal over the years."

"But I'm just some girl," I said uncertainly.

God's answer was silence, and then I understood that the greatest gift we, as human beings, have been given is our humanity. No matter whether I was immortal or supernatural or just plain old human, I possessed humanity and nothing could ever take that away from me. It was this character (flaw, some might say) that made me so special . . . and so important.

And it was the reason God had asked so much of me.

"So, now you see," God said.

"I do," I replied, as scary as it was to admit.

"Then go do what needs to be done," God said, his/her enthusiasm making me smile.

"I'll be watching."

i guess i shouldn't have been surprised by what I learned, but in the end, it made a strange kind of sense: a sense that in the days to follow would become even clearer.

jarvis was waiting for me when I returned. He wasn't on the couch anymore, though. Instead, he'd found his way over to the secretary's desk and was helping her put another ribbon on her old Remington typewriter. I took care to make as much noise as I could as I closed God's office door behind me, but they both looked up, startled, like I'd caught them making out or something.

"Get your lady friend's number," I said, heading back to the spiral staircase. "And then let's get the hell out of Dodge. We've got shit to take care of."

I didn't wait for Jarvis's answer, just started down the stairs, my feet rap-tapping on the white lacquer as I descended. A moment later, I heard Jarvis's matching steps behind me.

"What did God say, Miss Calliope?" he asked breathlessly.

I didn't stop, or even turn around, as I spoke.

"God likes this. All of this," I said, "He/she built this world for conflict and now we're gonna go give him/her a whole bunch of it."

As Jarvis mulled over what I'd just told him, the only sound was the staccato beat of our feet on the stairs. Finally, he asked:

"All right, then. So, where are we going?"

I laughed, enjoying the way the tables had turned. I was

usually the one asking where we were going, not the other way around.

"We're going to Hell," I replied. "The Devil and my sister have staked out Purgatory and left Hell all by its lonesome."

"How are we going to get there?" Jarvis asked. "I can't call a wormhole—the Devil will be watching to see if we attempt anything and then he'll know where we are."

"Oh, I've got all of that under control," I said, massaging my stomach while it burbled unhappily.

The pain had been more manageable while we were in Heaven, but now that we were leaving, the hard-core indigestion was back. I would've cursed Sumi and his magical jewel . . . if I hadn't had plans to use the gem for my own nefarious purposes.

"We have to get out of Heaven first," I continued. "Being here hampers the jewel's powers."

"You don't plan to use the wish-fulfillment jewel, Mistress Calliope?" he said incredulously, stopping midstep.

I turned around and put my hands on my hips. What I had to say to Jarvis, I needed to say directly to his face.

"Jarvis," I began. "First of all, I want you to call me Callie, not because I'm being impertinent, but because you're my friend and friends don't use the term 'Mistress' in front of other friends' names. It's just weird."

"All right," Jarvis said, turning over my request in his mind.

"And secondly: Damn straight I'm using the jewel to get to Hell—"

Jarvis opened his mouth to protest, but I overrode him.

"I don't think Sumi and Hyacinth are working for the Devil *or* Thalia. I think they're independent operators, using this opportunity to further their own agendas, whatever that may be. I want to draw them out, and the best way to do that is to use the jewel."

"Are you certain?" Jarvis asked.

"Very certain," I said, nodding. "The jewel is how Frank found me in the subway, and the more I think about that whole sordid experience, the more I think he used the jewel somehow to seduce me. Maybe it's just wishful thinking on my part, but who knows."

Jarvis's mouth dropped open.

"In his own totally screwed-up way," I continued, "I think he actually likes me, and seducing me wasn't even part of the bigger plan."

"Hmm, I suppose you could be right, Callie," Jarvis said. "But my worry is that their agendas, whatever they are, will not coincide with our own."

My brain was already one step ahead.

"It doesn't matter what they're really after," I replied. "Because for my purposes, all they have to do is just *exist*."

"Okay, then," Jarvis said, getting used to the idea. "You sound as though you know exactly what it is you're doing, so command me as you will."

I grinned and punched him in the arm.

"Jarvis, I command you to follow me down these god-damned stairs and then come with me while I go knock a few heads around."

Jarvis didn't hesitate for a moment.

"Sounds divine."

we tackled the remaining stairs with renewed vigor, cutting the time it'd taken us to originally climb them by half. They were still punishing, but not nearly as painful as they'd been on the way up. We were making great time and I actually found myself growing to enjoy each tip-tap our feet made on the lacquered stair, because I knew it meant I was one step closer to getting the hell out of there.

I was looking forward to throwing myself onto one of the very comfy yellow couches and resting my weary calves for a minute or two when we finally reached the bottom, but to my surprise, I saw that our subway train was still there, doors wide open and waiting.

"Looks like our chariot awaits," I said, gesturing to the empty car as we climbed aboard and fell onto one of the benches, the doors sliding closed behind us.

The train sprang to life, picking up speed as it sailed down the track. With my new take on life, I was in a much better frame of mind than the first time we'd boarded the train, and I found myself closing my eyes, the gentle rocking motion putting me to sleep. I wasn't too worried about missing my stop, because Jarvis was beside me, keeping an eye out for our destination, so I snuggled against the window, using my arm as a pillow. I realized it had been like a day and a half and I hadn't slept once. I figured I was due for a little nap—not that ten minutes of shut-eye could make up for missing a whole night's sleep.

I dreamed that the train was on a cloud, floating in the sky high above the earth. I could look out the window and see New York City, all swirls of gray and blue, far down below me. I felt untethered, like I was a million miles away from reality, even though I could still see the traces of my old life below.

"Callie?"

I woke up with a start. I was leaning against Jarvis's shoulder, a thin trail of my saliva on his ratty jacket sleeve.

"Sorry about that," I said, wiping my mouth with the back of my hand.

"You were snoring so loudly I didn't want to wake you," Jarvis said. "Well, actually it was so loud I did want to wake you, but I took pity."

The train had arrived at the 14th Street Station, and the doors were wide open, waiting for a few tentative people to climb aboard.

"I guess here is as good a place as any to do this," I said, my jaw cracking as I yawned. The nap had just served to make me groggier and hadn't refreshed me at all.

I stood up, leaning on Jarvis's arm as a crutch, and together we left the safety of the subway car—and when I said "safety," I meant safety. Standing outside on the platform, looking mightily pleased with himself, was Marcel, the Ender of Death. None of the people on the platform batted an eye at us, but they steered a wide berth around Marcel, as if they could sense the madness emanating from inside him.

"So, we meet again," he murmured as we approached.

I could feel Jarvis's arm stiffen around me, but I shook my head, letting him know he could relax because I had things well in hand.

"I guess that's just our fate, Marcel," I replied, only stopping when we were a few feet away from him, an easy enough space to breach if he chose to attack.

"I warned you that there were larger things at play here than you could understand," he said.

"Duly noted," I concurred.

"Have you figured it out yet?" he asked, grinning wickedly. It was nice that he hadn't underestimated me. He was one of the few creatures out there that'd known I hadn't been operating at my full potential.

"You're working with Sumi and Hyacinth," I said, letting the bombshell drop casually. "The Devil and my sister, they think you're in cahoots with them, too, but you know they'll just cage you once they get what they want."

Marcel clapped his hands together happily.

"It's amazing, isn't it? That I'm the big winner?" he purred. "No matter who comes out on top, I win."

I could tell Jarvis was appalled by Marcel's behavior, but I didn't think he truly understood how mad the Ender of Death had become—and that the fault lay squarely at my father's feet. He'd imprisoned Marcel—or Monsieur D, as he was called when I'd first met him—down in Hell as a way of keeping tabs on the creature that would eventually be the death of Death. The isolation had driven the poor thing crazy, had stripped him of his ability to do his intended duty.

It had left him a shell of his former self.

My father had done this to Marcel, not understanding the effects imprisonment and loneliness would have on the man, and because of that, fate had deemed that my dad's destruction should come at his prisoner's hand. It wasn't fair that my dad had to die, but at least I finally understood why he hadn't fought back:

He knew he couldn't outrun his fate forever.

"What should my dad have done differently?" I asked

Marcel. He seemed surprised, yet pleased, by the question and took his time to form an answer. As I stood there waiting, I wondered what God would make of what I was doing right then. He/she would probably be intrigued.

"If I were your father, I would not have imprisoned me," he began, "but as I mull over the question, I finally understand why he did as he did."

"He was trying to protect me and my sisters," I said. "Actually, more *me*, but still he did it for all of us."

Marcel nodded at the truth of my words.

"Death had never had a family before," Marcel continued. "So it had never figured into the equation."

"You've spent a long time sparring with Death, and then my dad took away your ability to perform, or try to perform, your job."

"I am the balance to Death," Marcel said. "Without me, Death becomes vulnerable, allowing others to try and fill the void I have left behind."

"Like my sister Thalia and her demon lover, Vritra," I added.

"Yes, it was your father's fault," Marcel said. "He loved you and your sisters so well that he caused his own demise."

"That's not true!" Jarvis said, wrenching his arm from mine and making a move to clobber Marcel.

"No, Jarvis!" I said as I grabbed his hand and pulled him back toward me. Jarvis turned on me then, his eyes full of fury.

"How can you allow him to say these things about your father? How can *you* say them? After all he did for you—"

I had expected Jarvis to react, but it was still painful to hear the anger and distress in his voice.

"Jarvis," I said, drawing him closer to me while all he wanted to do was beat the crap out of Marcel. "My dad was fallible; he made a mistake. I know you know it's the truth. You don't want to believe it and neither do I, but it was Dad's fault. He set all of this into motion when he chained the Ender of Death to a palm tree down in Hell."

"He was the best of men—" Jarvis said, still unable to accept what he knew was true.

"Yes, he was," I said. "He was the best dad in the world, and I wish I'd let him know that more."

Jarvis's eyes filled with tears and he started to sob.

"He loved you and your sisters so much. He only wanted what was best for you . . ."

"I know, Jarvi," I said, his words ripping my heart to pieces. "I know."

"You were marked from the beginning. It was foretold from your birth that you would follow your father, but he wanted to give you, more than anything, the freedom to choose," Jarvis said, wiping the tears from his face. "It had been so hard for him to adjust to the job himself, and he wanted only that *you* make the decision, not be forced into it by him."

All the years of acting out and fighting my fate and here I was, right back where I started. My dad had wanted to give me freedom, but instead, he'd wrapped the noose even more tightly around my neck.

Well, so be it, I thought.

I returned my gaze to Marcel, knowing I had to do this now, or I might miss the chance entirely.

"Marcel, the Ender of Death, I ask you to take leave of me now. Allow me to assume all the rights of Death, and then, when I'm at my full power, we'll meet at a place of your choosing and fight."

Marcel's eyes flared suspiciously as he listened to my offer.

"If I beat you fairly," I continued, "we'll revert back to the cat-and-mouse game that Death and the Ender of Death must always dance. If you dispatch me, then my job'll fall to another and I'm out of it."

"You swear it?" Marcel breathed, his whole body rigid with anticipation as he waited for my reply.

"I swear it."

"Then you are a witness," he said to Jarvis, who nodded stiffly.

Satisfied, Marcel proffered a low bow, which I returned with a curt nod.

"Thank you, Marcel," I said softly.

"'Til we meet again, Death."

And then the Ender of Death turned on his heel and silently disappeared into the midafternoon commuter crowd.

twenty-five

Jarvis sat on the ground, his back resting against one of the metal columns. He looked like a beaten man, his already pale face so drawn and pinched, one might think he was ill. Maybe he was. The body he now possessed was probably going through heroin withdrawal, but I doubted that was what was making him look so wan. I'd just laid my dad's shortcomings bare before his mortal enemy and Jarvis could be nothing but terribly conflicted by the turn of events.

Who deserved his loyalty more: my father—his former master—or me, his possible new one?

I couldn't answer that question for him, but I could shed a different-colored light on it.

"Jarvis," I said, squatting down beside him, "listen to me."

He opened his eyes, but he didn't really see me. He was still lost in his own thoughts, wrestling the demons that lived there.

"Jarvis," I said again. "You understand that my dad did what he did out of love. His humanity was what made him good at being Death, but it was his flaw, too."

Slowly, Jarvis began to nod.

"It's why God chose him, Jarvis—because he was human,

because he could be *both* perfect and imperfect at the same time."

"He was my friend," Jarvis whispered, returning my gaze.

"And as his friend, wouldn't he want you to protect the people he loved so dearly?" I asked.

Jarvis nodded again, finally understanding what I was driving at. I fluffed his hair.

"Will you help me?"

I reached out my hand and he took it, letting me help him to his feet. I guess all of this strangeness was par for the course down in the subway.

"It's what your father would want," he said softly.

"Yes, it is."

"So we're off to Hell, then?" Jarvis asked.

"I think now is as good a time as any," I said, placing one hand on my belly, where I could feel the stomach juices simmering away in my gut, and taking hold of Jarvis's arm with the other hand.

I took a deep breath, closed my eyes and said:

"I wanna go to Hell."

When I opened them again, we were there.

i make no bones about the fact that I dislike Hell. It's hot and miserable and I always lose like two pounds in water weight while I'm there. The desert part is all sandy and gross; the forested area is spooky and filled with odd creatures like the Bugbears. I get attacked, peed and slobbered on, or thrown down into a bottomless pit at least once every time I visit—and frankly, I'm getting pretty tired of the whole rigmarole.

Luckily, on this trip, the wish-fulfillment jewel was kind enough to avoid the desert *and* the spooky forest, setting us down, instead, right in front of the entrance to the North Gate of Hell.

"Callie!" a voice called from behind me, and I whirled around just in time to see my hellhound puppy, Runt, take a flying leap in my direction. We hit the ground hard, but I didn't mind because I was just so damn happy to see that she was okay.

Jarvis, who was smart enough to get out of the way, snickered at the sight of me being molested by a sixty-pound hellhound pup.

"What are you doing here?" she said, licking my face—something she'd never done before—her tail thumping rhythmically against my leg in happiness. "I'm so glad to see you!"

As I gave her a good scratching behind the ears, I noticed she'd gained about ten pounds since I'd last seen her, and her dark coat had gotten so shiny that it glowed. She was still wearing the pink rhinestone collar I'd magicked up for her when we'd originally met—it was the first, and pretty much only, spell I'd ever really done on purpose—but I could see it was starting to get too tight for her, something we'd have to remedy soon so she didn't choke herself on it.

"Okay now, enough slobber," I said, sitting up on my elbows and pushing the big black puppy off my lap.

"We've been hearing all kinds of rumors about what's happening in Purgatory," Runt said as she sat back on her haunches thoughtfully. "They say your dad and Jarvis got killed and that Clio and your mom are missing, but I know that can't really be true, because Jarvis is right here."

Leave it to a puppy to use her nose to root out the truth.

"I was dead," Jarvis said, "but Callie did such a bad job of it I was able to escape and secrete myself into this new body."

Runt nodded. "Yeah, Callie has a hard time focusing," she said sagely.

"Thanks, guys," I said, climbing to my feet and brushing off the dog slobber. "Where's your dad, Runt? I need to talk to him."

Instead of an answer, the puppy gave three short yips in rapid succession and, a moment later, received an answering howl in return. The howl was so chilling that it would make a normal person's blood run cold, but I was used to it, so I just grinned, happy to see Cerberus as he lumbered out of the forest, carrying a dead stag in his mouth.

"Dad was just showing me how to hunt," she said as she padded over to where her father, the three-headed Guardian of the North Gate of Hell, had dropped the dead animal in the dirt. He was about three times bigger than Runt, but I'd learned not to be scared of him, because he was just a big old softie at heart.

Hellhounds were like sea horses; the women bore the babies while the men raised them, teaching the little tykes how to hunt and look after themselves. That left the women free to go out and bring home the bacon or, in their case, the giant stag. I'd never asked Cerberus about his mate, but I got the impression that he was a single dad because, as I'd just witnessed, he could do both jobs, and admirably.

Runt, being the baby, was the last of the kids to go out and seek her fortune, and I knew Cerberus was enjoying having her around, especially because she'd spent her formative months hanging out up at Sea Verge with Clio and my parents. I'd "borrowed" Runt to help save my dad when he was kidnapped by my sister and her nasty demon husband, Vritra, but I'd fallen in love with the pup and then had had a hard time returning her to her dad.

Like all male hellhounds, Cerberus possessed three heads—one smart head (his bore a giant, all-seeing Cyclops eye) and then two normal but not very smart heads. I'd nicknamed the dominant head "Snarly"—not that I ever called Cerberus that to his face—while I referred to the other two as the "Dumb" heads.

Not very clever, but it did the trick.

"I would like to offer our sincerest apologies on your loss," Snarly head boomed, lowering all three heads in a low bow.

"Thank you," I said, touched. "It means a lot to me that you respected my father."

"Would that he'd had dominion over our domain, too," Snarly head said. "And not just Purgatory."

I couldn't have agreed more. I looked over at Jarvis and saw that the compliments Cerberus had paid my dad pleased him, too.

"What can the hellhounds do for you in your time of loss, Death's Daughter?" Snarly head asked.

"I spoke to God," I said, looking to Jarvis to offer confirmation. He nodded his head in the affirmative. "And now I need your help to get rid of the Devil and my sister before they take over Purgatory."

"What do you need from us?" Runt said, wagging her tail with the enthusiasm of a little kid.

I swallowed hard, knowing that what I was about to ask Cerberus to do went against everything that was sacred in Hell, but it was the only plan I could conceive that had a chance of shifting the Devil's attention away from Purgatory and back to Hell.

"I want you to open the North Gate of Hell and let all the souls out."

I don't think I could've shocked Cerberus—and Jarvis—more if I'd taken all my clothes off and done the hokeypokey right there in front of them. It was Runt, the hyperintuitive one, who came to my rescue.

"It's a brilliant idea, Callie," she said. "Overrun Hell with all the demons and damned souls trapped inside of the Gates, and the Devil will be forced to come back here and deal with us."

She turned to her dad.

"It's the revolution you've always wanted, Daddy!"

"I need to separate Thalia from the Devil," I continued, now that Runt had my back. "If we cause a riot down here, one of them—the Devil, I hope—will have to come and try to squelch the uprising. They've left Hell unguarded because they believe they've got you by the balls, that no one here would ever stand up to them."

"Putting it that way," Snarly head said, his unblinking yellow eye staring thoughtfully at me, "I think you may be on to something."

The other two heads drooled their agreement.

"What do you think, Jarvis?" I asked, turning back to look at my friend.

"I think if anything has a chance to work, this is it."

I smiled. Getting the seal of approval from Jarvis gave me the confidence to believe my plan might actually work.

"So be it," I said, my mischievous grin wide enough to include Jarvis, Runt, and Cerberus. "Open the gates."

the dead arrived in a flood.

In Hell, every religion or philosophy had its special area of punishment. Because we were at the North Gate of Hell, the province of the tormented Atheists, Pagans, and Satanists of the world, it was this marginalized group of dead who were the first ones to appear at the Gates. It didn't take long for the word to spread throughout Hell, and soon we were inundated with the damned souls of the more traditional religions: Christians, Muslims, Hindus, Jews . . . and from there the list went on and on and on.

The Devil had taken the Bugbear Guard with him in order to secure Purgatory, leaving a handful of loyal demons to oversee Hell. Needless to say, there were so few of them—versus so many of the aggrieved—that they didn't stand a chance. Besides, once the damned souls realized we'd provided them with an escape route, they took matters into their own hands, felling the other Gates and snaking out into the surrounding forest, free to do as they pleased.

"They're not going to want to go back in," I said as Jarvis, Runt, and I watched Cerberus rip the gate from its hinges, widening the gap for the escaping souls. He threw the splintered gate behind a boulder before loping over to where we were waiting.

"It will be Death's job to help re-collect them all," Jarvis said knowingly.

"Well, that's a bummer," I said, though I'd already expected that to be the case.

"I will mobilize all of the hellhounds," Snarly head said, "and have them alert the Bugbear families as to what is happening and tell them to stay in their houses. They live mostly in the deep woods, so I think the souls will leave them be, but the escaping demons could become a problem."

The great three-headed hellhound had agreed to become my commander-at-arms. He would mobilize all the creatures sympathetic to our cause and prepare the able-bodied to defend Hell upon the Devil's return.

"I know that the angels and Gods and Goddesses are in Purgatory fighting as we speak," Jarvis said. "But Callie, you have the power to command the Harvesters and Transporters. They work for Death, Inc., and will do your bidding if you ask them. They could be very helpful down here in Hell."

"What do I do?" I asked. "Just call them?"

"That's what your father would do," Jarvis said.

I took a step away from the others and placed my fingers at my temples.

I need you. Come help me! Long Live the New Reign of Death!

No sooner had I thought the words than the skies were filled with a sea of Victorian-garbed men and women, each holding an unfurled black parasol to guide their trajectory to Earth. There were thousands of them, every color and race and nationality that the world possessed. A veritable army of Death's finest, and they had all heeded my cry for help. It was awe-inspiring.

I knew the Devil would be major league pissed to see the North Gate of Hell overrun with my people, and if I'd had my phone, I'd have taken a picture and e-mailed it to him. That'd show him that while he'd been playing patty-cake up in Purgatory, Death had seized the opportunity and taken Hell by storm. I could only hope that once the rumors of our coup reached his malevolent ears, he'd take the bait and come down to restake his claim.

I waited until the last of the Harvesters and Transporters had arrived, sailing down from the sky to add to the already swelling crowd, and then I began:

"Thank you for coming!" I said, trying my best to project over the din. The Harvesters and Transporters, curious as to why they'd been called out, were talking quietly among themselves. There were so many of them, though, that "quietly" was a relative word.

"Try this," Jarvis said, twisting his hand to reveal a bullhorn he'd magicked out of the air for me. I placed the contraption to my lips and my voice exploded into the air.

"Thank you for coming!" I said again. "As you probably know, the Devil and my sister Thalia have taken over Death, Inc."

There was a chorus of boos from the assemblage—obviously they weren't too keen on the new management—but I waved them down.

"This means that they've left Hell vulnerable to us," I continued. "Which is why I've called you here. When the Devil realizes his mistake, he'll come back to Hell to protect his dominion, and that's when we'll strike. Let's show the Devil he can't mess with Purgatory!"

I wiped a bead of sweat from my forehead; the heat and the burning in my gut were making me woozy.

"So, are you guys down to do a little ass-kicking?" I screamed at the crowd, ignoring my own discomfort.

The roar of agreement nearly bowled me over.

"Jarvis here will be overseeing the battle in Hell." I looked over at my friend and winked. He looked surprised, then his cheeks flared pink with pleasure. "So, do what he says and let's show these pricks who's boss!"

Satisfied that I'd gotten the crowd riled up enough to ensure their help, I handed the bullhorn back to Jarvis. My gut was churning, but I kept my agony to myself. I wanted to get out of there before anyone else noticed how badly off I was. I needed to put the next step of my plan in motion, and I didn't want to have to explain myself in the process.

As Jarvis began to outline the plan of attack to the Harvesters and Transporters, I knelt down beside Runt. I wanted at least someone to know where I was going, in case I didn't make it back.

"Runt," I said, scratching the back of her ears the way I knew she liked. "I'm leaving now, but I want you to know where I'm going. It's not a secret, but give me a few minutes to get going before you tell your father or Jarvis."

"I don't want you to go, Callie," the hellhound puppy

said, her big pink eyes pleading with me. "You might never come back if you do."

"Then you understand why I have to go," I said. "Clio and my mom need me, and someone has to put a stop to Thalia before she knocks the whole universe out of whack."

Runt seemed to understand my predicament. She licked my hand, her way of letting me know she would do as I asked.

"I won't tell anyone until you're gone."

I leaned down and kissed the top of her furry head.

"Jarvis is gonna need all the help he can get," I said, standing up.

"Pop and I will keep him safe," she promised. "You do the same for Clio and your mom."

"Will do, Captain."

I gave Runt one final hug, then I took off for the tree line, following the same trajectory into the forest the damned souls had taken. A scalding wave of agony burned through my gut as I ran, and I just hoped that once we'd succeeded in dealing with the Devil and Thalia, I'd be able to find someone to remove the evil wish-fulfillment jewel from my belly.

As I got farther into the forest, I took a sharp right turn, veering away from the path the dead had taken and trudging deeper into the forest—away from prying eyes. The canopy of low-hung branches blocked out most of the sunlight, and soon I found myself walking through semidarkness, dodging exposed roots while I fended off a small swarm of gnatlike creatures that'd decided I was dinner.

After a few minutes of hard slogging, I came to a clearing in the woods where a stand of red maple trees—five large specimens grouped together in a circle—stood sentinel. I imagined this would be as good a place as any to make my play.

"Frank," I called, "you can come on out now!"

A light breeze filtered through the trees as the rustle of leaves filled the air like a ghostly whistle, and then a man stepped out of the forest, cowboy hat in hand.

"Hello there, Miss Death," Frank said, scratching an itchy

spot in his right muttonchop. He was wearing the same clothes I'd last "experienced" him in, and there was still a trickle of dried blood on his upper lip.

"You weren't playing very fair the last time we met," I said, keeping my distance from him. He seemed to understand that I didn't want him any closer to me than he was, so he stopped and sat down on a tree root.

I guess this was supposed to make him seem less aggressive, but I didn't trust the snake as far as I could throw him.

"Yeah, that wasn't right of me," he said, looking down at his hat. "I know that now. I just found you to be a very attractive young lady and, well, you know how it goes."

"No, not really," I said, my throat burning. I tried to swallow back the pain, but a coughing jag hit me hard, forcing me to bend at the waist and cover my mouth with my hand to hide my red-flecked phlegm.

When I was done, I stood up straight and glared at Frank. He was as much at fault for my distress as Sumi and Hyacinth, but as I stared down at him here in the copse of maple trees, he looked so pathetic that I found my heart wasn't really into hating him anymore.

"The wish-fulfillment jewel, it's my weakness, isn't it?" I said.

Frank shook his head.

"Nah, the jewel's the real deal. It's what's inside the jewel that's making you feel so rough."

"So, I have to ask. Why not just kill me outright?"

"We wanted you to help us," he said, threading his hat through his hands. "You were supposed to challenge your friend, Daniel, and kill him. When you didn't, Sumi released the promethium that was inside the jewel."

I started coughing again, but this fit wasn't as prolific as the last one and I was able to get it in check much more quickly.

So promethium is my weakness, I thought. *I just wonder how* they *knew . . . when even* I *didn't know what my weakness was.*

"I tried to help you," Frank said. "I sent Starr your way so she could warn you, but the damn fish is so mercurial I was worried she wouldn't tell you."

"She tried." I sighed. "She told me to ask 'smart' questions. I just didn't understand what she meant."

Frank nodded, as if he'd suspected as much.

"So, you've been following me, for what?" I asked. "I mean, *who* are you, Frank?"

"It's like this, Cal," Frank said sheepishly. "You know how you and your friend Daniel are Deaths-in-Waiting?"

"Yeah?" I said, not really seeing where this was going.

"Well, I'm, uh, another one."

"Another one what?" I said.

He stood up then, reinforcing something I already knew: He was *a lot* bigger than I was. And if he decided to come after me, well, in the state I was in, there wasn't very much I could do to stop him. But to my surprise, he stopped short of moving any closer and just stood there, a silly little grin plastered on his handsome face.

"I'm a Death-in-Waiting, too."

twenty-six

In the back of my mind, I remembered the Egyptian Pharaoh Hatshepsut (though she'd been in her guise as an aura specialist at the time) had once told me that there were actually *three* possible Deaths running around the world at any given time. I knew that I was one and Daniel was another, but until now, I'd never even had a clue as to the identity of the third possible Death. In truth, I'd never factored his/her presence into any of my equations because it hadn't really occurred to me to—but now that I knew who and what Frank was, everything clicked into place.

"You got real quiet, Callie," Frank said nervously.

"I didn't understand," I replied. "I needed a moment to process what you were saying."

This seemed to appease the wannabe cowboy.

"Sumi and Hyacinth, they want to kill you, Cal," Frank said. "It's so I can be Death, but I'm starting to get cold feet. I never even knew there was all this Afterlife stuff until I was a teenager—and even then, I knew more about the magic part and not very much about anything else."

So, Jarvis had been right. Sumi and Hyacinth were trying to usurp the Devil's power by destroying Daniel and me and setting their own Death on the throne of Death, Inc., in our place—and if they controlled Purgatory, that would put a pretty big kink in Thalia's plans. The Ender of Death had implied as much back at the subway station, but I hadn't understood the game I'd been playing until right that very moment.

"So, you'll help me, then?" Frank said pitifully, hat in hand.

I wanted to trust him, to believe he had nothing to do with Sumi and Hyacinth's plan—a plan, it appeared, they'd been hatching for a long, long time. I'd been working for Hy since I'd moved to New York and that had been years ago. Oh well, at least now I understood why she'd never promoted me: Being my boss made it way easier for her to keep tabs on my comings and goings.

"I'll help you," I said, not sure if I was sealing my own Death warrant by agreeing to the deal. I just knew I had to get out of Hell, and having Frank's help would only make things easier.

"Thank you so much, Cal. You're a real lifesaver," he said, reaching out and running his hands through his hair. It was a move I would've found sexy in another life, but I was so over Frank now that it wasn't even funny.

"Where are Sumi and Hyacinth?" I asked.

"They're in Purgatory. They're just waiting for the promethium to kill you, and then they're gonna try and crown me as Death."

The breeze—God knew where it had come from—picked up and wrapped itself sinuously around my sweat-soaked body. The thought of dying right then and there didn't frighten me at all. Maybe that was my fate; maybe I was supposed to tell Frank to go on to Purgatory without me, then when he was gone, I could just curl up on the forest floor and go to sleep.

Forever.

Maybe Death wasn't such a terrible eventuality. At least the idea of expiring in such a beautiful place, surrounded by burnt scarlet maple leaves and the rushing wind, was appealing. So appealing, in fact, that I almost told Frank to go suck on an egg—which would've thus ended my pathetic existence in one fell swoop—but then an image of my sister Clio came unbidden into my mind's eye. Her rakish face, Buddy Holly glasses, and mischievous smile as she laughed at some stupid joke I'd made . . . brought me back to reality like a punch to my solar plexus.

"Hold my hand, Frank," I said, taking a step toward him so I could slip my hand into his own larger one.

"I like you, Callie," he said as if he'd known all along I would do his bidding. "So much more than I ever thought I would."

I shivered as the wind whipped through my hair, sending chills of trepidation shimmying down my spine. I felt like I'd just traded my soul for absolutely nothing in return.

I put a hand to my belly, my gut twitching under my fingers.

"Take us to Purgatory," I said to the jewel.

And then we were there.

I purposely hadn't closed my eyes this time, keeping them open so I could see for myself how the jewel worked, but I learned nothing. One moment we were in a copse of red maple trees, the next we were in the lobby of Death, Inc.

"Wow," Frank said, looking around the place, "this is wild."

He wasn't talking about the building. He was referring to the frenzied fighting that was taking place outside the plate glass windows surrounding us. It was a battle of epic proportions: a chaotic shuffle of tattered and bloodied bodies, set against the stark emptiness of the Purgatorial landscape.

I walked over to one of the windows, pressing my face against the transparent surface so I could get a better look at the bloodfest outside. Instantly, a thread of white-hot heat shot through me, propelling me away from the window. Now I understood why the fighting had remained outside: someone had placed a protection spell around the entire building, so no one could get in or out.

Standing a safe distance away from the window, I watched as the fighting escalated so that I had a hard time separating the good guys from the bad ones. Once, I caught sight of Kali, her perfect feminine form bathed in the blood of her foes, teeth gnashing together as she ripped the head off a tall man in casual office attire, hungrily sucking down the hot, red arterial blood as it pulsed in time to his dissipating heartbeat.

I also saw a number of poop ball monsters—the preferred foot soldier of Thalia's dead demon husband, Vritra—and that was enough to make me superglad I was dying *inside* the building rather than out there with the walking poop patrol. Since I'd been eaten by one of them in the past, a repeat of the experience was not high on my list of things to revisit. There were also fauns and satyrs, Gopi and dragons, human-looking men and women in gold-plated chain mail, and beasts of all shapes and sizes. It was a menagerie of all the mythological creatures from all the different mythological canons the world had ever known.

"I wonder who's winning," I said to Frank, who'd come to stand beside me at the window.

"Looks like a stalemate," he said thoughtfully.

Struck by another round of gut-wrenching coughing, I was left with a specter of deep, red rose–colored sputum in my hand. Each coughing fit left me breathless, my body aching from the effort. I was getting weaker with every passing second and there was absolutely nothing I could do about it.

"I take that back, Cal," he said, eyes lingering on the carnage outside. "Maybe *both* sides are gonna be losers."

He moved away from the glass, his eyes roving over the darkened lobby as he took in the cold sterility of the place. The lights were off down here, but you could see the space had good bones—a real architect's construct of what a concrete and steel skeleton should look like.

"It's cold down here," he continued, pausing before the empty receptionist's desk. He ran a finger over the metal and glass desktop, then flipped through a crumpled beige folder that was spread out across the workspace, obviously left behind when someone was yanked away from their seat without warning.

"They keep the air conditioner set on high," I replied—but I had to admit I was glad for the chilly air. It was a welcome change from the penetrating heat I'd suffered through down in Hell

I noticed a mug of overturned tea on a glass-topped coffee table. I'd waited in the seat beside it the first time I'd been summoned to see the Board of Death with Jarvis. The liquid was still wet, but just starting to dry around the edges. A magazine lay smashed on the floor next to the seat, haphazardly opened to an article on breast-feeding.

"You think if we find your sister and explain the situation, she'll help me with Sumi and Hyacinth?" Frank asked suddenly, picking up the magazine and giving it a cursory look before throwing it down on a nearby chair.

So that was Frank's game, I realized. Like the Ender of Death, he was looking to play both sides and then he'd sidle up to whoever won.

What a jerk, I thought to myself. *And I'd actually felt sorry for the guy.*

Freed from any and all guilt where Frank was concerned, I decided I would apply his own double-crossing methods to my dilemma—only with better (I hoped) results.

"Well, if it were me," I said, leading him right into my hands. "I'd probably be up in the cafeteria hiding out, but since it's Thalia we're talking about here, I'd try my dad's office. She's always wanted the top job."

"And how do we do that?"

I pointed to the bank of elevators.

"We take a little ride."

I doubted Thalia would be up in the Executive Offices, but I had a strong suspicion that that was where she would've stored my mom and sister.

"Let's take a little look-see," he said, and he walked over to the elevators and pushed the flat gray call button marked UP. The light above the brushed steel door winked on and the machine whirred to life. Patiently, we waited for a car to descend to our level; then, as the door glided open, we stepped inside.

The interior was fashioned like a simple metal box, its only unique feature being the long panel of buttons demarcating the different floors. These buttons were so numerous that they ascended from the floor to the ceiling of one whole wall.

"What floor?" Frank asked.

I knew the Executive Offices were on the top floor, so I pointed to the uppermost button on the panel—one I couldn't have reached by myself without a step stool—and watched as Frank stood on his tippy-toes to press it.

"Good eye." Then he added: "You feel pretty bad, huh?"

That was an understatement. I'd gone from overheating to freezing and now my skin was blanketed in a slick of sickly sweat. Shivering was on the bill, too, but I drew the line at teeth chattering. The elevator door eased shut in front of us, and since I didn't feel like discussing my illness with the man who'd been a party to creating it, I used the hum of the upwardly mobile elevator to try to block him out.

"You really think your sister will be upstairs?" Frank slipped his cowboy hat back on his head.

"I think so," I murmured.

Exhausted, I leaned against the elevator wall, my body sprouting gooseflesh in the chilled air. I decided I didn't like the tenor of his questions one bit, and so silence became the elevator music of choice.

After a few minutes of strained silence, Frank reached out and took my clammy hand, giving my fingers a furtive squeeze. The move so set my teeth on edge I had to really fight the urge to slug him. He was so smarmy, and I was so *dying*, that it was hard for me to reconcile the idea of the two things being able to coexist at the same time. I just didn't understand how he, or anyone for that matter, could hold the hand of the person they were murdering and not feel badly about it. He obviously had a clear conscience—while I, on the other hand, was filled with loathing.

I was fast approaching the point where being trapped in an elevator with Frank was making me claustrophobic, but luckily the car chose that moment to reach its final destination, slowing to a stop and chiming twice as the door swept open to reveal a plain beige hallway, industrial-grade Berber carpet, matte beige walls, and a brass plaque listing all the suite numbers for the floor, fitted onto the wall directly across from us.

"This doesn't look right," Frank said, furrowing his brow uncertainly.

I ignored him, stepping out of the elevator and walking over to the brass plaque to get a better look at the suite numbers engraved on it. There were five of them for my perusal—372, 373, 374, 375, and 376—but I was only concerned with the last one.

"Nope, this is the place," I said, starting down the hallway toward Suite 376.

I didn't care if Frank was following me or not. Actually, I was hoping he'd take the hint and go away, because my tolerance for the guy was quickly hitting an all-time low. I couldn't believe I'd let the schmuck anywhere near me; just thinking about those double-crossing fingers running up and down the length of my body made me furious.

Setting his hesitancy aside, Frank chased after me, our feet making swishing sounds on the Berber carpeting as we walked. Each doorway we passed was identical to the next: all pale brown doors, brass doorknobs, and suite numbers engraved on brass wedges affixed to the doorframe. I liked the blandness of the hallway, the sameness of door and doorknob.

It was comforting.

"This is it," I said, stopping in front of Suite 376.

I rested my fist on the face of the door, but didn't knock.

"What're we waiting for?" Frank asked.

I opened my mouth to tell him that *he* should do the knocking, but a gaseous, foul-smelling belch escaped my lips instead.

"Oh, Callie, honey," Frank said, covering his nose, "that is disgusting."

I leaned my forehead against the door and shrugged.

"You know how it is," I replied. "When you're dying from the inside out, things can get kind of stinky."

Undone by the ferocity of that last belch, I lifted my fist and knocked feebly on the door.

As if Evangeline had been waiting there anticipating our arrival, the door flew open and I found myself shoved against the far wall, my head slamming into the opposite doorframe. But Evangeline didn't wait for my body to hit the floor before she attacked again. This time, to her own misfortune, she chose to ram her bald pate into my gut, thus releasing another hideous belch from my diseased stomach.

She may have anticipated our arrival, but no way in Hell did she expect that belch. Gagging, she turned away from me, surprise and disgust etched on her face.

"You're sick," Evangeline screeched, pinching her nostrils together to ward off the smell.

"Yes, I am," I said. "And this is Frank."

Frank took the hint, slamming his fist into the side of Evangeline's neck. She made a grotesque gurgling sound deep in her gullet then dropped to her knees, clutching her throat. Seizing the opportunity that had presented itself to him, he slammed his ample fist into the back of her head. I heard a tiny *pop* and then Evangeline went down face-first, her glassy eyes staring up at nothing.

I normally didn't condone murder, but I decided that Evangeline had had it coming.

Of course, the bitch chose that moment to blink, dashing my hopes for a quick end to my sister's henchwoman. Still, I knew she was too incapacitated to be much of a threat to anyone anymore—and that was good enough for me.

"After you," Frank said, gesturing to Evangeline's prone body.

I did as instructed, using her back as a stepping-stone, and crossed the threshold into the suite that had once been my dad's office.

It was almost too easy.

I flipped on the overhead light, adding to the meager glow

coming from the desk lamp, and found Clio trussed up on a brown leather sofa, her hands and feet bound with twine, a leather gag in her mouth. I saw the purple bruising around her eye and the split lower lip, and I was reminded of my father's last few moments on this earth—and the rage in Clio's eyes as she had watched him die.

Beside her, my mother sat similarly bound, her once beautiful face slack in the harsh fluorescent light. At first, I thought she was dead because her eyes were so dull and lifeless, but then they welled up with tears and I understood that she was very much alive, just locked inside the terrible grief she was experiencing. I could imagine what she was going through—and I knew the shock alone would be enough to drive anyone a little insane.

"Help me untie them—" I yelled at Frank, but stopped, the words frozen in my mouth when I saw two Bugbear guards waiting behind the office door. I instinctively threw myself down on the floor, out of the way of the punishing violet light emanating from the creatures' eyes.

But Frank wasn't so lucky.

Hit with a direct blast, he fell to the floor and started convulsing, his arms and legs twitching as both Bugbears focused their energy on him. Something I'd noticed during my last two run-ins with the Bugbears was that their laser beam eyes seemed to work best on corporeal flesh, not on inanimate objects—which had given me an idea of a way to protect myself. With the Bugbears otherwise engaged, I started crawling toward my dad's polished brown oak desk.

"Come on, you pricks!" I screamed, trying to draw their eyes as I crouched underneath a large, rectangular plate glass window. "I'm over here!"

Immediately Frank was forgotten in favor of me, the moving target. I crawled as fast as my hands and knees would carry me, sliding toward the safety of the other side of the desk just as the Bugbears unleashed their precision laserlike beams of light. The spot where I'd crouched only seconds before sizzled under their gaze, then the violet light faded as they realized I wasn't there. They moved to readjust their trajectory, but by then I was safely ensconced behind the thick wooden desk and completely out of their reach.

I would've given myself a pat on the back for my quick thinking, but my plan pretty much ended there. I'd bought myself a modicum of safety, but that wouldn't last very long once the Bugbears realized they could descend on me together and I'd be ripe for the picking. I racked my brain, trying to think of anything I could do to waylay them, but I was at a loss.

Struck with what we'll call Divine Inspiration, I started ripping the desk drawers out of their cubbies, digging around in each one, looking for some weapon I could use against the Bugbears. Drawer after drawer, there was nothing but papers. Finally, in the last drawer, I chanced upon a stapler and a red blown-glass paperweight.

"They're coming, Callie!" Clio screamed, having managed to worm her way out of her gag.

I grabbed the paperweight, hefting its bulk in my hand. Maybe I could throw it at one of the Bugbears, and if my aim was good, I could knock it out—

Oh, who am I kidding? I thought miserably.

I was a softball dropout who couldn't hit a garbage can with a crumpled wad of paper. It looked like the jig was up; I'd been outnumbered and outgunned and the best course of action was to just hold up the white flag of surrender (in this case it was a red paperweight of surrender) and hope the promethium killed me before my sister Thalia did.

I took a deep breath and raised the hand holding the paperweight up in the air. Suddenly, my arm was enveloped in a red-hot poker of pain as the Bugbears directed their laser eyes at my exposed appendage. I screamed and I dropped the smoking paperweight onto the desktop, my fingers sizzling as I pulled them back protectively to my chest. I heard a loud *crunch* behind me, and I quickly scuttled around to the other side of the desk, stifling another scream when I found myself face-to-face with a dead Bugbear, its eyes black cinders in an otherwise untouched face. I reeled away from the dead body, crawling backward until I was in the safe zone again, then I reached up onto the desk, scrambling for the paperweight—but it was gone.

"Clio," I yelled, my voice hoarse from screaming. "Do you see the paperweight? Where did I drop it?"

"It's right here," she said, her voice so close, I could've sworn she was right beside me, and when I looked up I found my baby sister standing over me, paperweight clutched tightly in her hand. "You got them both in one shot, Cal, when their laser eyes reflected off of the paperweight!"

Instantly, I was on my feet, wrapping Clio in a giant bear hug.

"But who untied you?" I said, squeezing her scrawny frame tightly in my arms.

"The Bugbears spelled our bindings," she said, her voice thick with emotion. "They just fell off once you killed them."

I released her and stared down at my dastardly handiwork, my heart slamming nervously inside me. I looked around, half expecting a few Harvesters to show up with condemning countenances, butterfly nets unfurled as they made ready to disparage me for committing two more murders. Yet after a few minutes when no one had arrived to collect the souls of the dead, I decided to proceed as if the Bugbears had committed suicide (which they had, *kind of*) and chalked the whole thing up to blind luck.

Still, the joke about Death being the worst mass murderer in history, well, it wasn't really a joke. All you had to do was look around at the legacy left there in that office by one Death, a little luck, and a paperweight.

twenty-seven

"Who's that?" Clio asked, her gaze fixed on Frank, who lay unconscious in the middle of the floor, his hair and mutton-chops singed by the direct contact he'd had with the Bug-bears' powerful laser eyes. His face appeared innocent and peaceful in repose, but I knew it was all a front, that underneath the handsome exterior lurked the soul of a snake.

"That," I said, pointing at Frank, "is a son of a bitch."

"Whatever you say, Cal," Clio replied, looking dubiously at the handsome stranger.

"He's another wannabe Death like me and Daniel," I continued. "And he's super bad news."

"We should tie him up," Clio said, grabbing a lamp from a side table. "Use the power cord to bind his hands."

It was nice to have Clio in my orbit again. Her brain moved much faster than mine, meaning she could figure out the solution to a problem in record time—she was great to have around in the middle of a crisis situation.

At Clio's suggestion, I dragged an expensive metal standing lamp over to where Frank lay prone on the ground and used the cord to tie up his feet. It wasn't perfect, but between my handiwork and Clio's, we got Frank's lanky body secured.

Our next order of business was to figure out what to do with our mother. She hadn't moved from her spot on the couch since I'd killed the Bugbears, and it didn't look like she was going to be coming back to reality anytime soon. I debated leaving her where she was but quickly discarded that notion, not trusting that Frank wouldn't find his way out of his bindings and hurt her.

"We could take her to the cafeteria," Clio suggested. "That's where they're holding most of the Death, Inc., employees. At least she'd be safer there."

"You'll both be safer there," I said, kneeling down in front of the couch and taking my mother's hands in my own.

"No way," Clio shot back. "You're not leaving me in the stupid cafeteria like I'm some kind of baby. I'm going where you go."

I wasn't going to argue with her. Not because I wasn't right, but because she was smarter than me and would win any argument she trapped me into.

"Fine," I said as a wave of fiery nausea hit me so hard I had to close my eyes to fend it off.

"What's wrong with you?" Clio said, concern written on her features, but I only shook my head. I didn't have time to go into specifics, and besides, I knew she would only freak out if I told her the truth, and I needed her functioning on all cylinders to help me get our mom down to the cafeteria.

"Just something I ate," I said, ignoring the irony of those words. "Just . . . help me get Mom out of here."

I turned my attention to my mother, trying to catch her eye, but her gaze was fixed inward, lost in some inner dream world where my dad was still alive and Thalia wasn't evil incarnate. I didn't know how much time I had left before the promethium breached the jewel's exterior and took full effect, but I at least had to try to get through to her while I still had the chance.

"Mom," I said, rubbing her freezing hands in mine. "I know that you're hiding in there because you'll fall apart if you come out, even for a second."

"We should really jet, Cal," Clio said from the doorway, where she was keeping watch over the hall.

"Just a minute," I said to my sister, then I instantly felt bad about sniping at her and apologized. "Sorry, just, please, give me a minute, okay, Clio?"

She nodded, watching my face intently for some sign as to what my damage was.

"Mom," I continued. "I just want to tell you I'm sorry. About Dad, about me, about everything . . . and that I love you. And I promise, if I get any say in what happens here today, I'll make the Ender of Death pay for what he's done to you."

I paused, my throat constricting.

"And that's all."

I leaned over and kissed her softly on the cheek, then I swung back around to face my sister.

"Let's get her out of here."

I grabbed one arm and Clio took the other and together we lifted her from the couch.

"Boy, she weighs a lot for someone with bird bones," Clio grunted as she slid her hand underneath our mom's armpit. I did the same and we started hustling her over to the doorway. Clio was right, though—for someone so tiny, the woman weighed a ton in deadweight.

"How're we getting her over that?" Clio said, gesturing with her chin to where Evangeline's body lay blocking the exit.

"We just step on her," I said. Evangeline had made her own bed and now she was gonna have to lie in it.

"All righty, then," Clio said, stepping onto Evangeline's spine with a sickening *crack*. "This is just gross, Cal."

"No kidding," I replied, repeating the same *crack*ing step once Clio had made it over to the other side.

We hustled our mother down the nondescript hallway, her weight pulling at my shoulder as her high-heeled shoes caught at the Berber carpeting. Our mother had always been small, but the shock of what'd happened to her seemed to have shrunk her density down to black hole–sized proportions.

We got to the elevator and Clio slammed her fist into the down button. Immediately, the door slid open—it'd never had a reason to descend back to the lobby after Frank and I had used it—and we climbed inside.

"What floor?" I asked, my gut churning, the fire pouring down my intestines and up my throat.

"Twenty-seven," Clio said without having to think about it. I'd forgotten she'd interned at the Hall of Death and therefore knew her way around the building.

"Twenty-seven it is, then," I said, grappling with my mom's body so I could press the button.

There was a shudder and then the door started to close.

"I hate to do this to you, kiddo," I said suddenly—and then I shoved my mom's body toward Clio, the deadweight pinning my sister against the wall as I slipped out the elevator door. I hadn't wanted things to go down that way, but Clio had left me no choice. I needed her and my mom out of the way in the event I died and they lost their immortality. Then, at least, when I was gone, they had a shot at getting away before Thalia could dispose of them for good.

As soon as the elevator door had closed, I ran back down the hallway and, ignoring the burning in my stomach and throat, crouched down beside Evangeline. I stuck my face right up in hers and screamed:

"Where's Thalia?"

The woman's broken body shuddered and she opened her eyes, her dilated pupils inches from my own.

"Don't . . . know."

I grabbed her ear and twisted, eliciting a pathetic keening noise from somewhere deep in her throat.

"Had enough?" I growled as she swallowed back a terrified sob. "Now tell me where she is."

She blinked back tears as I released her ear.

"Hall . . . of . . . Death," she hiccupped.

"Are you lying to me?" I said, grabbing her smooth scalp

in both hands and lifting her head off the carpet. She squeezed her eyes shut, as if that would make me disappear.

"No . . . please, no."

"You better not be," I whispered, leaning down so my lips were against the cartilage of her ear. "Or I'm gonna come back here and break all the bones in your face, *capisce*?"

"Yes," she slobbered into the carpet. *"I . . . understand."*

I dropped her head back onto the carpeting, leaving her to gag in her own spittle. My aggression spent, I stumbled back down the hallway toward the elevators, using the wall to hold myself up. I was getting worse, my body going haywire with the effects of the promethium, and time was not on my side. I was seriously starting to doubt I'd be able to get to Thalia before I kicked the bucket.

Relief washed over me when I reached the bank of elevators, my hands raw from gripping the wall so fiercely. I was convinced that if I could just get into the elevator car, everything would be all right. I jabbed my finger into the call button, leaning against the wall for support as I waited for the elevator to come. I stood there, my stomach roiling as I was hit by another wave of fiery nausea. My eyes swimming with tears of pain and humiliation, I dropped to my knees, clutching my belly.

"I don't want to die, God," I said, looking heavenward. There was no reply—but then I hadn't really expected one. I wasn't looking for an answer; I just wanted my opinion duly noted.

The elevator door finally slid open and I fell inside, crawling into the back of the car as the door closed like an accordion behind me. I used the wall to hoist myself back onto my feet, my face pressing into the cold metal to steady myself. I'd been to the Hall of Death before with Jarvis and I knew there was a trick to getting the elevator to take me there. I racked my brains, trying to remember exactly what buttons Jarvis had told me to press the last time.

"Seventy-three and twenty-one," I shouted as my memory unexpectedly kicked in. I slid my finger along the panel, counting to seventy-three, then I depressed the button. Next, I drew my finger back down the panel and punched twenty-one.

"Please hold on to the handrail," an electronic voice chimed—but before I could comply with the request, the elevator began to plummet downward, my body slamming into the ceiling.

"'rap," I said, my face pressed against the ceiling's smooth metal surface as the car dropped at G-force speeds.

Suddenly, the elevator came to an abrupt stop, chiming twice to announce our arrival, and my stomach shot up into my throat as the elevator/carnival ride of craziness dropped me back the way I'd come, my shoulder smashing into the floor. The elevator door folded open and I winced, the right side of my face aching from the ceiling hit I'd taken, but that pain was eclipsed by the agony I felt when I tried to stand up and found that my shoulder had separated in the fall.

I was still immortal. Which meant my cells should've started regenerating right there in the elevator, but the promethium was taking its toll on my body and all my energy was being funneled into just keeping me alive. So no matter how hard I willed it to move, my left arm remained immobile, hanging uselessly at my side. Part of me wanted to stay in the elevator and wait for the inevitable, but I fought against it, forcing myself to crawl out into the cramped antechamber marking the threshold of the Hall of Death. I vaguely remembered the space being painted a sickly mint green, but the lights had been dimmed, making it impossible to ferret out any real detail.

Banging my shin once on an overturned chair, I made it across the room without further incident, but when I tried to push my way through into the Hall of Death itself, I found only a blank wall where the entrance should've been. I knew there was a door somewhere—I'd seen it the last time I was there—but then I remembered how it had appeared invisible to Jarvis and me until our guide had led us through it. Pressing my good shoulder against the blank wall, I ran my hand over every inch of the smooth surface until my fingers found a thin crack, which I exploited by hooking my fingers inside it. Using my own body weight, I yanked backward on the opening with enough force to widen the gap just enough to allow me to slip inside.

Immediately, I stumbled over a fresh corpse on the other side of the door. In the darkness, I could see it was smaller than an average person's body, with thin limbs, longish hair . . . and a shirtwaist dress. I didn't stop to look at its face. Not because I meant the body any disrespect, but because I already intuitively knew it belonged to Suri, the Day Manager of the Hall of Death. I said a quick prayer for the dead girl in the doorway, who'd died defending this place from its enemies, but I didn't stop to wonder how long it would be before I joined her. Instead, I forged steadily onward.

The first time I'd been in the Hall of Death, I'd marveled at the beauty of the place: the humongous skeletal steel structure, the floors made from large cut limestone blocks, the oriental carpets bearing strange symbols I'd never seen before, and the walls hung with surreal and bloody medieval tapestries. All the disjointed architectural styles gave the space the austerity of a monastery coupled with the modernity of a skyscraper.

Now the lights were low, hiding the carnage that had been wrought on the place. I found the floors slick with blood; the bodies of Bugbears, humans, and other creatures lay intermeshed with the desecrated armor of the Hall's knightly guards. I'd had a run-in with the knights the last time I'd been here, but we'd been able to resolve the situation without bloodshed. My sister and the Devil hadn't been so lucky. Their people had been decimated here.

I heard raised voices down at the end of the long hall and immediately tried to fade into the darkness, hiding myself in the arched doorway of one of the myriad reading rooms that intersected the throughway of the Hall. I stood there a few moments without drawing a breath, using the wall as a support, but when I realized the voices were staying put, I relaxed. Whoever the voices belonged to, they had no clue about my presence. Emboldened, I stepped out of my hiding space and silently continued my journey down the hallway. I was careful not to make any noise that would give away my position, treading as lightly as my wounded body allowed. When I reached the end of the hallway, I slid into another archway and listened:

"I want all of them!" a woman screamed.

I peeked around the edge of the stone archway to see my sister Thalia pacing in front of the Hall of Death's scarred cherrywood Main Information Desk, her firm body encased in a pair of snug hot pink Juicy Couture sweats. With her hair pulled back into a slick ponytail and her feet encased in a pair of those stupid round-soled Shape-Up shoes that were supposed to tighten your ass while you walked, it appeared she'd dressed down for the occasion.

She stopped pacing and walked over to the desk, slamming her fists into its scarred top, making the giant sumo wrestler of a man sitting behind it quiver. I'd met the man, Tanuki, the last time I'd been to the Hall of Death, looking for a friend's Death Record. Back then he'd been a bubbling bowl of Jell-O, with an easy demeanor that could be either catty or playful, depending on his mood. Now, with his eyes red and puffy from crying, he looked beaten.

"The Hall of Death is an entity unto itself," Tanuki cried. "It decides who receives the Death Records . . . *and who does not*."

Having worked up his courage, he spoke the last few words with a poisonous disdain.

My sister was livid, her eyes wild as she pushed herself away from the desktop, walking around to the other side of the desk where Tanuki, nervous as a cat, sat in an oversized rolling chair. I thought she was going to strike the giant man, but to my surprise she walked past him, her eyes drawn instead by the allure of the humongous apothecary cabinet that towered over him, its face crowded with tiny wooden drawers. My sister stopped when she stood in front of its massive bulk, her hands running over the battered wood. Then, one by one, she began to yank the drawers out onto the ground like a whirling dervish, digging her hands into the empty cubbies, searching for something.

"Please, I beg of you," Tanuki wailed, but my sister, in her frenzy, ignored his pleas. Instead, she became even more aggressive, throwing the drawers—once she'd confirmed their emptiness—as far down the Hall as she could manage. Distraught, Tanuki put his head down on the desk and began to cry, while behind him, my sister systematically destroyed everything in her path.

As I watched Thalia dismantle the cabinet, I began to wonder why she was down here without any kind of guard. If the Devil had really fallen for our plan and gone off to Hell to deal with the uprising we'd started, he would've at least left my sister with *some* protection, right? It just didn't make any sense.

And then I had the epiphany.

The Devil *had* left her with protection. She'd just chosen to use her guard in a creative way. She'd sent them on a suicide mission to take the Hall of Death.

The Devil was pretty smart. He knew that the Hall was the most heavily fortified place in all of Purgatory, and he'd chosen to starve Suri and her guard out rather than attempt to force his way in. He probably thought they'd surrender peaceably once he'd installed his puppet (Daniel) as the President of Death, Inc., and assumed full control of both Purgatory and Hell.

But while the Devil had gone to take care of things down in Hell, Thalia had done as she liked, using her guard to descend on the Hall and take it—with maximum bloodshed. Of course, she'd greatly underestimated Suri and her knights, losing her whole guard in the takedown.

"Nice job, Thalia," I said, clapping, as I stepped out of the shadows and into the light. "You destroyed the Hall of Death and lost all your guards in the process. What's the next thing on your agenda? Killing your mother and sisters?"

At the sound of my voice, Thalia whirled around, her eyes scanning the darkened Hall. When she sighted me, an odd smile played at the corner of her lips and she shook her head sadly.

"I was really hoping someone else would've killed you by now," she said, leaving the confines of Tanuki's apothecary cabinet and crossing back around to the front of the desk, where she was closer to me.

"What happened to your buddy, the Devil?" I said, keeping my voice friendly. "He have a little accident down in Hell and had to leave his best girl here in Purgatory to hold down the fort?"

Thalia's eyes shone with menace.

"You bitch! You're responsible for what happened in Hell, aren't you—"

"I am most definitely the cause of and answer to all your problems, big sis," I shot back at her before she could get herself too worked up. "So, does the Devil know you've raided the Hall of Death in his absence?"

My well-chosen barb struck a nerve—Thalia's face turned white and her mouth dropped open in surprise. In my peripheral vision, I saw Tanuki slowly rolling his chair away from the desk. I wished him all the luck in the world—I wouldn't want to be caught between two very pissed-off immortal sisters dealing with some seriously screwed-up family issues.

"I was just doing him a favor," she said suddenly, backtracking. "He thought the Hall would be impenetrable, but look, it only took two hundred Bugbear guards and here we are."

"Here we are," I echoed.

She narrowed her eyes at me, irises glinting black in the overhead light.

I spat my next words at her: "Why'd you kill Dad, Thalia?"

My sister leaned against Tanuki's desk and laughed, but it was the sound of bitterness, not mirth.

"Calliope, you know why I had to do it," she said, the odd smile still playing across her lips. "He left me no choice. He took away my future and then he had me locked away. When the Devil came and offered me his help through Evangeline, what else could I say, but yes?"

There was no point in talking to Thalia, I realized. Nothing she said, no bizarre ramblings she indulged in, would ever give me the closure I wanted—because no matter which way you sliced it, ambition and insanity were not good reasons for murdering your family.

"It's over, Thalia."

She raised an eyebrow.

"Why?"

"Because I said so. You've done enough damage already, and now it's time to stop," I said, anger and nausea driving my words. "The Devil's not coming back. It was a trap. And without him, you're nothing."

She pursed her lips, her hand instinctively stroking her ponytail.

"You're lying. No one stops the Devil—"

"We did," I said, lying through my teeth. I had no idea if Jarvis and the others had secured Hell yet, but Thalia didn't need to know that.

Something behind me caught my sister's attention and she turned her head to get a better look. Her face went slack with recognition and she lifted her hand aggressively.

"What're you doing down here?" she said, uncertainty blooming in her eyes.

I turned around, too, wondering who'd decided to join the party now. To my shock, I saw my dad's attorney, Father McGee, standing in the middle of the hallway, looking about half as old and decrepit as he usually did. Beside him stood my old buddy, Frank, who shot me a knowing grin. I guess he'd figured out who had tied him up with the light cords.

"I'm afraid I'm here to put an end to your fun, Thalia," Father McGee said, taking something from his jacket pocket and holding it up to the light.

I had expected to see a gun or, at the very least, a Taser, but what I saw, instead . . . *was a package of airplane peanuts.*

twenty-eight

"Stay away from me!" Thalia screamed, bumping up against the edge of the desk as she tried to back away from the silvery-blue package in Father McGee's hand. I would've laughed at the absurdity of the scenario: my megalomaniac sister being terrorized by a bag of airplane peanuts—*except now I had an inkling what my sister's immortal weakness was.*

As a child, I'd known that Thalia was allergic to peanuts. We'd never had them in the house, and Clio and I were forbidden from buying peanut butter cookies and Reese's Peanut Butter Cups or ordering peanut butter and jelly sandwiches when we went out to eat—but I'd just never put it all together before.

Thalia had been born with the most common immortal weakness of all: peanuts.

And then, with a leaden certainty, I knew who had sold out my family.

It hadn't taken me long to realize that someone had been feeding Sumi the particulars of my family's immortal weaknesses—I just couldn't figure out who the culprit was.

I knew that the person, whoever they were, was close to my dad—that they knew every aspect of his life intimately, both personally and professionally, and that they were in a position of utter confidence within the Death, Inc., hierarchy. Since I could cross Jarvis off the list—my Dad's Executive Assistant had done nothing but suffer for my family—the only other person with the kind of access necessary to crush the Reaper-Jones clan was the man standing in front of me, shaking a bag of peanuts in my sister's face: Father McGee, my dad's lawyer and personal confidante.

"You bastard," I said under my breath. "You as good as killed my father—"

"No," Father McGee said, interrupting me. "I didn't kill your father. The Ender of Death has always known *his* weakness. I simply provided the necessary information about you, your mother, your sister, and Jarvis."

Father McGee's face glowed with power—yet upon closer inspection, I saw that it wasn't just power that was making him appear so sprightly. His skin was appreciably firmer, the lines around his mouth and eyes less pronounced. Even his hair was shinier, the color having molted from snow white to a more distinguished salt and pepper. It was almost as if he'd won a year's worth of Botox in the church raffle and had used the whole supply in one sitting. Gone, too, were the clerical trappings I'd always known, replaced now by a well-tailored black Armani suit and sockless white calfskin penny loafers that made him look like Bob Hope on a USO Tour to Hell.

I took a few steps forward, wanting to pummel the priest in his Benjamin Button face for what he'd done to my family, but it'd taken so much energy to confront Thalia that when Frank grabbed my arm to stop me, there was nothing I could do to fight him.

"Get off me—" I growled as Frank threw me to the floor, where I had to bite my tongue not to scream in agony when I landed heavily on my bad shoulder.

"Frank, go get the little minx," Father McGee said, pointing to Thalia, who was still cowering by the desk.

"Leave me alone," Thalia yelled, swatting at Frank with both of her hands as she tried to climb over the desk to get away from him. Of course, he was bigger and stronger than she was, so it was no contest. He scooped her up under his arm and carried her back to where Father McGee was waiting.

"What about her?" Thalia wailed, pointing at me.

"What about me?" I rasped.

"Why don't you kill her, too?" Thalia said, ignoring me. "She deserves to be put out of her misery."

Selling me out even now, I thought wryly. *What are sisters for?*

"You don't have to worry about her," Father McGee said, smiling as Frank dropped Thalia to her knees in front of him. "She's already been taken care of."

Thalia closed her eyes, then opened them again, nodding.

"Let's get it over with, then," she said, her voice even.

"Good. I knew you would eventually see things my way," Father McGee said, tearing open the package and presenting it to my sister.

"But I'll only do it if you let me administer them to myself," Thalia said quickly—and I wondered what devious plan she'd just conjured to save herself.

Father McGee motioned for Frank to release her. Frank let her go and she quickly moved away from the mutton-chopped henchman.

"Let me have the stupid nuts," she said, holding out her hand.

Father McGee lifted his hand to drop the package into her outstretched palm, but she moved like a flash, slapping the peanuts away and driving her elbow into his gut as she pushed past him, knocking him to the ground. I had to admire her chutzpah, but I quickly saw that she'd made a serious error in judgment. As soon as she'd knocked out the priest, she should've taken off as fast as her little Shape-Ups could carry her, but instead, her actions fueled by her gigantic ego, she'd turned back around and lunged at Frank. Grabbing a handful of his shirt and pulling him to her, she'd kneed him in the crotch the minute he was in nut-crushing range.

I decided not to encourage Thalia by cheering. Why remind her I was there when she still had her hands full with Frank?

Speaking of Frank, Thalia's crotch shot dropped the cowboy to his knees, his face going from milky white to scarlet in a heartbeat. I could see tears of agony forming in the corners of his eyes, but by then Thalia had turned her attention to me.

"I'm gonna kill you myself, Calliope, you dumb bitch," she spat at me, lifting her leg to kick me in the head, but I was too transfixed by the sight of Frank—muscling through *mucho* pain to drag himself onto his feet—to really defend myself. Reaching out a large hand, he easily caught hold of the back of Thalia's hoodie, knocking her off balance and dragging her backward so that her kick went wide, missing my head by an inch.

"Callie, help me!" Thalia cried, her eyes locking on to mine as Frank wrapped his arms around her torso, constricting her movement and forcing her back to where Father McGee was waiting, having used the opportunity to haul himself onto his feet. He looked pained by the fall, but he shook off his discomfort and lurched toward Thalia, the bag of peanuts back in his hand.

"Callie, please!" Thalia begged, her eyes full of terror—the realization that death was fast approaching, and there was nothing she could do to prevent it, blooming on her face.

After all we'd been through, after all the atrocities she'd perpetrated against me and the people I loved, after trying to kick my head in not even two minutes earlier, my sister still had the balls to ask me for my help. Jesus, the woman was unbelievable.

Whether or not I wanted to help her, there was nothing I could do. I was barely keeping myself alive, *and* deep down, if I was really being honest with myself, I knew that even if I could save her, the world would be a much better place without her in it. So I made the only reasonable choice I could: I sat on the floor and watched as Frank held my sister's mouth open and Father McGee poured the entire contents of the aluminum peanut wrapper down her throat.

The effect was instantaneous.

Thalia's body went rigid and then her arms and legs began

to flail like a marionette puppet as Frank held one palm over her mouth to prevent her from spitting out the peanuts. Bucking like a wild animal, she rocked against his restraining arms, her face turning white then puce and then the color of boiled beets, while the whites of her eyes shifted from ochre to oxblood red. Suddenly she screamed, the sound trapped behind Frank's hand. Her eyes began to roll wildly in their sockets, and then, without any kind of warning, her head exploded like a volcano, viscera flying everywhere as her headless corpse slid down Frank's body and crumpled to the floor. I was far enough away that I was saved from having bits of Thalia splattered all over me, but Frank and Father McGee both got slimed, the foul miasma of offal now exposed to the air coating them like a second skin. Secretly, it filled me with glee to think my sister—no matter how evil she'd been, she'd always be my sister—had had the last word, defiling Frank and Father McGee with the nasty gore of her own dead body.

"You get what you deserve," I said. It was directed at Father McGee and Frank, but it went for Thalia, too.

"I think that same notion can be applied to you, as well, Calliope," Father McGee said, fishing a clean handkerchief from his back pocket and beginning to wipe the gore from his face.

"My dad trusted you and you gave his family up for what . . . immortality?"

"Better than that," Father McGee said, handing the befouled handkerchief to Frank, who waved it away. "Eternal youth. Even now you can see the aging process being reversed, and soon, I'll look like I did when I was twenty-five—and I will remain that way forever."

"You may look young on the outside, but your conscience will be a black and foul thing," I said.

"As if I care about my conscience," he replied, laughing. "Of course, you wouldn't know anything about my motivations. You, who've been immortal your whole existence, who has never had your body ache with arthritis or your vision fail from glaucoma. You, who've never stared down the well of life and found only death and loss-of-self curled up at the bottom, lying in wait for you. You try being a mortal for one lifetime, Calliope Reaper-Jones, and then we'll talk."

"I guess I'll just have to save that for the next life," I said, clutching my stomach as a corkscrew of fire from my gut ratcheted up into my throat.

"You're a bright girl, Calliope," Father McGee said. "But I hope you come back as a fly."

"I'm gonna break you . . ." I said, crawling to my knees, my hands raised as if I were close enough to wrap them around Father McGee's scrawny old neck and squeeze the life out of him, but then a wave of fire spread through my body, black spots dancing before my aching eyes.

The promethium had hit me full force.

"It won't be long now, Calliope," Father McGee said as he slammed his palms into my chest, sending me sprawling onto the floor again. "You've done us so many good turns—sending the Devil back to Hell, disposing of Evangeline and her Bugbears so Frank could come rescue me—it would be rude of us to let you suffer unnecessarily."

I lay on the floor where I'd landed, unable to feel anything but the agonized burning of the promethium as it flowed through my bloodstream. My muscles gave out and I found my face pressed into the plush fibers of the oriental carpet I'd been lying on. Trying to quell the agony I felt, I pulled my feet up into my chest in a modified version of the fetal position. The relief it gave was minimal, but it was something. I was in so much pain I could hardly move, not even to lift my head up off the floor when Frank squatted down beside me, his features pinched with worry. He put a hand to my forehead, then brushed my hair back off my face.

"I'm sorry you're suffering so much, Callie," he said. "I'm gonna get Sumi to fix you up when he gets here. He promised I could have you."

My eyes burning, I nodded, but I had little hope that Sumi was going to reverse the death sentence he'd already laid on me. I closed my eyes, trying to ease the ache behind my eyelids, and when I opened them again, I saw Father McGee pulling a tiny, cell phone–like device from his pocket. He pressed a numbered code into the screen and the device beeped, a wall of flickering light projecting out from inside it.

I'd thought Thalia and the Devil had blocked anyone from entering or leaving the building via wormhole, but somehow Father McGee had called up one anyway. The priest caught my questioning glance and smiled.

"Who do you think showed your sister how to shut down the wormhole system?" he purred, pleased with himself. "You really believe she was so smart? No, she was a brute, using other people's expertise to further her own agenda—with an ego so large she could never believe anyone would ever double-cross her."

"You're a prick . . ." I started to say, but then the wormhole flickered between us, its gray light shimmering like static on a television set, and I watched as first Hyacinth then Sumi crossed through, entering the Hall of Death as if they owned the place. As soon as they were both safely through the wormhole, it flickered and then disappeared.

Sumi looked exactly as he had before—still wrapped in his kimono and grass skirt—while Hyacinth had slipped into something more comfortable: a pale linen and gold caftan with matching gold slippers. Her change of costume, coupled with her flaxen hair and rounded body, made her resemble a Wagnerian opera heroine.

"So good of you to hold up your end of the bargain," Sumi said, nodding to Father McGee.

"Of course," Father McGee replied, "the jewel you gave me is already working. My youth is returning as we speak."

I started laughing; I couldn't help myself, even though it hurt terribly to do it. I couldn't believe Father McGee had done the exact thing he'd just accused my sister of doing. By accepting Sumi's wish-fulfillment jewel, the good Father's big fat ego had just opened itself up to a whole lot of double-crossing.

Ah, such is the irony of life.

"What's so funny?" Hyacinth roared, bending over me as I lay on the floor, giggling to myself.

"Nothing," I moaned, hit by another wave of giggles that had me convulsing with pain and laughter.

"Tell me why you're laughing, Calliope Reaper-Jones!" she said, kicking me in the gut with the tip of her golden slipper.

Note to self: Never kick anyone suffering from promethium poisoning in the stomach.

The force of Hyacinth's blow, compounded with the nausea I'd already been marinating in, made me throw up, expelling a red foaming bile that oozed out of my mouth and poured onto the gigantic woman's slippered feet. She backed away, kicking off her shoes as she tried to keep the stench of my vomit away from her skin, the smell assailing not only *her* nostrils, but everyone else's, too. It was so gross I started gagging again even though I'd pretty much emptied out what was left in my stomach already.

"A jewel," I whispered huskily, my seared throat aching. "I ate a jewel, too, Father."

I didn't have the energy to laugh, but Father McGee's face blanched as he caught my meaning.

"Did you put something in my jewel?" the old man wailed, poking a bony finger into Sumi's chest, the gesture only making the Sea God cackle.

"You think I double-crossed you?" Sumi said, pushing the priest's hand away as he stepped in closer, so that they were now standing chest to chest.

"I don't know," the priest said, his lips trembling. "Did you?"

Sumi sneered at the pathetic priest, taking immense joy in the other man's terrified countenance and wild eyes.

"Of course I double-crossed you."

Father McGee took a step back, clutching his hands to his belly where death gestated inside him.

"You wouldn't dare," Father McGee whispered as he looked around wildly for an escape.

"I made it long-acting, Father," Sumi said, enjoying Father McGee's dismay. "It could be months before it kills you."

Father McGee dropped to his knees and wrapped his arms around Sumi's grass skirt.

"Please, for the love of all things holy, take it out of me . . ." the priest begged.

Sumi didn't seem at all fazed by having a grown man clutching at his legs. Instead, he leaned down, whispering into Father McGee's ear—but just loud enough for everyone else to hear:

"Get away from me or I'll kill you now."

Father McGee dropped his hands and sat back on his haunches. He stared up at the old Sea God, his jaw slack with fear, then he began to scuttle backward down the hall, making his escape.

"You said I could have her when you were done," Frank said as the priest disappeared into the shadowed hallway. "I wanna collect on that promise now. You said I'd be Death and she'd be my queen."

Sumi shrugged. "I say a lot of things."

Frank crossed the space between them, but Hyacinth stepped in between them, her bulk blocking Frank from getting too close to the duplicitous Sea God.

"Don't even think about it," Hyacinth said, her voice as calm as a snake right before it struck.

With Hyacinth holding Frank at bay, Sumi squatted down beside me, his fingers pressing into my skull.

"You a phrenologist as well as an asshole?" I rasped, my voice nearly gone. "'Cause if you're gonna tell me my future is shot to shit, I already know."

Sumi ignored me as his fingers continued to gauge how far gone I was. Satisfied I wasn't going to be making a miraculous recovery, he began to chuckle, pleased with himself and with his handiwork. I curled further into myself, trying to escape from his insidious laughter, but I was trapped in my decaying body, the pain roping me to consciousness, forcing me to endure every crushing ache and deleterious physical reaction I was suffering under the effects of the promethium.

"She will die soon," Sumi said blandly, returning to his

feet as he addressed Frank. "And she's a liability. She could challenge you—and win—and then this would all have been for nothing."

"But it's already for nothing," a seductive voice called out from the darkness.

Sumi stood at attention, his eyes narrowed as he peered into the shadows, looking for the owner of the voice. Hyacinth came to stand protectively beside him, but Frank, looking like a dog that'd just had its bone taken away, stayed where he was.

"Show yourself," Sumi commanded, his voice booming into the darkened Hall.

"Don't get your panties in a bunch, Watatsumi. It's just little old me."

And then like a ghost, the Devil glided out of the shadows.

"How are you here?" Sumi said, his eyes wide with surprise.

"Oh, I have a few tricks up my sleeve," the Devil said as he took off one glove then the other, dropping them onto the floor.

"And who is this lovely lady?" the Devil continued. He walked over to where I lay on the ground, and then, oddly, he knelt beside me. He removed the black silk top hat he was wearing over his slicked-back black hair and slid a silver, lion-headed cane under his arm, bending at the waist so he could look deeply into my eyes.

"This isn't the delectable Calliope Reaper-Jones, is it? Oh, yes, I do believe that it is."

I shut my eyes, wanting to disappear, but the Devil set his hand on my forehead and forcefully lifted one eyelid, then the other, checking for God knew what, and then, as if I were a cat, he patted the top of my head and stood.

"She's been rather a tricky dick," the Devil said, seemingly amused by the scene he'd stepped into. "But it seems as if you've finally accomplished what so many others could not. She'll be dead within the half hour.

"Well played," he continued, keeping his voice pleasant—but I noticed his wary eyes never left Sumi's face.

"We shall see," Sumi said thoughtfully. "She's not dead yet."

The Devil nodded, unclasping the silver lion broach that rested at the base of his throat and letting the black silken cape he wore slither to the floor. He kicked away the sinewy fabric—and the stupid thing flew in my direction, draping itself over my arm. Suddenly, I felt a cooling balm settle over my burning skin, and for the first time in hours, I could take a breath without feeling like I was going to retch. Even my dislocated shoulder stopped aching, although my arm still hung stiffly at my side, my range of motion shot. I didn't know why the Devil would do me this simple kindness, but I wasn't going to look a gift horse in the mouth—even though I knew I would invariably end up paying for it somewhere down the line.

"You sent me on a fool's errand to Hell, Sumi," the Devil mused. "One I easily quelled, returning the errant souls back inside the Gates where they belonged—it's just too bad Cerberus and his child had to be destroyed for their insubordination."

"No!" I cried, forcing myself on to my knees and dragging my body with numb fingers over to where the Devil stood, prostrating myself at his feet. The motion caused my shoulder to slip out of place again and a jagged knife of pain sliced up my arm and into my neck and back.

"Please, tell me you're lying," I said, an odd weightless feeling settling over me now that I was no longer underneath the protection of the Devil's cape. "Swear you didn't do it. Swear you didn't hurt them."

For a moment the Devil looked uncertain, not sure what to make of my protestations, but then he turned away, shooing me back with his foot. I wanted to scream with grief, but there were no tears left inside me; I was drained. Instead, I lay down beside him, utterly spent.

"Go back to where you were, you sniveling fool," the Devil growled, swatting at me again with his toe—but I was immovable. If Runt was dead, then I deserved to suffer. Her death lay squarely at my feet, because I was the one who'd come up with the idiotic plan that had gotten her killed.

"I said to go back where you came from," the Devil growled, his eye now on the cape where it lay spread out on the floor, unguarded.

Sumi watched our odd back-and-forth with an attentive eye, suspicion flaring in every synapse.

"Devil," Sumi said, thoughtfully rubbing his chin. "Tell me, how is it you hold me accountable for your troubles in Hell, when you know very well the real culprit lies there at your feet."

The Devil froze, his toe pointed in my direction, but then quickly regained his composure.

"I know no such thing," he said sullenly.

"*You* are no Devil," Sumi said, shaking his head. "Merely the Devil's protégé."

The glamour instantly fell away and Daniel stood above me, his face fierce with anger. I was in shock . . . If this was really Daniel, then what about Cerberus and Runt? Were they okay? Was Hell still the Devil's domain or had the revolt worked? A myriad of possibilities, all of them positive, swam before my eyes.

"Get back under the cape, Calliope," Daniel instructed—and his voice brooked no argument.

Using my good arm, I dragged myself back to the cape, but just as my fingers grazed the silken material, the thing was whisked away from my grasp. Spent, I watched as, with a flourish, Father McGee draped the silken cloth over his own bony shoulders, triumphant in his return.

Left with no further hope of salvation, I knew that now only imminent death remained.

twenty-nine

"You bastard!" I screamed, rage consuming every inch of me. I started crawling, bad arm and all, over to where Father McGee stood gloating—my cape, my salvation, wrapped around his torso.

I threw myself at his feet, biting into the top of his sockless foot, my teeth tearing into the soft flesh with a ferocity I didn't know I possessed. As my teeth sank into bone and sinew, a spurt of thick, warm blood shot into my mouth and I almost gagged. By sheer force of will, I held on to my prize, channeling all my anger into ripping his foot apart as I ignored the salty taste of blood.

"Stop it, you dog!" he screamed, attempting to shake me off, but only managing to trip himself up, so that, off balance, he stumbled backward, arms waving like windmills. I wrapped my good arm around his ankle and yank his bloodied foot out from underneath him, sending him sprawling onto his back. Dragging my broken body on top of him, so he was pinned underneath my weight, I leaned in as close as I could and whispered into his ear:

"I wish you dead."

I didn't know if it would work. I thought there might be a

slim chance it might, but in truth, I was really hoping for a miracle.

At first, Father McGee just stared at me, disgusted by the sight of his own blood smeared across my lips, but then, something amazing happened: His eyes flared, the whites so pronounced I could see where they rounded into his eye sockets, and he shuddered once, then lay still beneath me, all the heat dissipating from his body in death. I wrenched the cape from his dead shoulders and bundled myself inside the safety of its silken folds. I didn't know what magic the cape possessed, but I hoped it was powerful enough to keep the promethium from dealing its final, deathly blow.

I stuck my hand into the dead priest's clothes, extracting the strange wormhole-calling device from the depths of one of his pockets. I ran my hand over its screen and the thing sprang to life, a series of numerical buttons lighting up beneath my fingertips. I knew I needed to unblock the wormholes, but I didn't know how. But before I could attempt any trial-and-error tinkering, a heavy body smashed into mine, my head cracking against the stone tile floor as shooting stars of pain bloomed inside my brain. As I lay sprawled on the floor, I saw two tiny Asian women in Victorian garb chasing Father McGee's soul as it looped around the room. I wondered if Daniel and Frank could see the little ladies—but then a meaty fist slammed into my nose, changing the subject of my inner monologue. Dazed by the punch, I felt Hyacinth's enormous girth straddle me, compressing my lungs into pancakes so that I could barely draw a breath.

"Get off me, you bitch." I groaned, driving my fist into what I hoped was the hollow of her throat. To my surprise, the weight constricting my chest eased and I could breathe again. I opened my eyes, my nose smarting where Hyacinth's punch had snapped the nasal bone, and saw the Amazonian woman listing above me like a giant ship, her hands clutching her throat. I tried to drag myself out from under her, but she grimaced, and releasing her damaged neck as she grunted in pain, she made a grab for the wormhole-calling device in my hand, knocking it from my grasp so that it skittered across the floor, crashing into the leg of Tanuki's desk.

"Dammit," I growled. "Get off me!"

"You're stuck, bug," she laughed, pressing her hands into my chest in order to crack my sternum. Hyacinth wasn't wrong. I did feel like a bug, pinned and wriggling on a piece of wood.

"I wish you dead," I rasped, even though I knew it wouldn't work on an immortal like Hyacinth. Amused by my pathetic attempts to save myself, she relaxed her grip on my chest, allowing me just enough room to drag my right arm out from beneath her fleshy thigh, wriggling back with my shoulders and hips, until she was astride my waist instead of my torso. With as much forward motion as I could muster, I drove my curled fist into one of her massive breasts, the impact crushing mammary and rib cage like they were made of butter. I saw Hyacinth's eyes cross in astonishment as she slumped onto her side, clutching her injured breast.

Across the Hall, I saw Daniel and Frank locked in intense battle, each clawing at the other as if they could shred flesh with their bare fingers. I was pleased to see Daniel had the upper hand, but I didn't dare do anything to distract him, so I swallowed the cry for help that'd been brewing in my throat and took a deep breath. Wiggling my legs, I extracted myself from underneath Hyacinth's muscled bulk. Freed from my former boss's meaty embrace, I began crawling over to the desk. I could see the silvery glint of the wormhole-calling device where it lay underneath the desk leg, but as I stretched out my fingers to grasp it, Sumi's bare foot slammed down on my hand, splintering the delicate metacarpals into transverse sections of broken bone. I screamed as he ground his heel into my wounded hand, then bent down and plucked the device out of my grasp.

He turned to go, and I did the only thing I could think of to stop him from getting away—I bit down on his foot, sinking my teeth into the hard, calloused skin, which, I had to say, tasted an awful lot like old rubbery eel. Because of the horned nature of his skin, I couldn't get as good a grip on

Sumi's foot as I had on Father McGee's, but I still managed to inflict enough pain that he dropped the device. Ripping his foot away from my snapping jaws, he took a step back, then made a halfhearted attempt to kick my head in. I rolled away, scooping up the device in my good hand. I gritted my teeth as pain flooded into my bad shoulder.

"You cannot work the machine," Sumi said, blood pooling on the floor from his abraded foot. "Give it to me and I will show you the trick."

"Ha!" I replied, crawling to my feet. "Like I can trust you. You'll just double cross me like you double crossed everyone else."

"Suit yourself," Sumi said, bowing his head in what looked like prayer—but then the old man lifted his head and screamed, charging at me like a mad bull.

Instantly, his flesh fell away and his human body elongated, rippling and swelling as he shifted into the massive, red-hued Sea Serpent I'd ridden on in the ocean. Every cell in my body screamed at me to run, that the monster was going to crush me like a bug, but I held my ground—I wasn't about to leave Daniel alone to deal with Sumi *and* Frank by himself.

I want to be big like Sumi, I thought, desperately, squeezing my eyes shut and praying the jewel still had some juice left in it—but when, after a few moments, nothing had happened, I knew the promethium had obliterated the jewel's powers, leaving me no way to fight back against Sumi's monstrous new body.

With his transformation now complete, Sumi roared, the sound raising the hackles on the back of my neck as his crystalline eyes narrowed warily at me, showing his displeasure. I took an involuntary step backward, then another and another as the monster lowered its head and hissed, a fiery plume of smoke barreling toward me. I threw myself to the side, trying to escape the fire's wrath, but instead I lost my balance and fell forward onto my knees. Father McGee's strange device flew from my hand, and I watched, horrified, as it shattered into a zillion tiny pieces on the cold limestone floor.

My heart leapt into my throat as I realized that all was lost, but then, to my shock, I heard a static burst as the room suddenly became awash in the glow of a thousand wormholes flickering into being and filling the darkness—the blockade on wormhole travel in and out of Death, Inc., destroyed along with the device.

Suddenly, I found myself surrounded by Kali, Indra, and Runt.

"White girl, you look like shit," Kali said as she and Indra encircled me protectively, both holding bloodied weapons in their hands. Not wanting to be left out, Runt nuzzled up against me, licking my broken hand with her scratchy tongue.

"You're alive," I said, bending down and kissing the top of the hellhound pup's head. "I thought the revolt in Hell had failed, that the Devil had killed you."

Runt wagged her tail.

"The opposite, Callie," she said. "We won. Jarvis and Dad and your Death soldiers kicked some serious butt. Dad's beside himself with happiness; he's got the Devil and the Jackal Brothers guarding the North Gate of Hell in his stead. It's great!"

"I'm so glad," I said, automatically, scratching behind the pup's ears, while I distractedly searched the room for Sumi.

He'd been in sea serpent form when the device had been destroyed, so he shouldn't have been hard to spot, but after scanning the room twice with no luck, I had to accept the fact that he was gone, probably having shifted back into his human body and escaped in the flurry of activity that'd consumed the Hall when the wormhole restriction had been lifted. Still, I had a funny feeling this wouldn't be the last time I tangled with the mischievous Japanese Sea God—

"Callie!"

My thoughts were interrupted by Clio's singsonging voice as she burst through the melee and threw her arms around me.

"You're okay," she bellowed, squeezing me as hard as she could. My shoulder and hand protested against the attack, but I let her go on and squeeze as hard as she wanted.

"I'm all right," I said weakly, remembering Hyacinth's pythonlike embrace.

Speaking of Hyacinth, I was happy to see that both she and Frank had been trussed up like Thanksgiving turkeys by a contingent of Bugbears, who thankfully were out of the Devil's command now that we'd wrested Hell from his control. Hyacinth, livid with fury, shot daggers at me with her eyes as they dragged her away, kicking and screaming.

Frank was a different story entirely. There was no antipathy in him as our gazes locked, and I found myself feeling kind of sorry for the man again. He had been used by Sumi and Hyacinth, but that didn't free him from responsibility for his actions. He'd made his choices and now he was going to have to answer for them.

"Hey, I'm really pissed at you," Clio said, her voice abruptly cutting into my thoughts as she punched me hard in my bad shoulder, trying to get my attention. "You threw me in that elevator with Mom and then you just left me there. I could've killed you!"

Rubbing my poor dislocated shoulder, I apologized.

"It was the only way I could keep you guys safe," I said sheepishly. "If I'd died, then you guys would've lost your immortality and you'd have been sitting ducks."

Clio nodded, but I could tell she was still furious with me for ditching her. She opened her mouth to say as much but was silenced by a kiss from her boyfriend, Indra, who had snuck up behind her while she fumed. A few months back, I'd labeled him Mr. Sex on a Stick—and the nickname hadn't been far from wrong. Even covered with drying blood, he was definitely a hunk. It made me a bit uncomfortable to see him macking on my baby sister, but if it gave me a "Get Out of Jail" free pass, then I guess I was all for it.

"I was lost without you," Indra breathed into Clio's ear, and as my sister melted into her lover's embrace, I chose that moment to disentangle myself from their reunion and move into the swarm of bodies surrounding us. Now that the wormholes had been reopened, more and more people who had helped to fight against the Devil's aborted coup were coming into the Hall of Death to celebrate. As I pushed through the crowd, I knew there was someone I needed to do a little explaining to myself—and I needed to do it sooner rather than later.

I found Daniel helping Tanuki replace the drawers in the apothecary cabinet. The rotund man looked worn out—the face I'd only seen filled with laughter was now a mask of grief. I reached out and patted his shoulder and he jumped, before realizing I was a friend, not foe.

"I'm sorry about Suri and the others," I said—and I meant it.

"They fought very valiantly," Tanuki said softly. "And it is better to die fighting than to become a traitor like me."

The large man's face fell and he started to cry.

"What're you talking about?" I said, rubbing his arm. "There was nothing else you could've done."

He nodded, but he didn't look convinced.

"You could've given my sister the files she wanted, but you stalled her, hoping help would come."

"That's true," Tanuki said. "And then you arrived. As if in answer to my prayers."

"See," I said, smiling at him. "You did right by me and everyone here in Purgatory."

"Thank you," he said uncertainly, "I will get the drawers returned to their proper places before the day is over. I swear it."

I almost told him not worry about it, to just relax and we'd get things settled later, but he looked like he needed to keep his hands busy, so I simply nodded.

As Tanuki returned to the epic task of collecting drawers, I took a deep breath and wheeled around to face Daniel. I had expected anger, maybe even tears, but the cold veneer of civility he wore was enough to chill my heart.

He knows, I thought, guilt sweeping through me. *He knows what I've done.*

"Thanks for the cape," I said, launching into the most benign sentence in the universe, when what I really wanted to say was: *I'm an idiot. I love you.*

"May I see it," he said, holding out his hand for the cape. I gave it to him, and the moment he touched it, it shifted into the Cup of Jamshid. No wonder it'd protected me from the promethium. The Cup was what gave Death his/her powers—and it was the only thing that could've saved me from my immortal weakness. Even now, without the Cup's power, the burning sensation in my gut had started to return.

"Here, drink from it," Daniel said, offering me a sip of my own salvation.

"Wait," I said, holding up my hand.

We stood there in silence, neither one saying what we should've, both of us guilty of glossing over what we were really feeling. I opened my mouth, ready to plunge into the abyss, but Kali saved me from the executioner's ax. She was covered in gore and viscera from head to foot—and frankly she looked like she was in her element. She grinned at me, showing off her pearly whites.

"So, Boss, what's the first order of business?"

I stared at her.

"What are you talking about?"

She rolled her eyes heavenward.

"Still a dumb old white girl, no matter what title you give her," she said, shaking her head.

I looked to Daniel for confirmation and he nodded.

"But what about the Challenge?" I asked, my head spinning. I had no interest in fighting anyone for anything.

"I'll be overseeing Hell, re-collecting all the souls you let out . . ."

I rubbed my eyes with the heel of my palms.

"Okay, hold on, are you saying I'm Death now? And that you're the new Devil?"

"The nitwit has so much to learn," Kali snickered. "Our Jarvis will be a very busy man."

"But how . . . ? How did all of this happen?" I said, totally lost by this new turn of events.

"First, drink from the Cup," Daniel said, forcing the thing into my hands. I hesitated, then lifted it to my mouth and felt the warm nectar flow from my lips down through the rest of me, permanently squelching the promethium's fire. I would be all right again—or at least until the next time I ate a jewel filled with the stuff.

"Can you explain, Kali?" Daniel asked, "I need to return to Hell so I can relieve Jarvis and Cerberus from guard duty."

Kali winked at me.

"Oh, I'll tell white girl *everything*," she said. "You'd better believe it."

"Daniel, wait," I called out as he turned to go.

He stopped, his eyes heavy with raw emotion as he looked at me.

"I have to go, Calliope," he said, finally letting out the breath he'd been holding. "We'll talk later."

I watched him leave, my heart breaking into two jagged pieces.

"Kali?" I said, grabbing her wrist to steady myself. She seemed surprised by my touch, but she didn't shrug it off. "Can you tell me who Daniel is?"

"What are you asking me, white girl?" she said, eyes narrowed suspiciously.

"I just want to know who he really is," I said, my shoulders hunching with exhaustion. "Yes, he's the Devil's protégé, I know, I don't care, *whatever*. I want to know about before then—who he was and how he came to be under the Devil's control."

"We should be celebrating." Kali sighed, her sari stiff with dried blood, the pungent scent of iron floating around her like a perfume.

"Please," I begged.

"He was just a man, Callie. He sold his soul for immortality and was cursed to be the Devil's plaything . . . until you released him."

"And the Devil knew he could be Death?" I asked.

Kali sucked on her teeth like she'd eaten a raw lemon, but then she nodded.

"I would assume so," she said. "That was why he offered Daniel the bargain, right? Does that answer your question?"

"Sort of," I replied, though I'd sensed Kali was holding

something back, something important she wasn't supposed to tell me. Looking at the proud warrior Goddess, I decided to leave things alone for now. There'd be plenty of time in the future to pick Jarvis's brains about the subject.

"Let's get you in a bath, white girl," Kali said. "You smell like sick."

I snorted.

"Um, have you smelled yourself recently?" I asked, the beginnings of a grin stretching across my face.

"Ha!" she said, shaking her weapon at me. "I always smell as fresh as a daisy. That's *your* stench overwhelming mine, nimrod."

I decided being called "nimrod" was one of the nicest things anyone had said to me all day.

As I stood there, a disgusting dirty mess of my former self, and surveyed the chaos swirling around me, my soul was full of wonder. Around me, all the minions of Heaven, Purgatory, and Hell were working together, each doing their part to set the Hall of Death back to rights again. As badly as I stank, I had no intention of going anywhere, not even for a shower. My place was here, among my people; it was where I belonged. My father had known it, he'd seen it was my destiny, and he'd given me just enough rope to hang myself.

No, that wasn't exactly true.

Even though I'd fled from the family business my entire life, my fate had been sealed from the day I was born—I was meant to be Death. It was my calling.

I was my father's daughter.

I was Calliope Reaper-Jones.

I was Death.

epilogue

I'd spent most of the last forty-eight hours on-site at Death, Inc. The building was a mess, files and workspaces in disarray, the Hall of Death utterly ransacked, the Executive Offices filled with dead Bugbears and a very pissed-off bald woman. The consortium of Death, Inc., employees—Transporters, Harvesters, and other office drones—worked tirelessly to get the place cleaned up and back in semiworking order. I'd done what was needed here and there, ignoring my aches and pains as the Cup of Jamshid plied its magic on me. I had no interest in being anywhere but where I was—and no matter what Kali or Jarvis said, they couldn't tear me away from the office.

Finally, once things seemed to be progressing reasonably, Jarvis convinced me to take Clio and my mother back to Sea Verge. I hesitated, not sure it was fair to leave him and Runt in charge of everything after all they'd been through, nor was I sure I could bear returning to the place where my dad had been killed, but I had to do something with my mother, and the mansion seemed like the obvious choice.

We settled her into her suite of rooms, but we all knew there was little hope of recovery. Without my father, she was like a ghost of her former self. She just sat in a white upholstered Chippendale chair, staring out the plate glass windows overlooking the sea. Clio and I both tried to draw her out, to engage her somehow, but her gaze remained locked on the waves as they crashed into the jagged cliffs below.

Then, the next morning, we woke up to find my mother gone, a note left on the seat of her Chippendale chair written in her spidery cursive. It read: *I've gone to the sea.*

Thinking of Starr, I explained to Clio about my run-in with the Siren and how I didn't think Mom had committed suicide—her immortal weakness was snoring and I doubted there was much of that going on in the ocean—but instead, I believed that she had returned to her family. Clio had a hard time understanding why our mom felt comfortable leaving us to clean up the mess alone, but I knew better.

My father had been what tied her to this life. With him gone, there was nothing left to hold her to Sea Verge.

I couldn't fault her for grief.

With my parents missing, the house was terribly empty, and I found myself roaming the desolate halls, the scent of Daniel filling my nostrils as I steeped myself in memories of our time together. I kept my wanderings limited to the inside of the house, unwilling to venture outside where my dad had died. I just didn't have the heart to deal with any of that yet.

Neither Clio nor I was inured to the loneliness of Sea Verge, so when she asked if it was all right if she went and stayed with Indra, who was I to say no? She left her room as it was, but stuffed her laptop and enough clothing into her bag to last her more than a few weeks. I wasn't worried about her disappearing like my mom. I just knew she needed to get away from the house in order to heal, that it was the right thing—just like my mother's leaving had been—and that I should be happy she had Indra to help her pick up the pieces.

I sat on the front steps as Indra, in a very mortal move, came to pick Clio up in his red miniconvertible, one that had white racing stripes painted down its sides. As I watched her pile her stuff into the backseat, I realized that while I wasn't looking, my little sister had turned into a beautiful young woman. It made me want to cry, but tears were unbecoming to Death, so I composed myself, and by the time she'd come back up to give me a bone-crunching hug, the tears were nowhere to be found. With the innocence of a child, she asked me if I wanted to go stay with Indra, too, but I assured her I was fine at Sea Verge. Besides, how would it look if Death went and hid out at Indra's house like a crybaby?

When she was gone, I went back to my old bedroom, where I'd slept the night before, and curled up on the comforter. I thought of my apartment in New York and how it wasn't really mine anymore. That that part of my life was over and a new chapter had already begun.

I lay there for what seemed like hours, thinking about the implications of what all this meant, and then I heard a knock at my door. I'd assumed it was Jarvis, but when I got up to open it, I found Daniel waiting across the threshold.

"May I come in?" he asked, his dark hair unkempt, a day's worth of stubble on his face.

I gestured for him to enter, not sure I trusted my voice. He sat down on the end of the bed and I curled up by the pillows.

"Can I turn on the lights?" he asked. I nodded, not realizing I'd been sitting in the dark. He got up and turned on the bedside lamp, flooding the room with a pale yellow electric glow. He went back to sit at the end of my bed, the light casting shadows across his face.

"Calliope—" he began, looking down at his hands.

"I know," I said, interrupting. "We need to talk."

He sighed and ran a hand through his hair, his ice blue eyes neutral.

"I'm staying in Hell," he began again. "It's where I'm needed now that the Devil's been deposed."

"Runt said Cerberus had him and the Jackal Brothers guarding the North Gate."

That elicited a hint of a smile from Daniel.

"Yeah, it's kind of an amazing sight."

I smiled.

"Okay, so *you're* staying in Hell—"

"And *you're* needed in Purgatory and on Earth," he said. "You have some pretty big shoes to fill."

I have the Ender of Death to deal with, too, I mused—but I didn't share that thought out loud.

"And things haven't really been going that great with us lately. You're not happy, Calliope, and you cheated . . ."

There. He'd said it. The thing I'd been dreading for the past forty-eight hours.

"It wasn't really my fault," I started to say, but he held up his hand for silence.

"Calliope, you've wanted to be a free agent for weeks now," he said, his gaze returning to his hands. "I thought we had something important, something that was worth fighting for, but I was alone in that—and after everything that's happened, I just don't think I trust you anymore."

It was like having a nail driven through my heart. I felt light-headed, and the dark spots that descended on my vision made it hard to see.

"Then I understand," I heard myself saying. "If that's what you really feel."

Inside, I was screaming at myself, begging me to ask for Daniel's forgiveness, to tell him that I loved him more than anything, that I just hadn't understood that until he'd gone away.

But my internal pleas fell on my own deaf ears.

Daniel nodded and stood up.

"Then I guess that's it."

Nausea burbled in my throat and I felt faint. I took a deep breath to stay my racing heart and then I said:

"Thank you, Daniel. For everything."

His eyes went dark, but then he shook his head, dispelling whatever emotion he'd been feeling.

"You're welcome, Cal," he said.

We stared at each other, drinking in the last dregs of what could've been, and then he walked to the door. I watched him go, but as the door closed softly behind him, I let the words that had been running through my head silently slip between my lips:

I love you, Daniel.

DON'T MISS THE FIRST

CALLIOPE REAPER-JONES NOVEL FROM

AMBER BENSON

death's daughter

Calliope Reaper-Jones just wants a normal life—buying designer shoes on sale, dating guys from craigslist, Web surfing for organic dim sum for her boss...

But when her father, who happens to be Death himself, is kidnapped and the Devil's protégé embarks on a hostile takeover of the family business, Death, Inc., Callie returns home to assume the CEO mantle—only to discover that she must complete three nearly impossible tasks in the realm of the Afterlife.